LOVER'S
KNOT

The Hearts of Rebellion Series
Book Two

Louise Clark

Cover and Book design by eBook Prep
www.ebookprep.com

November, 2015
ISBN: 978-1-61417-774-6

ePublishing Works!
www.epublishingworks.com

REVIEWS & ACCOLADES

"A blend of romance, conspiracy, and hidden identities…with just the right mix of action and seduction."
~Susan Tanner, author of *Winds Across Texas*

DEDICATION

To Muriel Whitlock Gillespie Allen
Great Aunt Boots

CHAPTER 1

Southwest England, 1659

"I think we should visit him." Excitement, mischief and amusement colored Alysa Leighton's voice. The person she was speaking of was Sir Philip Hampton, a relatively new arrival in the small town of West Easton. He had inherited the estate of Ainslie Manor on the death of his uncle, but had only taken up residence at the beginning of February, one month before.

"After all," she continued, her vivid blue eyes challenging, "how will we know if he holds acceptable views unless we actually deign to speak to him?"

"Speaking to him is one thing, Alysa. Visiting him is another." Abigail, Lady Strathern, Alysa's stepmother, took a bite of ham from the well-filled breakfast plate before her. Plump and plain, Abigail enjoyed the everyday pleasures. She had learned long ago that life was too chancy to put off the little things. "You know very well that if your father condescends to visit Sir Philip, it is as much as admitting that the man should be accepted by the rest of the neighborhood."

There was no denying that Edward, Baron Strathern, had considerable influence in the countryside around West Easton. Though his title was only third generation, having been bestowed by Queen Elizabeth some one hundred years before, the Leightons came of old stock. Moreover, Edward's service to King Charles during the recent civil wars had further enhanced his prestige in this largely Royalist area.

"And why should he not be accepted?" demanded Prudence Leighton, Alysa's half sister.

Prudence was headstrong, impulsive and tended to view life with a refreshingly simple naiveté.

"Because he might be a Roundhead!" Abigail retorted, smiling affectionately at her daughter.

She was wearing a dark blue gown of a finely woven, but sturdy cloth. The bodice was close fitting and came to a deep point in front. Decorative details were done in pale blue, while the petticoat that showed beneath the full skirt was a mauve silk. The colors didn't enhance her mousy coloring, but they didn't detract from it either. "Don't you remember the story about the two nephews of Richard Hampton? When the war broke out one took service with the parliamentary troops, while the other followed the king. We're not sure if the man who is at Ainslie is the Royalist or the Roundhead brother."

"Why not ask him?" Prudence suggested practically. Unlike her mother, she wore a gown in magenta with the petticoat and details picked out in white. The bright color of the gown was typical of Prudence. Left to her own choice she would always select a vivid color, whether it complemented her sand-brown hair and hazel eyes or not.

Lord Strathern—a big, heavyset man of middle-age whose features were remarkably like those of his daughters— laughed indulgently. "I suppose we could, but I doubt it would do much good. If he is not the Royalist brother he will simply say that he is."

Prudence, just over sixteen years old, sighed. "Politics. I am so tired of politics! The war has been over for an age. Does it really matter if Sir Philip was once a Roundhead? The king was executed over ten years ago and it is almost eight years since his son, Prince Charles, attempted to return to England and was defeated at the Battle of Worchester."

"King Charles," Strathern corrected absently, brushing a

crumb from the dark brown cloth of his doublet. The suit he wore was well cut, but shabby from much use. The doublet, which covered a shirt of fine linen, was too long to be fashionable, and on this cool spring day Strathern was able to close all the buttons to the waist for warmth. His breeches were also too long for fashion and were adorned with only the minimum of ribbon loops at the cuffs to proclaim him a Royalist gentleman. The stockings he wore were wool, not silk, and his black leather shoes were tied with ribbon bows. It was the outfit of a practical man who saw no need to impress.

About to take a mouthful of eggs, Prudence paused, frowning. "Papa?"

"Even though he was in exile, the prince became king the moment his father died," Strathern explained patiently. "When Charles Stuart returned to Great Britain in 1651 he was already king."

"Oh." Uninterested in politics, she added with daunting brightness, "Prince or king, it makes no difference! We are living under the Lord Protector now and so continue to be."

"The new Lord Protector is not the man of strength and purpose his father was. Richard Cromwell has ruled England for little more than six months and already there are rumors that the army will not continue to support him. And the army is the pillar on which his power rests." Strathern's bright blue eyes were thoughtful. "I do not believe that Englishmen will allow Richard to rule simply because he is Oliver Cromwell's son and designated heir."

"Which means that change is coming," Alysa added, her fine blue eyes, so much like her father's, sparkling as she spoke. "And that is why it is important for us to know where the new lord of Ainslie Manor stands. Isn't that so, Papa?"

Lord Strathern cast her an affectionate look. Alysa was the daughter of his first marriage and she and her sister were as unlike as their mothers were. Blond hair the color of old gold, so like her mother's, was drawn away from Alysa's forehead, but allowed to fall in frothy curls on either side of her face, framing her features. Blue, heavy-lidded eyes, a short, straight nose and a chin with a determined jut to it had all come from him, but her sweetly bowed mouth was the image of her mother's, as was her creamy complexion.

Unlike her sister, Alysa chose elegant colors for her clothes. Today she was wearing a gown that was the color of fine wine with an underskirt of soft rose. The details of the gown were picked out in white.

Intelligent, intuitive and shrewd, Alysa could be trusted to find ways of interpreting the facts that came before her with uncanny precision. In the absence of his son, Thomas, who was in exile for his participation in the attempted rising in fifty-one, Strathern relied heavily on Alysa as his sounding board and second-in-command. "Exactly, my dear. In these troubled times it is well to know what each man believes. One can never be too cautious."

Caution was a virtue that Royalists in England had long ago learned to cultivate. Punitive taxes and ruthless suppression of their rights had taught them that defying the rule of the Lord Protector was a risky venture. Most Royalist families were like the Leightons, once wealthy and powerful, but now subsisting on reduced income because they had the misfortune of choosing the wrong side in the war. Indeed, the room in which the family sat was a good example of how circumstances had changed.

Small and cozy, the breakfast parlor was paneled in the carved oak so popular a century before. Sunlight flowed in through the leaded glass windows, warming the paneling, but emphasizing the scars on the old mahogany dining table and the worn upholstery on the seats of the straight-backed chairs. Though the furniture and faded carpet covering much of the oak parquet floor were of the finest quality, there was no money to replace the aging fabrics or repair the damaged furniture.

Too young to remember the way of life before the war, Prudence was more content than the rest of her family to accede to the changes that had come about. Her main concern was to find a husband and so acquire a household of her own. "I hope that Sir Philip is an acceptable gentleman, for he appears to be unmarried and the neighborhood will be better off with another eligible bachelor."

"Prudence!" Abigail said, scandalized. "Where do you get your ideas from! What a dreadful thing to say."

Prudence thrust out her jaw. It had the same stubborn jut as her sister's. "Alysa has the only gentleman of interest in the area languishing at her feet. Perhaps if there is a new man of marriageable age about she will decide whether or not to accept Master Ingram's courtship."

Alysa blushed. Uncomfortably, she fiddled with her sleeve, where the soft wine-colored cloth was slit to show off the fine linen of her chemise. "I find Cedric Ingram to be an amiable man, but I am glad he has not asked me to wed him, for I could not give him an answer."

Abigail's eyes twinkled. "When the man asks, you will know how to answer him, my dear. In the meantime, you must show him what courtesy you can, just as you would any other gentleman."

"Including Sir Philip Hampton."

Once again Prudence reduced the rest of the family to silence.

Finally Strathern said slowly, "Especially Sir Philip Hampton. If he is the Royalist brother, he will be an asset to our community. If he is not…." The statement hung ominously. There was no need for him to finish it.

"A Roundhead at Ainslie!" Alysa murmured. "It doesn't bear thinking about."

"We must proceed cautiously." Across the table, father's and daughter's eyes met. A message passed between them. Ainslie was one of the great houses of the area. It would be dangerous to have one of the enemy ensconced there. "Very cautiously indeed."

Later that day, Alysa followed her father to the stable yard, where he had gone to inspect a young mare who was about to foal for the first time. While he discussed arrangements with the head groom, she waited patiently, wandering from stall to stall to pat the heads of the horses stabled there. Only about a third of the stalls were in use—yet another reminder that the Roundhead regime had decimated Lord Strathern's finances.

As a punishment for his loyalty to the king, all but a tiny portion of his estates had been sequestered at the end of the war. He had been allowed to keep Strathern, the property on which his title was based, in order to provide for his family, but the rich lands from which he had once drawn most of his wealth were no longer his.

Strathern was a small manor compared to the one the family had used as their principal residence before the war and it was shockingly old-fashioned. It had been difficult to adjust to such reduced circumstances when they had relocated there after the king's execution. As well, there were other, more serious, problems. The lands had been ravaged during the war, the cattle stolen to feed the Roundheads, the horses requisitioned to mount Oliver Cromwell's formidable New Model Army. Rebuilding was a slow process, especially when there was little money to go around.

And so, the roomy loose boxes housed plebeian workhorses as well as the bloodstock used by the family for riding. To Alysa it made no difference as she patted the out-thrust noses while waiting for her father.

When he had finished his inspection, she said eagerly, "Papa, have you had word?"

Lord Strathern patted the mare's nose before saying carefully, "I have, Alysa. Come, let's walk over to the pasture. I want to view the cattle grazing there. We can talk while we go."

Though there was no censure in her father's voice, Alysa was reminded of the constant need for caution, because supporting an exiled king was a dangerous matter. Silently, she waited until he was ready to speak.

The cattle were pastured away from the house and main outbuildings. There was no one about to overhear Strathern disclose, "My contact in the Sealed Knot has confirmed that the emissary from King Charles will be your brother."

Alysa's breath caught with excitement. "Oh, Papa! How wonderful. When is he to arrive?"

"Soon. I was not given the exact date for security reasons, but I am sure it will be within the month." After ten years of republican rule, the Royalist cause was fragmented in England. There were those, like Lord Strathern, who accepted the Sealed Knot, a secret council of six men, as the coordinators of rebellion in England. Lately, however, other groups claiming to represent loyal Royalists and offering contrary opinions had arisen. With no clear voice on whether rebellion in England was possible or not, King Charles had decided to send envoys from his own court to acquire firsthand information about the country's state of readiness. Thomas Leighton was one of those men.

A pleased smile curved Alysa's mouth. "It will be wonderful to have Thomas home again."

Strathern turned from his thoughtful contemplation of the field of dairy cattle. Fixing a steady gaze on his daughter, he cautioned, "Thomas is not coming home for good, my dear. Nor will his visit be an opportunity for family rejoicing. The time he is able to spend with us will be brief."

Alysa refused to be daunted. "I know, Papa, but Thomas has been in exile for nigh on eight years now and I miss him. Just to see and speak to him again will be a treat."

"Yes," Strathern said, a little wistfully. "This wretched war has turned all our lives topsy-turvy. A pox on Oliver Cromwell and all Roundheads!" He turned back to his pensive study of the grazing cattle.

For a moment Alysa stood silently beside him. Then she tilted her head so she could watch him as she said, "Papa, when Thomas arrives, I will of course be there."

A muscle at the corner of Strathern's mouth twitched with amusement. It was typical of Alysa to announce her participation in a potentially dangerous activity, rather than to ask permission. As he had expected that she would want to be involved in her brother's welcoming party he had already thought the question through. "Yes, my dear, provided—"

Alysa bristled. "Conditions, Papa?"

Strathern nodded, his expression serious. "Conditions, Alysa."

Her lovely features twisted into a pout, but she sighed with resignation. "Very well, Papa." Suddenly her eyes twinkled. "I trust they will not be too onerous?"

A faint smile curled Strathern's mouth. "I do not think so, but you may, daughter." At Alysa's scandalized look, he laughed. "My dear, we must remember that Thomas is a wanted man. Should the Roundheads come to hear of his return to England, they will try to capture him. That would put Thomas, and all those meeting him, in danger of arrest. I would not like you to see the inside of a prison, Alysa."

"So," she said slowly, "I will only be allowed to go if you believe I will be safe."

"Correct, my dear."

"How will you know?" she asked simply.

Edward rubbed his chin thoughtfully. "In a small community like West Easton, it is difficult to keep news of any moment from becoming public knowledge. Anyone with a mind to pave his way into the good graces of our current rulers could supply information of Thomas's return, but I trust the people of West Easton not to do so. All, that is, except Sir Philip Hampton. His loyalties are a question."

"Even if he is the Royalist brother?"

Strathern nodded. "Yes. He has been allowed to inherit a valuable estate by the Roundheads. There is usually a price to be paid for such generosity."

Alysa's eyes narrowed. "You think he has been sent to spy on us?"

"I cannot say for sure, my dear, but I think it is possible. In any event, he might have had to compound in order to inherit. If so, he will not want to be involved in our activities." The Roundhead government levied a heavy estate tax on all Royalists. In order to inherit, or retrieve his estate from the government, a Royalist gentleman had to pay the hated tax. This was called compounding. If a man compounded, it usually meant that he would be reluctant to participate in any further attempts to restore the king. "I want to know more of the man before Thomas arrives."

A gleam of mischief appeared in Alysa's eyes. "I would be happy to engage in discourse with the gentleman, Papa. After all, he is unmarried and so eminently eligible. What could be more natural than for me to show an interest in him?"

Relief and consternation fought in Strathern's expression. "Cedric Ingram could become jealous. Or he might decide that you are too flighty for his taste. I would not want to see your chances with him ruined because of this, Alysa."

She cocked her head. "You do not intend to tell Master Ingram of your suspicions?"

"A man is entitled to be given the benefit of the doubt, until the crime against him can be proven. I would not like to voice my suspicions of Sir Philip Hampton to anyone until I feel certain that he is not what he claims."

Alysa nodded. The sentiment was typical of her father's attitude toward his fellow man. He acted honorably whether others did or not. "Master Ingram may assume that his suit would be accepted should he choose to proffer it, but he has not offered for me and I have not agreed. Until we are betrothed we are nothing more than friends." Her chin rose a little, emphasizing the jut in the gentle rounding, and the sparkle in her eyes became more pronounced. "Besides, I believe it would do Cedric Ingram good to recognize that he is not the only gentleman considered to be a catch in West Easton!"

Strathern laughed, curiously relieved. Though he worked closely with Cedric Ingram to keep Royalist hopes and spirits high in this corner of Southwest England, there was something about the man that he did not like, something he couldn't pinpoint. The idea of his beloved Alysa wed to Ingram nagged at him, even though the whole neighborhood thought it an excellent match. It did him good to hear Alysa speak so blithely of Ingram, for he had been half afraid that her heart had been lost to him. He touched her gleaming golden hair gently. "Remember, Alysa, be careful. This is not a game."

Her eyes danced. "Of course, Papa! But I shall enjoy probing into the motives of Sir Philip Hampton no end!"

The sleek black stallion arched its crested neck and tossed its handsome head. Philip Hampton automatically gentled the animal with firm hands and knees as he rode down the main street of West Easton. Instinct dictated his moves, rather than conscious thought, for he was very much aware that he was being watched surreptitiously by the people of the village. It was fortunate that he had been riding since he was a tiny child and had been a cavalry officer for so long that he was as one with the horse he rode. Thus, he did not have to waste conscious thought on managing the spirited stallion.

Instead, his senses were able to capture the small nuances of the town: the main street muddy from the March rain, the solidly constructed frame buildings that housed the shops, the ancient stone church at one end of the town and the timber smithy at the other. Behind the commercial buildings were the dwellings of the merchants and beyond them the cottages of the lesser folk. In the distance could be heard the lowing of cattle or the bleats of sheep. There were smells too. The rank scent of drying earth fought with the pungent odor of burning wood and the sweet smell of flowering fruit trees.

All in all, West Easton was a village like any other village, with one exception. It was where Philip Hampton must make his home from now on, and until he had been acknowledged by Edward, Lord Strathern, he would always be an outcast.

His restless gaze sharpened as he noted three ladies emerging from the mercer's shop. Thoughtfully he drew his horse to a snorting stop, and in one smooth movement, he dismounted. Catching the bridle in his hand, he strolled toward the shop, regardless of the mud sucking at his boots.

"Lady Strathern," he said, removing his broad-brimmed beaver hat, jauntily cocked on one side and embellished by a curling ostrich feather. With a flourish, he swept the hat downward in an elegant bow, very conscious of the image he presented to the three women. His short, skimpy doublet, buttoned only halfway down so that the fine linen of his shirt could show through, was in the forefront of fashion, even if it was somewhat drafty on this brisk spring afternoon. The cloak he wore fastened at the neck was thrust negligently over his shoulders, providing little extra warmth. His breeches were wool, but they stopped at the knee in a froth of ribbon loops. Fortunately he was wearing stirrup hose and ankle socks under the soft leather of his long boots. The hose ended in a froth of lace where the flexible leather had been folded down into a cup-shaped top.

He knew he was the epitome of a fashionable Royalist gentleman. He knew it, but still he could feel the tension tightening his nerves and stiffening his muscles. "What a pleasure it is to meet you, my lady. Allow me to introduce myself. I am Sir Philip Hampton of Ainslie Manor."

Abigail, who was dressed very sensibly in a riding habit of sturdy dark brown cloth, which would not readily show either dirt or wear, nodded coolly and said with a small, polite smile, "How do you do, Sir Philip?" She hesitated, as if unsure whether or not to continue, then added, "This is most irregular, but allow me to make you known to my daughters, Alysa and Prudence."

The charming smile he used infrequently, but to excellent effect, curled Philip's lips. "My pleasure, Mistress Leighton, Mistress Prudence. I am delighted to make your acquaintance."

Prudence stammered something polite while Alysa returned Philip's smile with a small, tantalizing one of her own. The expression in her blue eyes was masked by her carefully lowered lids. In another woman, Philip might have thought the look one of modesty. For Alysa Leighton, he was not so charitable.

"Sir Philip, how delightful to meet you at last," she said. "You have no idea how much we have all wanted to make your acquaintance."

Philip raised his brows. Ainslie abutted on Strathern property. It would have been a simple matter for the lord of Strathern Hall to have bundled his family into a carriage and driven them over to the manor. If there was anything Philip disliked in a woman, it was dissembling. He had seen too much of it in the past and known the damage it could do to those who were victims of it. His antipathy gave him the comforting feeling of being well armored against Alysa Leighton's undeniable charms.

For Alysa Leighton was, to Philip's mind, a typical Royalist beauty. Her face was round and, in a more innocent lady, would have been described as sweet, but the sharp intelligence lurking in Alysa's vivid blue eyes made sweet an adjective unlikely to be used for her. The jut to her rounded chin and the pouty cast to her bowed lips further emphasized that she was a lady used to getting what she wanted from the men in her life.

Even the obviously well-used riding habit she wore could not detract from her beauty. The bodice, tailored in the form of a doublet, shaped her breasts, and the froth of fine linen that showed through the open buttons suggested a slender waist, even as the ample material masked it. Her creamy skin and blond hair were seductive against the dark blue of the sturdy cloth, making Philip ache to see her dressed in satin or silk. He suspected she would be exquisite.

However, though he might dislike the ploys used by Mistress Alysa and her ilk to snare unwary males, Philip had no hesitation in making use of the lady in order to achieve his ends. He was quite happy to play whatever game Alysa was planning, as long as he was the eventual winner.

Though these cynical thoughts didn't show on Philip's face, Alysa seemed intuitively to have understood that he would not be an easy conquest. She laughed softly and touched the back of his hand with her gloved one. "What a burden it is to be the prominent family in an area. The people all look to us, you see, for the lead they are to follow. Papa had to be certain…that is, that you are a respectable person."

This time a smile of real amusement twitched Philip's lips. "And am I?"

"Papa has given us permission to speak to you," Alysa murmured, lowering her eyes demurely. "He would not have done so if he believed it to be inadvisable."

Tantalizing the mere male seemed to be second nature to Mistress Alysa, Philip decided. Drawing upon skills he had learned from his father, who had been a prominent courtier at the late King Charles's court, Philip maintained a bland expression as he bowed elegantly. "Lord Strathern is a wise man, mistress. In these troubled times, one can never be sure whether or not an individual is what he seems."

"Exactly!" Alysa beamed.

To Philip's surprise, the smile seemed natural, which didn't fit with his view of Royalist women. Long ago, he'd learned they were cold, scheming and heartless, despite the charm of their manners. If a man allowed one to get near to him, he would find himself losing his independence, and everything else he held dear.

An entrancing dimple danced into life in Alysa's cheek. "And so, Sir Philip, pray tell us how you find England after your long exile on the Continent."

"The longer I am at Ainslie Manor, the more content I become." His answer surprised him, for he realized it was the truth.

"That is not unexpected, Sir Philip," Abigail said. "I'm sure a family manor in England is much more comfortable than a rented lodging on the Continent, even if the manor is in need of refurbishment." The cautious glint remained in her brown eyes, but there was also a question there as she glanced at Alysa.

Philip noted that curiously. Evidently she was surprised at the manner in which Alysa was acting. Or was the surprise over what Alysa was saying to him? Possibly Lady Strathern preferred to keep conversations with strangers to a bare minimum. That would not be surprising, for in an England where brother had fought brother for years and the vanquished had suffered from the heavy yoke of the victor, it was not wise to trust too easily.

Philip decided not to give Lady Strathern an excuse to slip

away too soon. He would keep the conversation going and at the same time reinforce his story about the past. "I rarely had contact with my Uncle Richard before the war and after...." He shrugged. "What happened to Ainslie, and to other estates hereabouts? I had not heard that any skirmishes were fought in this vicinity."

"Ainslie Manor, like other properties in the area, was attacked and looted by marauding troops. In the years since, there has not been the money to restore them." There was an edge of bitterness to Abigail's soft voice. "Once West Easton was a place like any other. There were those who supported the king and those who did not. After the town was devastated by the parliamentary army, there were only Royalists in West Easton." Very deliberately, she added, "I would not want to be a Roundhead sympathizer if I lived here."

Once more Philip raised his brows. "Then I am glad to say I am not."

Alysa interjected gently, "You must have had time to look into Ainslie's condition, Sir Philip. How do you find the estate?"

Philip answered evenly, but there was a question at the back of his eyes. Alysa Leighton clearly wanted his attention focused on her, and he wondered why, though it suited his purpose admirably to have the lady fascinated with him. "Ainslie is not as prosperous as I remember it being when I visited as a child, but I believe that with careful management and much work, I will be able to bring the estate back to its old glory." He paused, then added deliberately, "I also believe that the political climate will soon be more favorable to those who lost much in the war."

Alysa smiled approvingly, but a shutter came down over the expression in Abigail's eyes. Caution gave way to vigilance. "I do not indulge in the discussion of politics, Sir Philip. I think you will find that few in this area do. We have suffered much through the unrestrained results of political disagreements. All we ask is to be left in peace."

The warning in Abigail's words could not be missed, and

like the good strategist he was, Philip knew when it was time to retreat. "My pardon, Lady Strathern." A rueful light glinted in his dark, almost black, eyes. "I fear that my years on the Continent have made me forget my manners. With little to occupy our time but the desire to return to our homes, we perhaps indulged in plotting and political speculation a trifle too much. Now that I am returned, I find the habit hard to break."

Though Abigail did not appear to be appeased by his comment, Alysa responded warmly, "Indeed, Sir Philip, you are most fortunate in being able to return. Is it true that you have a brother who adheres to the Roundhead cause and who was willing to plead your case with the Lord Protector when your uncle died, leaving you heir to his estate?"

"Alysa!" Abigail said reprovingly.

Alysa raised one dark blond eyebrow, her blue, heavy-lidded eyes amused. To his surprise, Philip felt an answering humor twitch his lips. "Alas, Mistress Leighton, it is true that one member of my family had the poor taste to follow the late Oliver Cromwell. As a result, he throve while the rest of us endured political misfortune." A sardonic note entered his voice. "Perhaps his conscience bothered him after all these years and he decided to help me claim my legal rights in order to salve it."

"Perhaps." Alysa added gently, "Or perhaps he thought that the gift of Ainslie would persuade you to join the Roundhead cause as he did."

Her bluntness sat oddly with the image Philip had created of Alysa as a subtle, insidious schemer. For a moment, his eyes narrowed dangerously, before he was able to hide his thoughts behind a bland mask. "My brother's reasons are his own and not of my concern. We have always gone our separate ways, merely retaining friendly contact. Politics do not enter into our relationship."

"Then you must be the only family in England that it doesn't!" interjected Prudence. As clear and easy to read as Alysa was complex and confusing, she said fiercely, "I'faith, I grow impatient with the discussions of the past I hear around me. The war is over! Best we all remember that and look to the future instead."

"I suggest you moderate your tone, daughter," Abigail said stringently, before she softened. "However, your words do make some sense. Now, if Sir Philip will excuse us, I would like to visit the bootmaker before we join your father. He said he would be no more than a half an hour at the smithy." She nodded her head in dismissal. "Good day to you, Sir Philip."

"And to you, Lady Strathern. Mistress Leighton. Mistress Prudence." He bowed politely as he watched them leave and silently thanked Lady Strathern for advising him where her husband was to be found. Having implemented the first part of the rough plan he had concocted, he might as well push to achieve the second.

The smithy was at the far end of the village, set a little apart to minimize the danger of sparks from the forge starting a fire that would involve the whole community. A young boy who was hovering near the front entry shouted, "Hello, sir! Are you coming to see my papa, the smith?"

He hurried over to hold Philip's horse while he dismounted. Acknowledging that was indeed what he was planning, Philip asked the boy to walk the horse while he went inside. He was already halfway through the door as the lad pulled his forelock and promised to take great care of the stallion.

The heat from the forge was stifling, despite the dampness of the spring day. Philip could not help wondering what made a man like Edward, Lord Strathern, spend a half an hour inside the overheated shed, when his authority and status entitled him to command the smith come to him.

A gesture of respect from one man to another involved in the same dangerous plotting? A need for privacy, perhaps? The presence of the youthful guard at the door suggested the latter.

Since interrupting Lord Strathern was his purpose, not eavesdropping on his conversation, Philip called loudly, "Hallo, smith! Are you there?" He paused in the doorway to allow his eyes to adjust to the dimness of the interior.

"I am," said the smith, a stocky man with broad shoulders and a sturdy independence to match. "What would you like—Sir Philip, is it not?"

"Aye, it is," Philip acknowledged amiably as he proceeded into the building. "I need several of my horses shod and wondered if you could come out to Ainslie Manor this week to see to it." He caught sight of Strathern, standing by a table on which several bridle bits of excellent workmanship had been laid. Bowing, he added, "But I am interrupting! Pray do not mind me. I will happily wait until you're finished."

"Indeed, my business here is done," Strathern said. He turned to the smith. "I will have a half a dozen of these new bits, Wishingham. Send them to Strathern Hall when they are ready."

Barnabus Wishingham, the smith, bowed. "Of course, my lord." He turned to Philip. "Now, sir, you were asking when I could come to shoe your horses."

"Any time will do," Philip said, waving the smith away with thinly disguised impatience. "Strathern, a moment, if you please."

On his way out, Edward paused. He observed Philip through shrewd, wary eyes. "A moment only. I have promised my wife and daughters to meet them and I have already lingered over-long."

Philip's mouth twitched in what could have been amusement. "The ladies are behind times themselves. I met them but a few minutes ago and they were on their way to the bootmaker."

"I see."

There was a cool edge to Strathern's voice that Philip was able to make use of. Feigning hesitation, he said, "It was of your daughter Alysa that I wished to speak to you, Lord Strathern."

"Alysa?" Curiosity colored Edward's voice. "Why?"

Philip drew a deep breath. "As you know, I am newly returned to England. Now that I am once more a man of estate, I feel it my duty to marry and start a family. Mistress Alysa has a very fine reputation in the area, and now that I have met her I can see why. I need not mention that her loveliness is such that any man would be delighted to look upon her every day of his life. In that and many other ways, I believe that she would make me an excellent wife. Consequently, I wondered if I might have your permission to visit her in order to press my suit."

Not surprisingly, Strathern was startled by the request. He was silent for a moment, his shrewd eyes examining Philip's face, seeking sincerity in his expression. At last he said dryly, "My daughter has a will of her own, Sir Philip. Yes, you may call upon her, but she will say if she wishes the visits to continue."

Philip bowed. "I can ask for nothing fairer."

With a nod, Lord Strathern left the smithy.

Philip stared after him, his expression enigmatic.

And so, he thought, *the game begins.*

CHAPTER 2

The family sitting room where Alysa and Prudence were mending sheets on this dull spring day was a small, cluttered chamber. Though the room was not normally used for entertaining, Jenkins, the elderly butler, brought the gentleman who called directly there. After all, it was only Cedric Ingram and he was almost one of the family.

Cedric Ingram was a small man with a tight, humorless smile and pale gray eyes that were rarely warm. Though fine boned and even featured, his face was not a memorable one, for no spark of life animated his expression. He dressed, however, with the style and panache befitting a man of his status, for in the West Easton area, he was second in rank only to Lord Strathern.

As Jenkins ushered him into the room, the full glory of his attire made Alysa blink and Prudence sigh with pleasure.

A canary-yellow doublet was paired with slightly darker breeches. The doublet was very short and skimpy, showing a great deal of fine linen shirt at his waist, while the legs of his breeches were very wide. White ribbons adorned the bottoms of the breeches and large white rosettes embellished the outside seams. His artfully curled hair fell past his shoulders, and in the front, two thick locks were tied with white ribbons in the fashion known as love locks.

Over his shoulders was a cloak of canary-and-white silk, which matched the suit. His tall black boots were made of soft Spanish leather and folded down below the knees in a cup-shaped cuff. Stirrup hose frothed at their rims.

The garments proclaimed Cedric to be an avid Royalist, but apart from making eager promises, his loyalty had never been tested. During the war he had let his brother, the Earl of Easton, carry the family honor into battle. Cedric's contribution to the Stuart cause had been to offer shelter to the young King Charles during his flight from England after the battle of Worcester and to manage his exiled brother's remaining estate. However, he was passionate in his belief that Charles would one day return to England and that was something Alysa liked about him.

Now in his mid-thirties and still unmarried, Cedric had been courting Alysa in a lazy way for the past year. Lately, he had begun to act as if their betrothal had already been announced.

As he entered, Alysa put down her sewing and smiled, but Prudence greeted him with flattering pleasure. "Master Ingram, how delightful to see you." She dropped her sheet and hurried forward, plucking at the soft folds of her sky-blue gown to straighten it. "How kind of you to come to brighten our gloomy day!"

Cedric's pale eyes swept over Prudence with the cold calculation of a snake assessing its prey. His glance passed her, disdaining her as unworthy, and came to rest on Alysa. Dressed in a gown of soft violet wool, with ice-blue trimmings and petticoat, her golden curls framing her lovely features, she was a woman any man could be proud of. Imperceptibly the cool gray of his eyes warmed. "I came to speak to your father, but find that he is not in."

Resentment surged through Alysa, not on her own behalf, but for Prudence. More and more often lately she found herself angry at the things Cedric said or did, and she was not sure if it was because she had changed since he had first begun to court her, or if Cedric had changed. It was, she suspected, a little of both.

Now her anger was focused on his thoughtless disregard of her sister. She had no doubt that Cedric had indeed come to visit Lord Strathern or that he had decided to stop in to speak to the young ladies of the house simply as a courtesy, but he had no right to squash Prudence's pleasure with such careless ease.

There was little she could do to reprimand him, however. It was not her place and Cedric wouldn't listen anyway. "My father is expected back within the hour. I shall be happy to tell him you called."

Cedric smiled at her, a tight upward twitch of the lips that was devoid of emotion. "You are too kind, Mistress Alysa. However, I find I have a moment or two to spare. If you will suffer my presence, I shall be happy to wait for him."

Alysa gestured to a chair at the same time as Prudence burst out, "Oh, how delightful! Of course you must stay, Master Ingram! Your company will undoubtedly drag us out of the doldrums we are suffering this morning."

Alysa waited tensely for Cedric's reply. It would be too cruel of him to snub Prudence's enthusiasm yet again.

Ingram, however, smiled at Prudence, thanked her for her kind invitation and sat down on a high-backed chair that creaked dangerously.

Blossoming under Cedric's notice, momentary as it was, Prudence flung herself down on the edge of a settee that was close to his seat. The satin of her peach petticoat rustled alluringly. "Master Ingram, I understand you have recently purchased a new horse for your stables. Is this part of a breeding program to enhance the bloodlines in your stud?"

Abigail, Lady Strathern, always said that the best way to attract a man was to ask him about what interested him, then look engrossed when he replied, no matter how boring the subject was. As Lord Strathern was deeply involved in the husbandry of his lands, Prudence naturally assumed Cedric would have the same interests.

She was wrong. Ingram shrugged his narrow shoulders and looked down his high-bridged nose. "I have no idea. I bought the animal on the advice of my head groom." He turned to Alysa and smiled indulgently. "You have been very quiet, Mistress Alysa. Are you feeling quite well this morning?"

"I feel fine," Alysa said softly. Her deep blue eyes flickered over Prudence, noting her sister's downcast expression. Alysa was well aware that Prudence thought her incredibly fortunate in having attracted Cedric Ingram, for the younger girl could not imagine any female not being instantly and always enamored of him. With his cool aristocratic airs and patrician features, he was the epitome of a perfect cavalier gentleman. In Prudence's opinion, the woman who was lucky enough to capture Cedric's attentions and eventually his hand would be blessed indeed. She had once told Alysa that if her sister had not been amongst those vying for his attention, Prudence would happily have entered the contest herself.

As a result, Alysa was equally aware that Prudence could be easily hurt by Cedric's often arrogant actions. He never failed to make it perfectly clear that he felt himself to be far superior to those who did not possess the power or importance to be of value to him, and Prudence, unfortunately, fit this category perfectly.

A deep affection for her sister made Alysa say gently, "I'm surprised at the loose rein you keep on your servants, Master Ingram. My father always says that it is important to allow one's staff to act independently at times, but he would never blindly follow a servant's advice without first making the decision on his own."

Ingram raised his brows and smiled in a supercilious way that Alysa found extremely annoying. When he had first begun to court her, he had been flatteringly attentive, discussing issues with her as he might with another man, listening to her opinions with apparent interest. Now that he thought he had all but won her, he treated her with the carelessness he might show to a longtime retainer. "As I know your father's lands to be in excellent condition, I am sure he keeps a close eye on their maintenance. Should I wish to discuss land management with him, I am confident that his advice would be sound. You and I, Mistress Alysa, have a different set of subjects on which to converse."

Alysa stabbed her needle through the linen sheet with a

violence that didn't show on her serene features, or sound in her soft voice. "My father taught me that we all owe obligations to the land and the people who work it, Master Ingram. Thus, I am always interested in the subject of its management." When annoyed color flooded his cheeks, she added peaceably, "But I know Prudence would prefer to discuss other matters and so we shall. Have you heard that Miss Meacham over at Broughton House will be leaving to visit Lincoln in a week? She tells me that her sister is soon to be brought to childbed and is desperate to have one of her family with her when the time comes."

"But why?" Prudence asked, her youthful naiveté coming to the surface.

Alysa shot her an indulgent look and said, "Having family near during a time of crisis is important, Prue. Think how lonely it would be if you could not see Mama or Papa whenever you liked."

Prudence considered that for a moment. "Oh, the way you miss Thomas, you mean."

Alysa's eyes clouded at the mention of her beloved brother. "Exactly."

Cedric said smoothly, "Family is always important." His voice was as cool as the expression in his pale eyes. Alysa knew that he and Thomas had never been friends and was not surprised when he turned the conversation back to area gossip. "Did you hear that Nathanial Morton has asked Miss Atherton to become his wife?"

Alysa allowed herself to be diverted. Her questions about Cedric's suitability as a husband were coming more and more frequently. Worse, the questions were no longer arising from nagging little irritations, but now emerged from a deeper insight into his character and beliefs. For the moment, however, Alysa was content to let the relationship continue as it was. At least until Thomas had visited and fled once more. So she exclaimed with pleasure and asked Cedric about the details of their neighbor's upcoming nuptials.

Thus they were able to pass the remaining time until Lord Strathern returned in harmony. But when Cedric had gone and the ladies were once more alone, Prudence demanded bluntly, "Alysa, have you lost interest in Master Ingram? Though your voice was sweet, your words were hardly flattering. In sooth, if you do not take care, he will stop courting you!"

Alysa paused in her sewing as she looked up, a thoughtful expression on her face. "If he loses interest in me, so be it, sister! The other day I told Mama that I would not know how to reply if he asked for my hand and I meant it. There are times when the man can be perfectly charming and I think he would make a fine husband. But then at others I could gladly hit him, and I congratulate myself that I am not bound to him for the rest of my life." She shrugged. "There is a fault in my makeup, I suppose, that I want more than just a marriage of form. I cannot help it, but there it is. I want to marry a man I can respect, but also one I can love." She paused before adding, "And I do not love Master Ingram."

Prudence's eyes widened and hope filled them. "You do not?"

"No. Nor do I know any man in West Easton who can fulfill my dreams," Alysa added with a sigh.

"That's because you have known all of the men in the area forever," Prudence said practically. "How can you fall in love with someone you know very well?"

Alysa laughed. "Indeed."

Prudence nodded thoughtfully. "Of course, there is someone new hereabouts. Sir Philip Hampton." She grinned at her half sister. "A fine gentleman and one who seemed quite taken with you when we met the other day. You must open your heart, Alysa, and see where this leads."

Alysa smiled, a deep, secret smile. "Perhaps I will," she said softly. "Perhaps I will."

"Are you ready, Alysa? Prudence?" Lord Strathern accepted his black beaver hat from the hands of the elderly Jenkins. The hat was good quality, but old and well used, like the burgundy doublet and breeches he wore under a loose cassock. "I want to be off and back before the storm strikes."

A mischievous dimple peeped into life in Alysa's cheek as she drew on the embroidered leather gloves that matched her dark blue riding habit. "Of course we're ready, papa. Indeed, we have been waiting this age for you!"

Strathern grunted, fully aware that he had been delayed, though most reasonably, by his dairyman, who wanted to discuss the way his herd was producing. "Very well then, let us go!"

Laughing, Alysa shot Prudence an amused look, then linked her arm with her father's. "Now, sir, pray do explain why you think it will rain when the sky is perfectly clear."

As they walked down the steps to the drive, where three spirited horses waited, Strathern said with amused admiration, "Apart from the fact that it is March and it always rains in March, Bailey told me. The man has an uncanny knack for getting the weather right. Mayhap it is his cows who advise him. I have never seen a man who cares so much for the animals he tends."

A groom tossed Alysa up into the saddle. She frowned as she gathered up the reins. "Do you think it is wise to say such things, Papa? There are those who would use such a light-comment to condemn Master Bailey."

His eyebrows raised, Strathern responded mildly, "The only ones who heard were our own people. I trust them implicitly."

Alysa nodded. Under her gentle control the chestnut mare she rode stood quietly, confident in its rider. "Our people can be trusted, but what of others? A chance remark here, an amused comment there and Master Bailey is suddenly accused of being involved in the dark arts."

Lord Strathern listened grimly to his daughter's reply and didn't like the edge of cynicism he heard in her words, but he could not deny her soundly practical judgment. Mounting his large gray stallion, he paused to find his stirrups and gather his reins before replying. "You are correct, daughter, I did speak without thinking. Damn these mealy-mouthed Puritans and their authoritarian ways! There are times when I long for the old days, when England was ruled by her rightful, lawful guardian. King Charles may have aspired to more arbitrary power than a monarch should have, but I would rather be ruled by a Stuart than by a Cromwell! I'll be happy when King Charles II is restored to his crown."

"I think you are both jumping at shadows," Prudence commented. Dressed in a vivid green habit much like Alysa's in cut, she had been paying more attention to the very fresh bay mare she was riding than to the conversation. Now that she had the animal under a tight rein, she sallied closer to her father and sister and joined in. "England has been peaceful for years now and I for one am glad! Nor do I consider these restrictions you complain about to be so onerous. Our people are safe and our lands are able to prosper again. What is so bad about that?"

Strathern raised his brows, but he waited until they were underway before replying sternly, "There is more to life than a full belly, Prudence. A man's honor, his right to express himself freely, to live without suspicion or the fear of sudden arrest are but a few of the intangible freedoms we have lost under the domination of the army and Oliver Cromwell. I will never support the Protectorate. I refuse to. And I will do all I can to ensure that our rightful monarch is restored to the throne."

Though they were riding through relatively open country, Alysa could not resist a quick look around to reassure herself that they were alone. Ever since Thomas had followed young King Charles into exile, Lord Strathern had worked for the restoration of the king, for when Charles Stuart returned so too would Thomas Leighton.

Though it was no secret in West Easton that Lord Strathern was an ardent Royalist, it did not do to state such feelings openly. Alysa knew from past discussions that the more Prudence argued with their father the harder and more bitter Lord Strathern's opinions would become.

Something must be done to interrupt.

Alysa dug her heels into her horse as she issued a laughing challenge. "A race, from the elm tree to the pond in the next field!"

The breeze caught her words and carried them away, but it was the daring glint in her eyes and the reckless smile on her full, bowed lips that made Strathern nod and spur his own mount forward. In her fearlessness, Alysa was the image of her dead mother, even if her features had come from her father. Not to be outdone, Prudence urged her spirited mount alongside her father and sister.

The horses galloped eagerly. Obstacles such as fences meant nothing to bruising riders like the Leightons. Blood pounded in Alysa's ears as the breeze, now a wind, tore ruthlessly through the pins holding her hair and threatened to steal away her hat. Beneath her, the chestnut mare pulled and fretted, wanting to give its all, but Alysa had a strategy she intended to follow and not until the perfect moment would she allow the final burst of speed needed from her horse.

The pond was in sight. Alysa eased her hold on the mare's mouth. She was rewarded by a surge of power that left her laughing and breathless. Beside her, neck-and-neck, was her father, a grin of pure competitive pleasure on his face. Prudence, she noticed vaguely, was scarcely a length behind.

Gently, oh so delicately, Alysa tightened her reins. Not enough to noticeably draw up her mare from its headlong gallop, but enough to slow the horse and allow her father to pull a little ahead.

As he took the lead, Strathern bellowed out a victory cry. He clapped his heels against his stallion once more and slapped its neck with one hand, urging ever more speed to ensure his win. He reached the pond scant seconds before Alysa and well ahead of Prudence.

Laughing, all three paused by the water to catch their breath and permit their horses to cool down. "That was delightful," Alysa said, panting a bit. "But Prudence and I must tidy our hair. It would not do to arrive at a tenant's cottage looking all undone." She slid down off the horse so she could peer at her reflection in the pond while she rectified the damage wrought by the wind. Prudence followed suit and in a few moments the two girls were giggling lightheartedly without apparently having much success in their project.

Strathern remained on his horse, holding the other two, so it was he who first saw the lone rider emerging from the woods that sheltered the north side of the pond. The man sat tall and straight in the saddle and rode at a lazy canter with all the grace and elegance of one totally at ease on the back of a horse. Even from a distance it was possible to identify him as Sir Philip Hampton.

Strathern watched thoughtfully for a moment, before remarking casually, "Girls, I believe we have a visitor." His eyes twinkled at the squeaks of feminine embarrassment that ensued as Prudence and Alysa abandoned their attempts to beautify themselves and dove for their respective horses. A few seconds later Sir Philip appeared to notice their little group and turned his sleek black stallion toward them.

Unlike Lord Strathern's well-worn suit, Philip Hampton's clothes were new. His doublet was dark blue velvet and his breeches were fine black cloth. A black cloak swung from his shoulders with a casual elegance that belied the need for warmth on this cool March morning. The only parts of his outfit that had the look of being well used were his tall black boots and his hat.

Strathern waited silently until Hampton hailed them. Then he said curtly, "Sir Philip. I trust you are not aware that you are trespassing on my lands." The pond was on the domain farm and too close to the main house for Strathern to allow a stranger to move freely about. Philip Hampton removed his broad-brimmed beaver hat politely as he kept his restive mount still with knees and a light hand, the effortless control of an expert rider. Holding the hat in one hand, he contemplated the jaunty feather in its cocked brim thoughtfully. When he looked up, his long, tanned face was expressionless, though his eyes were cool. "I do apologize, Lord Strathern, if I have caused you any disquiet by being on your property. I had no idea the people hereabouts were so very possessive. In my youth people were more…generous."

Strathern's eyes hardened, but he was a just man. "You will not find us ungenerous for the most part, Sir Philip, but times have changed. Of necessity we are more cautious now. And so I ask again, why were you emerging from my woods just now?"

Hampton raised a dark brow. "As I said, Lord Strathern, my apologies. I did not know I was trespassing on your lands. I was exploring, as I have done since I returned. I can remember certain things about West Easton and its area, but I have not been here since I was a lad. I was merely trying to acquaint myself with the district, as it were."

Somewhat mollified, Lord Strathern nodded. The border between Strathern and Ainslie was an irregular line that followed the natural contours of the land. In this particular spot there was a small ridge that pointed like a finger toward Strathern. Here the boundary crossed through the woods that lay between the slopes of the ridge and the pond where they now were. It would be easy enough for Sir Philip to have misjudged the exact line of demarcation. "Perhaps, Sir Philip, you would enjoy your explorations more by riding along with us. We are visiting some of my tenants today. You might find it informative to see how other properties in the area are performing."

Executing a sweeping bow that brought him low over the withers of his mount and would do justice to the most polished courtier, Philip said, "I should be delighted, Lord Strathern." As he clapped his curly beaver over his dark, flowing locks he shot a sideways look at Alysa. "I could not ask for more charming company."

Alysa's faintly mischievous smile tugged at her bowed lips. "Sir Philip, my sister and I will become quite ridiculously puffed up in our own esteem if you continue to shower us with compliments!"

Philip inclined his head and bestowed one of his devastating smiles on Alysa. "I have no fear of that, sweet lady, for my remarks are more than merely shallow flattery."

Alysa laughed, enjoying the repartee and not believing one word. "Indeed sir, you are too kind. But come, we are delaying my father and he has it on good authority that the afternoon will be marred by rain." She shot Edward a mischievous look and Prudence rolled her eyes.

Amusement in his eyes, Strathern agreed that they should be going and led the way to their first stop.

At the cottage of the third tenant, Alysa and Prudence went inside to talk to the farmer's wife while Edward introduced Sir Philip to the farmer and pointed out various improvements that had been made on the property since the area had been devastated during the war. The repairs had the fresh look of recent work, as if there had not been the money for them earlier. The scars of war ran deep in West Easton.

Leaving Philip to examine some fencing that had been recently installed, Strathern went off with his tenant to the barn. Philip was still alone when Alysa and Prudence emerged from the cottage. The perfect gentleman, he offered to help them remount, but Prudence suddenly remembered that she had meant to ask the farmer's wife for a recipe and darted back into the house, a whirl of bright green cloth and sand-brown curls.

Alysa watched her sister's precipitous departure with rueful amusement and hoped that Philip Hampton had not noticed Prudence's contrived attempt to give them a few minutes alone together.

He hardly seemed aware that Prudence had gone, and as he spoke, he watched Alysa steadily. "I must compliment you on your riding skills, Mistress Leighton. I saw your race as I was riding through the trees and was positive that you would emerge the winner."

"Oh!" Alysa wasn't sure how to respond to that. She thought she discerned an edge of contempt in his deep voice, and she guessed that he'd noticed her deliberate loss to her father. Embarrassed color stained her smooth cheeks; then her blue eyes began to sparkle challengingly. "Indeed, sir, I do enjoy riding, but my father is the better of me." She slanted him a sideways look as she deliberately changed the subject. "But you do not mention my indiscretion at the pond. How thoughtful of you! The wind is most unkind to ladies who give in to the urge to race."

A smile twitched at the corners of Philip's mouth.

Strangely, for Alysa was used to the grim, humorless smiles of Cedric Ingram, the look was full of warm amusement. Her stomach did a little flip and she found herself suddenly breathless. The laughter died out of Philip's face as his eyes met Alysa's and saw her involuntary response. His voice lowered a notch as he said huskily, "The wind transformed a veritable goddess into a delightful nymph."

The words were nothing more than the usual flowery phrases Royalist ladies expected from their cavaliers, but the rough passion in Philip's voice gave these a meaning beyond the obvious. For a moment Alysa could only stare at him, disconcerted. Then she managed a shaky laugh. "Sir Philip, you go too far! We are ordinary country folk here, not creatures of myth. I promise you that you will see us looking less than perfect more often than not!"

Prudence returned at that moment and Philip didn't reply. Instead, he repeated his offer to help the ladies mount, tossing Prudence up first, then Alysa.

The action was that of a gentleman helping a lady, but the effect was far more than that. From the moment he put his hands around her waist, Alysa was vitally aware of him. As he lifted her, their bodies were so close that she could smell the warm, clean scent of him. She breathed deeply, enjoying the heady fragrance, even as her flesh tingled with an unexpected pleasure. Never before had a man had this affect on her. She found it unsettling.

Once in the saddle Alysa tried desperately to collect herself, but his eyes were intent upon her, firing her blood and making her heart thump. They could have been the only people for miles about, so lost was she in the depths of his dark eyes. She started to say something, but at that moment her mare issued a high-pitched scream and reared up on its hind legs. She almost lost her seat, but instinct took over and she clung precariously to the horse.

"Alysa!" Prudence shouted. Thoroughly agitated, the mare dropped back to the ground and bolted. Alysa had lost hold of the reins, so all she could do was hang on to the mane and pray that the horse exhausted itself soon.

The mare was charging across a muddy field that had not yet been plowed. The earth caught and sucked at its hooves, slowing the beast, but directly in its path were a stile and a row of trees that separated this field from the next. With no control of the bolting mare, Alysa did not think that she or the horse would come safely over the obstacle. She gritted her teeth, refusing to accept that a nasty fall was inevitable. Slowly, she leaned against the mare's neck, reaching for the flapping reins. The horse stumbled, almost unseating Alysa. She shrieked and clung to the flying mane, thoroughly frightened now.

Ahead of her, the stile loomed perilously close. Alysa knew that if the mare tried to jump the fence, she would not be able to keep her seat. Worse, she feared that the horse would not take the jump cleanly and would injure itself. Her heart beat rapidly as she desperately tried to think of a way to save both her mount and herself. No brilliant ideas came to mind, however, for panic had begun to take hold of Alysa's emotions.

"No!" she screamed, oblivious to everything but the straining horse beneath her and the dangerous obstacle ahead. She tugged at the mane in a last desperate attempt to turn the horse, but to no avail.

From somewhere close she heard the low thunder of a second galloping horse. Hope surged in her, but she didn't dare risk looking behind to see who the rider coming to her rescue was. Besides, it wasn't necessary. She knew her father would never allow her to come to harm.

But it wasn't the gray Lord Strathern rode that gradually drew abreast of Alysa's sweating chestnut, but Sir Philip's sleek black stallion. Admiration for his riding abilities drove the panic from Alysa's mind, because he was guiding the powerful horse with only his knees as he edged the stallion close to her mount. As the horses raced neck and neck he leaned over and plucked Alysa from the saddle as if she were nothing heavier than thistledown.

She gasped and couldn't help crying out as she was suspended in the air, but Philip's arms were strong around her and she was soon safely settled before him. Gradually, the big stallion slowed, responding to silent signals Alysa couldn't interpret.

"Are you all right?" There was none of Philip's usual flowery charm in the words. Right now he was the man of action, stripped of the superficial panache he used as a disguise.

Deeply shaken, Alysa's eyes searched his face. "Yes, I'm fine, thanks to you."

He shrugged away her thanks, as if they were not necessary. "What happened to make your horse bolt?" he asked, as abruptly as before.

She frowned. "I have no idea." Now that the danger was over exhilaration seized her and laughter warmed her voice. "I was rather busy making sure I didn't take a nasty tumble, you see. I wasn't able to pause and find out."

"No doubt," he replied curtly. He turned his big horse toward Alysa's mare, which had come to a trembling stop just before the stile.

His continuing abruptness made Alysa's eyes widen. "Sir Philip, I assure you that beyond a scare I was not harmed in any way. Your dismay over my mishap is flattering, but you need not be so concerned on my behalf!"

Philip frowned for a moment; then his features emptied as he cleared his face of all expression. A moment later he was smiling and Alysa wondered if she had imagined that little moment of careful blankness.

"Allow me to tell you how delighted I am that you are safe and unharmed, Mistress Leighton. Your father and sister must be beside themselves with worry. If I catch your horse, would you feel able to ride to rejoin them?"

"Of course." Alysa couldn't help staring at him, for the difference in his manner was so pronounced from that of moments before. Moreover, he had withdrawn from her in a very tangible way. Beneath the flowery statements there was none of his earlier passion. He was like a man reciting a poem without knowing the meaning of the words.

They reached the mare, who sidled skittishly away as they

approached. Sir Philip crooned softly to the frightened animal, calming it with nonsense words until he was able to get close enough to grasp the trailing reins. The mare snorted and tossed her head, but didn't try to escape. He jumped down from his stallion, heedless of the mud dirtying his boots, and reached for Alysa. She slid into his outstretched arms, confident he would keep her safe.

For a moment he held her against him. They were so close that she could hear the thump of his heart and feel the warmth of his body. A shiver of excitement ran through her and she looked into his eyes, wondering if he had felt the same flaring of emotion she had. Satisfaction enhanced her pleasure, for burning in the dark depths of his eyes was an awareness as keen as hers.

"Your steed, fair lady," he said huskily, tossing her up into the saddle. "Allow me to escort you back to your father and sister."

"I should be delighted, kind sir," she replied, keeping her tone as light as his. He kept up an easy flow of conversation as they slowly returned to the cottage and Alysa let him talk while she thought. Once they reached the house, Lord Strathern thanked him profusely, while Prudence exclaimed volubly. The tenant and his family added their own delighted relief to the conversation, creating a pleasant confusion that lasted until Philip announced that he must take his leave and Strathern decided to curtail his visits for the day. Besides, the rain Bailey had predicted now appeared imminent.

As they rode home Alysa allowed her horse to lag a little behind and Prudence joined her.

"What a splendid man," Prudence remarked enthusiastically. "It was fortunate that he was there to rescue you, was it not?"

"Fortunate indeed. What would I have done if he had not been able to catch me before my horse reached the stile?"

"I know what a good rider you are. I'm sure you would have come to no harm," Prudence said cheerfully.

Alysa looked her sister in the eye. "Did you somehow arrange for my horse to bolt, Prue?"

Opening her eyes wide, Prudence contrived to look

injured. "Alysa! How could you think I would do such a thing?"

Alysa sighed, her hunch confirmed. "Prudence, there are other, easier ways of throwing me together with Sir Philip, if that was your plan."

Prudence laughed. "But none so effective, dear sister." She kicked her horse into a canter and joined their father. Alysa remained behind, thoughtfully remembering her short discussion with Philip Hampton. Her interest in the man had indeed intensified, but not quite in the way Prudence intended.

CHAPTER 3

Clouds covered the moon and stars, making the footing difficult for Philip Hampton's sleek black stallion. He let the horse pick its way slowly through the undergrowth, which covered the flanks of the low ridge that jutted like a pointing finger into Strathern land. Despite its proximity to Strathern Hall, the thickly wooded hill was the perfect place for a midnight rendezvous, for the top of the ridge was covered by an old stand of mature trees, which provided a relatively clear space to meet, but also gave adequate cover for men who did not want to be seen.

Men like Philip Hampton and his government contact, Sir Edgar Osborne.

As the stallion nosed through the wild tangle of saplings, blackberry vines and bushes, Philip reflected that the hillside, like the arable lands in the area, gave evidence of the depredations of war. Once the whole ridge had been covered by large, mature trees like those that crowned the top, but a wanton fire, caused by parliamentary soldiers when they were camped on the hillside, had burned off the ancient growth, leaving nothing but barren landscape behind. In time vegetation returned, but it would be many years before trees of any size again stood on this hillside.

The night was very quiet. The sounds of the stallion's hoofbeats and the snort of its breathing were loud in the dark silence, but Philip was certain he could hear no other telltale sounds. That meant he was the only one in the area, which pleased him, for he wanted to be settled at the rendezvous point when Osborne arrived. Having control of the meeting ground would give him a slight advantage over the other man, and when dealing with Sir Edgar Osborne, he needed every advantage he could get.

When the stallion breasted the rise, Philip pulled it to a standstill so that he could survey the terrain. His practiced eyes picked out a spot that provided the maximum cover, while at the same time was an excellent vantage point. Without any undue hurry he urged the horse in that direction.

There he dismounted, tied the stallion where the shadows hid its bulk and settled down to wait. Creative waiting was a skill he had long since mastered. He would use the time to run over his preparations in his mind, making sure that he had not forgotten any obscure details; then he deliberately turned his thoughts away from the crisis that was about to happen. To worry over what could not be changed would only make him tense and edgy, which could affect his judgment when he most needed to be coolheaded and quick thinking.

So, once he was satisfied that he was ready to cross verbal swords with Sir Edgar Osborne, he began to think of other things. Creature comforts came first. For the first time in a month he did not have to wear the frivolous fashions that a Royalist cavalier would choose. Instead of a skimpy doublet of velvet or satin he was wearing the oiled-leather buff coat of the military. He'd owned the jerkin for years and it shaped to his body in a most comfortable way. Moreover, it was warm, unlike the garments he was required to wear in order to further his claim that he was a Royalist just returned from exile.

He shifted uneasily as he thought about the deception he had become involved in. When he had agreed to come to West Easton, it all seemed very simple and very logical.

Osborne had approached him in Scotland, where he was serving under General Monck. Philip had recently been promoted to the rank of colonel and he was discovering that he spent more time at headquarters than out on patrol with his men. Headquarters, to Philip, was the court in miniature. Officers fawned on those in power, while their wives gushed and flirted and often gave their favors to whatever man they thought able to promote their husbands' careers. Officious clerks cited rules and regulations to every request and made even the smallest requisition difficult.

Philip hated it.

However, his life was the army and he had no private fortune that he could fall back on should he resign his commission, so he had gritted his teeth and accepted what he could not change.

Then Osborne had come to Edinburgh with the information that Philip had inherited Ainslie Manor. He suggested bluntly, that, as a loyal subject of the Lord Protector, Philip should take up residence at his new property and keep an eye on the Royalists in the area for his ruler.

Initially Philip had rejected the suggestion. He was a plain, honest man, not a spy, and he disliked slippery, untrustworthy men like Sir Edgar Osborne, to whom he took a quick and very active dislike. Not only that, but Ainslie was his by right of inheritance. Since his uncle had been neutral during the war and Philip had been an active supporter of parliament, there were no crippling taxes that must be paid before he could inherit, as there were on Royalist estates. He could go down to Ainslie any time he wanted without having to agree to spy on his new neighbors in order to gain his property.

Osborne quickly disabused him of that cheery notion. Philip was a Roundhead. West Easton was Royalist. If Philip did not agree to Osborne's plan, Osborne would make sure that everyone in the neighborhood was aware that the new owner of Ainslie Manor had supported parliament and later the Lord Protector Cromwell. There would be no point in Philip's trying to take up his inheritance, for life at Ainslie would be uncomfortable in the extreme.

Philip's immediate reaction to this blatant piece of

blackmail was to damn Osborne and throw his threats back in his face, but his father, the courtier, had taught him well.

Always think things through, Philip. Never act impulsively. Impulse is a weakness your enemies will take advantage of. A well thought-out strategy allows for mistakes and errors. No man can defeat an opponent who can outthink him.

Philip's careful planning and attention to detail had brought him through several major battles and a dozen skirmishes unscathed. He was not about to change his tactics now.

So he had lifted the corners of his lips in a semblance of a smile and told Osborne that he would consider the matter, even as fury and outrage burned through his soul.

Days had passed. Philip had not bothered to contact Osborne with an answer. Perhaps Osborne had guessed that Philip's silence meant a refusal, or perhaps it was simply in his nature to try to coerce his victims in every possible manner in order to get the response he wanted. Whatever the reason, Osborne had gone directly to Philip's commanding officer, General Monck, with his proposal and asked Monck to intervene with Philip on his behalf. Monck had done so, but not quite in the way Osborne intended.

General Monck had pointed out to Philip that the army did not trust Richard Cromwell and would not support him as commander-in-chief. Since Richard refused to appoint a military man to that post, sooner or later there would be a confrontation and Lord Protector Richard would fall from power. Military rule would follow, something Monck didn't think England would tolerate for very long.

Settle yourself at Ainslie, lad. Tell Osborne a few secrets to keep him happy. He won't be bothering you for long, I'll wager my army on that. Once he's gone you'll be free and well out of whatever's to come.

Philip had followed the advice of both his father and his commanding officer. He had thought about Osborne's offer, considered his options and wished he had a looking glass that could see into the future. In the end he had decided that Monck's advice was sound. Ainslie was solid, real, and it was his. Osborne was a passing problem who could be dealt with in the fullness of time. So, he had resigned his commission and headed south to his future.

When he left Scotland he had no idea how difficult he would find impersonating his brother, the ardent Royalist, to be. Living at Ainslie forced Philip to come to grips with the fact that he would never see Anthony Hampton again. Until the war had pushed them into different camps, he and Anthony had been close. They had been allies against the loneliness of growing up on the edges of the court, part of that small, tight world, yet not part of it. Their parents had been kind, but Anthony Hampton Sr. had relied on his position in the king's household to support his family and he could not afford to offend those in power or to be seen to be lacking in any way. He spent more time at Whitehall than he did at the London lodgings he rented for his family.

As they grew, Philip had resented his father's absences, both for his own sake and his mother's, and he blamed them on court life. While Philip vowed he would never allow himself to be sucked into the intrigue and politics that spread like a virulent disease through the court, Anthony became fascinated with the life. He took up with a rather wild bunch of young bloods and would come home at all hours, laughing and boasting of his night of revels, or whispering extravagant word pictures of his romantic conquests, to his impressionable younger brother.

Now Anthony was gone, consumed by the incessant plotting and bickering of a court-in-exile. Because of his death Philip must pretend to be the brother he had loved and lost. It hurt, sometimes unbearably. At those moments of anguish, he blamed Sir Edgar Osborne for his pain.

He glanced at the sky, wondering how long he had been waiting for the odious Osborne, but clouds blocked the moon and stars. Over the years Philip had become adept at estimating the passage of time and he guessed that he had been waiting a half an hour or more. Perhaps Osborne was lost. Philip found that the idea suited him just fine, for it gave him another slight advantage over the Londoner.

Thinking about how he had come to be here tonight had

started anger bubbling again through his veins, so he forced his thoughts into different paths. Random fragments of conversations about Ainslie and the needs of the property flitted through his head; then he focused on the chance meeting with Lord Strathern and his daughters. There he paused to linger on memories of Alysa Leighton.

Alysa as she crouched over the lake, frantically trying to tidy her windblown hair, her lovely features alight with laughter. Or later, as she sat the bolting horse with all the skill of one of his own well-trained cavalry, her face pale with strain and a fear she wouldn't admit. He had rescued her from, at best, a nasty fall and to his surprise she had felt good in his arms. Her laughing indifference to the danger she had faced sat oddly with his image of a Royalist lady. He wondered now if Alysa was as clear and honest as she seemed, or if she was as duplicitous as the women who had pursued his father during his time at court.

From some distance away came the sound of a twig cracking. Philip shook himself out of his reverie with the speed of long experience. Every sense was alert as he strode over to the edge of the old growth and peered into the night. The shadows were as black and heavy as the clouds above, but he thought he detected the shape of a horse and rider heading toward him. Cautiously, he melted into the shadows and waited for the newcomer to arrive.

Sir Edgar Osborne entered the old growth with reasonable stealth, given that he hated woodland areas. He couldn't resist uttering an oath when Philip silently emerged from the trees behind him. "'Od's blood, Hampton! What the devil are you playing at?"

Philip raised his brows. "I was merely being cautious, Sir Edgar. Were you followed?"

Osborne was thoroughly fed up with his jaunt through the countryside. He fiddled with the lapels of his dark wool cassock, a long, loose coat he wore over a black doublet and narrow breeches. "Damn it, no. That wretched undergrowth is so thick I can't imagine how anyone could possibly keep another person under observation."

Philip considered him wryly as he dismounted. "There would be no need to see you, Osborne. You were making enough noise to wake the whole area. I was able to track you from a mile away."

"Indeed!" Osborne said stiffly. He didn't like being criticized by one he considered an underling. Deftly, he turned the subject. "Let's have your report and be gone from here. As poor as my accommodations are, I would like to be in my bed before sunrise."

Ignoring the sarcasm, for it was hardly gone midnight, Philip shrugged. "There is not much to report. I have no proof that the leading Royalists in the area are associated with the Sealed Knot, though I believe they are. Nor can I prove that they are actively plotting to overthrow the Lord Protector. I have made contact with Lord Strathern and he appears willing to grant that I am a Royalist returned from exile. Once he has accepted me, I shall be welcomed in the area and I can begin to find out more about the Sealed Knot and its activities."

"You don't have time for that."

Philip raised his brows again at the snap in Osborne's voice. "How so?"

"Our agents in the Low Countries have sent word that Charles no longer trusts the gentlemen of the Sealed Knot. Because of that, he has decided to bypass the Knot and send emissaries to Britain directly. Their mission will be to decide if another rebellion is possible. Apparently his spies here are telling him that Richard Cromwell does not have the support his father did. Charles wants to know if that is true before he acts."

"The conduct of a wise man," Philip murmured without thinking.

"Or a coward," Osborne sneered.

Philip shrugged. He wasn't going to get into an argument with Osborne. "Do you know when these envoys are supposed to arrive?"

"Within the month." Osborne allowed a heartbeat to pass before adding, "And I know the name of the man being sent to this area."

Something about the way he said the words, perhaps the

mockery in his voice or the delight in his eyes, prepared Philip for what was to come. He was able to ask quite casually, "And who is being sent to West Easton?"

"Thomas Leighton."

Philip leaned against a broad tree trunk. His lazy posture and thoughtful tone belied the thumping of his heart. "This could be a problem. I'm sure Thomas Leighton knew my brother in exile. He will know that Anthony is dead. Even if he isn't aware that I chose the parliamentary side in the war, he will question why I am allowing people to think that I was in exile with young Charles Stuart."

"You seem damn calm about the whole thing!"

Philip pulled away from the tree. "What would you have me do, Osborne? Shout with rage and tear my hair out?"

"Eliminate Thomas Leighton."

The words fell like a blow. "Eliminate? What the devil do you mean by that?"

Osborne's face creased in a smile of triumph, for he had at last cracked Philip Hampton's calm aristocratic mask. "You have a week, mayhap two, and if you are lucky, nearly a month, to penetrate the local Royalist organization. We are certain the leader is Lord Strathern."

"Well? What has this to do with the danger of my charade being exposed?"

"Find out when Thomas Leighton is to arrive in England and I will see he never meets his associates here in West Easton. That way he will not be a danger to you."

"An excellent plan," Philip said, in control of himself once more. "But impractical. Lord Strathern is an intelligent man. Moreover he is a cautious one. Even if he accepts me as a true Royalist, he wouldn't let me into a secret as important as when and where the king's emissary is to arrive."

Osborne smirked. "No, but his daughter would, if you used her sensibly."

"His daughter!"

The ugly smile continued to play on Osborne's lips as he nodded. "We know that Lord Strathern is besotted with the girl. He tells her any number of inappropriate secrets. It is unlikely that he would be able to keep from her the time and date of her brother's return."

Though Philip had already decided that Alysa was the way to gain Lord Strathern's confidence and thus to find out more about the local Royalists, he found that he didn't like the notion when it came from Sir Edgar Osborne. His tone was absurdly indignant as he demanded, "What do you expect me to do? Seduce the girl?"

Osborne shrugged. "Why not give yourself some pleasure? I understand Mistress Alysa is quite handsome in her way."

It took all of Philip's self-control not to put his hands around Osborne's neck and throttle him. Instead he contemptuously turned his back on the man as he strode over to his tied horse. He led the animal into the clearing and as he mounted, he said simply, "I will contact you when I have news." Without waiting for a response he guided the horse into the dense undergrowth.

It was not until the darkness had swallowed him up that the stiff tension left his body. He had allowed Osborne to penetrate his thoughts and feelings tonight and that was a mistake. As long as he remained an enigma, Osborne had nothing to use against him. Exposing his indignation let Osborne see a little of his deepest soul and Philip did not doubt that Sir Edgar would use the knowledge, eventually.

There was nothing he could do about it now, beyond putting a careful guard on his emotions in the future. His mouth hardened. Though he did not like the tangled deceptions he was being forced to engage in, he was more than capable of maneuvering his way through them. Somehow, he would ensure that his goals, and not Osborne's, were the ones that were reached.

Keyed up and wary of being seen, he kept his spirited mount to a careful, mincing walk until he had reached the park around Ainslie Manor. Only then did he allow the horse to stretch its legs in a canter. The fluid motion relaxed him and his thoughts roamed freely, trying to solve the problems that had presented themselves that evening.

It was damn bad luck that the agent being sent to the West Easton area was Thomas Leighton. Much as Philip resented admitting it, Osborne was right—he would have to make some kind of arrangement to ensure Leighton didn't identify him as an impostor. But what?

Coaxing information about her brother from Alysa Leighton was not the answer. The lady was intelligent, observant and critical, qualities that made her extremely dangerous in Philip's opinion. She would wonder why he was asking the questions he was, and before long she would have guessed that Philip Hampton was not the loyal follower of King Charles he claimed to be.

There was another, softer reason for Philip's refusal to use Alysa as Osborne had suggested. Even in the short time he had known her, he sensed that Alysa Leighton was a lady of deep loyalties and strong beliefs. She would be devastated if she discovered later that her words had caused her brother to be arrested upon his arrival in England. Philip could not bring himself to do that to her.

No, he would have to find another way to deal with Thomas Leighton. The stallion's hooves rang hollowly on the slate that paved the courtyard around which the Ainslie stables were built. Philip dismounted and led the animal to one of the roomy loose boxes, where he quickly brushed it down before putting away the saddle and bridle.

The stable yard was quiet and no servant came to disturb Philip as he worked. That annoyed him and made him forget the thorny question of how to deal with Thomas Leighton. A thief could easily come in and steal all of his horses without any of the stablemen being aware of what was going on. Which only proved that West Easton was a safe area, unprepared for the more devious transgressions of mankind.

Something that was about to change.

"Sir Philip Hampton to see Miss Alysa." The elderly butler's eyes rested with tolerant amusement on Alysa's surprised face for a moment before he blandly glanced at his mistress.

"Where have you put him, Jenkins?" Abigail asked.

"In the King's Salon, my lady." Jenkins paused, then added serenely, "I thought you would want him to be properly impressed."

A smile flickered across Abigail's face, then was gone. She looked over at Alysa. "Your father told me that Sir Philip asked leave to court you—"

"He did?" Prudence interrupted, her eyes wide. She turned to her sister. "Alysa, did Papa tell you he'd done that?"

Alysa was saved from replying by Abigail, who said sternly, "Enough, Prudence! Jenkins, tell Sir Philip that we will be with him directly. Oh, and find Lord Strathern. He will want to know that Sir Philip has called."

"Yes, my lady." The butler departed without hurry.

"Now then, Alysa," said Abigail, eyeing her stepdaughter critically, "do you feel comfortable in what you are wearing, or would you like time to run up and change?"

Alysa glanced down at the rose gown with the silver-blue petticoat she had donned that morning and shook her head. "No, I am quite happy wearing this, Mama."

"Your hair is newly washed and curled and the knot at the back is still neatly bound," Abigail noted, thinking aloud. "I like the caul you have put over it. The blue satin and net highlights the gold in your hair."

Alysa touched her head tentatively. The fashion was to comb the hair at the forehead away from the face, leaving the shorter hair on the sides to frame a woman's features. The long hair at the back and the hair on the top of the head would be bound in a small, tight bun, which would be covered by a tiny cap called a caul. If a lady chose, she might leave a few strands at the nape loose and curling to emphasize the long line of her neck, as Alysa had done this morning. Though she knew she was well dressed and looked her best, Abigail's cool assessment was disconcerting, to say the least. "Mama, you do not fuss so when Cedric Ingram visits."

A little color pinked Abigail's cheeks. "You have known Cedric Ingram this age, Alysa. Sir Philip is a virtual stranger to us. I want you to make a good impression." She looked critically at Prudence. "Prue, your gorget is crooked. Straighten it before we go in to see Sir Philip."

"Am I invited too?" Prudence said artlessly as she dutifully rearranged the fine linen shawl, which covered the low décolletage of her daffodil-yellow gown.

"Of course you are!" Abigail said impatiently. "I do not want Sir Philip to think that Alysa is the sort of girl who would throw herself at an eligible man." She smoothed her tan skirt over the green petticoat and made sure the white bows that held the skirt back were straight. "There now, we are ready. Very well, we shall go in. I do hope that Jenkins has found your father. I think he should be there the first time Sir Philip calls, don't you?"

Prudence shot Alysa a look so full of affectionate amazement that Alysa almost laughed. Instead, she said soothingly, "I am sure Sir Philip will not be overly critical of my appearance, Mama. After all, he did see me in the village, and when he went with us to visit the tenants the other day, I was wearing my old, well-worn riding habit and my hair was quite windblown!"

Abigail bustled through the vast, high-ceilinged Great Hall, her daughters trailing behind like obedient ducklings. "How many times have I said you should not race, Alysa! You never know whom you will meet and just see the damage that can be done!"

"I don't think there was any damage at all," Prudence observed bluntly. "Sir Philip seemed quite taken with Alysa and he was most happy to rescue her when her horse bolted."

Abigail paused in front of the closed door to the King's Salon. "We are here. Now, both of you, mind your manners!"

Philip stood as the women entered. He looked very fine in a deep wine-colored suit laced with gold. A black cloak fell from his shoulders to his knees and at his waist was a beautifully wrought sword with a jeweled hilt. Evidently exile had not left him in financial hardship.

"Sir Philip, how very delightful of you to call," Abigail

said, extending her hand to be kissed. None of her fussy concern of a minute before was visible on her calm features.

Philip took her hand in his and made the deep reverence of a courtier. "Madam, the pleasure is all mine, I assure you. How could it not be when I am in the presence of three such lovely ladies?"

Abigail smiled carefully as she removed her hand from his. "Sir Philip, your tongue is as polished as your bow is. Pray do sit down, sir. Would you like some refreshments? Some wine, perhaps?"

Settling himself on a chair that was near Alysa, but a proper distance away, Philip said, "Thank you, Lady Strathern, I would enjoy a glass."

A sparkling crystal decanter and glasses resided on a beautiful table that had obviously been lovingly kept. Philip's gaze rested briefly on the polished walnut and a flicker of emotion remarkably like abhorrence danced for a moment in his eyes, then was gone so quickly that Alysa, who was watching him closely from beneath demurely lowered lids, wondered if she had imagined it.

He thanked Abigail as she handed him a glass; then he sampled the wine with grave pleasure. "A fine vintage. Pray convey my compliments to Lord Strathern on his choice of wines."

"My husband will be with us in a few minutes. I am sure he will be happy to hear your compliment himself, Sir Philip."

Philip nodded, sipped the wine again and shot Alysa a considering look over the top of the glass. "I hope that your dangerous ride the other day has caused you no injury, Mistress Alysa."

Alysa smiled and the mischievous dimple appeared in her cheek. "Indeed, sir, it has not. Thanks to your timely intervention all I had was a momentary scare and even that has faded over the past days."

He raised an ironic black brow. "Then you have no lingering fear as a result of your misfortune?"

Laughing, Alysa retorted, "I have always enjoyed a good

gallop, Sir Philip. I refuse to allow the fear of a tumble to keep me from the saddle."

"Then it seems that my mission here today is unnecessary." Philip's lips curved in a small, enigmatic smile that fascinated both of the young women in the room. While Alysa considered the meaning behind his words and smile, Prudence rushed into speech.

She clapped her hands together with enthusiasm and said with her usual bluntness, "Sir Philip, pray do tell us what your plans are! I know Alysa is just as intrigued as I am to know your secrets!"

Involuntarily, Philip stiffened.

Alysa noticed the movement and her expression turned thoughtful. Then her beautiful, sweet smile blossomed on her lips. "My dear Prudence, we must be polite and allow Sir Philip to keep his secrets if he so chooses. Ah, Papa, you have come to join us. I'm sure Sir Philip will be delighted. We were just talking about the secrets he is hiding from us all."

Philip sent her an annoyed glance as he rose to greet Lord Strathern. His look only made Alysa's smile all the sweeter. A muscle flexed in his jaw, but he said smoothly, "Indeed, sir, my only secret is my heartfelt appreciation for your eldest daughter."

Strathern smiled with amusement and Alysa's brows rose teasingly. A dull flush colored Philip's cheeks, branding him as not the courtier he claimed to be or an honest man truly attracted to a lovely young woman.

Lord Strathern was willing to accept that second, more obvious, explanation. He said mildly, "I have not had the opportunity to thank you properly for your assistance to my daughter last week. It was most fortunate that you were there to rescue her."

Philip bowed. "I was happy to be of service, Lord Strathern. Indeed, my mission today was to see if Mistress Alysa had quite recovered from her fright—"

"As you can see, I have," Alysa interrupted breezily.

"—and to ask her if she would care to ride with me this afternoon."

His offer was greeted with an interesting response. Abigail folded her hands in her lap and cast a quick, sharp look at her husband, Prudence gasped and Alysa froze momentarily, her eyes wide with questions.

Strathern smiled at his daughter. "Alysa must decide, of course, but I believe the afternoon will be fine. An excellent day to spend on a pleasure outing."

At her father's words, Alysa stood. "As you say, Papa, it would be a shame to waste this lovely afternoon. Sir Philip, if you would consent to wait while I change into my riding habit I will be but a moment."

He bowed. "I should be delighted, Mistress Alysa."

"I must go and help Alysa to dress," Prudence said. "It has been lovely seeing you again, Sir Philip." She cast Abigail a conspiratorial look that was not lost on Philip before she hastily followed Alysa from the room.

Edward chuckled softly at the quizzical look on Philip's face. "My daughters are very close. Undoubtedly Prudence wants to discuss your invitation with Alysa. Now then, Sir Philip, I must caution you to avoid the area around the Easton River marsh. The footing is treacherous there. Much better to take Alysa to the Fenwick Cliffs. The ride is a pleasant one and the view from the edge of the cliffs is spectacular. I trust you know the area I am speaking of?"

"I do not, my lord, but I am sure that your daughter or her groom can supply me with directions."

"It is an easy ride through open countryside." By sending Alysa and Hampton to the Fenwick Cliffs, Strathern was ensuring her safety. The terrain would make it possible for the groom riding behind to keep Alysa and Philip in sight, thus guaranteeing that no harm would come to Alysa should Sir Philip prove to be more a cad than a gentleman. "My daughter is a very daring rider, Sir Philip. She seeks challenges and may tease you to choose another, more demanding path. However, I rely on you to keep her from any precipitate action."

A smile Philip couldn't control quivered on his lips. "I shall do my best, my lord."

The expression in Strathern's eyes hardened. "Alysa is very precious to me, Sir Philip. I would not have her come to any grief."

Philip said forcefully, "Not at my hands, Lord Strathern," and for the second time that day he flushed.

Strathern took his reddened cheeks as further evidence that Philip was indeed a man besotted with a young lady and kindly offered him another glass of wine. As he poured, he said, "Tell me, Hampton, how do you find your uncle's lands?"

"Ainslie Manor is in worse repair than I'd expected," Philip replied ruefully. On safe ground, he talked freely of the problems he had encountered and the methods he'd used to solve them. He concluded by saying, an edge of bitterness in his voice, "I had not realized what a toll the war had taken on this area."

"And not only on your lands," Strathern said heavily. "There is no one hereabouts, from landowner to tenant, who hasn't had cause to curse the day the Roundhead troops rode into West Easton."

"Surely not everyone was affected!"

"Everyone," Strathern said flatly. His eyes were hard as they bored into Philip, but his voice was even. "After the Battle of Worcester young King Charles hid in this area while trying to escape to France. Cromwell's troops were frantic to find him. They burned crops and houses, harassed and even raped our women and threatened to hang the influential men of the area, your uncle among them, in their efforts to force us to give up the king. Before that time this was a moderate community. There were those who supported the monarchy and those who were for parliament. After that there were only Royalists. You have known exile for your beliefs, Sir Philip. You must be able to understand."

Philip nodded, his expression hooded. "I believe West Easton is not the only area in England to feel so strongly. King Charles need only choose his moment carefully and he will be able to regain his throne without difficulty."

There was a moment of silence as Strathern scrutinized

Philip's face. When he replied at last, his voice was careful. "As to that, I cannot say. I only know that we of West Easton have suffered greatly under the care of the Lord Protector." He shrugged and smiled, dismissing the subject as he resumed a proper public facade. "Indeed, if Richard Cromwell is a wise man he will be a kinder master for England than his father was."

Philip raised one black brow skeptically. "I hope you do not count on that, Lord Strathern. Richard Cromwell is not the man his father was."

"My point exactly," Strathern said dryly. "England is fortunate that Oliver Cromwell no longer rules. The time has come for change and Richard will help to effect it."

Philip looked deep into his glass, then lifted it high. "To change then."

"Peaceful change," Abigail added softly.

"Amen to that," said Strathern, drinking deeply.

Up in her bedroom Alysa had sent a servant to have her horse saddled and was watching her maid lay out her riding habit when Prudence surged into the room.

"I knew it! Sir Philip is attracted to you!" she announced dramatically as she flopped inelegantly onto the bed.

"Don't let Mama see you do that, Prue, or she will have you walking the halls with weighty books on your head to ensure you have the proper deportment."

"Poo! Mama is busy helping Papa ascertain if Sir Philip is a proper escort for you." Prudence shifted restlessly. "Honestly, Alysa, I cannot understand how Papa can doubt the man's integrity. After all, he did rescue you, didn't he?"

Alysa shot her a level look. "After you jabbed my poor beast with a hatpin and scared it half to death, Sir Philip did the only thing a gentleman could do!"

"But you heard him, Alysa! He said he was most affected by you."

Alysa sat down on a low stool while her maid began untying the laces at the back of her gown. "I must admit that

Sir Philip is an interesting man. I believe there is more to him than appears on the surface."

"Aha! I knew it!" Prudence bounced a couple of times on the bed to her sister's amusement. "You are as attracted to him as he is to you!"

Alysa smiled at her enthusiasm. "I would not put it quite that way."

Prudence looked down at her hands. "He makes Cedric Ingram seem quite dull, don't you think?" she remarked casually.

The gown came free and the maid pushed it from Alysa's shoulders. Distracted, Alysa waved her hand for the servant to stop while she considered what Prudence had said. "Prue, are you harboring a fancy for Cedric? Because if you are…."

"Don't be silly!" Prudence said gaily. "In sooth, Alysa, your precious Cedric is safe from my wiles."

"I didn't mean anything like that, Prue! Only that you would be better not to think of Cedric in that way. I believe his tastes run to more mature women." Alysa allowed the servant to resume her task. The bodice was removed and she stood to allow the maid to untie the loose folds of her skirt.

Prudence, who was only sixteen and just out of the schoolroom, blushed hard. "I will be older one day." She blinked and managed a bright little smile. "But that is not what we were talking about! Alysa, you are the most dreadful of sisters for finding anything about. Do you like Sir Philip Hampton? There, I have asked you straight out. Be so kind as to favor me with an equally direct answer."

Alysa loved her half sister dearly, so she laughed and gave Prudence as honest an answer as she was able. "I find Sir Philip to be an enigma. At times he seems to be the perfect courtier, as he was when he first arrived today. Then words tripped from his tongue and he was all charm. It was easy to believe him to be a Royalist gentleman just home from exile. Then later he became tongue-tied and blushed like a schoolboy over words that should have flowed off his tongue like honey. And then I wonder."

"What do you wonder?"

The maid slipped the long, full skirt of the riding habit over Alysa's head and arranged it around her slender waist before fitting the bodice, fashioned in the form of a man's doublet, over her shoulders. When it was buttoned, Alysa said softly, "Whether Sir Philip is truly the Royalist brother or if he is the one who chose to follow the Roundheads."

Prudence gasped. "Alysa! Are you mad? If he is the Roundhead brother we could all be in terrible danger."

"That, dear little sister, is why I plan to see as much as possible of Sir Philip Hampton," Alysa said lightly, pausing before a mirror to put on the low-crowned hat with the jaunty feather in the brim that matched the riding habit.

"Cedric Ingram may not understand," Prudence warned. Her voice sounded hopeful.

Alysa smiled at her reflection. "That is a risk I shall have to take."

CHAPTER 4

From the top of the Fenwick Cliffs it was possible to see for miles. Below, fields made the landscape a patchwork, until trees marked the abrupt break into a sandy beach that curved in a small cove. Where Alysa and Philip had stopped their horses the cliff top was rocky and bare, but to either side the slope allowed for the growth of thick stands of trees. As Lord Strathern had said, the ride there was an easy one and the view was spectacular.

Philip wasn't looking at the scenery, however. Instead he watched Alysa Leighton. Sitting tall and straight in the saddle, she was a lovely, vibrant woman and he was disconcerted by the growing pleasure he found being in her company. Indulgently, he let her fill his eyes and thoughts.

On the ride to this spot they had been able to gallop several times and the wind had put roses in the smooth creamy skin of her cheeks. Her eyes sparkled with pleasure, deepening the blue to a glittering sapphire, while the smile that curled her full lips eased the pouty bow that was their shape in repose. As he watched her, he thought she seemed more open, more innocent, than when they had met before.

This observation was confirmed as she looked over at him with glowing eyes and said softly, "I have been here many times, but I never fail to enjoy the fine prospect. Would you mind, sir, if we dismounted for a moment?"

"Of course, Mistress Alysa." He turned to the groom, who

was riding a discreet distance behind, and ordered him to hold the horses. Then he dismounted and helped Alysa down from her perch. She slid easily into his arms, feeling like a featherweight. Inadvertently, his hands closed more tightly around her slender waist as he held her inches from the ground. She was smiling, but slowly the smile died as they both became aware that she was a woman and he a man.

She said his name softly. It was the polite protest of a lady to a gentleman who was encroaching too far, but her eyes were warm on him, expressing her pleasure more strongly than the mild protest. Philip felt the heat in her gaze burn through him. Giving in to a whim, he drew her closer as he lowered her to the ground. Alysa's breath caught. So did his. He felt as if he was on fire in every place she touched.

Shaken, he said the first thing that came into his mind. "The view is as fine as I was led to believe."

Alysa's eyes widened, for he was staring directly at her. "I have always loved this particular spot. Would you care to walk a ways, Sir Philip?"

He nodded soberly. The longer they stood so close together that their bodies were almost touching, the more difficult it became for him not to indulge in a further whim and bend his head to taste the moist freshness of her lovely, pouting mouth. However, to give in to that indulgence would be mad, for not only was a servant a mere few feet away, but he had sworn that he would not seduce Alysa Leighton while he sought to ingratiate himself into Royalist life in West Easton.

They ambled along the edge of the cliff admiring the neat, well-kept fields and the blue-green of the sea as it lapped against the gold of the sandy beach. "Permit me to compliment you on your riding skills, Sir Philip," Alysa said after a moment. She cast him a sideways glance that was flirtatious, but totally controlled. "I was not in a position to do so when you so gallantly saved me, but I did notice then, and again today, that you ride with the ease of one born to the saddle."

Philip smiled, once more on his guard. The beautiful,

natural woman who attracted him so dangerously a few minutes before had been lost behind the artificial airs of a Royalist lady. The game of thrust and counterthrust had begun again. With a careful blend of truth and innuendo, he said, "I learned from my father, who was famous at court for his riding ability." That Philip had polished his skills during his long years in parliament's and later Cromwell's cavalry was not at issue here.

"How interesting." Alysa's slanting gaze remained flirtatious, but lurking beneath there was a glimmer of hard intelligence. "I do not remember your uncle, Sir Richard Hampton, as being a particularly good rider."

Philip laughed. "To hear my father tell it, he wasn't. Uncle Richard didn't quite hate horses, but he saw them only as a means of transportation. Apparently my grandfather had a penchant for rather wild horses and my uncle had the misfortune of trying to ride one of the half-broken stallions when he was still only a lad. He broke his arm rather badly, as well as several ribs. After that Uncle Richard was more cautious about his choice of mounts."

"That explains it then. Your father, I gather, was always able to master your grandfather's string of wild horses?"

Philip nodded, lost in memories of the past. In his mind's eye, he could see his father stroking the nose of a particularly unruly stallion, gentling it with his touch and the quiet murmur of his voice. "My father had a way with horses and it seems my grandfather respected him for it. Richard was never allowed to forget that, even though he was the heir, it was my father whom my grandfather favored. That was why, when my grandfather died, my father exiled himself to court. The animosity bred up because of that simple difference between the two brothers was so strong that it drove them apart permanently."

"Exiled! What a strange word to use. I thought court life was in your blood."

The surprise in Alysa's voice brought Philip back to the present with a start. *Careful!* He thought.

He smoothed his expression as he once more assumed the

role that had been laid out for him. "My father served the king and so we lived in London during my growing years. Occasionally my brother and I would be brought to court to play with the young princes, but it was not really until after the war and I was in exile, that I assumed a position, albeit a minor one, at court. As children, my brother and I were allowed to visit Ainslie a few times and it seemed to me that to live in the country was the perfect existence." He smiled faintly. "Whenever we visited Ainslie our tutors stayed in London, so we were allowed to run free, which we were never permitted to do in London. I think that colored my view of country life considerably."

Noticing a particularly large rock, he took Alysa's arm to guide her around it. Not only did the warmth of her flesh heat him in ways he should have been able to control, but their bodies leaned close to each other for a few short moments and the brush of her skirts against his thigh sent a shimmer of sensation lancing through him.

He should have dropped her arm after they were well away from the obstacle, but he liked the warmth of her in his hand and he found he could not easily give it up. It struck him that they were virtually alone together in a beautiful setting that was the perfect site for a romantic tryst. Grimly he pushed the thought away. But he did not let go of her arm.

"You must have found exile very difficult then. I understand that everything is more intense—all the gossip, the fighting for position, the emotions that are roused." There was a tiny revealing shake in Alysa's voice, which told Philip that she too was affected by their proximity. He noted as well that she chose to remark on his more serious comment rather than his last, light observation.

He smiled enigmatically, once more using the truth to substantiate a lie. "I did prefer my days in the cavalry."

Alysa looked at him sharply, a question in her vivid blue eyes.

Hastily, Philip clarified his statement, once more cursing himself for underestimating Alysa Leighton's sharp intelligence. "I was speaking of the time I spent serving His

Majesty during the war, Mistress Alysa. I was in the cavalry. Despite the desperate times, I found there was much to recommend the life."

Alysa laughed. The sound was brittle, as if she was relieved by his answer. "Oh, yes, we are back again to your riding ability."

Philip followed her lead and chuckled too. "I didn't intend to bring the conversation a full circle, but it seems most appropriate, does it not, to end it here?"

They had reached the point where the cliff softened into hillside. A thick forest clung to the slope and they could walk no farther. Philip released her arm and stepped back, watching as Alysa wandered over to a huge old oak that stood on the edge of the woods. She rubbed her hand along the gnarled trunk, glancing up at the spreading branches. Then she smiled as she looked over at Philip. "When young King Charles stayed with us after the Battle of Worcester, he told us how he had nearly been captured by some Roundhead troops. He hid in the branches of an old oak like this one, and while his trackers milled about below searching for him, he watched them with his heart in his mouth, every moment expecting to be captured. Did he ever tell you that story while you were in Europe together?"

Philip discovered that he hated the dreamy look that had stolen into her eyes as she spoke of the Black Boy, as King Charles's enemies called him. The nickname had been given because of the young king's swarthy skin, long black hair and dark eyes, but it could be applied just as easily to Philip himself. He forced himself to smile grimly. "His Majesty and I were never close enough for storytelling, ma'am. I was by way of being a very minor functionary at his court-in-exile."

"So you did not know him well?"

"To my deep regret, I did not."

Alysa raised her arched brows. "A pity. He is a charming man. Despite the danger he was in, he had time to spend with those who supported him. I shall always remember the way he spoke so easily to me. He was entirely natural, despite his great rank."

Alysa's words told Philip more than he wanted to know. He envisioned a young, impressionable girl swept away by the aura of danger that emphasized the lazy charm of a young man who had always had a way with people. There would have been no time for Alysa to see beyond the carefree facade Charles used to hide his true feelings. All she had seen was a man who had been treated with great unfairness and she resented that treatment and the men who did it.

Philip found that he wanted to smash Alysa's idealistic vision and replace it with something closer to the truth. His truth. Very gently, he said, "The young man escaping from England after a desperate attempt to regain his father's throne was charming. His years in exile may have hardened him more than you care to know."

"All the better for when he is king once more." Alysa's eyes snapped.

Philip laughed, without amusement. "A valid point, Mistress Leighton. A little hard seasoning might have made Richard Cromwell more secure in the position his father left him."

Alysa turned away from the oak and began walking back the way they'd come. Philip strolled along beside her. "Tell me about Richard Cromwell," she suggested lightly.

Philip shrugged, trying to appear cool. "Like His Majesty, I hardly know the man."

"But you must have met him when he agreed that you could return to Ainslie!"

"I met more of his advisers," Philip said ruefully and with complete honesty. "I was told how I should act and what I should say if I was approached by anyone seeking to reinstate the king."

Alysa's lovely blue eyes opened wide. "And what was that?"

"Mistress Alysa, I have already been pardoned once for my participation in a rebellion. I would not be given the same consideration again."

"No, I suppose not." She looked thoughtfully at his set

features. "Did they make you give your parole?"

There was danger in this line of conversation. He could only stretch the truth so far and he hated lying. He wondered too if Alysa's probing questions had a purpose beyond personal interest. "No, they were so busy telling me what I must do that they forgot to ensure my agreement. I fear the present Lord Protector and his henchmen are not as skilled at enforcing their will as the late Oliver Cromwell was."

"All the better for those who support King Charles," Alysa said with a suppressed passion that spoke volumes on her intense belief in the restoration of the monarchy.

They were almost at the horses again. Philip halted and brought Alysa to a stop beside him by catching her hands in his. "Alysa, take care. As inept as Richard Cromwell and his supporters seem, they still have all the weight of the government behind them. The Sealed Knot is rotten from within—"

Her hands curled around his fingers. "What do you know of the Sealed Knot?"

"Everyone knows about the Sealed Knot!" he said impatiently. "The court-in-exile, the Lord Protector and his men. It is an open secret that King Charles authorized six men to link the Royalists in every region of England so that an isolated revolt could become a country-wide rebellion. But someone in the Sealed Knot is selling their secrets to the Lord Protector."

Alysa pulled her hands away and crossed her arms over her chest. Her expression was stricken, but mutinously defiant. "The Sealed Knot is only six men. Though it is true they have great influence with the king, they are not the ones who would rise against the Lord Protector and his men. It is men like—" She stopped just short of saying a name, but Philip knew that she was speaking of her father. She drew a deep, steadying breath, then demanded, "Who told you the Lord Protector knows of the Sealed Knot?"

Philip hesitated. He knew he had already admitted more than he should.

"Who!"

Reluctantly, he said, "My brother."

"Your Roundhead brother."

"Yes."

Alysa shivered. Though the members of the Sealed Knot never actively participated in acts of rebellion, they were the Royalists' link with the king-in-exile. As the most prominent Royalist in the area, Lord Strathern was in contact with one of the members of the Sealed Knot. That was how he had learned that Thomas was being sent to England. "I must tell my father." Though there was urgency in her voice, she was able to smile. "Thank you, Sir Philip, for this information. My family will be indebted to you."

There was nothing Philip could do but try to make use of his slip of the tongue. "Pray tell you father that I shall be happy to be of whatever assistance I can." He caught her waist as he prepared to toss her up into the saddle. Once more the hot, instantaneous response to her nearness rushed through him and when she smiled at him he felt a fierce flush of male pride.

"I shall," she said softly, moistening her lips in a way that told Philip that she was as affected by their proximity as he was. As she settled into the saddle, he moved away. "And, Sir Philip, you need have no fear that we here in West Easton will expect more of you than you are prepared to give. An honorable gentleman's word is as important as his actions."

Philip didn't reply. Absurdly, her remark made him feel like a traitor. He swung up onto his horse in one lithe motion, and by the time he was mounted, he was again in control of his emotions.

More than once on that ride home, as he kept their conversation on bland subjects, he was aware of Alysa looking at him with questions in her eyes, wondering why he had suddenly reverted to the enigmatic man who kept his own counsel. There was no doubt in his mind that Alysa Leighton represented danger to him.

In more ways than one.

* * *

"Do you know, Mama, that we have not had company at Strathern Hall for quite some time." Prudence, dressed in her favorite sky-blue gown and peach petticoat, set a stitch in the handkerchief she was sewing.

The Leighton family was ensconced in the shabby sitting room they habitually used. Dusk had fallen and the candlelight gave the wood paneling a soft glow that made the room seem cozy rather than worn. The chairs they were using were clustered around the fireplace to catch the warmth that took the edge off the crisp spring evening. The ladies were busy with needlework while Lord Strathern idly read a London broadsheet. He occasionally entertained his womenfolk by indignantly reading out what was printed and commenting tartly on the information afterward.

Abigail responded to her daughter's comment with considerable relief. Politics was not her favorite subject. "These times do not lead to revelry, Prue. The Puritans frown on levity."

"That is not quite true, my dear." Strathern looked up from his broadsheet. "Remember when Cromwell's daughters were married, what was it, a year or two ago? From all accounts the celebrations were quite rowdy. Not only was dancing allowed, but I understand some of the guests became quite intoxicated."

"What is acceptable for the Lord Protector is not necessarily acceptable for his subjects, especially those who are known supporters of the king." Abigail snapped her thread in a pointed way that emphasized her words.

Prudence laid the handkerchief she was stitching in her lap. Her expression was indignant. "I was not thinking of a ball, Mama! Merely a small gathering of some kind." She contrived to look innocent. "For instance, we might hold a reception to welcome Sir Philip Hampton to the area now that Alysa has determined he is truly a respectable person."

Alysa lifted her golden head and looked at her sister. Her expression was indignant. "You make me sound quite awful, as if I were a grand inquisitor or something!"

"Well, are you not in a way? Are we all not scrutinizing

him? The neighborhood takes its cue from us, especially Papa, of course. If we are seen to accept Sir Philip, then he is assured of welcome in West Easton. You told us that you believed Sir Philip was a man of principle. Well, is that not enough?"

Lord Strathern's expression turned thoughtful. Idly he flicked at a piece of fluff that had adhered to the black cloth of the breeches he wore with a dark green doublet. "I think Prudence has a point. Sir Philip has already made excellent progress in gaining the allegiance of the Ainslie tenants and word has it that he is bringing a fresh viewpoint to the thorny problem of how to return the lands to profitability. We should make it known that he is welcome in West Easton."

"But, Papa! Would it not be better to wait until after Thomas has left the area?" Alysa protested.

Strathern smiled. It was a remarkably pleased expression that boded no good for anyone who was not of his point of view. "Arrangements have to be made for Thomas's arrival. I have been cudgeling my mind for some way of having a meeting without drawing notice. What could be more natural, or seem more innocent, than deliberately welcoming a stranger into our midst at this time? It is perfect! We can invite all of the respectable people of West Easton and the surrounding area on the pretext of introducing Sir Philip. Once the party is well begun my committee and I can retire to the King's Salon and make our plans. When we are finished we simply return to the party and no one is the wiser."

"Then we are agreed!" Prudence said with delight. "Mama, we must start making arrangements for the party immediately. Shall we hold it a sennight from now?"

Abigail glanced at her husband, who nodded. "That should give us enough time. We will have an informal evening gathering. First Edward must make certain that those gentlemen he wants to confer with are able to attend; then we must invite Sir Philip. After that we will ask those who would expect to be invited to a party of this sort." She glanced at her family, a general in a ruby gown and white petticoat marshaling the troops. "Now, we have much to do and not much time to do it in. Edward, you must prepare invitations for those you want to meet with so that we can send them off at first light. Alysa, you help your father. Prudence and I will make a list of those who should be invited and begin the other preparations."

Strathern cast a rueful look at his daughter and said, "Come, my dear, I believe we have been given our orders."

Alysa willingly set down her stitching. She stood, smoothing the quilted green petticoat she wore under a royal blue gown. "Papa, I know the others will be against it, but I do hope that you will remember to find a way for me to participate in Thomas's homecoming."

Abigail sent Alysa a long, level look. "Your papa would be exceedingly sensible if he chose not to let you be a part of your brother's landing. My heavens, Alysa! The Lord Protector has spies all around us! Do you honestly think that Thomas's return will remain a secret?"

Alysa lifted her chin. "Sir Philip Hampton was able to return to England."

Abigail snorted with unladylike vigor. "Sir Philip has a brother who supports the Lord Protector. Moreover, Sir Philip fought in the Civil Wars, not young King Charles's rising in fifty-one. His crimes have been paid for long since."

"And Sir Philip is not here to foment rebellion," Prudence added, finishing her sewing and holding up her handkerchief to admire her needlework.

Alysa's jaw hardened. "He is my brother, Mama. I would be there when he comes home."

"Enough!" Strathern said, holding up his hands. "One thing at a time. Alysa, come with me. We must begin if we are to get those invitations written tonight."

When they had left the room Abigail shook her head and sighed. "Prudence, I hope you do not intend to use your sister as a guide on how to make your way in life. There are moments when I fear that she will come to no good with her nonsensical ideas."

Prudence said seriously, "No indeed, Mama. Alysa is

beautiful and she can have her pick of the men hereabouts, but her ideas are such that I do not think she will ever be willing to commit herself to anyone. She expects too much. I am much more practical. I would like to wed a man of property and position who is not repugnant to me. I do not expect my heart to be involved."

"Good." Abigail neatly put her serving away and began to tick names off on her fingers. The subject of Alysa's inept handling of her matrimonial prospects was lost in the more pressing issues of who was to be invited, what was to be served and what the ladies should wear that evening.

The next few days were busy ones as the invitations were sent out and the acceptances received. Strathern's committee members were quick to reply, so it was not more than two days later that a note was sent to Sir Philip asking him if he would consider attending a small evening party that Lord and Lady Strathern were holding. Sir Philip too was pleased to accept, so the final set of invitations was sent out.

In the meantime, preparations were going on apace. The house was cleaned thoroughly. The furniture in the Great Hall and the nearby Music Room, so named because of the harpsichord there, was polished until it shone. Alysa sat down at the instrument one day and, a little wistfully, played a lively tune upon it, but she knew that dancing would not be advisable. It was disconcerting, though, to realize that the man she envisioned herself dancing with was not Cedric Ingram, but Sir Philip Hampton.

When all of the guests had arrived and Sir Philip Hampton had been properly introduced to each and every one, Strathern decided it was the prudent moment to slip away with a few other gentlemen to discuss the details of Thomas's arrival. Hampton was well occupied and the other guests would not question the disappearance.

"The King's emissary is to arrive a fortnight from now. The man chosen to visit this area is my son, Thomas, whom you all know." He paused and looked carefully at each man in the room. "I recently received disturbing information that one of the members of the Sealed Knot cannot be trusted, but I do not know if it is true or not. Nor do I know who the man is. Consequently, I sent Thomas a message telling him that he should land at Fenwick Cove at midnight a fortnight hence. I deliberately changed the time and place of his arrival, so that only those of us in this room know when he is to land. I do not think that there is any danger that we will be met by any of the Lord Protector's troops. However, I think it wise to keep the greeting party small. Two dozen or more on a lonely beach at midnight would be remarked upon, but a small party of gentlemen meeting a smugglers' brig will not seem out of the way. We will have a lookout of course, but that too would be normal."

The four gentlemen in the King's Salon listened with grave expressions. Cedric Ingram was the first to speak. "A sensible observation, Strathern. Smuggling is rife on this coast, and although the Lord Protector and his henchmen have tried to put a stop to it, so far we have been able to keep it running. Even if a patrol should happen to come across us, they would not suspect the real cause of the gathering."

"They will arrest us just the same!" said Sir Henry Ballentyne, who was a nervous man. His estate was a dozen miles from West Easton and he was Strathern's contact with Royalists in the western part of the county. He was the sort of man who was full of opinions, but poor at backing them up. However, men willing to risk their necks in the service of the king were not always easy to find, so Strathern had to overlook his inadequacies.

"We will remain in the shadows until the ship arrives," Strathern said soothingly. "No patrol will catch us, I assure you, Ballentyne. Now then, I would like you, Cedric Ingram, young Graham and one other to be on the beach that evening. We will ask Barnabus Wishingham, the smith, to act as our lookout."

Asked point-blank to attend, Sir Henry Ballentyne could not decline, though from the reluctant way he accepted, Strathern suspected he would have preferred not to. The others agreed with alacrity.

"Very well, we will meet on the beach at midnight, a fortnight from now. Thomas will go with one of you on that first evening...."

"He'll come here, of course," Cedric Ingram said, raising his brows.

"Not necessarily," Strathern replied coolly. "His commission is to meet with as many groups in this county as possible, so he will have much ground to cover. It has not yet been decided where he will begin."

"Sensible," said the nervous Sir Henry.

Strathern nodded. "I will convey the details to the person chosen to harbor him initially as soon as the decision is made. Until then, gentlemen, I suggest we return to the party so that our presence will not be missed."

Cedric Ingram lingered behind when the rest had gone. "Who will be deciding Thomas's first stop?"

Strathern shot him a long look. Cedric didn't flinch. "I will," he said at last. "Though the Knot has arranged for an emissary to be sent to every region of the country, it is the local supporters of the king who are to plan the itinerary. You know, of course, that there are those advocating active rebellion who have managed to get the king's ear. The gentlemen of the Knot believe that rebellion now would be premature. With two such disparate opinions being offered him, His Majesty thought it best to send his own emissaries. The Sealed Knot is certain that these envoys will find exactly what the Knot has been claiming: that rebellion would fail and worse, it would push the republicans together as they sought to defend themselves from the threat of a royal return."

"You and I must agree to disagree on this subject, Strathern," Cedric said stiffly. "I am of the opinion that we have accepted the yoke of the Puritans too long! We must show them that we are men and dangerous men! I would gladly engage in rebellion."

"I know," Strathern said quietly. "You will be allowed to voice your opinions, Ingram, when we meet with Thomas. If the majority agrees with you, then Thomas will take that back to the king. Now, I do not want to be missed. Shall we rejoin the party?"

There was nothing Cedric could do but agree and he did so with a smile and a willingness that said he was not harboring any grudges about the difference of opinion.

When they emerged, the Great Hall was empty. The sound of the harpsichord tinkling merrily drew them to the Music Room. There Abigail sat at the keyboard playing a cheerful tune, while the rest of the party danced. Since dancing was officially frowned upon, the element of risk further enhanced the pleasure everyone was having as they moved to the music.

"This is not a good idea," Cedric muttered to Edward as they paused just inside the doorway of the room. "What was Lady Strathern thinking of to be persuaded to permit dancing?"

Strathern resisted the urge to swear. Virtually all of the neighbors who had been invited were convinced Royalists, but that did not mean that the rules could be flouted so obviously, especially at a time like this. However, he was not about to admit to Cedric Ingram that his wife had made an error in judgment. He dealt with the man in matters relating to the restoration of the king, but they were not friends. Nor was he a son-in-law. Yet. "Undoubtedly my lady had her reasons for agreeing to this activity. I shall discover it in due course. Until then I think it best to put as good face on it as we can."

Cedric grunted. Then, with a flash of boyish charm that was rare and in its own way endearing, he grinned. "I must own that I shall enjoy partnering your daughter. Where is she? Can you see her?"

Unfortunately, Edward could. In the center of the dancers were Alysa and Philip Hampton. Dressed in a gown of marine blue, the bodice picked out in silver, the petticoat striped ice blue and silver silk, Alysa was a vision of elegant loveliness as she looked up into Philip's face. On her lips was a smile that was calculated to melt any man's heart. The mischievous dimple in her cheek was peeking enticingly as she spoke and her vivid blue eyes sparkled with pleasure.

Strathern glanced at Cedric Ingram. His expression was bleak, then suddenly became furious. Curious as to what had caused the sudden passionate response, Strathern looked again at his daughter and Sir Philip Hampton.

Philip, also dressed in blue, was a dark contrast to Alysa's pale beauty. His suit was cut with the perfection that no small-town tailor could match and had a stylish flare that spoke of Continental styling. The dark blue satin of the wide sleeves of his doublet rippled in the light as did his cloak, which was flung over his shoulders with a jaunty air. He bent his head to whisper intimately in Alysa's ear.

She laughed, then shook her head teasingly. To an observer, she appeared more than merely appreciative of a witty sally. She looked like a woman flirting with a man she was attracted to.

"'Od's blood! Who does he think he is?" Cedric bristled. "How dare he speak to Mistress Alysa that way?"

Strathern heard the jealousy in Cedric's voice and understood it. For a year Cedric had been Alysa's most prominent suitor and recently he had begun to view her as already won. It would be difficult for a man with Ingram's high sense of self-worth not to feel dismay at seeing his ladylove respond so prettily to another man.

Especially a man who wore the sometimes outrageous fashions of the cavalier gentleman with an undeniable masculine authority. Philip made Cedric, who had always prided himself on being the most fashionable man in the neighborhood, look rather silly in his green suit, the color of new leaves, that was embellished with silver and darker green ribbons. Everything about Cedric Ingram was exaggerated, from the absurdly skimpy doublet, to the width of his breeches and the rows of ribbon loops that adorned their hems. Everything about Philip Hampton was understated confidence. He cast Cedric Ingram in a shade the other man could not abide.

"Since Sir Philip is our guest of honor and Alysa is by way of being a hostess of this event I can see no problem in their dancing together. I am sure my daughter will be quite happy to dance with you when the next set is formed."

Cedric glowered. "I know she will be pleased to dance with me. However, I cannot like the way that fellow—a mere stranger to us—looks at her."

Strathern chuckled. He couldn't help it. "'Od's blood, Ingram, he's a guest in this house! I believe you are making too much of this."

"Perhaps." Since Strathern had not yet given his blessing to a match between his daughter and Cedric, both men knew Cedric could no more lay claim to Alysa than any other man could.

"I see my daughter Prudence is coming to greet us. Say hello, Ingram, and stop worrying about Alysa and Philip Hampton." He glanced at Cedric's set features and decided to add a little sweetener to the command. "I've asked Alysa to talk to Sir Philip to find out more about his politics. That is most likely why she seems so intrigued by him. You know how passionately she feels about returning England to its natural political order."

Cedric seemed to stiffen even more. "By all that is holy, Strathern! I cannot believe that you would trust such a delicate assignment to a mere woman, whether she be your daughter or not! I—"

Prudence, a vision in rose and white, stopped beside her father, her hopeful gaze fixed on Cedric. "Papa, Master Ingram, welcome back. We missed you." She smiled shyly at Cedric. "I hope you will consent to participate in the dancing when the next set forms, sir. We were hard put to convince Sir Philip that he should join the fun, but at last we did and he seems to be enjoying himself thoroughly."

"I can see that." Cedric glowered at Philip and Alysa as the steps of the dance brought them together once more. "By your leave, Strathern, I see young Johnston by the harpsichord. I must go and have a word with him."

He strode off, skirting the dancers and glaring at Alysa and Philip as he went. Strathern watched him go, the expression in his eyes concerned, while Prudence gazed regretfully at his retreating back. "Well, Papa," she said after a minute, "I think we can safely say that Alysa has truly captured Master Ingram's heart."

"His heart or his pride?" Strathern returned sardonically. He looked down at his youngest daughter. "Prudence, my dear, have you taken a liking to Master Ingram?"

Prudence's eyes filled. She blinked rapidly to clear the moisture forming there, but she shrugged with deceptive unconcern. "He is the most eligible gentleman in the area, Papa, but he is Alysa's suitor, not mine."

The music stopped and everyone clapped enthusiastically. Abigail struck up another tune. Cedric shoved his way through the dancers to claim Alysa's hand. "Come," Prudence said with false cheer. "Dance the next set with me, Papa, since Mama is otherwise occupied."

Lord Strathern did not think that the dancing was a good idea and ordinarily he would have refused to participate, but he sensed the heaviness in his youngest daughter's heart and would do nothing to increase it. "I would be delighted," he said, smiling and leading her onto the floor.

Prudence flushed prettily, but her eyes were all for Cedric Ingram.

CHAPTER 5

"Blame the dancing on me, Papa," Alysa said after they had ushered the last guest from the house.

"I do not want to *blame* anybody!" Strathern replied with asperity. "I just want to know why dancing was permitted—no, encouraged—in my house."

"I take full responsibility, Edward," Abigail interjected, glancing at her stepdaughter as they returned to the Music Room to inspect the debris left from the party. The servants were already busy picking up the empty glasses and removing the extra candlesticks that had been brought in to light the room. "Alysa convinced me that it would be a good idea and I concurred with her reasons."

Lord Strathern sighed. "Fine! What were those reasons?"

Alysa bowed her head, then looked up, straight into her father's eyes. "I thought, Papa, that it would be a good way to test Sir Philip."

"Test? How so?"

"I wanted to know if he could dance."

Frowning, Lord Strathern considered Alysa's reply. "A courtier would undoubtedly dance extremely well."

"Exactly!" The gloom on Alysa's face lifted and she smiled mischievously. "And I can report that Sir Philip is an excellent dancer. Prudence can confirm my findings as well."

"Sir Philip did dance beautifully," Prudence agreed, but her expression indicated that she was indifferent to the man and his abilities. She wandered about the room, picking up glasses, then putting them down restlessly. Her family watched her with concern. Noticing their worried expressions, Prudence flushed. "I feel rather tired. I think I shall retire for the night, if you don't mind, Mama."

"Of course not, dearest. Sleep well."

Prudence nodded and went out. Alysa sighed. "There are times when I would like to hit Cedric Ingram! He did not dance with her once this evening. Indeed, he never spoke to her that I am aware of. Surely he could have been polite and asked for her to join him in at least one set."

Lord Strathern moved to the fireplace and frowned down into the low flames. "Ingram was shocked that we would allow dancing. I don't think he enjoys the sport." He turned back to his wife and daughter. "Your test of Sir Philip was most ingenious, my dear Alysa. But did you consider that both of Anthony Hampton's sons were virtually brought up at court? It was not until they were adults that the younger one made the choice of joining the parliamentary side. I'm sure the Roundhead brother dances as elegantly as his Royalist sibling."

Crestfallen, Alysa said, "I hadn't thought of that, Papa. Now we are no farther ahead." She paused thoughtfully. "Or are we? Sir Philip was reluctant to dance."

"For the same reason I was reluctant to allow the activity, Alysa—because of the possible repercussions," Abigail reminded her. "Once we had persuaded him that all were to be trusted he was most willing to participate." Her eyes twinkled. "In fact, he made no secret of his enjoyment of partnering you in the first set."

Alysa blushed, but looked pleased. "He is so very light on his feet; he is a pleasure to dance with. Oh, Papa! I did think I had hit upon the most perfect test as to whether Sir Philip is to be trusted or not. Now what shall we do?"

"Concentrate on what we know." Edward came away from the fireplace to sit beside his wife on the settee. With Alysa only a few feet away on a chair, they made a compact group.

He lowered his voice so that only they could hear. "The decisions have been made about meeting Thomas."

Both ladies stiffened. Alysa's eyes gleamed with excitement. "Papa, tell us!"

"He is to arrive in a fortnight and will be brought to Fenwick Cove by a smuggling boat. Six people are to be there to greet him."

"Who are the six, Papa?" Anxiety colored Alysa's voice. There was no guarantee that her father had been able to include her in the welcoming committee, much as she wanted to go.

Strathern's expression was full of tolerant affection. "Myself, Cedric Ingram, Ballentyne, young Graham and one other are to wait on the beach. Barnabus Wishingham is to be the lookout."

Hope flared into life in Alysa's eyes. "Who is the other person, Papa?"

Strathern smiled.

Alysa laughed delightedly. "I am!" she said, clapping her hands together. "Thank you, Papa. I promise you I shall wear a man's riding clothes so that I do not stand out—"

Abigail interrupted tartly. "There is no possible way for you to disguise your femininity, Alysa. A person just has to look at your sweet face and he will know you are a woman."

"All the same," Strathern said, "Alysa is right. If she wears a man's garments with a cloak over top and pulls a hat low over her face, a chance glance will not indicate who she truly is."

Abigail looked at him sharply. "Do you fear the Lord Protector will be sending a welcoming committee as well?"

"I would not include Alysa if I did not think it would be safe," Strathern replied after a long moment. "But one must always be prepared for the unexpected to happen."

"Everything will be fine!" Alysa's face glowed with excitement and pleasure. "I cannot believe we will actually be seeing Thomas so soon."

"Alysa, I know how deeply you love your brother, that is why I am allowing you to meet him when he lands. But remember, this is far from a pleasure visit for him. He is to meet with preeminent Royalists in at least a dozen communities in this part of the country. He will come to West Easton last, and for his safety, he will not even be staying here at Strathern Hall. This is the first place the Protectorate troops would look should they hear of his arrival. I am afraid that there is every likelihood that you will not see him after that first night."

Even her father's sober assessment of her brother's activities could not put a damper on Alysa's enthusiasm. "Of course, Papa! I do understand." Once again a mischievous smile curled her lips. "Papa, was Master Ingram grumpy this evening because you told him that I would be with you on the beach? I know how reluctant he is to admit that women are able to do anything at all beyond bringing up children and managing a household."

"There is nothing wrong with either of those occupations," Abigail interjected vigorously.

A soft chuckle escaped Alysa's lips. She had heard this sort of lecture from Abigail before. "Of course not, Mama. But you must admit that his view is rather narrow. Why, there are times when Cedric Ingram reminds me of the most ferocious Puritan! I think if the Lord Protector had been of Stuart blood he would have been quite happy to serve him."

"Alysa, enough of that kind of talk!"

"Shame, Alysa!"

Lord Strathern and his lady protested at the same moment, their frowns equally heavy.

Alysa opened her eyes wide. "I'm sorry, Papa, Mama, if I have said anything out of the way. I did not mean to cast any aspersions on Master Ingram's integrity. It was just an observation I have made from time to time."

Strathern drew a deep breath. "Cedric Ingram is loyal to the king." His expression hardened. "Your brother's fate depends on it."

West Easton was a small town where everyone knew everyone else, so it was not long before news of Thomas

Leighton's visit percolated through the population. Barnabus Wishingham, the smith, got the gossip going. He was married to a managing woman who liked to know where he was every minute of the day. Usually he was busily at work in his forge just outside the house they shared on the edge of town, but he did have one activity that took him away from his forge and hearth at irregular times: he was a committed Royalist and had been so ever since King Charles II had deigned to notice him during those desperate days when Charles had taken shelter in the area.

Barnabus Wishingham was Lord Strathern's link with the lesser members of the West Easton community. A man whose physical strength made him fear few men, he was always willing to speak out for those more timid than he who were daunted by the trappings of power. Strathern respected him and accepted his opinions, a simple act that had won Barnabus's loyalty as effectively as an exiled king's pleasantry had made him a Royalist for life.

Barnabus had no use for most members of the aristocracy, men like Cedric Ingram who could not be bothered with someone as low as Barnabus Wishingham. Barnabus had a sturdy sense of self-worth and he gave the gentry their due, but no more. Cedric Ingram got a polite greeting and Barnabus's usual fine work, but no favors. He had to wait for his goods like the rest of the townsfolk.

Strathern duly informed Barnabus about the envoy being sent by the king and asked if he would consent to be the lookout. Thrilled at being invited, Barnabus agreed without hesitation. He immediately told his wife, Ruth, of the event, for he wanted to give her plenty of time to get used to the idea that he would be roaming the countryside at midnight a fortnight hence. If there were arguments, he intended to get them over with early, rather than have to fight with his wife on the night of Thomas's arrival.

His good wife was not pleased by his plans, but she could do little to keep him from participating, beyond arguing fiercely against his role. Ruth Wishingham was not the committed royalist her husband was. She was keenly aware that involvement with such a group could lead to arrest and trial for treason if her husband was caught. However, Barnabus refused to listen to her good sense on this issue and continued to plot and plan with his betters. So, she took her frustrated anger to her sister, who was the confidante of all her marital troubles.

Ruth's sister was married to the town joiner and more than a little jealous that Barnabus, and not her husband, was the nominal representative of the little people in West Easton. Full of indignation, she told her husband of the time and place of the meeting and urged him to join the others there. Her husband was a timid man and of no mind to become involved in anything so dangerous as being on the beach when a condemned Royalist illicitly landed in England, but he was quite willing to pretend that he had been asked.

In fact, he bragged of his involvement to his parents and brothers one evening when the family was altogether. To prove to his disbelieving relatives that what he said was true, he announced the date and time of the arrival. Suitably impressed, his family proceeded to boast of the event to virtually everyone they knew. By that point, the secret of Thomas's arrival was as public as if it had been published in a London broadsheet.

Philip heard about it three days before it was to occur, in plenty of time to relay the details to Osborne. He was standing in the mercer's shop, looking over some cloth he planned to purchase to make livery for his house servants, when he over-heard an excited woman proclaiming the details of the arrival to one of her friends. He stood very still, his ears straining to hear each fact, his fingers absently testing the cloth, his mind racing.

This was the opening Osborne needed. This was the reason Philip had been sent to West Easton. In one quick instant he could fulfill his obligation and ensure that Thomas Leighton never returned to expose his masquerade. Simple.

But the picture had become more complex since the day when he had reluctantly agreed to take this assignment. He liked living at Ainslie Manor. He enjoyed being tied to the land after years of having no home but his regiment. To betray Thomas Leighton would jeopardize his position here in West Easton. If Thomas Leighton was apprehended he would, at best, spend years in prison. More likely, he would be tried for treason and executed. If the people of West Easton guessed who had turned him in, and eventually they would, they would view that man as a viper, and would be justified in doing so.

Then there was the Leighton family itself. Philip had discovered that he had a great deal of respect for Lord Strathern, who was an upright, honest man. No matter that he and Philip were on opposite sides. There were so few men of character these days that it was a pleasure to come across one, whatever his political stripe.

Lord Strathern would be distraught if his son was captured, but he was a gentleman and knew the dangers of duty. Alysa, on the other hand, would never forgive the man who had betrayed her brother. With a woman's unerring insight, she would condemn the crime for what it was—deceitful, underhanded, vicious—and she would do all in her power to avenge her loss. There would be no room in her heart for a Roundhead gentleman who had just been doing his duty.

The shrill, gossipy voice changed tone, then went on to discuss some other subject of no interest to Philip. He motioned to the shopkeeper hovering nearby that he intended to purchase the fabric without really having an idea of what the cloth looked like. As the man took the bolt to the counter to wrap it, Philip's thoughts continued to be on the news he had just heard, so he was a trifle abstracted as he handed over the coins. The honest merchant laughed pleasantly and told him he was being too generous. Brought back to the present, Philip smiled easily and told the man to keep what was left over. Gratified, the merchant thanked him profusely, promised to send the purchase to Ainslie Manor and bowed Philip from the shop, holding the door himself.

Philip emerged into the bright sunshine, still undecided about what he should do. His duty?

Or what his heart told him was right?

* * *

The night sky was clear of clouds, allowing the moon and stars to shed their light on the gently curving beach of Fenwick Cove. From the point of view of the little group waiting for the smuggling boat to arrive, the night was too bright for complete safety. Even wearing dark clothes, as they all were, a man was clearly silhouetted whenever he emerged from the safety of the shadows, while out at sea the moon cast a brazen glow over the water. If Thomas had been betrayed, his pursuers would have no difficulty spotting his arrival.

The welcoming party Lord Strathern had assembled had not been particularly pleased when they realized that the youth in an oversize doublet and baggy breeches was Alysa Leighton. It was Cedric Ingram who discovered her identity first and he had yelled so sharply that the rest of the group had shushed him nervously, then gathered round Alysa to see if what he said was true. Now Sir Henry Ballentyne was worried about her safety, young Graham kept looking at her with an awed and somewhat lascivious expression on his face while Cedric Ingram fumed.

Strathern silenced him with a curt comment spoken in a voice the brooked no disagreement.

"The longer we remain here, the more danger there is that we will be spotted and betrayed," grunted Sir Henry Ballentyne.

"We cannot leave until my son's ship arrives," Strathern said mildly, but with the same inflexible tone that had silenced Ingram. "Until then we are in no danger."

Ballentyne snorted nervously. "I beg to differ."

"What can we be accused of?" Strathern countered patiently. "We are a group of men out for an evening ride, nothing more."

"Of being conspirators," the other man said grimly. "Who else would be abroad in the small hours of the morning, huddled in the shadows, hiding from every man?"

"Your conscience is overpowering your good sense, sir." Strathern's voice grew a little impatient. "Or have you lost your taste for the king's cause?"

"No," Ballentyne growled. "Not that. But I am far from sanguine about this expedition! Why needs the king send emissaries from the Low Countries? Cannot he trust the messages the Sealed Knot sends to him about our readiness to rise? Why does he doubt us?"

Good questions. Ones Lord Strathern had no intention of debating, because there were no answers that he could be sure of. If the rumors were true, there was a traitor in the ranks of the Sealed Knot. Strathern was inclined to believe the story, since Philip Hampton had inadvertently confirmed it to Alysa. That was why he had taken precautions to ensure that the day and time of Thomas's arrival was not known to the central committee.

As to Charles's reason for sending envoys to England, Strathern suspected that it stemmed from the king's experiences after the Battle of Worcester. He had learned caution from that first attempt to lead a revolt. Then he had found himself without the followers he'd been promised, at the mercy of the covenanting Scots, forced to deny his religion in order to survive. Intelligent and flexible, Charles Stuart would listen to all the promises made to him, but in the end he would make his own decisions.

"Papa!" Alysa urged her horse beside Lord Strathern's. Keeping her voice low, she pointed out to sea. "Papa! Isn't that a sail? There—over by the headland?"

Strathern peered into the gloom. Was she right? The breeze picked up and something white fluttered at the edge of the cove. Strathern allowed the breath he hadn't even been aware of holding to ease from his lungs. "Yes! It is a sail! Come, gentlemen, our wait is almost over!"

A few minutes later the ship rounded the headland and its sails were fully visible. "Oh, Papa," Alysa said on an excited sigh. "I can hardly believe that Thomas is almost here! When will the ship reach us? How can we bear to wait? Why is it taking so long?"

"The ship will stand to in deep water and row Thomas ashore," Lord Strathern said, smiling at her excitement.

Unlike the rest of the party, his eyes were not fixed on the fast little brig gliding silently into the cove, but roved freely, searching the land, looking for a shadow that moved or should not be there, watching for evidence that they had been betrayed.

"The boat's over the side," Cedric Ingram said, his voice unnaturally high with nerves. "He is committed now."

"We are committed," grunted Sir Henry Ballentyne.

The moon glittered off the droplets of water falling from the oars as the seamen began to row. Those on the sand waited with ever deepening impatience, for each stroke seemed to take an eternity.

With agonizing slowness the skiff gained in size as it neared the beach. Now the waiting party could make out the laboring seamen bent over their oars and the erect figure seated in the center. Tension radiated from the men, making the horses snort and stamp their feet. While Thomas remained on the water his return could still be aborted. Once the skiff touched land and he came ashore there would be no going back. They would have taken the first step toward rebellion.

The sailors pulled at the oars, propelling the boat ever closer. Alysa watched, her gaze fixed on her brother. In the dim light she could not see his face clearly, for it was just a white blur in the darkness, but she remembered his posture. He had always held himself proudly, his back straight, his head high. Anticipation of their meeting slithered along her nerve endings. At last he was here again.

A grinding sound told those on the beach that the skiff had reached the shallows. There was a flutter of activity as Thomas leapt from the boat into the lazily curling surf, uncaring of the wetting his boots were getting. He raised his hat to the sailors and threw a pouch full of gold to them; then he turned and scanned the beach.

Slowly, so as not to alarm him, Lord Strathern urged his horse from the shadows. The seamen pushed the boat back into the salt froth of the whitecaps to return to the ship as Thomas waded through the rushing water toward dry land. A smile dawned on his face as he saw who had come first to welcome him. He raised a hand in greeting.

His movement seemed to be the catalyst that set the rest of the party into action as they followed Strathern from the shadows. Alysa kicked her mount into a trot, impatient to be close to her brother. She was leading the extra horse that had been brought for him and had to jab sharply at the animal's reins to make it move as quickly as she wanted. She saw her father reach her brother and lean down to clasp his hand. Her heart soared.

"Thomas!" she cried, keeping her voice low. Still, it sounded unpleasantly loud in the midnight silence.

Thomas looked toward her. "Alysa?" He glanced at his father. "You allowed Alysa to participate in a dangerous activity such as this?"

Lord Strathern was rueful. "Your sister is as hotheaded as you are, my son. Come, she will give you your mount and then we must be off. I mislike remaining in such an open area."

"You think we are betrayed?" This was from Cedric Ingram, who had followed Sir Henry Ballentyne and the rest from the dark rim of the beach.

"Ingram!" There was surprise in Thomas's voice. "I did not expect to see you here tonight."

Strathern shot his son a quick, searching look, but didn't remark on his comment. Instead he replied to Cedric's question. "No, but there is always danger in this sort of work."

Thomas had grasped the reins of his horse from Alysa and was mounting as his father spoke. He found the stirrups and gathered up the reins before leaning over to give Alysa a hug. "My darling sister, you should not be here, but I am delighted to see you all the same."

Alysa laughed and returned the hug. "Thomas, you cannot know how much I've missed you!"

On the low rise above the beach where a small copse of trees sheltered the headland, there was a shiver of movement, movement that no one noticed, including

Barnabus Wishingham, who was standing guard. Until now they had been no indication of any danger, so his attention was fully focused on the activity below.

There Thomas was saying briskly, "Very well, then. What are the plans?"

"Let us ride while we describe them to you." Strathern kicked his horse into motion to emphasize his suggestion. The rest followed. "You will be going west first, to...."

On the rise there was the stamp of a shoed hoof. The smith knew the sound well and he also knew his own mount had not made the noise. Panic seized him as he scanned the trees from which the sound had come. Were there shapes there that should not be?

Yes!

He kicked his horse into a gallop and careened down the path to the beach. "Fly!" he screamed. "Fly! We are betrayed!"

CHAPTER 6

The smith was a man of powerful lungs and his warning carried clearly on the night stillness. On the beach there was a moment in time when every action ceased, then a flurry of movement as men urged their horses into a run. Sand spurted from hooves digging into the beach for purchase, horses neighed, men shouted. From the trees there was another burst of activity as a troop of cavalry, warned of what was afoot, moved into action. Twenty men mounted on quick, light horses thundered from their hiding place and galloped in pursuit of the Royalists.

All around there was a chaos of sound and fury. The darkly clothed cavaliers flew like shadows from the bright scarlet coats of the seemingly unstoppable Roundhead cavalry, which rushed down the hillside with ferocious speed. They closed rapidly on the Royalists until their horses reached the precarious footing of the soft sand; then they slowed.

Near the water's edge, where Thomas and his well-wishers were, the beach was tide washed. There the harder sand gave the horses a better footing, but to escape they had to cut across the soft sand before they reached the land's edge. By prior, unspoken agreement the group broke apart, each man bent on saving himself. Only the Leightons stuck together.

As the horses galloped along the tidal sand, Lord Strathern shouted to his son, "Thomas! Ride to Broadview Abbey. It is not the place I intended for you to go to first, but I fear that whoever betrayed us tonight might know of our original plans! At Broadview you will be safe until we can make other arrangements. It is far enough away that the Roundheads will not look there, not at first, and you know the way and the family."

Thomas nodded. Cautiously, he drew his mount from a gallop to a canter, for they were nearing the deep, dry sand where the footing was treacherous. "What happened Papa? Who betrayed us? Do you know?"

Lord Strathern slowed his horse to keep pace with Thomas. Alysa's mount continued its forward momentum, pulling ahead of the other two. Beside Thomas, Strathern shook his head grimly. "I can pinpoint no one," he said bitterly. "News of your arrival was all over the village this past sennight. The traitor could have been anyone."

Suddenly a scream echoed through the night, overwhelming even the pounding of hooves and the shouts of men. Lord Strathern's voice abruptly stopped, for Alysa's horse had stumbled in the loose sand. She pulled desperately at the reins, urging the animal to move more carefully, but her caution was too late. A detachment of the Roundhead troops, their horses cantering steadily, were gaining ground. Soon they would reach her.

The Leighton family had never been inclined to follow the safest path and on this night there was more reason than usual for acts of foolhardy daring. With Alysa in danger, both Lord Strathern and his son immediately turned their horses toward the oncoming soldiers, prepared to engage them so that Alysa could escape.

Their gallantry was not needed, however, for the midnight rendezvous had been attended by another unsuspected observer. A dark-haired gentleman, dressed in the serviceable buff coat worn by many officers during the wars, had also been observing from the security of the trees. When he saw that the little group was in danger of being captured he did not pause to question why two men had stopped to defend another. He simply acted. Clapping his heels to the smooth black flanks of his stallion, he charged into the fray, his sword raised.

None of the troops expected an attacker to be coming from their rear and the cavalier's intervention threw them into confusion. When confronted with the armed might of the Protectorate, Royalists usually fled, as this group of conspirators was doing. A deliberate assault was so unusual as to be unheard of.

As the soldiers faltered and lost momentum, Lord Strathern and his son wheeled their horses to follow Alysa, who was now rapidly drawing away. Thomas raised his hand in a salute of farewell. "God willing, I will see you within the month." He flashed a cocky grin. "Watch for me!"

With that, he kicked his horse into a headlong gallop and turned its head to the left, drawing several troopers deeper into the soft, treacherous sand. Two others paused to meet the mad cavalier charging on them, leaving only one man to chase Lord Strathern and Alysa.

The soft sand pulled at the hooves of the horses. Any step could be the one that would hobble the Leightons' mounts and so end the chase. The hillside loomed ever closer, but never quite seemed within reach. Alysa risked a quick look behind that made her redouble her silent urgings to her horse. Inexorably, the Roundhead trooper was gaining on them, and from the grim smile of satisfaction that twisted his lips, the soldier was confident he would soon make his capture.

A triumphant shout made Alysa risk another glance over her shoulder. The lonely cavalier had won through the troopers opposing him, leaving one man nursing a wounded arm and the other picking himself up off the sand as his mount cantered riderless toward the trees. The valiant champion pulled his spirited black horse to a prancing stop, wheeled and set off in pursuit of the lone Roundhead following Alysa and her father.

Their rescuer's horsemanship was superb. Recognition flashed in Alysa's mind, but she dismissed it. Surely this was not Sir Philip Hampton. How could it be? He did not know that Thomas was to arrive in England tonight. Or did he? Had it been he who had alerted the Roundheads of the time and place of the meeting?

Questions danced in her mind, then were forgotten in the danger of the moment. The trooper chasing them had decided to ignore the man who was following him and seek the glory of a capture instead. He urged his horse to run faster, but the extra speed was his undoing. A depression in the sand, hidden by tufts of coarse sea grass, was in his path and his flying mount could do nothing to save itself as it put one hoof into the hole. The animal tripped, fell to its knees and the trooper flew over its head into the soft sand. Winded, but otherwise unhurt, he was able to stand after a minute and watch his prey fade into the gloom, followed by the wild cavalier, who had emerged from the shadows. Cursing softly, he brushed himself off and went to see to his horse.

Safe on the high ground, Lord Strathern and Alysa slowed their horses and looked back at the beach. Several Roundheads lingered there, but there was no sign of Thomas, the other members of the greeting party or the elusive rescuer. Alysa shivered. "Do you think Thomas escaped, Papa?"

Lord Strathern was silent for a moment; then he smiled rather grimly. "If the Roundheads had captured Thomas there would have been a great cry of success. Yes, Alysa, I think your brother was able to escape."

They rode on, heading for Strathern Hall by indirect means. On the familiar roads and paths, Alysa felt secure enough to voice the questions that had nagged at her on the beach. "Papa, how could someone from West Easton betray us to the Roundheads? Everyone in the village has suffered at their hands. I thought we were all agreed that it was best for England to overthrow the Lord Protector."

Strathern was grim. "Evidently not everyone is what he pretends to be." He turned to Alysa. "I was a fool to allow your protestations to override my good sense. You should not have been there this night, Alysa. Had we been caught—" He broke off, shaking his head. "If it had not been for that unknown gentleman riding out of the darkness and surprising the Roundheads we would have been caught."

"Not unknown, Papa," Alysa said somberly. She waited for her father to question her silently with a look before continuing, "I believe the man was Sir Philip Hampton."

"Hampton! What the devil was he doing there tonight?" Lord Strathern's expression hardened. "Alysa, listen to me. Now that Thomas is in England and the Roundheads know it, we will be under scrutiny. You must be careful! Not only do we have to contend with the Roundhead troops, but we have a traitor in our midst."

Alysa shivered. "Sir Philip?"

Strathern sighed. "I don't know. I can think of no reason why Sir Philip Hampton would have been at Fenwick Cove tonight. If he was the one who betrayed Thomas he would have stayed away. Certainly he would never have ensured that your brother was able to escape. Be that what it may, the question remains: why was he there?"

Not, Alysa hoped, because he was indebted to the Protectorate for his inheritance and willing to do anything to pay them back. For some reason, she did not want to believe that Philip Hampton was capable of betraying his friends. But she could not be sure. Nor, she acknowledged as they neared Strathern Hall, could she rest until she had discovered who the traitor was.

The next day, West Easton and area became unpleasantly aware that the Protectorate was not entirely without teeth. The soldiers were out early, despite their late night, patrolling the roads, combing the woodlands, pushing their way into the houses of the lower orders and pounding on the doors of the better class of people. Oliver Cromwell might be dead, but the military machine he had created continued relentlessly on.

Philip Hampton was visited shortly after dawn. He had expected a house-by-house search and had deliberately retired to his bed, even though he had returned to Ainslie late and had not yet been asleep. Appearances were everything in a situation like this. If questioned, his servants would not have to lie about rousing him and if the troops took it into their head to surprise him in his room, he would be innocently in bed and grouchy at being awakened so suddenly.

He hadn't been surprised last night when he'd seen the troop of cavalry burst from the trees. Long years of experience at court and in the army had taught him that the safest secret was one that remained unspoken. The more people who knew, the more likely it was that the secret would be whispered into the wrong ears. It was far too difficult to convince people that keeping a confidence meant telling no one, including one's nearest and dearest.

He had heard the details of the rendezvous spoken of in a normal tone in broad daylight in a public place, which meant that the arrival of Thomas Leighton was being discussed by virtually everyone in the vicinity. After considerable soul-searching, Philip had decided that he would not tell Osborne of the news he had learned. After a devastating event like the arrest of Thomas Leighton, the good people of West Easton would feel the need to lay blame, and what better candidate for scapegoat than the stranger in their midst. Philip would immediately be suspected and that would not suit his long-term goals at all.

There was another, less personal reason for his decision. Osborne would not stop at arresting Thomas Leighton. He would also apprehend every man who was there to greet the returned Royalist. Inevitably that would include Lord Strathern. Despite his duty to the Lord Protector, Philip could not bring himself to arrange the downfall of a good and honorable man.

So he went to Fenwick Cove with the idea that he would follow young Leighton to his first place of sanctuary, then tell Osborne of the hiding place. Thomas could be arrested quietly, in such a way that no one would suspect Philip of informing on him. Moreover, only Thomas would be caught and charged with treason. His father and the other gentlemen who met him at the cove would no doubt be chastened by their flirtation with danger and would desist in their rebellious activities.

This ingenious plan still left Philip feeling somewhat ashamed of himself, for treachery was not something he enjoyed. So, although he was surprised when he saw the soldiers exploding from the trees, he was also relieved. The decision whether or not to turn in Thomas Leighton had been taken out of his hands.

The arrival of the soldiers raised an interesting point, though. It meant that Osborne had another spy in West Easton, and since Philip was the only stranger in the area, Osborne's spy must be one of the local people.

He thought of that now, as his butler, dressed in a rather hasty fashion, breathlessly told him that an officer was waiting to see him downstairs. Philip nodded, ran his fingers through his long, tousled dark hair, rubbed his stubbly chin and generally acted like a man who had just been wakened from a deep sleep. Grumpily, he demanded his nightgown, a long, loose garment made of an exotic damask silk, which he wrapped around his muscular form.

"Where did you put the fellow?" he growled, knotting the sash. The rich crimson of the shimmering cloth brought out shiny highlights in his black hair.

"I left him in the Great Hall, Sir Philip. Young Lealand is watching him."

Ashton, the butler, eyed Philip in a nervous, wary way as he spoke. Philip noted this grimly. Someone in West Easton had betrayed Thomas Leighton, but it had not been him. Nevertheless, even his own people were questioning whether or not he was the one who had laid the information. Anger sizzled in him. He had never liked being blamed for crimes he had not committed.

As he descended the great staircase, he heard a loud, bullying voice saying, "You know more than you are telling, lad, and don't think that you can get away with hiding it from me! We'll find that scurvy devil or we'll arrest half this county for harboring a traitor!"

Philip paused. The voice was unknown to him, and from

what he could see, so was the officer who was ruthlessly interrogating his servant. The man was wearing the red coat of Cromwell's Ironsides. Regimental facings of a bright green told Philip that he was part of a unit stationed here in southern England. Philip knew the name of the colonel of the regiment, but none of the man's officers. Somewhat reassured, for he had been half afraid that his impersonation would be exposed this morning, he considered how best to handle the coming interview.

Should he act like an innocent man unjustly accused? Royalists tended to be a prickly lot, especially when confronted with their own wrongdoing. They usually began by denying any responsibility and often continued so until the bitter end. There were those in the hierarchy of the Protectorate who delighted in breaking such men. Philip had never been one of them, but he had the uneasy feeling that the officer below could be classed among their number. If that was so, it would be better to present a mild front and pass off any malice the fellow might exhibit with a smile and a shrug.

Better, but not possible. Philip despised men who used their rank and power to intimidate others. Moreover, he had been an officer too long to suppress his training. A fractious subordinate was one who must be put securely in his place.

Shrugging, he continued down the stairs. He would see how the interview went and he would follow his instincts.

Hearing footsteps on the stairs, Lealand looked over with undeniable relief. "Sir Philip," he said, stammering a little in his haste to say what he had to and be gone. "This is Lieutenant Weston. He is here to ask some questions about the doings last night."

"What doings?" Philip growled, running his fingers through his thick hair, supposedly to straighten it, but really to increase the look of ruffled dishabille.

"A convicted rebel returned to England last night," Weston announced, puffing out his chest and deepening his voice. He abandoned Lealand, who promptly scuttled away to a safer haven in the servants' quarters. "We're searching the area to locate him."

"He's not here," Philip said grumpily. He glared at the lieutenant, sizing him up with the speed of long experience. The man had the fervent glitter of a fanatic in his eyes, but he also had the sharp, uneasy manner of an inexperienced man given a task that was beyond his skills.

"Don't lie to me!" Weston said menacingly.

Philip suppressed a mischievous little wish that he had the lieutenant under his command so that he could teach the man some manners. However, since that was not possible, he ignored the man's rudeness. "Is that why you woke me up? To see if Ainslie was harboring a returned Royalist?"

Weston, who had all the subtlety of a dull nail, sneered. "Lying abed late because you were out at all hours meeting a smuggling boat? If the Royalist isn't here, then I'll wager you know where he is!"

Philip replied with an enviable, icy calm. He'd long ago trained himself not to lose his detachment once involved in an engagement. Too many mistakes were made by men who allowed the passions of the hour to overset their good judgment. "Then you would lose that bet. I do not know where your Royalist is, nor do I care. If that is all, Lieutenant, you may leave."

"Not so fast," Weston said roughly. "I'm not finished."

Philip raised black brows. "Then continue, but pray do so quickly. Now that I am awake I would like to break my fast and enjoy a mug of ale."

The lieutenant colored at the haughty tone in Philip's voice. "I'll proceed at my own speed!"

"Sir," Philip said softly. Dangerously.

Weston blinked. "What was that?"

"When you speak to me do so respectfully. 'I'll proceed at my own speed, *sir.*'"

"Respect must be earned," Weston sneered.

"And information is freely given," Philip shot back. "Use your head, Lieutenant. No one in West Easton is going to welcome you with open arms, especially if you do your best to alienate every potential ally you might have."

Contempt skittered across the officer's face. "You consider yourself a potential ally? I think not! We know West Easton is a hotbed of Royalists. Last night we almost caught the ringleaders in the act of welcoming an exiled traitor back to England. They managed to escape by the merest hairbreadth of chance. Rest assured, Hampton, we will not make the same mistake again! We know the Black Boy's henchman is in this area. We know it and we will find him. Even if we have to tear down every building for miles around!"

Weston's eyes were glittering with fervor and his face had begun to turn a bright pink. Philip had no doubt the officer must be kept from abusing the power he'd been given, or the people of West Easton would have another reason to hate the Protectorate. He drew a deep breath. "Get out of my house, Lieutenant. Now!"

"You haven't finished answering my questions."

Violence was a language a man like Weston understood. He would scorn an opponent who returned a soft answer, but he would fear, and so respect, one who unexpectedly used him as ruthlessly as he liked to use others.

In two quick strides Philip was beside the officer. He took Weston by the arm in an iron hold and marched him swiftly to the door. Throwing it open he pushed the man onto the porch. "Hear me, Lieutenant Weston. Do not return to Ainslie Manor again. Do not harass my tenants. Do not seek to question my servants. Above all, do not attempt to speak to me again. Am I understood?"

Weston had almost fallen from the momentum of Philip's push and he was flushed with temper as he righted himself and straightened his tunic. His men, who had waited for him in the forecourt while he went to interrogate Philip, observed the altercation silently. Very much aware of the watching eyes, Weston put on a bold face. "And if I choose not to obey you?" he sneered. "What do you think you can do to me? I can burn your tenants' houses and rape their women for sport and you can do nothing to me!"

Philip moved until he was only inches away from the man.

Fury at this petty creature was mixed with a real fear that Weston would do exactly what he said if he wasn't stopped. Deliberately allowing the force of his feelings to show in his blazing eyes, Philip spoke in a voice icy with promise. "You think you are invincible? I promise you, you are not! Should I hear that you have acted in any way beyond what is right and proper, I'll tie you to an oxcart myself and whip you until you beg for mercy. Then I'll cut off your ears and feed them to the pigs! I can do it and I will do it. Do you understand me, Lieutenant?"

He read the fear in the man's eyes and was satisfied. "Good. Now go. And do not think that I will remain silent regarding this. I shall be telling the other landowners in the area and we will all stand against you should you harm anyone—anyone!—in your attempts to discover this Royalist's whereabouts."

A small group of servants had gathered in the doorway. The butler stepped forward when Philip finished. He was holding a mug of ale, which he offered to Philip. Somewhat surprised, Philip took it and sipped while he watched through narrowed eyes as the lieutenant hurried down the stairs to his waiting men, roughly ordering them to mount up as he went. As they rode off down the drive Philip drank the ale and thought about the visit.

His butler's voice brought him back from his reverie. "That was perhaps not wise, Sir Philip."

Philip glanced at Ashton. The wariness that he'd seen in the butler's eyes earlier was gone. Now the expression there was one of respect and concern. "How so?"

"You have been away from England for a long time, sir. The government is empowered to apprehend those it deems suspicious, whether there is reason for the arrest or not. The lieutenant might just decide to give your name to the Committee of Safety for no other reason than you annoyed him."

A chill ran through Philip. He thrust the now empty mug into the butler's hands. "No one is going to arrest me," he said grimly, as he stomped into the house, "or any other householder in this area if we are willing to stand together against them."

He headed for the stairs. Behind him the butler muttered uneasily, "I hope you are right, Sir Philip. England is not the land you once knew."

Later that morning Philip Hampton visited Strathern Hall. He was shown into the shabby morning room, where Lord Strathern sat with his wife and eldest daughter. "Sir Philip, this is an unexpected surprise."

Just inside the room, Philip stopped. His brows rose fractionally as his eyes scanned the small, cluttered chamber. It was nothing at all like the elegant King's Salon.

After that short pause to get his bearings, Philip strode into the room with the decisive walk of someone used to command. After bowing to the ladies, he addressed Lord Strathern. "I had a thoroughly unpleasant visit from a troop of Cromwell's Ironsides earlier this morning, Strathern. I am particularly concerned about an odious lieutenant by the name of Weston who believes his position gives him the right to allow his baser instincts free rein."

Cautiously, Strathern nodded. "We were also visited by troops this morning." Watching Philip closely, he added, "I must confess, I did not expect you to come to me with this particular complaint."

Philip frowned. He was dressed in a comfortable riding outfit. The brown cloth suit was not as opulent as some of his other clothes, but looked just as new. "Why not?"

Lord Strathern shrugged noncommittally. Unlike Philip's, his green doublet and black breeches were of the finest silk and decorated with a vast number of ribbon loops. His hair had been carefully curled and two lovelocks fell past his shoulders. It was as if he had dressed to annoy any Roundhead interloper who might have the temerity to invade his privacy.

Philip colored at Strathern's unspoken slur. "Because of my brother, the Roundhead?"

"You are new to the area, Sir Philip. The troops would

have no reason to believe that you are involved in Royalist plots," Abigail said pacifically. Like her husband she was very carefully dressed. Her gown was of blue silk over a pale blue quilted petticoat and a fine lawn gorget circled her neck and fell to the top of the gown, adequately covering the skin exposed by the low-cut bodice. Despite her impressive garments, strain shadowed her eyes.

"And so you think that they would have left me alone while the rest of the neighborhood was thoroughly searched." Philip's expression was sardonic. "I see you have a very poor opinion of the care taken by the Lord Protector's servants."

"Roundheads are given preferential treatment in the Lord Protector's realm," Alysa burst out. Her lovely blue eyes were marked with the evidence of too much worry and not enough sleep, but like her parents she was impressively garbed in a gown of violet with a petticoat of ice blue. "With your family connections it is most likely that you would be safe." She paused for a fraction of a second before adding deliberately, "Unless they identified you as the unknown champion who deprived them of their pray last night."

Philip looked at her sharply, his expression at first surprised, then guarded.

There was an uneasy silence until Abigail said, "Do sit down, Sir Philip. Would you like some refreshments?"

Philip sat, but he declined the refreshments.

Lord Strathern considered Philip a moment before he said heavily, "I do not think it is wise to speak of last night any more than is necessary, but I must ask, Sir Philip, why were you there? To my knowledge you were not invited. As well, I wish to know how you discovered the time and date of the meeting."

The blank expression Alysa had seen several times before fell over Philip's features as he considered his reply. "If I may, I'll answer your second question first, Lord Strathern. I learned that Thomas Leighton would be visiting England and the date of his arrival from a conversation overheard in the village. Two ladies talking. Loudly, I might add."

Strathern nodded morosely. "I was afraid of that. I suspect that is how the Protectorate learned of it too."

"As to my reason for being there." Philip shrugged. "I guessed that if I had overheard, others might too. Through hard experience I have learned that it is always best to expect the worst. I thought, rightly it turned out, that you just might need the assistance of the unexpected."

Lord Strathern's eyes bored into Philip's. At last Strathern spoke, apparently satisfied with what he saw. "I thank you for your assistance, Sir Philip. Without it I fear that the situation might have ended differently. Now tell me about your visit from the infernal Roundhead, Weston."

"The man made threats. Dangerous threats." Philip glanced deliberately at the ladies.

Strathern frowned once more. "You have been out of the country, Sir Philip. No doubt exile has little to recommend it, but I promise you, living under the tyranny of Cromwell's dictatorship has less."

"Papa!"

He waved Alysa's instinctive protest aside, and although he answered her, his eyes were fixed probingly on Philip's face. "My dear, there comes a time when a man must speak out, no matter what the consequences. I gather Sir Philip has seen for the first time how the Lord Protector's troops treat England's citizens. I'll wager it was something of a shock, was it not, Hampton?"

Philip looked at him ruefully. "More than a shock, Strathern, a revelation." A faint smile curled his lips. "I fear I reacted not as a cowed civilian might, but as an officer with an insubordinate trooper would."

Strathern raised his brows in cool question, although amusement warmed his eyes.

"I threatened to horsewhip Weston and do certain, er, other things to his person that he would not like. He left my property in a great hurry."

"That may not have been wise, Sir Philip," Abigail said kindly. "The military has been allowed to do pretty well what it pleases since Cromwell took power. Your officer will not like being dressed down, especially by a Royalist landowner."

With surprising fierceness, Philip said, "With all due respect, ma'am, whether the lieutenant liked it or not, he deserved the snub I gave him." He turned to Lord Strathern. "If we stand together, Strathern, we can defeat this riffraff."

"Yes, we could," Strathern said softly. His eyes were watchful, but approval glowed within their depths. "You have seen firsthand what we have borne these last ten years, Sir Philip, but you must understand what you are suggesting."

Philip raised his brows questioningly. "And what is that?"

"Rebellion."

"Papa," Alysa said again, softly, pleadingly.

Strathern indicated her with a nod of his head. "You see what happens when that word is used, Hampton. Our women cringe, even as daring a soul as my daughter here. We have seen enough of the results of rebellion here in England."

"And so you lie down like dogs and wait to be kicked?"

"Sir Philip!" Abigail said, shocked.

"Shame!" cried Alysa, jumping to her feet. She went to stand in front of Philip, who had stood as soon as she had. She looked up into his eyes, her own glittering fiercely. "There are none who would like to see the Protector overthrown more than the people of West Easton. We have been loyal to the monarchy since the war began and the Protector and his barbarians have not hesitated to try to show us the error of our ways. But we have not broken! No, no matter what was done to us, we have kept our secrets. And we will continue to do so. So do not think that we are submitting to the tyranny of the current regime, for we are not. What we are doing is appearing to submit and you will find, Sir Philip, that there is a vast difference between the two!"

Philip drew a deep breath. His features were taut with unexpressed emotion. "I beg your pardon, Lord Strathern. I will relieve you of my company." He bowed politely. "I came today merely to warn you that troops are in the area and are seeking your son. You may rest assured that I gave them no information."

As he was about to leave, Strathern said coldly, "A moment, Hampton."

Philip turned slowly. He looked from Strathern, straight and formidable, to Alysa, still stiff with her defiance, her lovely face glowing with spirit.

"Yes?"

"Did Lieutenant Weston mention that the man they sought was my son?"

A faint smile curled Philip's lips. "No, Lord Strathern, he did not. To my knowledge the troops do not know the name of the man they are seeking, or else they would have taken you into custody before now. I learned the identity of the Royalist emissary four days ago, along with the date and time of his arrival, in a shop in the village, as I mentioned earlier." A grim amusement colored his voice. "If you plan to indulge in this sort of conspiracy in the future, I suggest you strive for a degree of confidentiality when you make your plans, sir." With that parting shot, he bowed again and turned once more to leave.

"How dare you!" Alysa flared at his retreating back.

Philip didn't acknowledge her passionate outburst, but at the doorway he paused. "I dare, Mistress Leighton, because I care."

He was gone before anyone in the family could think of a reply.

CHAPTER 7

There was complete silence in the shabby parlor after Philip walked out.

"Well, well," Lord Strathern said at last, his voice thoughtful. "What do you make of that?"

His question was addressed to both his wife and daughter. It was Abigail who answered first. "I would not have thought that a man used to being at court would speak so—bluntly."

"Perhaps not, but an honest man, angry at an injustice he does not expect, would." Strathern nodded his head. "I like the way Hampton handles himself. He has a care for his tenants, he is decisive, but not imperious, and he acts without asking how he will be rewarded. Most of all," Strathern shot a serious look at Alysa, "I think he is a match for my headstrong daughter."

"Papa," Alysa said, a little breathlessly. "I hardly know the man! Indeed, you asked me to find out what I could about him, and I have learned nothing! Oh, he speaks of what is inconsequential, but he does not discuss the important things."

"Such as what? Think carefully, Alysa! If the man is not what he purports to be I must warn the people of West Easton of his duplicity. The townspeople will not be kind to Sir Philip. He will find his life at Ainslie to be a lonely one." Strathern paused, then added heavily, "If you are wrong in your assessment, you will be condemning an innocent man."

Alysa bit her lip. She thought of Philip Hampton, risking his freedom, perhaps his very life, to save her from the Roundhead trooper the night before, of the way his eyes sparkled with an inner amusement while his lips remained serious, of the way he looked at her, with a masculine appreciation that was both frank and respectful. Then she thought of those moments of careful blankness when she had caught him off guard, and the way he spoke smooth nothings when asked about his life on the Continent or of his political beliefs.

Was he the Royalist brother or the Roundhead?

Should she condemn him to be ostracized by the people of West Easton because she wondered why his expression would hide his thoughts at some moments? Was that enough reason to denounce a man? But with Thomas in England, and in danger, could she afford to give Sir Philip Hampton the benefit of the doubt?

Alysa felt the weight of her father's eyes watching her expression as she considered what she should say, but she did not rush into speech. Her decision was too important to be made lightly. "Papa, I deem Sir Philip to be a just and honorable man. I do not believe that he was the one who betrayed Thomas's arrival to the troops, but I do not know him well enough to say whether you should admit him to your councils."

Edward sighed and sat down beside his wife on the sofa. "I grow tired of this constant mistrust. It should be enough that a man is honorable and upright. Why must we always be questioning which side he is on?"

Abigail patted him on the hand. "I believe you have answered yourself, husband. A just man would not betray a friend. If you have decided Sir Philip is such a man, then you must, perforce, trust him."

Her husband blew gustily through his lips. "My dear, an excellent point! I believe Sir Philip would be a valuable addition to our organization. He has qualities we need and he will bring a fresh viewpoint to our discussions."

Alysa's uneasiness continued. "Are you sure, Papa? With

Thomas in England, is it not dangerous to admit a new member at this time?"

She waited nervously, half hoping her father would dismiss her remark as nothing more than silly female fears. When he did not answer right away, she felt her heart sink.

"You have a good point, my dear. Thomas is vulnerable. There *is* a traitor somewhere in West Easton, and as Sir Philip pointed out, to date our security has been lamentable. It could have been virtually anyone in the village or the surrounding area who alerted the authorities of Thomas's arrival, including Sir Philip himself. But," Strathern added emphatically, "I do not think it was Philip Hampton who did the foul deed. My sense of the man makes me believe that he would not have flown to our rescue last night or shown himself here today if he had betrayed us the night before."

"Then you are decided," Alysa said, relief flooding her.

"The king needs new supporters, Alysa, especially now. If he does decide to return we will require all the loyal men we can muster to follow him. As to the danger to Thomas, this is a good time, not a bad one, to involve a man of Sir Philip's qualities. I would like his opinion on whether or not a rebellion would be successful, should we be able to raise the men and supplies. He will be able to add a great deal to our deliberations."

"I suppose I need not encourage him any longer?" Disappointment colored Alysa's voice.

Her father caught the sound and smiled. "Only if you choose not to."

Alysa wandered over to a carved table set against the wall. There she fiddled with the wax tapers fixed in plain pewter candlesticks, straightening them when they needed no straightening. Her back was to her family as she considered what she should do. After a long minute she turned, her face set. "Cedric Ingram has come to believe that I am his for the asking. If I continue to invite Sir Philip's attentions Cedric will assume I prefer our new neighbor to him. He will be jealous."

"A little jealousy would not do Cedric Ingram any harm,"

Abigail said calmly, glancing at Alysa with a small smile. "You are a lovely young lady, Alysa. I have always thought it a shame that there are so few gentlemen of quality in the neighborhood. You deserve to have men tilting with each other for your token. Master Ingram must realize that there is no legal tie between you and that he has no claim on you until there is."

Alysa felt a pang of sympathy as she listened to her stepmother. Abigail had never had the opportunity she had just wished Alysa could have, and obviously she regretted it. She had been all of four and twenty when she had come from a tiny hamlet in the north to care for the son and daughter of her recently widowed cousin, Edward, Lord Strathern. Their marriage not long after had been a match of convenience that had grown into a close, loving bond. But Abigail had not had the opportunity to pick and choose from among many suitors. Evidently, no matter how happy her marriage was, that lingered in her mind as one of life's cheats.

Strathern added his support to his wife's. "If Ingram makes a fuss, leave him to me, my dear. Do what your heart tells you you must regarding Sir Philip. You have our support in whatever you decide."

A sweet and very beautiful smile bloomed on Alysa's face. "Thank you, both! Yes, I would like Sir Philip to continue his courtship. Perhaps nothing will come of it, but...." She laughed, a happy, free sound. "We will see what the future brings."

The woods were very still on this dark, brooding night. Philip Hampton thought about the message he had received, which had been more of a command that he appear in the little copse at the top of the rise at midnight than a request for a meeting. The demand had saved him from contacting Osborne himself, for he wanted the London man to know that he would not put up with Lieutenant Weston terrorizing the people of West Easton.

As was his custom he arrived at the meeting place well

ahead of time. The property was his, the woods were his and he had no intention of letting Osborne have the run of them because he couldn't bestir himself to arrive early.

Heavy clouds covered the moon, almost obscuring the path to the top of the hill. Within the undergrowth there were few sounds. Philip reflected that the wild animals respected the portents of a storm to come and had retreated to the safety of their lairs. Only rash humans were abroad tonight, and few of them at that.

He waited in the shadows, absently stroking the nose of his horse while he listened for the sound of Osborne's arrival. He was wearing the warm buff coat that branded him as a military man, the same coat he'd worn on the night of Thomas Leighton's arrival. The leather was soft and well-worn. If Lord Strathern or his daughter had seen it close up, they would have questioned why a man who had spent the past few years at a court-in-exile would possess such an unfashionable, but obviously well-used garment. At midnight on a blustery spring night, Philip welcomed the insulating quality of the coat and didn't care about what people might think.

Time passed and the scent of moisture in the air grew stronger. He judged they would be in for a storm soon and if Osborne didn't hurry up they would both be caught in it.

Some twenty minutes after the time arranged Osborne did finally arrive. He was dressed in his usual black doublet and breeches. The garments helped him blend in with the shadows and gave him the appearance of a creature of the night. Beneath a broad-brimmed black hat, his face was a blur of pale, frowning features. "These damn woods are blacker than Hades itself! I lost my way a dozen times before I found the path! Damned country life. Next time we meet, we'll do it in some more civilized place."

"Such as at the inn where you are staying?" Philip suggested sardonically, his control a strong contrast to Osborne's irritation. "That would be perfect. Then all of the area would hear that the Puritan from London is meeting with the foreigner who lives at Ainslie."

Osborne stiffened and his voice grew cautious. "I'm not staying in West Easton."

"I know that," Philip shot back. He was regretting his sarcasm, for Sir Edgar Osborne was an astute man, quick to pick up nuances other men would miss. "West Easton doesn't have an inn to speak of. However, I know you must be within a short ride of the town or you would not be able to keep such a close watch on events."

"Very true." Osborne smiled, apparently satisfied that Philip didn't know the location of his hideaway. One of the absurdities of this whole episode, in Philip's mind, was Osborne's insistence that his headquarters be a secret.

It wasn't. Within a few days of arriving at Ainslie, Philip had decided that the more he knew about Sir Edgar Osborne, the safer he would be. So he had followed the Londoner back to his lair one evening. Osborne was staying at a decrepit inn a few miles outside of West Easton. Since the war the place had fallen on hard times, though it had never been a very prosperous or respectable inn.

Built in a sturdy post-and-beam construction, the inn had strong walls, but the foundation had shifted and the roof was in dire need of repair. Whitewash and paint had not been applied to the exterior in some time and here and there the protective coating had peeled away to expose the bare wood beneath. A ramshackle stable abutted one side of the building, which was longer than it was wide. This created a vague sort of a courtyard, where guests of the establishment would leave their horses or carriages and expect a servant to deal with them.

On the night that Philip had followed him, he had watched Osborne shout for a groom to tend to his horse, but the hour was late and whatever servants the place could afford had long since gone to bed. Philip had found it rather satisfying to see the imperious Osborne forced to tend to his own mount.

"Enough of this talk of inns," Osborne continued firmly, unaware of Philip's thoughts. "I want a report on what you've discovered so far. You missed a fine opportunity when you did not warn me that Thomas Leighton was arriving two nights ago."

Philip retorted mildly, "As I have mentioned before, Osborne, I have not been accepted by Lord Strathern to the degree that he would tell me a secret such as the date and time of his son's return to England." He shrugged dismissively, then tried what he feared would be a forlorn hope, for he badly wanted to escape from the trap he found himself in. "Evidently my services are not needed, for you have a well-informed spy in the Royalist ranks already. Certainly a more capable spy than I shall ever be."

Eyes narrowed, Osborne said calculatingly, "What do you mean?"

Real amusement lit Philip's features. "Come now, sir! There is no need to dissemble with me. Half the county has been the recipient of a visit from the troops you brought here to capture Thomas Leighton. As I was unable to tell you when and where he was to arrive, I must infer that someone else did."

Osborne's eyes snapped wide open and he assumed a look of innocence. "And how did you know that my men were at the traitor's arrival?" He cocked his head. "There was an unknown cavalier there who spoiled the perfect chance to capture Leighton. I've been wondering who that was."

Philip's heart began to pound, but he let none of his dismay show on his face. He cursed himself roundly, though, for forgetting to guard every word he said to Sir Edgar Osborne. "I knew because I visited Lord Strathern today. He made mention of it. As to the unknown rider, I cannot help you, for I was not there." Philip allowed himself a grim smile. "Perhaps if I were a better spy I would have been. Now then, what is the point of keeping me involved in this unhappy affair when you have a man who can supply you with the information you need?"

A crafty look appeared on Osborne's face. He thoughtfully examined his boots for some moments before replying to Philip's remark. "And if I do have an agent secreted in the ranks of the local Royalists, what business is it of yours?"

"None whatsoever," Philip agreed blandly. "I wish to know nothing about the fellow. In fact, since I plan to stay awhile in West Easton, I would prefer not to learn which of my neighbors is selling out his friends for thirty pieces of silver. I am glad, however, that my dubious services will no longer be needed by the Lord Protector."

Osborne's head snapped up. "Who says they will not?"

Philip's jaw hardened. "You have one informant, Osborne. Is not one traitor enough?"

"You see yourself as a traitor?" Osborne hissed, his gaze probing.

Philip realized the trap his words had set and sighed inwardly. In the unsettled atmosphere of Lord Richard Cromwell's reign, the Protectorate had become a nest of suspicion. Every word a man said could be taken, twisted and ultimately used against him. Though Philip would have liked to have walked away from the loathsome Osborne and his innuendoes, he knew he could not. Therefore, he carefully clarified his remark. "I am posing as a friend to these people. Though their beliefs are not mine, I am pretending that they are. While I am not a traitor to my real loyalties, I do feel as if I truly am a traitor when I am among them."

"You're too soft," Osborne sneered.

Philip stiffened. "I am a simple soldier, Osborne, nothing more."

The Roundhead agent snorted. "Don't pretend to be naive to me. You were brought up at Charles's court. You know what politics are all about."

Philip stroked the nose of his mount. He used the movement to help dissipate some of the anger Osborne's words and manner had generated. "You are quite correct. I did grow up at court. I also joined the parliamentary army because I believed that the system needed to be changed."

"As did all of us who supported the Lord Protector," Osborne intoned piously.

Philip thought of the ruthless restrictions that had been placed on the defeated Royalists and never lifted, of the brutal bullying an officer like Weston believed he could get away with, and he abandoned the careful rein he kept on his tongue. There were times when caution was not a man's best policy. "I wonder now whether or not ten years of war did any good whatsoever."

Osborne's eyes bulged. "I cannot believe I am hearing this! From you of all people! Explain yourself, sir!"

"No! You explain yourself, Osborne! What the devil did you mean by sending the dregs of the army to West Easton?"

"The dregs?" Osborne sounded honestly puzzled.

"Now who is being naive? I'm referring to the overbearing Lieutenant Weston and the pack of wolves with him you ordered to capture Thomas Leighton. When they could not, you had them comb the neighborhood for him."

"Ah! Lieutenant Weston." Sir Edgar observed Philip thoughtfully. "While it is true that the man is not the flower of our officer corps, I would not call him the *dregs* either."

"I would," Philip retorted, his professional pride injured.

"Weston serves his purpose," Osborne said, dismissing him. He pointed a finger at Philip. "I suggest, sir, that you do the same."

A muscle twitched in Philip's jaw. "You do not need my participation in this scheme. You have an excellent spy already in place."

"Perhaps I do, Sir Philip Hampton." Osborne used Philip's full title quite deliberately, emphasizing that he would not have been allowed to inherit had it not been for the goodwill of the Lord Protector—and the fact that he would be useful located in West Easton. "But my agent runs a terrible risk of being caught out and since I have the good fortune to have a replacement carefully burrowing his way into the core of the Royalist organization in the area I will accept it. That way I have two men on the scene. If one is apprehended the other can carry on. And I am able to rest easy that the information I need will continue to flow my way."

Philip's horse tossed its head, catching the restless tension that burned through him. He stroked the animal's nose again, to soothe it and himself. "Very well then, it appears I must continue to make myself agreeable to Lord Strathern and his family."

Osborne laughed nastily. "That is one way of putting it." He mounted his horse. As he gathered up the reins he said, "I don't know why you are so set against this, Hampton. I would find romancing a young woman as pretty as Mistress Alysa to be no hardship at all."

Rage traveled like wildfire through Philip and seared into a white-hot fury that was all the more potent because it had to be contained. As Sir Edgar turned his horse to go, Philip said in a low, forceful voice, "A moment, Osborne."

The spymaster paused.

"There is one matter on which I will not bend."

Osborne raised his brows. He did not make the mistake of underestimating the potential for violence at this precise moment. "What is that?"

"Give your lieutenant a lesson in manners. If Weston makes any attempt to harm the people of this area in any way, I shall expose your whole dirty plot and raise a force against him. Do you understand me?"

Osborne lowered his head in a mock bow. "You are very clear, Sir Philip. Now, if you will excuse me? I must be on my way."

He left without saying anything further. Philip let him go, idly rubbing his horse's cheek as he watched. He stood there for a long time, stroking the horse and thinking about himself, Sir Edgar Osborne, and a traitor in the ranks of the West Easton Royalists.

Philip mounted his horse when he felt the first spattering of rain. While his mount picked its way through the undergrowth he remained relatively dry, but when he reached open ground there was no shelter from the shower and he was soon soaking wet.

With a slight grimace, he put his heels to the horse's sides and urged it into a gallop. As a cavalryman he had spent many wet nights like this. Though his leather jerkin was well-nigh waterproof and his beaver hat kept his head dry, his breeches clung to his skin and rain leaked down the sides of his boots. He well knew how to endure the discomfort of sodden clothes, but he was loath to do so unless he had to.

His route home took him through Strathern land. He didn't like trespassing on Lord Strathern's property after a meeting with Osborne, but there was no easy alternative path. The feeling of treachery that grew on him every time he considered what he was doing made him think again about his dialogue with Sir Edgar Osborne. He loathed the hold the man had over him. What he had agreed to do out of lingering loyalty to Oliver Cromwell's memory, Osborne had despoiled with lies and innuendo. The man was totally devoid of honor. His whole existence was empty, pragmatic cynicism.

Moreover, Philip was a man used to being in charge. As a senior officer in the parliamentary army he'd had the respect and obedience of his men and most of his fellow officers. He did not like being the one ordered about. It went against the grain. Even worse, he didn't trust Osborne. The man claimed he wanted to keep Philip active in his service simply for the security of having an alternate agent. That was possible, but more likely he had other plans for Philip in the future.

That was a thought that made Philip very nervous, not to mention angry.

For a man who had chosen the straightforward command and obey of army life, the duplicity of someone like Osborne was anathema. Though it was true Philip had been raised at court and so could reasonably be expected to be hardened to the games people played, he had also quite deliberately selected a different way of life. Not only that, but he had supported a new government, pledged to reform the old ways and clear away the deceptions of the Royalist courtiers.

Men like Sir Edgar Osborne made him doubt anything had changed, however. Had so many men fought and died simply to put a new set of duplicitous rogues into power?

The answer was becoming very clear to Philip, but he was not yet ready to decide what he ought to do. He did know that he was sick of this underhanded business.

His path took him through the trees to the lake where he had watched Alysa Leighton riding like the wind. He slowed, his thoughts naturally going to the lovely, golden-haired woman. A grim light entered his eyes as he remembered Osborne's remark about her. How dare the odious fellow sully her name!

A rather warm feeling rose up in him as he thought of Alysa. He believed she was responding to his advances in a most positive way, but he had to acknowledge that his reasons for courting her were flawed—he was using her to get to her father. Lord Strathern was a fine, respectable man whose only crime, if it was one, was that he had sworn allegiance to a king and had never broken that oath.

Alysa Leighton was a beautiful, intriguing woman whom Philip could very easily learn to feel affection for, if he allowed himself to admit his feelings, and her father, Lord Strathern, was a man Philip respected. He hated lying to both of them.

When he had agreed to take on this task it had seemed easy. Royalists were the enemy and he never dreamed that he would find himself being tied emotionally to one of their number. Yet here he was, respecting Lord Strathern and attracted to his daughter, while the distaste he felt for Osborne, a representative of the Commonwealth Philip had sworn to serve, was rapidly growing into hatred.

Over the years he'd cushioned himself by creating an image of Royalists as cynical manipulators who would stop at nothing to achieve their ends. Men like that were easy to hate—and easy to kill. The image had kept him sane through years of war when he had wondered before every battle if one of the men on the other side was his brother—and if, as his unit charged across the field, he would be raising his sword to hack down upon his brother's head as they broke through the Royalist lines.

He had never faced his brother in battle, and Anthony had died a dissolute death in exile, but the image Philip had used to protect himself still remained.

But the image he'd held and what he'd found when he came to West Easton were two very different things.

If the image was one of ruthless cynicism, the reality was solid, honest men pushed to the limit of their endurance and finally refusing to be pushed any further. Despite the mandate King Charles had given to the Sealed Knot, the Royalists were not cohesive, but fragmented. Organization, as evidenced by Thomas Leighton's near capture, was not their strong point.

Osborne did not need two spies in West Easton. Let him acquire what information he could from his turncoat Royalist. Philip would use his discretion in deciding what he would tell Sir Edgar Osborne. Should he hear something vital to the safety of the Protectorate he would certainly pass it along. But otherwise…let the turncoat do the day-to-day spying while Philip concentrated on making a life for himself at Ainslie Manor.

The skies opened in a deluge that made Philip put aside his thoughts of Alysa Leighton and the future. He urged the horse to increase its speed as much as possible over the slick mud of the clay path, but the stallion slipped in the sloppy going. Philip held it steady, avoiding a nasty spill and a long walk home in the heavy rain, but he was relieved when he had again reached the shelter of the trees.

In the woods the darkness was complete, since the canopy of leaves blocked what little light remained in the night sky. Philip's pace slowed to a crawl, but at least he was somewhat protected from the rain.

He emerged from the forest on Ainslie property. From here his route led him through a series of open fields, past a thick copse of oak trees that fringed the home park, then on to Ainslie Manor. The spirited stallion snorted and shook its head, sensing that the warmth of the stables was not far away. Philip let the animal have its head and it broke into a canter.

As he neared the trees Philip thought he saw a shadowy movement in them. He frowned, wondering who or what might be abroad on a nasty night such as this, but he didn't take any precautions. Why should he? This was Ainslie land.

His land.

The shot that rang out could have been thunder. Philip was close enough that it deafened him like thunder. He was fortunate that the accuracy of the weapon, or the man handling it, was poor. The musket ball made contact with Philip's upper thigh, passing through muscle and flesh before escaping to inflict a shallow graze on the horse's flank. Philip's wound was painful, but not overly dangerous. A seasoned campaigner and an accomplished rider, he kept his seat as the stallion shied, then let it have its head to run for home.

Without a weapon of his own, there was nothing he could do to the person who had shot him. As every old soldier knew, it was wiser to retreat and fight another day than to march headlong into certain death.

For now he would have to retreat. But later....

Later he intended to find out who had lain in wait for him and why.

CHAPTER 8

Lady Strathern had always maintained that gossiping with servants was unacceptable behavior for any member of the Leighton family and for the most part her daughters obeyed the dictum. On this sunny afternoon, however, Prudence couldn't resist listening to the tidbit of news her old nurse brought from the village. The information made her open her eyes wide and she could hardly wait to rush into the house to tell Alysa what she had just heard.

She found her sister in the parlor, dressed in a serviceable gown of dark brown cloth, the skirt closed in the front and with no ornamentation on the bodice. She was instructing a new maid, whose dress was not much plainer than Alysa's, on the art of the curtsey. Prudence interrupted unceremoniously, unable to contain her excitement. "Alysa! You have no idea what has happened!"

Alysa looked over, her expression amused. "You are quite correct, little sister, I don't. But I have a feeling you are about to tell me."

"It is the most awful thing, Alysa!" Prudence flounced down on the sofa, the skirt of her yellow gown flung wide, showing the peach petticoat beneath. She set her lips together and stared pointedly at the servant.

Alysa frowned, then suddenly realized that Prudence wanted her to dismiss the maid so that she could impart her news privately. "You may go, Matilda. I will send for you when I am ready to resume our lesson." She waited for the girl to close the door behind her before saying, "Very well, Prue. Now that we are alone pray do give me your news, or I fear you will burst before my very eyes!"

Prudence leaned forward, her eyes bright with anticipation, but her countenance suitably serious. "The most terrible thing has happened."

"So you said before," Alysa commented when Prudence stopped speaking and began to nibble her lip nervously. She smiled encouragingly and said, "Prue, do stop trying to find the right words and just blurt out what you know! It is the best way."

Prudence gave her a rueful little smile and nodded. "I'faith, you are right, Alysa! It is just that I thought…but no, if I am to pass these bad tidings to you I must do it truthfully and clearly."

Alysa paled. "What is it, Prue? Has something happened to Thomas? Have the Protectorate troops captured him?"

"Thomas? Heavens, no! My news is not about Thomas!"

"Then who?"

Prudence looked surprised. "Why, about Sir Philip Hampton, of course."

Alysa relaxed a little, but her body remained tense. "What about Sir Philip?"

"He's been shot!"

"Shot!" After a stunned moment Alysa was able to add, "By whom?"

"No one knows. That is what is so terrible! He was riding back to Ainslie last night and someone shot him in his home woods. He was able to stay on his mount and reach the manor safely, but there is no telling what might have happened to him if he were not such a fine horseman."

"Who told you this?"

Prudence cocked her head as she scrutinized her sister. "Nanny Green. She says it is all over the neighborhood."

Nanny Green's name put paid to the possibility that this

was nothing more than wild gossip, like the sort that had been circulating in West Easton ever since Thomas had landed in England. However, since old Nanny Green was well connected in the village, she could be relied on for reasonably accurate news.

An unnatural calm settled over Alysa's features. "Do Mama and Papa know about this?"

Prudence opened her eyes wide and managed to look surprised. "I have no idea."

Her contrived innocence made Alysa cast her a sharp look as she stood decisively. "Then let us go and tell them, shall we? Is Nanny Green still about? She should be with us to supply the details when we announce the news."

Prudence fell into step beside Alysa. "Nanny doesn't know any more than what I told you. She heard the story from the barber who went to Ainslie Manor to attend to the wound." She looked at her sister critically. "You are so calm, Alysa. I thought sure that you would be distressed that Sir Philip was hurt. Instead you prosaically ask if Mama and Papa know and suggest we tell them. I'm disappointed."

A grim, little smile curled Alysa's fine lips. "My dear sister, the man is nothing more than a neighbor. Of course I am concerned about his mishap, but…."

Prudence made a sound that was suspiciously close to a snort. "Of all the fustian! Admit it, Alysa, you like Sir Philip!"

"I hardly know the man," Alysa said gruffly.

Prudence cast her a disbelieving look.

"Yes, all right, I do like him, perhaps too much!" Alysa's emotions rose to the surface and poured out freely.

"Well then, don't you care that he has been shot?"

Alysa stopped abruptly, the expression on her face mutinous. "Yes, I care! However, there is nothing I can do, beyond making sure that Papa knows that a brigand is afoot in the area. He will do all he can to find the culprit."

"In the meantime, Sir Philip might die!" Prudence allowed the melodramatic words to lie in the air between them. She smiled with satisfaction as Alysa's skin paled.

"Surely not!"

Prudence shrugged. "Nanny Green said the wound was not bad and the barber thought it should heal fine, but," she added, shaking her finger for emphasis, "one never knows with a gunshot wound, does one?"

Alysa hesitated, her large blue eyes shadowed. Suddenly she lifted her brown cloth skirt and whirled away from Prudence. "Sister, I charge you with ensuring that Papa is informed of this heinous crime. Pray tell Mama that I will be home whenever possible. I will send a servant with a time when I have a better idea of how long I will be."

Prudence's eyes lit up. "Alysa, what are you doing?"

"I'm going to Ainslie," Alysa tossed over her shoulder as she headed for the door. "To nurse Sir Philip back to health."

Prudence laughed delightedly. "Wait for the coach, dear sister. You will get there much faster than by walking!"

Alysa looked over her shoulder and wrinkled her nose at her sister. "Don't forget, explain to Papa."

Prudence nodded at her sister's departing back. She was well satisfied with the effects of her meddling.

As the coach lumbered up the curving drive to Ainslie Manor, Alysa peered out the window, searching the weathered stone facade of the building for evidence that its owner had not been swept away by the tide of events. The house dozed in the afternoon sunlight, serene and peaceful. Alysa, who had been expecting at least some activity, wondered fleetingly if Prudence had decided to play a trick on her and had invented the story. Seconds later she dismissed the errant thought. Prudence wasn't capable of creating such a tale.

At the front steps, the coach drew to a halt. Ashton, the butler at the manor, opened one side of the imposing double doors, just as a footman jumped down from the coach to help Alysa alight.

"Good day, Mistress Leighton," Ashton said, eyeing Alysa

dubiously. She had paused to throw a sturdy black cloak over her shoulders while the coach was being readied, but hadn't taken the extra time needed to change into a more elegant gown.

"Hello, Ashton," Alysa replied, smiling. "How is your good wife? In health, I hope."

The butler, who had lived all of his life in West Easton and married one of the maidservants from Strathern Hall some four years before, unbent considerably. A broad smile crossed his face. "I'm right pleased to say that she be with child, Mistress Alysa. She's due mid-August."

"Why, that is wonderful news!" Alysa said, climbing the steps and gliding into the house. As she shrugged off her cloak she noticed that the wood paneling on the walls had a high gloss to it that she had never seen before and that the slate floor had been scrubbed clean. Her brows rose as she handed the cloak to the butler.

He nodded. "Sir Philip likes a clean house, he does. Soon as he arrived he set the maidservants—and some of the men too—to work polishing and scrubbing. The manor has taken on a whole new face thanks to him."

Another of the positive things she had heard about Sir Philip Hampton. Unbidden, the dismay she had felt when she heard of his accident rose up and threatened to suffocate her. Desperately, she clung to her calm. "Now then, Ashton, I have heard of Sir Philip's mishap and have come to see him. Take me to him, if you please."

The butler looked at her dubiously once more, but he bowed obediently. "Of course, Mistress Leighton. This way please."

Alysa was somewhat surprised when Ashton led her, not up the grand staircase to the second floor where the bedrooms were located, but to one of the parlors that looked out on the back of the house.

"Mistress Alysa Leighton," Ashton announced in stentorian tones as he opened the door. He stepped aside to allow Alysa to enter and she automatically did so. The room was furnished with several high-backed chairs and a sofa set before the fireplace. A table decorated with carved leaves and flowers rested below one of the windows, which pierced the exterior wall and bathed the room in light. Alysa's eyes widened as she saw Philip stretched out on the sofa, reading a book.

He was wearing a long, loose garment known as a nightgown, which was tied by a broad sash at the waist. One leg was propped up on a pillow, but there was no other evidence that he had been injured. Some of the worthy sentiments that had supported Alysa's bold decision to come to Ainslie began to dissipate.

At his butler's announcement, Philip looked up. His face was set in its habitual serious expression, but when he saw Alysa, he smiled.

Alysa felt her heart leap. Sir Philip Hampton did have a truly charming smile.

"I hope you will forgive me for not rising, but the local sawbones tells me I am fortunate that I was wounded only slightly. Even so, if I want the injury to heal quickly I must not move about any more than necessary."

"Then it is true." Alysa moved rather hesitantly toward him.

The grimness returned to Philip's features. "That I was shot on my own lands last night? Yes, it is true enough."

"But you are not seriously hurt."

Philip heard the tremor in Alysa's voice and hastened to reassure her. "It is naught but a flesh wound. I will be on my feet again in a day or two. The ball passed through some muscle, unfortunately, which makes walking awkward. Otherwise, I would ignore the good barber's advice and go about where I pleased."

"I thought you were on your deathbed!"

Philip's sweet smile warmed his features. "Rumor has, as usual, outdone itself. I promise you, Mistress Leighton, that a month from now I won't remember this happened."

Alysa sank down on a chair, clutching her hands together. "I...I really don't know what to say. I feel like such a fool."

Philip continued to watch her with warmth in his eyes. "You have nothing to apologize for, Mistress Alysa. Indeed, I am flattered that my mishap brought you over here so quickly."

Alysa was becoming very aware that she was alone in the room with a very handsome man. The light touched his black, shoulder-length hair with gleaming highlights and the figured crimson silk of his garment made his dark skin look more swarthy than it was. His coloring was very much like that of the young King Charles, whom Alysa had always considered to be a very romantic figure of a man.

Philip Hampton did not resemble the young king she remembered, however. Though both shared a thin face, a long, straight nose and a wide mouth with firm, well-shaped lips, it was in expression, more than anything, that Alysa saw a difference. There was no light laughter in Philip's dark, heavy-lidded eyes and his lips were usually closed tightly together, as if he was keeping secrets. Alysa knew that his mouth could curve upward in a sweet smile that would melt a lady's heart, but he did not cast his smiles about casually, unlike King Charles, who had smiled often, even in the direst of circumstances. To Alysa, Philip's rare smile was as priceless as a precious jewel.

Being with Philip now was giving Alysa thoughts a well-brought-up woman shouldn't have. Thoughts such as how his firm lips would taste under hers and what his long fingers would feel like stroking her skin. She blushed, suddenly very aware that when she had rushed over to be by Philip's sickbed she hadn't bothered to change out of the old, plain gown she wore for working around the house. With his dark eyes warm on her skin she wanted to look her best for him.

Her composure in shreds, she said the first thing that came into her mind. "You were kind enough to rescue me when my horse bolted, sir. I suppose I was just returning the favor."

"And I am most grateful."

As Philip studied her thoughtfully, Alysa forced herself to meet his eyes, despite her shyness. Her heartbeat speeded up while her breathing slowed. She moved her hand, almost as if to reach out for him, and the spell was broken.

"I hope you will stay and join me in refreshments. Though I am not badly injured, I am bored with my own company. I cannot be up and around as I would like," Philip explained with a whimsical little smile. "Your presence would mean a great deal to me."

Alysa knew she should go, but the words of refusal never came to her lips. "I would be delighted, Sir Philip." Her conscience got the better of her. "I cannot remain long. Indeed, I should not have come over here without my sister or Mama for company."

Philip glanced ruefully at his bandaged leg. "I promise not to compromise your virtue, fair lady."

Alysa had to laugh. "Thank you, sir. You are most kind."

He fumbled for something beside him on the sofa and came up with a brass bell, which he rang. Ashton reappeared with such speed that it was apparent he had been waiting just outside the door. Alysa sent Philip a speaking look, full of amusement. His eyes twinkled as he gravely ordered ale for himself, a glass of sweet wine for Alysa and a plate of cakes.

After the butler had departed, Alysa said dryly, "I fear every word we speak will be grist for the gossip mill. We must take care, sir, to choose topics of general interest."

"Such as?"

"Why, the subject which is on everyone's lips, sir—your unfortunate mishap. Have you any idea who shot you?"

He frowned. "None. As you know, the night was dark, with rain clouds obscuring the moon and stars. Whoever the scurvy rogue was, he lay in wait for me in the shadows. All I saw was a shape."

"Why would someone attack you on your own lands? Do you think it was one of the soldiers in the area?"

"No. The man was alone and he aimed directly for me. Soldiers rarely act independently and a cavalry man is better at wielding a sword than hitting a target he aimed at with a musket."

"You sound as though you speak from experience." Ashton returned with the refreshments and Alysa helped herself.

"I do," Philip replied, taking his tankard of ale and one of the cakes, his favorite kind, from the tray. "Armies, and the men in them, vary only in the colors they fight under."

Alysa sipped her wine and thought about his statement. "That is a very cynical opinion, Sir Philip." She cocked her head and looked at him more closely. "Indeed, it sounds as though it comes from a man who has dedicated his life to the military."

"I did."

"Oh!" Alysa's eyes widened. "But I understood you had spent most of your life at court and that it was your brother, your *Roundhead* brother, who was the professional military man."

Philip stared at her blankly for a second or two before his features assumed an amused, mocking expression. "Unfortunately, Mistress Leighton, all men who fought in our civil wars, whatever side they espoused, were professional soldiers. Four or five years in the army will make a soldier out of a courtier, whether he wills it or not."

The teasing light in Alysa's eyes died. "Yes, Sir Philip, I guess you are right." She frowned. "With these awful troops of Cromwell's in the area I tend to think of them as the only soldiers England has known."

"That is very natural. The war has been over for almost ten years."

"And you were in exile for most of them," Alysa said softly. "What was it like?"

Philip paused a moment before replying, "Boring."

When he didn't add anything more, Alysa smiled faintly. "I believe you are a man of industry and action, Sir Philip. I can tell that you would not have taken your years in exile easily."

Philip answered her gravely. "That is why I agreed to return to Ainslie Manor. I thought there would be more here to interest me."

Alysa laughed. "We are a small village, sir. What did you expect to find in West Easton?"

Philip looked her directly in the eyes. "A great deal less than what I did find, Mistress Alysa."

Philip's voice had softened, becoming a husky caress that charged the atmosphere. Alysa could feel her cheeks heat, with pleasure, not embarrassment. Making a show of finishing her wine, she set aside the glass and plate. "I must go." Her voice lacked its usual decisiveness. Indeed, there was a wistful note underlying the words, as if she was only saying what she felt she must, not what she really meant. Philip was watching her, his black brows lifted quizzically, his brown eyes tender. Alysa smiled rather hesitantly, wishing she could bask in the warmth of his gaze forever.

There was a quiet shuffling sound on the other side of the door. Philip looked past Alysa, a frown on his face, and she came alive to the dismaying improprieties of the situation. "I really must go, Sir Philip." She stood, hesitating as if she didn't want to conclude the visit. "Perhaps…perhaps, I might visit you again while you are laid up. With my Mama as a companion, of course."

"I would like that, Mistress Alysa. I would like that very much indeed."

Alysa returned home to find that Prudence had told Lord and Lady Strathern of the attempt on Sir Philip's life, but had neglected to add that Alysa had rushed to his bedside. Though Alysa appreciated her sister's attempt to be tactful, she was not prepared to lie to her parents, even by omission, so she owned up over dinner and, as a result of her honesty, received a sharp lecture on the behavior expected of a gentlewoman. Prudence was read an even sterner lecture, but she seemed to be more put out that Alysa had confessed than she was by her parents' disapproval.

The next day Lord Strathern rode over to Ainslie Manor to find out what he could about the shooting. Although Alysa asked if she could accompany him, he refused, saying that this would be a conversation between gentlemen only.

What was said that afternoon, Alysa didn't know, but her father returned from Ainslie looking grim. She could only guess that he was worried about the lawlessness that had seized the area since Thomas's return.

Alysa was more successful in convincing Abigail that they should pay a duty call to Sir Philip while he was unable to get around easily. The two ladies went over to Ainslie in the coach the fourth day after Philip had been shot. Alysa prepared carefully for the visit, dressing in a gown of a deep indigo blue with a silver petticoat. The colors did wonderful things for her eyes and skin, making them glow with an inner light. Over the gown she wore a rich cloak of black velvet and on her gleaming blond hair she pinned a broad-brimmed straw hat at a saucy angle. Abigail was content to choose a more somber gown of earth brown with a tan petticoat and her cloak was a matching dark brown. She was quite willing to allow her stepdaughter to shine alone.

When they reached Ainslie, they found Philip limping about, dressed in a fine linen shirt, wide black breeches, gray stockings and black shoes tied with large bows. He moved with the aid of an ornately carved ebony cane and he was visibly relieved to have company. He soon confessed that the inactivity was more difficult than the injury itself.

Since it was a fine day, Abigail suggested that they sit out on the terrace at the back of the house. Sir Philip called for one of his servants to fetch him his doublet, while others moved chairs out into the sunlight. Abigail directed the placing of the furniture, while Philip and Alysa wandered over to the edge of the terrace to enjoy the sunshine.

"Your father asked me to join his counsels," Philip said eventually.

Alysa smiled warmly at him. "I'm glad. It means that Papa has accepted you. He believes your opinion will be most valuable now that a decision whether or not to rise is near."

A shadow passed across Philip's features and he turned his gaze to the sloping lawns beyond the terrace. "I hope Lord Strathern does not intend to rely too heavily on my views, for if he does he will never participate in a fresh rebellion. I hate the idea of another war. It is so useless. Men are killed or must go into exile or lose the lands that have been in their families for generations. And for what? The opportunity to put a new tyrant on the throne of England."

Of all the things in her shaky world, Alysa believed fiercely in the need for a Stuart restoration. "Tyrant, sir?" she said in a low, passionate voice. "How can you speak of our lawful monarch that way?"

Philip glanced over at her and his bleak features warmed. His dark eyes caressed her, dousing Alysa's fiery anger and leaving her confused.

"That's right," he said softly, smiling. "You have met the Black Boy. From the time he was a small child he was always able to bewitch women."

Alysa thought it odd that Philip would use the common nickname based on Charles's black hair and swarthy coloring, but she was willing to accept that Philip knew the king much better than she and perhaps felt close enough to the man to refer to him in a familiar way.

A teasing dimple appeared in her cheek. "Men are not so easily swayed by his charm?"

The corner of Philip's mouth curled in a wry smile. "When he wishes, the king can enchant even the most hardened of those against him. But only for a time." He paused, looking inward. "I fear that not even Charles's ability to haunt the minds of men is enough to create a successful rebellion."

Alysa scanned his face. "Does that mean you would not participate in a rising?"

Philip looked down into her questioning eyes. His own were sad. "Before I inherited Ainslie I took an oath. In good conscience, I could not."

He stood before her, tall and strong. Alysa sensed that he was troubled by the promise he had made, but saw no way out of obeying it. She hated to see his inner turmoil and sought to lighten it by changing the subject. "Would you return to court, sir, if the king were to be restored to his throne?"

At that Philip smiled and answered freely. "No, indeed

not! The court is a tricky maze that is almost impossible to negotiate successfully. My father was considered to be one of the late king's most trusted friends, but it was only his death that saved him from disgrace in the years before the war. He had the temerity, you see, to give His Majesty advice that the king didn't want to hear."

"You sound bitter."

"Do I?" Philip smiled down at her. The warmth of his gaze brought an answering smile to Alysa's features. "I should not. I too might have wasted my life at court if the king had seen fit to accept my father's sage counsel. Instead he listened to those who repeated his own sentiments back to him and became more and more set on provoking the Commons against him. War became inevitable."

Alysa shivered. Her memories of the war were of fear and insecurity. News had traveled slowly, more slowly than roving armies. The residents of Strathern had not known from one day to the next if a skirmish might happen on their own lands or in West Easton. And there had been the loss of the men of the area, both loved ones and neighbors, as they went off to join the king's array. No one had known if those men would ever come back or if the war would take them forever.

As she listened to Philip, she began to realize that for him the war had come as a blessing. It gáve him a cause to believe in and a focus for his life that had been missing before. Moreover, in the beginning, when he joined, as a young lieutenant, army life had lacked the tricky byways that were so evident at court. In the army there was only obedience, coping with the small realities of day-to-day living and the sharp thrust of kill or be killed. The life had suited Philip to a tee.

At first.

He hadn't reckoned on how deeply a civil war could rend a country. Or how angry each side would become. Or the lengths to which men would go to ensure that their cause was the winning cause. Atrocities had occurred on both sides during the war years and Philip had participated in his own share of events he would like to forget, but couldn't.

Alysa listened to him intently, suffering his disillusionment with him and aching for his loss of innocence. "And so, when the king was captured you fled to France," she said eventually.

Philip smiled at her and said lightly, "And was forced to learn to speak French, for they did not seem at all inclined to learn English to please me!" Alysa laughed and he added gently, "Now, my lady, I am afraid that I must beg your indulgence and retreat to the chair that was brought out for me."

At once Alysa was all solace. "Oh! Is your leg paining you? Sir Philip, you should have spoken sooner. Come, let me help you over to the chair. Lean on me, if you wish. I'm sure that cane is useful at times, but on this uneven stone it is not what you need."

The gleam in Philip's eyes told Alysa that he was seriously considering doing as she suggested, but after a moment he shook his head and said softly, "Mistress Alysa, I will curb my natural desires and refuse your thoughtful suggestion. You look very enticing in that fetching straw hat and the deep blue of your gown enhances the color of your beautiful eyes. I should be delighted to hold you close against my body, but I fear that your good mother would not be so pleased."

The mischievous dimple appeared in Alysa's cheek again, but there was a telltale warmth in her eyes. "Mama could protest, of course, but not until the act was begun." She cocked her head, peaking out from under the wide brim of her hat. Her eyes gleamed bright blue. "I must confess that I did not make the offer simply from a sense of altruism."

Her words hung heavily between them, charging the air with currents of meaning. At last Philip sighed and said with a rueful smile, "I think it best if I decline your kind offer and use my cane. I would like to be allowed to see you again and I fear that I would be banished from your company if I followed my instincts."

Alysa blushed, but her smile was warm. "I would not like

you to be banished either, so I will accept your wise decision, Sir Philip. Now I see that Mama has finished her refreshment and will soon be ready to depart. We should go back and join her for a moment or two. And your poor leg! Come, let us go over to the chairs and sit down."

Philip laughed and allowed himself to be shepherded over to a seat. "Why, Mistress Alysa, I had no idea you were such a managing female."

"She has a mind of her own," Abigail said, overhearing. "Beware, Sir Philip, for she is not one to accept the strictures that others bow to."

"Mama! What a thing to say!" Alysa fussed about Philip until she was satisfied that he was comfortably bestowed in a chair. Only then did she allow the conversation to flow into a more general topic.

It was not until later, when she and Abigail had returned to Strathern Hall, that Alysa began to wonder about some of the things Philip has said that afternoon. His feelings about the court were sharp and unhappy, yet he had joined Charles's court-in-exile and stayed for many years, following the new king from France to the Low Countries. That suggested a deep dedication to the Stuart cause.

Or that part of Philip's story was a lie.

Was it possible that Philip was not the Royalist brother, but the Roundhead one? And if he was, what of her own brother, Thomas? In less than a week Thomas was to come to West Easton to participate in a meeting of the prominent Royalists in the area, a meeting her father had asked Philip to attend. If Philip was the Roundhead brother and thus the spy in their midst, Thomas was in danger. For that matter, so were her father and Cedric Ingram.

Had Alysa been certain Philip was the Roundhead brother she would have taken her concern to her father and let him deal with it, despite the warm feelings Philip Hampton generated in her, but she had no proof that Philip was not what he claimed. All she had was an insubstantial fear based on a few suppositions and that was not enough to condemn a man.

No, she would trust her instincts and say nothing. What her instincts told her was that Philip Hampton was not the person who had betrayed Thomas to the authorities. Someone else had done that, because Philip Hampton was too direct and too honorable a man to participate in such an underhanded scheme.

And she wondered too if the person who had betrayed Thomas had also decided to assassinate Philip. The thought made her shiver. It suggested a far greater plot than her experience of life had prepared her for. Unbidden, one of Philip's descriptions of court life leapt into her mind.

A dangerous maze had been erected at West Easton. She only hoped those trapped inside it had the skills to find the key.

CHAPTER 9

The meeting of prominent Royalists took place in an unexpected setting, to ensure that the soldiers combing the area would not accidentally discover its location. Lord Strathern believed that most, if not all, of the great houses were being kept under observation and so he asked his loyal follower, Barnabus Wishingham, the smith, if the meeting could be held at his home.

Much flattered, Barnabus immediately agreed. When he eventually told his wife, she raised her eyes heavenward, but didn't protest. Since Thomas had almost been captured she had been much chastened, for Barnabus had not hesitated to attribute the near disaster to her loose tongue.

Using the smith's residence was a stroke of genius on Lord Strathern's part. Attached to the forge was a large barn, which Barnabus used to store various necessities of his trade, as well as to house horses sent to him for shoeing. The interior of the barn was a roomy open area with rails for tying animals for short periods of time. There was ample space to stable the horses used by the Royalists attending the meeting, so that no Roundhead patrol would chance to see a large collection of horses and wonder what was afoot.

Some twenty-five men had been invited to the meeting. They represented all levels of local society, from gentlemen like Cedric Ingram, through honest merchants such as John Wilson, the village mercer. All were men who had long professed to support the Stuarts and so had the king's best interests at heart.

Just after Philip had been shot, he had been invited to the meeting by Lord Strathern. On that day, with his leg aching and his thoughts surprisingly concerned by the fact that Strathern had not brought his daughter with him when he'd come to visit, Philip had agreed to attend.

He'd been aware of the danger, for it was almost certain that he would meet Thomas Leighton that night, but there was nothing else he could do. To refuse the invitation would have been almost as damning as meeting Thomas Leighton face-to-face.

As the day of the meeting neared, Philip wondered if he could avoid participating by using the excuse that his leg was bothering him. He considered that for a minute or two before he dismissed the idea. The wound was virtually healed and he now used the cane he carried more as a fashion accessory than a means of support. No one would believe that he had been laid low by a relapse.

Then too there was the possibility that the meeting would be interrupted by the authorities, despite Strathern's attempts to find an unobtrusive location for the discussion. Thomas's return had been betrayed by a spy. The meeting of local Royalists could well be similarly informed on. If this were to happen the whole area would be suspicious of the man who had found a convenient excuse not to attend.

So, on the night of the meeting Philip clothed himself as a courtier would, in a doublet of blue silk and wide black breeches heavily adorned with ribbon bows and ribbon loops. Then he shrugged a short cloak of black silk over his shoulders and prepared to go boldly into danger.

The smith's house was a sizable dwelling for one who practiced such a humble occupation. Constructed of wood, it was an old-fashioned, half-timbered building in the style popular some seventy-five years before, during the reign of good Queen Bess. The parlor where the Royalists assembled took up the length of one side of the house. Though it was a large room, the twenty-five men attending made the space seemed cramped. Philip arrived late and deliberately mingled with the groups of earnestly talking men, staying away from Lord Strathern and the tall young man who stood beside him.

Philip had never met Thomas Leighton, but he had no doubt that the man with Strathern was his son. Not only were their facial features remarkably similar, but there was a certain aura of pride about Edward that marked him as a loving father.

While pretending to listen to what an earnest gentleman was saying, Philip studied Thomas Leighton. Surprisingly, it was not Edward, Lord Strathern, that Thomas most resembled, but his sister Alysa. Thomas's face was a bit rounder in shape, but there was the same firm chin, bowed upper lip and full lower one. Like Alysa's, his eyes were a vivid blue and heavy lidded, but beneath his left eye his face was marred by a long scar from a saber cut, presumably acquired at the Battle of Worcester.

There were other differences beneath the similarities. His mouth had a harder set to it, as if experience had forced from him the sensitive vulnerability that characterized Alysa's fine features, and there was a cynical world-weariness in the blue eyes that Philip hoped he would never see in Alysa's expression. But there was bright interest in those blue eyes as well. Evidently exile had not killed all of the optimism in Thomas Leighton's soul.

Barnabus Wishingham, moderately dressed in black, unlike his gaily-hued guests, was serving ale. Philip helped himself to a tankard as he explained to the smith that although he still carried a cane, he used it infrequently. Wishingham shook his head over the lawlessness in the area, blamed the Roundhead soldiers and moved on to another of his guests.

Philip sipped his ale while he studied the men about him. Unlike the smith, he did not believe that a soldier was responsible for his wound and he wondered if one of the men in this room was the one who had shot him. Over the past few days he had considered the problem from virtually every angle and he had come to the conclusion that his assailant and the turncoat who was working for Edgar Osborne were one in the same. He hadn't figured out why the man would use him for target practice yet, but he would.

His eyes scanned the group over the edge of his pewter tankard. It was an interesting cross section of West Easton society and a man's position could be identified by the clothes he wore. Prosperous landowners like Lord Strathern and Cedric Ingram predominated. They were dressed in bright-hued doublets made of satin or velvet and their breeches were fashionably wide, with rosettes at the knees and ribbon loops at the hems. Fine linen shirts could be seen through slashes in the balloon sleeves of their doublets and on their heads were hats made of expensive beaver felt. Long feathers, as precious as the beaver felt, curled from the brims of the hats, an elegant echo of their long, gleaming locks.

There were also prosperous merchants and craftsmen like the smith at the meeting. Their garb was less costly than that of the gentlemen, and the colors were more subdued, but their expressions were as serious. Plotting rebellion was not a matter to take lightly.

As Philip examined the faces, he decided that overall these men, though somewhat nervous, were firm in their commitment to what they were doing. That in itself was daunting to one who supported the other side. Had the Royalist organization been focused on any one group, such as wealthy landowners or the merchant class, the desire for revolution might be dismissed, but the men at this gathering represented the most influential sections of British life. If they were all allied against the Commonwealth, then Richard Cromwell's government was doomed.

There was a movement in the crowd and Philip was momentarily exposed. Lord Strathern caught sight of him, said something to Thomas and began moving toward him. Philip felt his heart begin to pound, as it did before every battle. Those thoughts that didn't relate to the coming engagement slipped from his mind as he focused on the issue at hand—survival.

There was a little stir as Cedric Ingram arrived and for a moment Lord Strathern was deflected from his intent as he paused to greet Ingram. Still keyed up, Philip watched assessingly as Thomas bowed coolly to Cedric. Curiosity flared briefly in Philip's mind, for Thomas's greeting had been barely civil. Evidently Thomas Leighton did not like Cedric Ingram. Philip wondered why.

He didn't bother to ponder this interesting question, though, for moments later Lord Strathern was once again on his way over to him.

Close up, Thomas Leighton reminded Philip even more forcefully of Alysa. His nose was slightly flared, while hers was straight, but each was short and neatly made. His hair was chestnut and darker than hers, but of the same texture and with the same wayward curl. But most telling was the cool intelligence Philip could see in the vivid blue eyes.

"Thomas, I want to introduce you to our new neighbor, Sir Philip Hampton."

Thomas bowed, the same reserved movement he had used with Ingram.

Philip responded in kind, his expression mocking and faintly amused. None of the trepidation he felt showed on his composed features, but he knew that his masquerade could be exposed at any moment. Depending on how Lord Strathern worded the rest of the introduction, though, he might be able to avoid the confrontation he expected.

His hopes were dashed as Strathern continued, "Sir Philip has lately inherited Ainslie Manor from old Richard Hampton. Prior to that he was in exile. Perhaps you know him?"

There was a quizzical twist to the question, for Strathern was no less intelligent than his offspring. He was watching the meeting between the two men intently and it was obvious that Thomas had not instantly recognized Philip. Thomas's blue eyes grew colder, more assessing, and they bored into Philip, who met them bravely, raising his dark brows defiantly. He expected to be unmasked at any time. When Thomas spoke, relief washed over him, but he hid the betraying emotion.

"I believe we have been introduced, but I am afraid I do not recollect the meeting in any detail. How is it, Sir Philip, that you were able to return home and inherit your father's property?"

"My uncle's," Philip replied calmly. Thomas inclined his head in acknowledgment. "And I was able to return because my brother has some influence in the Lord Protector's government. He arranged to have the interdiction against me lifted."

"You are indeed fortunate to have such a generous brother," Thomas said coolly. "Surely with you proscribed, he could have inherited himself had he done nothing."

Philip shrugged, his expression carefully blank. This had always been a weakness in Osborne's plot. He was surprised the question had not come up before this. "The wars have been over for some time now. Family ties are beginning to speak louder than political ones."

At this, some of the cool hostility on Thomas's face eased. He nodded glumly. "England does look very sweet from the vantage point of the Low Countries."

"Yes," Philip said softly. "As we grow older the ties that bound us as children become stronger—to our families, to our land, to our country."

Amusement flashed in Thomas's bright blue eyes. "Are you suggesting that the time is ripe for a return to a monarchy?"

"Is that not what we are all here to discuss this evening?" Philip parried, not wanting to commit himself to an outright lie.

"Precisely," Strathern said. "And it is your objective opinion that I would like to hear tonight, Hampton. Pray do not hesitate to speak up should you wish to contribute."

Philip smiled and agreed. As he watched Lord Strathern lead his son to the front of the room to call the meeting to order, he pondered the brief encounter. Apparently he had been able to convince Thomas that he was indeed the Royalist brother. He must have. Why else would Thomas not have exposed him then and there?

Was it possible Thomas had never met Anthony Hampton? There were thousands of supporters of the Stuarts living in exile in Europe. Not all of them were as intimate with the king as Thomas Leighton was. To Philip's knowledge, his brother had been on the fringes of the court, occasionally being allowed to attend the king, but more often observing from the outside. Exile had been hard on Anthony and he had drunk heavily, a vice that men like Edward Hyde, King Charles's former tutor and now most trusted adviser, did not want their charge to become addicted to.

So Anthony Hampton, despite his excellent lineage and the fact that he had known the young king since childhood, had been exiled once again, this time from the very man he'd given up his freedom to follow. Philip had heard that his brother had died a wasted, bitter man. The news had simply confirmed Philip's opinion of court life and the stupidity of putting one's fate in the hands of kings.

Thus, it was indeed possible that Thomas Leighton had met Anthony Hampton only briefly while on the Continent. Thomas was part of the second wave of Royalists who had followed King Charles into exile after the Battle of Worchester. They were too young to remember the old regime and had no preconceived idea of what court life should be like. They accepted their king and their new life with more ease than the members of the old guard like Anthony Hampton had.

As long as Thomas Leighton had not heard that Anthony had died, Philip thought he might well be able to carry his impersonation through successfully. The family resemblance between the brothers was strong and any differences Thomas might see he could very well put down to the positive effects of a cessation of heavy drinking.

Philip's rapid assessment of the danger he was in was brought to an abrupt end as Lord Strathern held up his hands to call the meeting to order. "Gentlemen! Thank you all for coming this evening. We have much to discuss, so I would ask you to find a seat so that we can begin."

There was some shuffling, the odd sound of laughter as

two men attempted to take the same chair and polite protestations as each offered to give it up to the other. At last the company was settled and there was silence in the room.

Strathern looked around, smiling. "My son needs no introduction, but I am proud to say that he has been chosen by King Charles to visit our area to discover how dedicated we are to the possibility of joining a revolt to reinstate the monarchy—" He stopped abruptly as the door to the room was flung open by the smith's wife.

She stood in the aperture, wringing her hands, clearly agitated. "I'm sorry to interrupt, sir, but we have an emergency."

Wishingham stood up, very flushed in the face. "It had better be a good one, mistress!" he said roughly. He was still smarting from the knowledge that it was his wife's loose tongue that had put Thomas Leighton in danger on the night of his arrival.

The poor woman blanched and swallowed. "It is, husband. I swear! I waited this long to disturb you in hopes that we could put it out, but—"

"Put it out?" someone said with concern. "Is there a fire?" Fire was always a danger that no one wished to have to deal with.

Mistress Wishingham nodded eagerly. "It started in the smithy, sir, and at first we thought we—that is my children and I—could deal with it. In faith, we did try! But now we fear, that is, our eldest boy is trying to lead your horses from the barn, gentlemen, so they will not be burned—"

"The barn is in danger of catching the blaze?" Strathern demanded.

Again she nodded. "Aye. It abuts on the smithy, you see, and—"

"Why didn't you bring this news earlier, woman!" Wishingham bellowed, outraged.

"Well, with this grand company I did not want to interrupt and—"

"Quickly," Thomas said. "Now is not the time to talk. We

must help fight the fire."

"Agreed," Strathern growled. He broke the group up into parties, one to draw water from the well, another to take charge of the horses and by far the largest to work on beating out the blaze. Within minutes a disciplined force of men poured out of the parlor to do their best to save the smith's home and livelihood. For Philip, who led the party responsible for controlling the horses, due to his well-known ability with those animals, the fire and Lord Strathern's handling of it proved that when action was called for the man was an excellent organizer and a respected leader. Should a rebellion come to pass, Charles Stuart would be well served by Edward, Lord Strathern. Philip wondered how many more of the supporters of the exiled king were of the quality of Lord Strathern. Not too many, he hoped, or the Commonwealth was doomed.

The blaze had not yet taken hold of the barn when Philip arrived, leaning heavily on his cane as he tried to trot as quickly as possible from the house. The smell of the smoke and the heat of the fire had panicked the horses and the poor beasts screamed with terror as they reared up, fighting the ties that bound them to the hitching rail or kicking fretfully at nearby animals. Philip quickly organized the members of his party, telling them to start with those horses stabled closest to the forge and reminding them to wrap cloth over the animals' eyes before attempting to lead them out. Throwing his cane aside, Philip ignored his aching leg and joined the others in the desperate work.

Within ten minutes they had cleared the barn, and not a moment too soon, for with a terrifying whoosh the hay in the loft caught and the old timbered structure went up in an orange fireball. From his position by the horses a safe distance away, Philip watched the inferno, his eyes narrowed thoughtfully.

The barn had gone up quickly, too quickly. Admittedly, it was an old building and full of inflammable material, but that fireball was not the normal result of burning hay. To Philip the speed and intensity of the blaze indicated one thing—gunpowder. That meant the fire had been deliberately set, unless the smith had taken to keeping his own store of munitions in his barn, which Philip thought doubtful.

If someone had set the fire, then who? And when?

More importantly, why?

Find the man who set the fire in the smithy, Philip thought grimly, and he would find the man who had betrayed Thomas Leighton's arrival to the Roundheads. For there was no doubt in his mind that they were one and the same man.

He thought too that he would also find the man who had tried to kill him.

"I'm going out to the kitchen garden," Alysa said to Jenkins, the butler, as she fixed a broad-brimmed hat over her long tresses. "I want to see how the herbs did over the winter." It was a beautiful spring day, sunny and warm, perfect for inspecting the garden and planning what to plant for the summer. "If anyone wants me, that's where I'll be."

She was crouching down beside a bed of lavender, snipping off the dead bits, when a large masculine shadow loomed up beside her. She smiled as she looked up, expecting to see her father or perhaps her brother. But the man who was standing there was Philip Hampton, not one of her relatives.

Alysa blushed. When she'd told Jenkins to send out anyone who asked for her, she hadn't meant for him to include visitors. The gown she was wearing was the same well-worn one she had been dressed in when she rushed over to Ainslie Manor to tend to the ailing Philip, and even though he'd seen it before, she still felt as if she was underdressed for receiving company.

Moreover, her hair was unpinned. It cascaded over her shoulders and down her back in a glorious stream of golden silk. Alysa enjoyed letting her hair flow freely, but only when she was alone or with family. She felt she should wear her hair in a more formal style when greeting a guest.

Especially a male guest as attractive as Sir Philip Hampton.

Hastily, Alysa rose from her crouching position, dusting off her hands as she stood. "Why, Sir Philip, what a surprise! I did not expect to see you here."

Unlike Alysa, Philip was dressed in clothes befitting a social visit. His doublet was expensive wine-colored silk and his matching breeches were adorned with rosettes and ribbon loops. Stirrup hose frothed at the top of his soft black boots and over his shoulders was a fine black cloak. In one hand he held a bouquet of fresh flowers. At Alysa's words he looked down at the blooms with a rueful smile. "I thought you would be indoors, so I brought some flowers to remind you that spring is truly here. I did not expect to find you in a garden."

Smiling warmly, Alysa took the flowers from his hand. Accidentally, their fingers touched. She felt a surge of excitement that made her heart thump. Suddenly, she was very much aware that they were alone in the sunny, walled enclosure. "What a charming thought, Sir Philip." She bent to smell the fragrant blooms. "I adore fresh-cut flowers. How thoughtful of you to bring me some."

Philip smiled, apparently with relief. His eyes caressed her face, bringing Alysa as much pleasure as his words did. "The flowers reminded me of you. Beautiful at all times, but glorious in the bright sunlight."

His voice had deepened as he spoke, growing softer and rougher at the same time. Instincts Alysa didn't understand were pushing her in directions she had never been before. "Philip, I don't know what to say. I—"

He smiled at her obvious confusion and tipped her chin up with the edge of his hand. "Then don't say anything."

They were very close. The sun beat down, encasing them in a sultry isolation that suspended time. For Alysa, all that seemed real was what could be sensed: the heady scent of the pruned lavender, the warmth of the sun, the touch of Philip's hand on her skin, the sight of his face so close to hers. Lost in the dark depths of his eyes, she parted her lips.

For a moment, Philip hesitated; then he lowered his head. Alysa closed her eyes as his face loomed nearer. But when his lips touched hers in a kiss that was little more than a chaste brush, she was unprepared for her own reaction. Her senses exploded in a rainbow of sharp, bright colors that were immensely pleasurable.

Obeying the primitive response he roused, she shifted closer. Philip's arm slipped around her waist and urged her more tightly against him. Still clutching the flowers he had given her, Alysa put her hand on his shoulder and let her body follow his command.

Her hat tipped from her head as he caught a handful of her long, silky hair in his hand. His fingers burrowed through the thick mass as his kiss hardened. Alysa responded instinctively, willingly. Her inexperience didn't stop her body from giving what nature demanded. She opened her lips under his.

Fire raged through her as his tongue invaded the moist softness of her mouth and rational thought became impossible. Her body heated under the flame of his kiss. Urges from somewhere deep inside made her melt against him.

"Alysa," he groaned, framing her face with his hands as he released her for a moment, only to take her again in another fierce, potent kiss. She lost track of time and place. Her whole being was centered in Philip Hampton. Whatever he cared to do to her at this moment, Alysa would willingly accept. The kiss went on and on, branding her as his as surely as if he had taken a hot iron and burned his initials in her.

And then he was drawing away, his breathing uneven, his eyes glazed with the same drugged passion that held Alysa in its sway. She knew, without a doubt, that it had taken every bit of integrity he possessed to keep from laying her down on the fragrant herbs and taking her to him then and there. She was unutterably disappointed but, at the same time, deeply relieved. Overall, she was profoundly touched that he would put her reputation and feelings above his own.

Dropping his hands, he stepped away. Gradually, the passionate glaze faded from his eyes, leaving him achingly vulnerable. "Mistress Alysa, I am sorry."

Alysa blushed and looked down. "Sir, you need not be. You did not force me; I was a willing participant." She bent to pick up her hat, then rather self-consciously brushed her hair back over her shoulders before she placed the hat on her head once more. From beneath the broad brim, she peeped up at him enticingly. "I shall not forget the kiss, sir, but perhaps for propriety's sake we should pretend that it did not happen."

"That will not be easy," he murmured, his voice gruff with suppressed emotion.

She peeked at him through her lashes, the dimple in her cheek in evidence once more. "I know that, sir, but any man who is able to save every horse in Master Wishingham's barn must be capable of great feats."

It was Philip's turn to color. "Oh, you heard about that."

"Of course! Papa returned home blackened and reeking of smoke. Mama immediately made him tell us what had happened."

"It was a most unfortunate business," Philip said grimly. He bent to pick up the cane he had dropped while he was kissing Alysa. "Have you seen your brother since? We had just started the discussions when the fire was discovered."

"No. Papa sent Thomas away as soon as it became clear that one extra person would make no difference to the outcome. He was afraid that the flames would bring the troops and he did not want Thomas lingering overlong."

"I see."

The innocent conversation had helped Alysa recover her equilibrium and she was very much aware of how isolated they were in the secluded garden. "Would you mind if we went into the house so that I could have these put in some water?" She held up the now somewhat bedraggled flowers.

Philip looked at them doubtfully and her smile deepened, as she said, "I will have them put by my bedside, where I can see them when I go to sleep at night and when I first wake in the morning."

A surprised pleasure flashed in his eyes. He looked around at the walls that blocked out the rest of the world and nodded. "Of course."

He leaned rather heavily on his cane as they walked. Alysa was instantly solicitous.

"I hope you suffered no injury from your heroic efforts at the fire last night."

Philip smiled deprecatingly. "Like everyone else, I only did what was necessary. I must admit that I was more concerned with saving the animals than worrying about my game leg, so I probably did more than I should have."

"When we get inside you must sit down and rest for awhile. I would not want you straining your wound further."

Philip laughed. "Mistress Alysa, thank you for the charming offer, but I believe I should be on my way. I hope, though, that you will allow me to visit you again soon."

"I should be delighted, sir." The sincerity in her voice could not be doubted.

The next day, Philip was surprised when he received a message from Alysa requesting that he meet her at the small lake near the woods that bordered the property lines of Strathern Hall and Ainslie Manor. He read the message twice, searching for a clue to explain the purpose of the meeting, but could find none.

Still, something about the note made every one of his senses wary. If writing him was something Alysa had never done before, requesting a meeting away from prying eyes was even more unusual. Briefly, he wondered if she wanted a repetition of the kiss they had shared yesterday, but he dismissed the notion. He did not believe that Alysa Leighton was the sort of woman who would lightly plot an illicit rendezvous with her lover.

Philip considered the messenger, who was waiting for a reply. The man was not wearing Strathern livery and appeared to be one of the outdoor staff, for his skin was weathered and there were deep lines about his eyes, as if he squinted into the sun a great deal. He might be one of Lord

Strathern's servants; then again he might not be.

If he was not, someone was using Alysa Leighton's name to draw Philip into a trap. That did not sit well with Philip. His eyes narrowed dangerously, his decision made. Briskly, he told the messenger that the answer was yes.

The man tugged his forelock and went away, leaving Philip to plan and prepare in peace.

Two hours later he rode to the appointed meeting place. As was his custom, he was early. It did not take him long to be certain that the person he had come to meet had not yet arrived. It took him even less time to find a spot in the trees where he could see, but not be seen. Dressed in a sturdy doublet of a mud-brown color that faded into the undergrowth, he was near invisible. When, not long after he had settled himself, he saw Thomas Leighton ride into the clearing, he knew that his wariness had been justified.

The note had not come from Alysa at all, but from her brother. That explained why her name had been used to draw him here, but still Philip wondered what had made Thomas want to meet with him. Obviously the Royalist knew more about Anthony Hampton than he had let on. But why had he not exposed Philip that night at the Smith's house?

The answers would not come until Philip had spoken to Thomas Leighton. He urged his horse into motion with knees and a light twitch on the reins. Picking its way carefully, the animal emerged from the trees, if not as silently as any wild woodland creature, at least more quietly than the average horse. The stallion had been well trained. Philip had seen to that.

Thomas had stationed himself where he could watch the path that led to Ainslie Manor, evidently expecting Philip to come from that direction. So, when Philip emerged from the dense trees, Thomas was clearly startled. He jerked at the bridle and his horse shook its head and sidled.

"So, Roundhead," he said, his blue eyes cold, hard chips, "you arrived before me." He glanced around, rather disdainfully. "Is there a troop of cavalry waiting for the perfect moment to snare me this time too?"

Philip stopped his horse a short distance from Thomas and allowed the reins to lie loosely on the animal's neck. "I did not betray your arrival to the military."

"Yet you come early to a meeting and hide yourself away, like a man with something to conceal."

There was a sneer in Thomas's voice, but Philip ignored it. After all, the man did have a point. He was not one to quietly let another gain the upper hand, however. "Just as you did," he said, taking the battle to the enemy camp. The stallion shifted uneasily from leg to leg. Philip swayed with it, at one with his mount.

"I am a marked man," Thomas countered.

Philip shrugged. "And I am always wary when I smell a trap."

Surprisingly, Thomas grinned. "What did I do wrong? Was my penmanship not at all like my sister's?"

"I have no idea," Philip said mildly, "for your sister has never written me a note. Nor has she offered to meet me secretly, in the woods or anywhere else. It was that which made me wonder what was afoot."

Thomas nodded. "Good point. I must remember that. Rumor has it that you are courting Alysa and that she is near besotted with you. Cedric Ingram becomes livid if your name is spoken with hers. And since you have won over my father, I half expect to hear that a marriage is being arranged."

"With a Roundhead?" Philip jeered.

"With a Royalist," Thomas retorted. "My father firmly believes you to be loyal to King Charles."

Philip shrugged again. He didn't know what to say to this young man who had spent the last eight years of his life in exile.

Thomas was watching him carefully. "Why are you pretending to be what you are not, if indeed you do not intend to betray my family?"

That was a very good question, one that had been nagging at Philip's conscience off and on for quite some time. One he had not yet found an answer to. "My brother is dead," he said finally. "You know that."

Thomas nodded.

Part of Philip wanted to ask about what his brother's life had been like in exile, but the disciplined part knew that he should not indulge in idle chatter with his enemy. "Though I am legally the heir to Ainslie, this is well-known to be an area loyal to the king. I do not want my life here to be made uncomfortable by old animosities, so I allow people to think that I am my brother."

"Such a simple reason," Thomas murmured. "But the Roundhead brother was fanatically loyal to Oliver Cromwell."

"Oliver Cromwell is dead," Philip said steadily. He watched Thomas through hooded eyes, assessing the man's reactions. He didn't think he was convincing him.

"That is true enough. But Oliver's son lives and Oliver gave him England to rule, just as if he was of the blood anointed. Your loyalty could easily pass from father to son."

"Richard Cromwell is an ineffectual ass," Philip said with more force than he expected. He'd always known that he disliked Richard Cromwell, but until now, until he denied his loyalty to Richard, he hadn't realized how much. "I've had enough of the man and England would be better off without him."

Thomas nodded; then he too shrugged. "So, you've abandoned your past and settled on a new future. Why join the Royalist organization? Why not simply remain neutral?"

Philip allowed himself a small cynical smile. "I am pretending to be a Royalist returned from exile. I could hardly claim that I don't want to see the Black Boy returned to his throne." He deliberately used the derisive nickname for King Charles II.

Thomas raised a brow at that, but didn't comment. "If you are not the spy in our midst, who is?"

"That I do not know," Philip replied honestly. "But I will tell you this, Thomas Leighton. The fire at the smith's was deliberately set. Find the arsonist and you will find your spy."

"How do you know it was deliberate?"

"I fought in seven major actions and skirmishes too numerous to count. I know gunpowder, how it works, what it smells like when ignited. That fire was set, I promise you."

Thomas stared at him consideringly. At last he nodded slowly. "I believe you. However, I can think of no reason why the spy would set a fire and cause the meeting to be aborted. Surely, if he knew where we were to meet, he would have been better served to call in the soldiers again, as he did the night I arrived."

"That would seem the sensible path," Philip agreed. "Perhaps he did, but something went awry."

Thomas's cold, hard eyes bored into Philip. "Perhaps. So, Roundhead, what do we do now?"

Philip shrugged and smiled. "The options are all yours, Leighton. You either betray me to your father and make me a pariah in my own home, or you keep my secret. Your choice."

"And if I say nothing, will you stay away from my sister?"

"I cannot," Philip said softly and realized he meant it.

Thomas stared at him for a minute. "And when my sister discovers your true identity? How will you explain to her that you have lied to her all this time?"

"I will deal with that when I must." Philip tightened the reins, signaling his horse that they were about to leave. "Well, Royalist, what do you plan to do with my future?"

Amusement leapt into Thomas's eyes. "Nothing at the moment. I shall make my decision before I leave England."

Philip jabbed at the reins, an unconscious gesture of annoyance. "Very well," he said, swinging his horse around. He inclined his head politely. "Until we meet again."

"Until then, Roundhead," Thomas replied. There was an irritating note of laughter in his voice that plagued Philip as he rode away.

CHAPTER 10

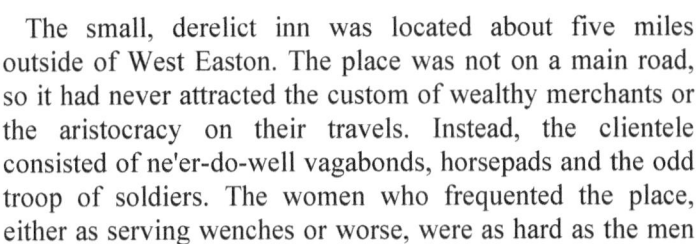

The small, derelict inn was located about five miles outside of West Easton. The place was not on a main road, so it had never attracted the custom of wealthy merchants or the aristocracy on their travels. Instead, the clientele consisted of ne'er-do-well vagabonds, horsepads and the odd troop of soldiers. The women who frequented the place, either as serving wenches or worse, were as hard as the men who drank there. No decent woman would be seen on the premises.

Just after dawn on the morning after he had spoken to Thomas Leighton, Philip came to this inn. His purpose was to talk to Sir Edgar Osborne.

Officially, he was supposed to leave a message in a special place where both knew to look if Philip required a meeting with the London man. The paper was to be wedged between two rocks in a stone fence that separated Ainslie Manor from the public roadway and there was only a certain time of the day when it would be checked. The secret place was to be used only in emergencies, for there was always the danger that someone would notice that a stranger was oddly interested in the fence.

Though Philip had agreed to this fragile method of communication, he'd made it his business to discover Osborne's lair. A good military man learned all he could of the enemy's position, and more and more now, Philip saw Sir

Edgar Osborne as the enemy.

On this morning he was glad he had gone to the effort of tracking his contact down. He wanted to surprise Osborne, to catch him in a vulnerable moment, in the hope that he would be able to pry at least a small part of the truth from him.

Roundhead troops were busy grooming and saddling up their horses when Philip arrived. They eyed him critically as he dismounted, noting the plain buff jacket he wore and the moderate width of the well-worn breeches that had no frothy ribbon loops at the hems. In contrast to these sober garments was the length of his hair and the jaunty angle at which he wore his hat, which proclaimed him to be a gentleman of Royalist sympathies. None of the hard-eyed troopers stopped him from striding into the building. However, they watched with the dangerous stillness of predators prepared to strike.

The inside of the inn was new to Philip, for he had only tracked Osborne as far as the forecourt. As he entered the building, he paused to get his bearings. Just inside the door was a worm-eaten counter on which a slatternly looking woman leaned casually, her chin propped on the heels of her hands, her rather dirty elbows resting on the top of the counter. She watched Philip curiously as he scanned the surroundings. He ignored her.

From the narrow hallway, stairs led to the upper floors where the bedrooms presumably were located. The hallway continued on to the kitchen and the innkeeper's quarters, which were located at the rear of the building. A dozen paces from the counter there was the doorway to a long, narrow room from which a low buzz of conversation could be heard. Philip identified this as the taproom, where the public and those guests who could not afford a private parlor would come to eat or while away the day and evening. He thought for a moment of checking the room for Osborne, then dismissed the idea. Despite his vocal complaints about the discomfort of his current situation, Sir Edgar Osborne undoubtedly had the best that this shabby establishment had to offer.

The slatternly wench behind the counter broke into Philip's

thoughts, as she coyly demanded his pleasure. Philip politely asked where he could find Osborne. Her face twisted with contempt as she snapped out directions. Philip raised a quizzical brow. Evidently Sir Edgar Osborne had not endeared himself to the staff at the inn.

The second floor was a long corridor with rooms opening off either side. Osborne's bedchamber and private parlor were halfway down the north side of the building. Philip found the room without difficulty, for as he neared the door he could hear a high-pitched feminine squeal united with the deeper rumble of a man's laughter. Philip had never heard quite that pitch in Osborne's voice, but he was certain that the sound belonged to him.

Surprise was the first and most powerful strategy a soldier learned. Philip used it now to disconcert Osborne and put him at a disadvantage. He opened the door to the parlor without knocking and found Osborne sitting in a loose nightgown, another of the inn's serving wenches perched on his knee. This girl was clearly enjoying her work. One hand rested on Osborne's chest as she rubbed the skin suggestively, while her head was buried in his neck. When Philip entered, Osborne stood abruptly and the girl shrieked as she was unceremoniously dumped onto the floor.

Osborne automatically reached for his sword, but he had left the weapon elsewhere. He swore softly. Philip smiled wryly.

"Such a touching little scene."

"Get out," Osborne said to the girl. She shot a calculating look at Philip, noted the sword at his side and hastily obeyed. Osborne waited until the door closed behind her, then snarled, "What the devil do you mean by coming here?"

"I wanted to speak to you," Philip said, inspecting the room. Like the rest of the inn, it had a dilapidated air. The sparse furnishings included nothing more than a small, round dining table and two wooden chairs, a pair of straight-backed chairs with seats covered in horsehair and a serving table that was little more than a slab of oak set on four legs. A low fire burned lethargically in the hearth, which was heaped with ash, as if it had not been cleaned in days.

"We have a system arranged for that." Osborne glowered at him. "Do you realize what you are risking by coming here?"

"I am perfectly aware of what I am doing," Philip countered. He stared at Osborne, his expression cold. "I want to know why the smith's buildings were set afire three nights ago."

Osborne sat back down on one of the horsehair chairs, a rather wicked grin on his thin lips. "That was a nice piece of work, wasn't it?" he said, as Philip cautiously settled onto one of the crude, but sturdy, wooden seats by the table.

Though the taunt was meant to annoy, Philip kept his expression bland. "Since the blaze almost destroyed a horse I have spent years training in the arts of war, I cannot agree. Moreover, you missed a fine opportunity to lay your hands on Thomas Leighton. He was there that night."

Osborne stared at Philip consideringly. "You did not tell me that."

"I did not know." He kept his gaze locked with Osborne's. "I was invited to a meeting of ardent Royalists. I was not informed of the reason for the gathering. Evidently the fine gentlemen have discovered the benefits of security since Leighton arrived in England."

A smug smile quirked Osborne's lips. "I knew Leighton would be there that night."

"Then why did you not take him? I cannot believe that the fire was an accident."

"It wasn't." Osborne laughed. "It was a very clever stratagem to break up the meeting and force the Royalists to hold another assembly, at a time more convenient to us."

"More convenient…. Then you were unable to get your troops to the smith's in time to apprehend Thomas Leighton?"

"Unfortunately you are correct." Osborne's expression became annoyed. "That idiot, Lieutenant Weston, chose that night to allow himself to be distracted by one of the serving wenches. He consumed too much spirituous liquor and decided to give his men a night of leave. Most of them were too drunk to move before I realized what was going on."

"So you had your spy set the fire."

Osborne shrugged. "I told him to interrupt the meeting. How he chose to do so was his decision."

Philip's hard gaze bored into Osborne. "You don't need me," he said softly.

Osborne grinned. "Not now, Hampton. Not yet. But you can be sure I will call upon you." He tilted his head thoughtfully. "You have some excellent skills that I may need to make use of. Unfortunately, you are encumbered by a set of moral values that are useless in this business. They have tended to obscure your vision at times. But you do have your uses."

Philip stood. "I'm a soldier, Osborne. I have a soldier's straightforward view of life."

"Precisely," Osborne sneered. "You are a man who can kill on command. I may have need of that."

Philip ignored the slur. His brows knit in a frown. "Do you intend to murder Thomas Leighton?"

Osborne scratched absently, very relaxed. "If I must. I would prefer to capture him and imprison him. He could then be used to keep his father from doing anything foolish."

"As a hostage, you mean."

"Of course." Osborne examined his fingernails. "However, capture may not be possible. In that case, I would have to dispose of him."

"And you expect me to do the deed."

Osborne's oily smile appeared again. "I congratulate you on your perception, Hampton." He folded his hands comfortably over his belly, still smiling evilly. "I will have another little duty for you to perform once this group of Royalists is rendered impotent."

An instinct for dangerous situations, which had saved him many times, sent a shiver creeping up Philip's spine. Though he thought he knew what was coming, he merely raised his brows in a question.

"We will have to dispose of the spy. He has been most helpful, but his loyalties cannot be guaranteed."

There was silence as the two men stared at each other. Then Philip said softly, "Poor fool."

Osborne laughed, though his expression was cruel. "You're too soft, Hampton. The man is a traitor to his own kind and a superb liar. He has betrayed his friends without a qualm. Would you have the Lord Protector reward him?"

"Since you sought his services, yes."

"Bah! The man came to us. Announced he had information, if we were willing to pay for it. He is totally without scruple."

A muscle in Philip's jaw jumped. "Then I will defend him no more." He turned on his heel, planning to leave. Osborne waited until he was at the door before he called Philip's name.

Pausing reluctantly, his hand on the knob, Philip glanced over his shoulder. "Yes?"

"Be prepared. As soon as Thomas Leighton is taken I will be done here. I will call on your services then."

Philip wrenched open the door and strode out. The resounding thump as it slammed behind him did nothing to soothe the dread within him.

The thunder of galloping hooves drowned out all other sounds in Alysa's ears, leaving her free to concentrate on her riding and the frustration that had already marred this day.

She had come out on this fine, sunny morning to visit Thomas. Although his whereabouts were usually kept secret, in order to ensure his safety, last night her father had accidentally let slip that Thomas was staying at the cottage of one of their tenants. During a largely sleepless night, Alysa had debated whether or not she should go to see her brother, for she badly wanted to talk to him. Just after dawn she awoke from a restless doze, her decision made. She would ride out to the cottage and catch him before he flitted off to his next hiding place. There would not be much time for conversation, but enough, she hoped, for her to learn what she needed to know.

Unfortunately she missed him by no more than ten minutes and his kind hosts had no idea where he had headed. Alysa knew that this secrecy was necessary while Thomas was a fugitive in England, but she couldn't help feeling annoyed. She wanted to talk about Sir Philip Hampton and Thomas was the only person who would know what Philip's life had been like in exile.

At one time the reason for her questions would have been purely practical, because she sought to discover if Philip was truly a Royalist home from exile. Now she simply wanted to learn what details she could of his past, so that she could better understand the man she was falling in love with.

The field she was crossing was bordered by a thick hedge. Alysa felt her horse gather itself beneath her, then launch into the air as it jumped the obstruction. As it always did when her horse took flight, elation seized her while they soared above the ground. The irritations and frustrations of the morning disappeared in the pleasure of the moment.

Abruptly, her exhilaration fled as she saw the rider coming down the road that bordered the field. His speed was such that he would be almost directly in her path when her horse returned to the ground. A collision seemed inevitable.

Horror filled her and she screamed. Frantically she dragged the horse's head around, forcing it to twist its body and change the direction of its landing. Still, she was afraid that she would land on top of the other rider.

Luck was with her that fine morning. Her hasty redirection and the quick wits of the other rider were enough to avert disaster. As her horse touched the ground she hauled sharply on the reins, pulling it to a snorting, rearing stop. The other rider did the same.

"'Od's blood!" said Sir Philip Hampton, much discomposed by the near disaster. "Mistress Alysa, are you all right?"

Alysa nodded shakily. "Yes, I'm fine." Her eyes began to sparkle as the shock wore off. "I must say, Sir Philip, that

was a fine piece of riding! I feared I should land on top of
you, even though I was able to turn my horse a trifle."

The concern died out of Philip's eyes as he listened to her
cheerful voice. "Are you mad, woman?" he demanded
angrily. "Jumping that hedge without so much as a glance for
what is on the other side. Why, you must have come on it at
a full gallop for you to have gained that much momentum."

Alysa nodded, the irrepressible dimple quivering to life in
her cheek. "It's too high to take at a slower pace." She
laughed at the outrage on his face. "I've jumped it many
times before, Sir Philip. I promise you I have yet to come to
grief."

"You came damned close today," he growled, not a whit
mollified.

"There are not usually any riders on the road at this hour of
the morning," Alysa pointed out sensibly. She looked at him
thoughtfully, noting the practical buff coat he wore instead
of a more fashionable doublet and cloak, and her expression
became curious. "Indeed, your presence here is most
unexpected, Sir Philip."

The careful blankness came down over his features. Alysa
watched him, puzzled. She searched back over what she had
said, but could find nothing untoward. She wished, rather
anxiously, that she knew why he sometimes closed himself
off from her this way.

She was surprised when he said levelly, "Don't do that
again, Alysa," and even more surprised when she replied, "If
it disturbs you, Philip, I promise you I will not."

He nodded, his eyes dark with an emotion she thought was
concern and something more. Her heart began to beat rather
wildly as she waited for the kiss she was sure was to come.

But he did not move. Instead he sat watching her with an
expression in his brooding eyes that sent shivers of desire
surging through her. Gently, she touched her heels to her horse,
urging it nearer to his mount. Something flared in Philip's eyes
as the skirt of her blue riding habit brushed against his leg. The
look assured Alysa he had recognized her action as deliberate.
She smiled, half enticing, half rueful.

Her horse's nose touched his mount's flank. They were inches apart now, facing each other, alone again in the warm sunshine. The magic that had surrounded them in the kitchen garden came to life once more, burning away doubts.

"I've never kissed a man on a horse before. Will you show me how it is done?" Alysa murmured, lowering her lashes demurely, then slowly and provocatively raising them so that she could look Philip directly in the eyes.

His breath caught. A wry smile curled his lips. "I fear, Mistress Alysa, that this is a new experience for me as well."

"Then let us experiment together." She shifted in the saddle, leaning toward him.

Philip could resist no more. Dropping the reins, he mastered the horse with his knees only so that he could use both hands to catch Alysa firmly by the shoulders and draw her close enough to kiss.

She made a soft murmuring sound deep in her throat as his mouth covered hers. The pleasure she had felt in the garden flooded back to her, but even more intensely.

This time there was no delicate brush preceding the hard, demanding kiss that forced her lips apart. This time Philip took her quickly and inside the sweet, moist cavern of her mouth his tongue teased hers, coaxing her to participate in the swift, sensual dance.

As before, Alysa surrendered to the demands of her senses and willingly allowed Philip to assume control of her responses. The near disaster had sent the blood flowing faster through her body, but now the kiss, awkward as it was, inflamed her ever more. Only the sudden movement of her horse brought Alysa back to reality. Less well trained than Philip's mount, it took advantage of her slackened grip on the reins to sidle away. Alysa was wrenched from Philip's grasp, even though passion still held them in its sway.

"Damn!" Philip said, grabbing her mount's bridle near the bit while Alysa shakily gathered up her loose reins.

She wasn't sure if he was expressing disappointment that their embrace had been cut short, or if he disapproved of what they had done. Her mind was still whirling from the pleasure of the kiss and she was not in a fit state to analyze anything.

In control of her horse once more, she smiled at him shakily.

Immediately the fierce expression faded from Philip's eyes. He brought his mount beside her again and lightly stroked her cheek. "My lovely Mistress Alysa, we must stop doing this. You have a devastating effect on my composure and I do not know how long I will be able to continue being a gentleman."

"Or I a lady," Alysa murmured. Her smile fell away. "Philip, I did not expect this…this fierce emotion that arises every time you touch me. I do not know how to cope with it."

He sighed, his eyes warm on her face. "Nor I. I think, Alysa, that from now on we should take care to remain in the presence of others if we are together. The time is not yet right for me to approach your father and I would not like to go to him with an uneasy conscience."

Alysa swallowed and silently agreed. Mention of her father made her very much aware that she was breaking every rule of good behavior that had been drummed into her. The knowledge that Philip did not think any the less of her for it buoyed up her spirits and made her smile mischievously again. "I do believe, sir, that you would have no difficulty winning my father over to your cause should you decide to speak to him this very morning, but I do appreciate your thoughtfulness in waiting until things are more settled here. When Thomas is safely away we will all be ready to discuss more private issues."

The shutter closed over Philip's expression again, agonizing Alysa as she vainly tried to understand what it was that had caused him to hide away from her. Try as she might, she could find nothing she said that was out of the ordinary. Then Philip smiled and the moment might never have been.

"I must go." He added gently, "And so must you, or questions will be asked."

Alysa pouted prettily. "I know, but I do not want to leave you, Philip."

"Or I you," he said ruefully. "But needs must. Now go, lovely lady, before I forget my good intentions and take you off that horse to give you a proper kiss."

"Is that a threat or a promise?" Alysa teased.

"Both," he retorted huskily. Then he added seriously, "Go, Alysa. We both know you must."

Though she made a little moue of distaste, she turned her horse and began to trot away. Unable to resist, she looked back at Philip to blow him a kiss. He was watching her leave, his expression grave, his gaze hooded.

The kiss withered on her hand. Dressed in the buff jerkin, sitting at ease on the sleek black stallion, he looked like nothing so much as one of the soldiers who had come to West Easton after the Battle of Worchester. They had devastated the land and the town in their attempts to discover the whereabouts of King Charles II. Those men had been tough, war-hardened soldiers who kept their feelings secret behind blank expressions and emotionless eyes, and to Alysa they represented the ultimate danger.

Rather desperately she dug her heels into her horse's sides. Obediently it launched into a ground-eating canter. Every time she thought she understood Philip Hampton, something would happen that would make her wonder again if he was all that he seemed. But he must be what he claimed to be, for if he was not, she was falling in love with the enemy.

"Alysa? May I come in?" Prudence stuck her head into her sister's bedroom and observed her hopefully.

Alysa smiled. "Of course." She turned to her maid. "That will be all for the moment. I will call you if I need you again."

The maid curtsied and went out, gathering up Alysa's riding habit to be aired as she passed.

"Now then," Alysa said when she and her sister were alone. "I know that look, Prudence. You have something you want to talk to me about."

Prudence settled down on the daybed that was in front of

the fire. She watched her sister brush out her long golden locks for a moment before she spoke. "Alysa, Mama tells me that you are smitten with Sir Philip Hampton."

Alysa colored vividly. Hastily she bent her head, staring down at the sky-blue petticoat exposed by the open skirt of her gown. The sweep of her long hair shielded her expression from her sister. "Smitten is hardly the word I would have used, but...I can hardly believe that Mama would use it either."

"She didn't really," Prudence admitted airily. "She said that you preferred him over Cedric Ingram. Is that true?"

"Well, yes, it is. But what has this to do with whatever it is that is troubling you?"

Prudence folded her hands in the lap of her magenta gown and ignored Alysa's question.

"Does this mean that you are no longer interested in allowing Master Ingram to court you?"

Alysa caught her breath. Slowly she looked up, brushing her hair back from her face so she could see Prudence clearly. "I think it is up to Master Ingram to decide whether or not he wishes to court a lady."

Prudence waved this away as trivial. "It is not Master Ingram's sentiments I am trying to discover, it's yours! Alysa, do you love him?"

The surprise on Alysa's face was entirely natural. "Love Cedric Ingram? Heavens, no!"

A smile broke out on Prudence's face. "That is what I thought. Good, then I need not worry that I am stealing him from you."

Amusement chased away the shock in Alysa's eyes. "I take it you have decided Master Ingram would make a suitable husband for you."

Prudence smiled mischievously. "I have. He does not know it yet, but soon he will be dancing to my tune."

The words sounded ominously smug to Alysa. She hesitated, then decided that in the interest of her sister's future happiness she should be blunt. "Prudence, Cedric has never yet shown any interest in you. What makes you think he will in the future?"

"He has shown no interest, dear sister, because of you." Prudence raised her shoulders in elegant denial. "If you were committed to another he would soon turn his eyes elsewhere. In the meantime, I can continue with my plan."

Alysa was beginning to feel seriously concerned about what Prudence had in mind. "What plan?"

"Why to get him to notice me, of course."

"Of course," Alysa murmured, twisting her hair into a knot. "And how are you going to do that?"

Prudence leaned forward conspiratorially. "Mama is always saying that the way to attract a man is to get him to talk about himself. In that manner a woman can convince a man that he is the most fascinating creature on earth, for there is nothing a man can talk about so well or so long as himself."

"Yes," Alysa said cautiously. She too had heard Abigail say that many times, and she had found the trick to be an excellent way to break the ice with a gentleman. But it wasn't an ideal method of building a solid relationship.

"Well," Prudence continued, her eyes gleaming with enthusiasm, "I realized that I know next to nothing about Cedric, beyond that he is the second son of the Earl of Easton and that he manages the Ingram estates for his brother, who is in exile. I do not know how he likes to spend his time, if he prefers a lamb chop to a beefsteak, or where he goes when he rides from his house. So I have begun to find out."

Alysa gazed at Prudence wide-eyed. There were times when she was truly amazed by her sister's thought processes. "How?"

Prudence settled herself more comfortably on the daybed. "First of all, I convinced my maid that she should strike up a friendship with Cedric's body servant. That way I can learn all his little habits. And I have been talking to people in the village about him, hearing what they think and have noticed."

Alysa thought that Cedric Ingram didn't have much of a chance against her sister's determined pursuit of him. She said so and Prudence laughed. "But wait! There is more! Haven't you noticed that I have been absent quite often over the last few days?"

Alysa thought back. "I must admit that I have not seen you about the house that much, but I assumed it was because I have been busy and we simply haven't been in the same place at the same time."

Prudence shook her head. "No, that's not it at all." She leaned forward, her eyes twinkling brightly. "I have been following Cedric to see what he does!"

Alysa's breath caught again. This time she let it out in a long, concerned sigh. "Prudence! How could you?"

"Very easily. I stay a good distance behind. He rarely looks back, you know, but if he did I would find some reason for my presence. Besides, if he does discover me he will be flattered. What man would not if a lady went to such great lengths to get to know him?"

Alysa opened her mouth to protest, then closed it again. Prudence did have a point. Although strictly speaking it was very forward of her to do what she was doing, Cedric might well be so flattered that he would overlook the impropriety. "Tell me, then, what exactly does Master Ingram do when you follow him throughout the countryside?"

Prudence made a face. "Nothing exciting. Nothing very interesting, in fact. He does a great deal of visiting, with the other landowners in the area, not his tenants. Indeed, I have not yet seen him stop at a farmhouse. Isn't that odd, Alysa? Papa makes sure he visits our people regularly."

"Perhaps Master Ingram has not yet had the reason to call on a tenant. And his visits to other landowners are perfectly reasonable. After all, he is assisting Papa to organize the local resistance. He is probably making sure the other committed Royalists are kept up-to-date."

"That is what I thought," Prudence agreed, nodding. "He was stopped by the odious troops one day and was forced to talk to the lieutenant for quite a long time. I was worried about his security then. I wondered what I could do to intervene."

Horrified, Alysa said forcefully, "Prudence, should that ever happen again you must come home immediately and tell Papa! He can get help. Putting yourself in danger would do Master Ingram no good!"

Prudence nodded, but she didn't look convinced. She hastily changed the subject. "Alysa, I haven't been able to follow Cedric in the evening, and I think it is important that I do."

"Why?"

"So I am able to get a balanced picture of him," Prudence retorted sweetly.

"Prudence, no sane woman goes out at night. It's dangerous! Besides, what would our parents say?"

"Alysa, I need to do this," Prudence said forcefully. "If I do not appear at dinner one evening, will you say I am not feeling well, or some such thing? I know Mama would understand what I am doing, but Papa would probably be upset."

"He would be furious," Alysa retorted dryly. "And I doubt that Mama would be very sympathetic."

Prudence grinned. "It is all her idea, so she ought to understand. Please, Alysa! I do not want Mama and Papa disturbed for no reason."

Alysa said dryly, "I would hardly call learning that your daughter is gadding about the countryside after dark no reason to become upset."

Prudence shrugged. "I will do this, whether you approve or not, Alysa." She abandoned her studied nonchalance. "Dear sister you must help me! I have been in love with Cedric Ingram for months and this may be my only chance to capture his fancy."

Prudence didn't say that she was desperate, or that she was sick with unrequited love, but Alysa knew both were true. Slowly, she felt herself nodding her head. "All right. On one condition, Prudence."

"Name it." A smile had broken over Prudence's face.

Alysa remained grave. "You must tell me what you intend before you go out so that someone will know where you are, even if it is only in a general way. Agreed?"

"Agreed!" Prudence bounced over to her sister to give her a big hug. "Thank you, Alysa. You won't regret this."

Alysa hoped not.

CHAPTER 11

The run of good weather continued unabated. Farmers in the West Easton area prophesied a good crop and planted their seeds early. At Strathern Hall the members of the household made excuses to get out into the spring sunshine, but on this fine day Alysa and her stepmother were stuck in the library. They were going over the estate records, discussing which of the tenants would probably need some sort of assistance over the next few months and what could be done to help them.

The longtime butler at Strathern interrupted their serious discussion. Though his voice was grave, there was an undisguisable twinkle in his eyes. "Sir Philip Hampton has come to call on Mistress Alysa. Shall I put him in the King's Salon or should I have him come here?"

Abigail cocked her head and thought for a moment. A smile twitched her lips as she watched Alysa sit up a little straighter. With her hands clasped together atop the desk, Alysa was the model of feminine propriety, but there was a subdued anticipation glittering in her eyes that Abigail could not miss.

Suppressing her smile, Abigail said mildly, "No, not in this room. Take Sir Philip out to the terrace. Alysa will join him in a few minutes. I will continue to work on these documents." She looked at Alysa and allowed her smile to break free. "You and Sir Philip will be alone on the terrace, but remember—I can see you from the window!"

Alysa laughed. "I will be good, Mama, I promise!"

Abigail laughed too. "Of course you will, my dear." She watched with considerable amusement as Alysa paused to shake out the skirts of her wine-red gown and straighten the rose colored petticoat beneath, then carefully inspect her hair in a mirror. She patted a few stray hairs back into place and pinched her cheeks to add a little more color before heading outside.

Philip was standing by the stone balustrade when Alysa stepped through the doorway. Though he was resting one hand on the stone surface he was not leaning on it as he had when his leg was troubling him. As he came toward her, Alysa saw that he had abandoned his cane completely and now walked with only the trace of a limp. When he reached her he smiled his devastating smile and took her hand in his to be kissed.

Though his lips lingered overlong on her skin, Alysa didn't mind. She did murmur, however, "Mama has decided to allow us to meet alone, but she is just in the library and could look out the window at any time."

Philip raised his head, but continued to hold her hand in his. "I would do nothing to compromise your reputation, my lovely lady. Come, let us walk over into the sunlight where we can be easily seen and no one can accuse us of skulking in the shadows."

Alysa laughed and let herself be guided over to the balustrade. She thought that Philip looked every inch the Royalist gentleman in his blue velvet doublet, black cloak lined with matching blue satin and wide black breeches, extravagantly fringed with blue ribbon loops and rosettes. She gazed up at him admiringly and said sincerely, "I doubt that you would ever skulk, my dear Philip. You are too forthright for that."

He turned his head away to look at something to the left of them. The wide brim of his low-crowned beaver hat hid the expression on his face. "Look," he said softly, pointing. Not far away a goldfinch, returning early from its annual migration, hovered over the balustrade, then gently landed for a brief respite. The beautifully marked bird was there but an instant before it was again on its way, yet for that short time both Philip and Alysa admired its fragile beauty. When it had flown away, Philip turned back to Alysa, smiling. "The goldfinch is a beautiful, delicate creature, much like you, my lady Alysa."

Warmth washed through Alysa. Though Philip's words could be nothing more than the empty compliments of a courtier, the expression deep in his eyes was sincere. She blushed, but deliberately turned her hand so that she could twine her fingers in his. "I thank you for the compliment, Philip," she said in a low, husky voice, "but I am merely a flesh-and-blood woman with all the faults and needs that state entails."

A light flared hotly in his eyes. "And I am but a flesh-and-blood man. Alysa, I would speak to your father, but I cannot at this time. I must wait, though I do not want to."

Excitement, elation, satisfaction and a dozen other emotions shivered through Alysa. This was a proposal of marriage, no matter how obliquely Philip had couched it. Then an image of Thomas on the beach, being chased by the Protectorate troops sneaked into Alysa's mind and put a momentary damper on her delight. She nodded quickly. "I understand, Philip, of course I do! Papa has too many immediate problems to concern himself with my future."

Philip squeezed her hand, before gently removing his. "If he gave his permission for us to marry, Alysa, how would you feel?"

The excitement returned, stronger than before. Alysa laughed and cupped his face in her hands. "You have to ask?"

"Yes," he said seriously, but he was smiling at her jubilation.

"I did not think I would ever find a man who could move me as you do, Philip." Her eyes and voice had become as serious as his. Her hands remained warm on his face. "In many ways you are a mystery to me and yet I trust you implicitly. From the beginning you intrigued me, even when no one in my family was sure whether you were a Roundhead spy or a loyal Royalist—What is it?"

Philip's expression had tightened forbiddingly. He caught her wrists and pulled her hands away from his face. "You thought I was a Roundhead spy?"

Relief flooded over Alysa, drowning her momentary dismay. She told herself that it was good that they were finally having this conversation, for doubt had hovered between them for too long. "The question did come up from time to time. You must remember, Philip, that you were a stranger here. Old Sir Richard Hampton rarely spoke about his two nephews and no one had seen you in years. With the country in confusion after the death of Oliver Cromwell, those loyal to the king were hopeful that a rebellion would finally bring him home for good. We were very aware that we could not afford to have an agent of the Protectorate in our midst."

Grimly, Philip said, "What made you decide that I was what I appeared to be?"

"Time," Alysa said simply. "When you seemed attracted to me, I offered to encourage your advances so that I could get to know you better. Papa was reluctant at first, but eventually he agreed to my plan." The expression on Philip's face was still and dangerous. Alysa hurried on, determined to complete her confession and get the worst behind them. "As you courted me, I learned that you were a man of honor, as well as one I could respect. I told Papa that I did not believe that you would seek to harm our family, and I believed it, then and now."

She gazed up into his fathomless brown eyes, pledging him her trust and promising her love. His eyes searched her face, probing the depth of her honesty, but his own expression was unreadable. After a moment he pulled away to stare unseeing across the broad green lawns. "You shouldn't have done that, Alysa."

She touched him tentatively on the shoulder. "Are you telling me that you are not the Royalist brother, Philip? That my family should be wary of you? That you are the spy who has been plaguing West Easton?"

He drew a deep breath and let it out again forcefully. "No. I am not the spy who almost cost your brother his freedom. You must look to your own ranks for that. But I am not what you imagine me to be, Alysa. I am a simple soldier who has retired from active duty, nothing more. Do not make me into what I am not."

Her grip on his shoulder firmed and she turned him toward her. "What I see in you, Philip, I have not imagined. We are all more than we think we are or can be. I know that if the time came for you to make a decision, you would make the right one. I know it!"

Taking both her hands in his, Philip rubbed the soft skin with his thumb as he gazed deep into her eyes. The movement had a slow, seductive rhythm to it that hypnotized Alysa. "By whose definition of what is right?"

She smiled up at him, her eyes trusting. "By yours, dear sir. For I know that your definition and mine are the same."

With the troops in the area, the need to set a date and a site for another meeting of those committed to seeing the king restored became both imperative and impossible. Lord Strathern believed it was necessary for his son to complete his business and leave England as soon as could be arranged, but at the same time, a meeting of a large number of men would be noticed and commented upon, thus alerting the military. They would naturally investigate and would most likely arrest Thomas as well as all of the prominent gentlemen attending.

So the question of where and when to hold the meeting remained while Thomas skipped from hiding place to hiding place. He seemed to be safest in the cottages of the tenant farmers, for Lieutenant Weston had apparently taken to heart Philip Hampton's promise of retribution should any lowly innocents be harmed. The lieutenant made a habit of avoiding these dwellings. Possibly, he assumed a man of Thomas's rank would not demean himself by residing in a peasant's cottage.

Whatever the reason, Thomas was never close to being captured while he stayed at one of the lowly cottages. He did come near to it, though, on the one evening he visited Ingram Abbey.

He had gone there to consult with his father, Cedric Ingram and one or two others on what to do about having the meeting. Since Lord Strathern suspected that he was being watched, Cedric Ingram convinced Thomas and the others that it was too risky for Thomas to leave the abbey after the discussion was over. Instead he suggested that Thomas stay the night in a room in the oldest part of the house, which had been boarded up since the war had curbed the fortune of the Ingram family. Cedric was certain the troops would not think to search there.

Thomas had accepted the suggestion, but once he was in the tiny chamber, he had second thoughts. The room was very dark, for shutters had been placed over the only small window. Dust lay thickly over everything and the air had a dank, musty smell caused by being closed up for years. The unpleasant conditions were not as bad as some Thomas had endured, but still he was edgy. He paced about the small room, telling himself that the lack of light and the neglect were friends, not enemies. No matter how many ways he tried to convince himself, however, he could not. He felt caged—trapped and vulnerable. He knew he could not spend the night in this shabby place.

He slipped out of the room as soon as the house was asleep. For some reason he didn't want anyone to know that he had left the hiding place. Perhaps his caution was the result of tension caused by being shut into the small closed cell, or perhaps it was simply basic survival instinct. Whatever the reason, he obeyed his inclination without question. His intuitive sense had saved him in strange situations before.

A full moon guided his steps as he emerged silently from the house to the grassy park outside. He headed for the stables, where his horse, a nondescript brown cob, had been settled for the night. Though it was a beast no one would pick from a herd of farm horses, Thomas wanted to be sure it had been properly bedded down so that it looked as if it belonged with the other Ingram horses.

He found the cob in a large loose box between a finely boned chestnut stallion and a lean gray hunter. With the two well-bred horses on either side, the little cob stood out like the scar on Thomas's cheek. He frowned, for it seemed to him that his mount had been stabled elsewhere when he arrived. He shrugged, assuming he was mistaken. Silently he drifted about the abbey outbuildings, looking for a more suitable place to house the cob.

He found it in a barn where hay was stored and several sturdy workhorses used to plow the fields or pull carts were tied in narrow stalls that allowed them little room to move about. It took him but a moment to discover that there was space for another horse. Swiftly, Thomas decided he would move his mount here, rather than leave the grounds altogether, for the troops would never believe an excuse if he was caught riding about the countryside at night.

After he had tied the cob with the other workhorses, he climbed up into the hayloft and settled in for the night.

Some hours later his precautions were justified. He woke to the sound of men shouting and horses stamping their hooves on the hard-packed earth around the outbuildings. He listened tensely as the grounds were searched, his ears straining to catch a word or two about the conclusions that had been reached.

His luck, which had been with him since his arrival in England, held. Like every other outbuilding, the barn was checked, but the searchers cast only a casual glance over the utilitarian animals stabled there. They made an equally cursory inspection of the loft, completely missing the spot where Thomas had created a secure place for himself.

"We're wasting our time," he heard one man say in disgust. "His horse is gone and there's no sign of him. We've missed him."

Evidently, this was the opinion of the officer in charge, for the troops left soon after. Much relieved, Thomas settled down in his hiding place to snatch a few more hours of slumber. He left the abbey grounds in that dark time just before first light, hoping that any soldiers who might have been left to watch for him had long since fallen asleep.

Again, his luck held. No one followed him and he was able to reach his next hiding place safely.

Word of Thomas's near capture spread quickly. Lord Strathern decided that a meeting must either be held or the idea of one abandoned completely. The original problem still remained, however. Where in tiny West Easton could a sizable number of people meet without causing comment?

The answer proved to be quite simple: the village church.

Though the minister was a Presbyterian, he was a moderate man who had come to believe that freedom for England could only be found with a Stuart on the throne. When Strathern approached him about using his church for the meeting site, he was more than willing—he was enthusiastic.

And so, the planning began again. This time only the vicar, Lord Strathern, Cedric Ingram and Thomas were in on the secret. There was no need to inform the other Royalist sympathizers, because the meeting would be held on Sunday, after the service was over. If any wished to leave they would be free to do so. Otherwise, everyone who attended church that day would be invited to say his piece.

It was not a foolproof plan, but it was the safest one Lord Strathern could think of. It was also a final effort. If this failed, Thomas would leave England with only the information he had collected so far. Strathern, and his contact within the Sealed Knot, believed it would be better for Thomas to get safely away with part of what he had been sent to discover than not to get away at all.

The note was written in a gently flowing script that could only have been penned by a woman. Philip scrutinized the missive, searching for hidden meanings behind the flowery message that Alysa Leighton would be in the village at eleven in the morning and that if he should also happen to there at that time she would be delighted to speak to him.

There could be no doubt that this was a request for a meeting, even though it was couched in terms that did not demand, or even specify, the event. He smiled slightly. That point, if nothing else, proved to him that the note came from his lady Alysa. Though she might be forthright at times and heedless of convention, she was a Royalist lady born, with all the subtly of the breed. She wanted to see him, yes, but it was not in her nature to demand outright.

He wondered what it was that had made her so distraught that she could not wait until he called upon her to talk to him. The contents of the letter told him nothing, but the delicate script was heavily underscored where she wrote that she would be happy to speak to him, signifying her agitation.

Whatever was bothering her, Philip was intensely flattered that she would turn to him for assistance in solving her problem. That proved she was coming to trust and care for him. He had long since abandoned the pretense that he was courting her in order to gain entry into local Royalist circles. Alysa had moved into his heart with all the smooth subtlety he expected of Royalist ladies. Without his wanting it, she had slipped beneath his barriers and lodged herself so tightly he had no means of getting her out. Not, he'd discovered, that he wanted to.

He arrived early in the village and paid a visit to the mercer's shop, where he had noticed a fine lace shawl that he thought Alysa would like. After purchasing the shawl, he sauntered down the street to what was left of the smithy. There he paused for a few moments, inspecting the charred remains of the buildings. The events of that evening went through his mind and merged with his last conversation with Osborne.

Who was the spy? Who in this small village appeared to be loyal to the king, but was truly more devoted to his own private interests?

It could, of course, be one of the merchants, or a tenant of one of the large landowners. Most Royalist support came from the propertied classes, but after years of rule by the radical Independents and the army, many of those who had originally supported the parliamentary side during the civil wars would have been happy to see a Stuart king on the throne of England once more.

Philip didn't believe that it was one of the common folk, however. He thought it more likely that the spy was a prominent person who was leading a double life, smiling at his friends while he did his best to betray them. Philip had told Osborne that he didn't care who the spy was, but that was not precisely true. Starting the fire in the smithy was the act of a coward, just as the assassination attempt on him had been. Philip was quite certain that one man had perpetrated both acts and he wanted to know who it was. He had a debt to settle with the gentleman.

Taking one last look at the ruins, Philip shrugged. The question of the spy's identity could wait until another day, for now it was nearly eleven o'clock and he did not want to keep Alysa waiting. In any case, the ashes held no clues, gave him no answers to his questions. He turned away, his thoughts already of Alysa.

She had walked to the village with only her maid for company. They met in front of the cobbler's establishment, as she had suggested in her note, and she smiled prettily as he greeted her. In her eyes was a warm approval of what he was wearing. Philip came as close to preening as was possible for one of his temperament. He had dressed carefully for the meeting, in a burgundy-colored doublet and matching breeches. The clothes were rich without being opulent, for he did not want anyone guessing that he had not run into Alysa by accident. At the same time, he wanted to look his best for her.

"Sir Philip! How delightful to meet you this morning," she said, brushing the hood of her black woolen cloak from her gleaming blond hair. The dimple in her cheek danced into life, and in that instant, Philip thought her the most beautiful woman alive. "Are you in the village for any particular purpose? I have come to have some boots fitted, as you can see." As Alysa waved airily at the shop, her maid discreetly moved away. Alysa sighed.

His eyes twinkling at the harmless game, Philip said gravely, "Though I am most pleased to see you, Mistress Leighton, I must not keep you from your appointment." He was rewarded by a smoldering look of disapproval from her fine blue eyes that made him laugh. "Evidently, your appointment is not critical. Would you care to walk a ways with me, my lady, so that we might talk?"

Alysa's face brightened and the mischievous dimple appeared in her cheek. "Oh, what a splendid suggestion, Sir Philip! Of course I will walk with you." She turned to the servant. "Mary, do tell Master Horner that I will be in directly."

The maid bobbed a curtsey, then hastened to do her mistress's bidding, leaving Alysa alone with Philip. One of the townsfolk passed and smiled. Alysa greeted the woman in an open, friendly way. Evidently, she did not care that gossip about them would soon be all over the village. The thought warmed Philip.

When they were alone together, Alysa smiled at him. "Thank you for coming, Sir Philip," she said in a low voice. Her fingers twitched nervously at the skirt of her sapphire-blue gown where it opened to show the ice-blue petticoat beneath. "Perhaps I am being a fool, but I felt I needed to talk to you and I did not want to do it at Strathern."

He looked at her sharply. "No?"

"No, I—" She hesitated. After a quick glance into his eyes, she looked down quickly. "Philip, my father has enough to worry him without having to deal with the fears of a daughter and sister."

Enlightenment dawned on him. "You are concerned about Thomas."

She nodded. Lifting her face to his, her eyes wide and vulnerable, she said, "Thomas is in such danger! He was almost caught a few nights ago at Ingram Abbey and it was only by the greatest good fortune that he escaped. I am so anxious about him!"

Ingram Abbey. Philip hadn't heard of the near capture

before now, but he thought the news more interesting than Alysa could possibly know. She was watching him with those huge frightened eyes, waiting for him to say something that would make her concerns fade away. He desperately wanted to reassure her, but he couldn't find the words.

Instead he said slowly, "Ingram Abbey. Why was Thomas there?"

She waved her hand impatiently. "Papa wanted to discuss the general meeting with him and he thought Strathern would be too dangerous for Thomas to come to, so Cedric Ingram suggested they use the abbey." She added in a small voice, "Philip, it is as if someone knew and deliberately told the military that Thomas would be there."

Someone indeed. A heaviness settled over Philip. Osborne had every right to feel cocky about the spy he had recruited, for the man had access to the most intimate details of the Royalist plans. The spy was Cedric Ingram.

Philip now faced the dilemma of how to alert Alysa that her suitor was a traitor without telling her that he, Philip, was not what he pretended to be. Thomas Leighton's words echoed eerily in his brain. *And when my sister discovers your true identity? How will you explain to her that you have lied to her all this time?* He would have to tell her why he had come to West Easton and how meeting her had changed his life.

But not today. Not while she was so distraught. Taking her hand, he said reassuringly, "Thomas was not caught then, and I am certain that wherever he is hiding, he has made sure that it was well away from Ingram Abbey. Remember that he is safe, Alysa, and rejoice in that."

The hand resting in his trembled a little, but she smiled bravely. "Thank you, Philip. Yes, he is safe for now and he will soon be gone."

Philip didn't want to speak the words, for he knew they would lead to a decision for him, a decision he did not want to make. He said slowly, reluctantly, "Then a time has been set for the meeting of Royalists?"

Alysa smiled up at him, her eyes trusting. "Yes, but only

Papa and a few others know the details. Even I have not been apprised of it." She paused then added fiercely, "And I am glad of it! I would hate to think that some idle conversation of mine might put my brother in jeopardy. This way I need not fear that I will harm him."

Relief flooded through Philip as he realized he would not have to make the ultimate choice yet. "A wise decision on Lord Strathern's part," he said gravely. Smiling, he touched Alysa's cheek. It was a reassurance and a caress at the same time. "Take heart, my lovely lady! For the moment your brother is safe hidden and soon his duty here will be fulfilled and he will be able to get safely away."

"Yes," Alysa said, smiling up into his eyes. "Now that I have talked with you I can see that my fears were groundless. Thank you, Philip. You have given me much comfort today."

These were heady words to a man who wanted nothing more than to please the lady who spoke them. Philip was almost light-headed with pleasure. He grinned down at Alysa, feeling younger than he had in years. "My pleasure, lovely lady." He extended the package he had been carrying under his arm. With a slightly wry smile, he said, "Though I am sure that you care more for your brother's fate at this moment than personal adornments, I would be most pleased if you would consent to accept this small token of my feelings for you."

Slowly, Alysa took the package. It was wrapped in plain cloth and tied with string and the very ordinariness of it made it look terribly innocent. But it was not. Instead it was a symbol, a promise of a union that couldn't yet be spoken of. Philip watched, breathless, as she turned the package in her hands. Then she pulled the string to untie the bow that held it closed.

Philip's heart leapt. She was committed now, just as he was committed. Though nothing had been said, Alysa had just acknowledged that her feelings toward him were strong and true.

Soon, he thought, exultant. Soon he would speak to Lord

Strathern and ask for her hand.

Unbidden, Thomas's words echoed in his head once more. *And when my sister discovers your true identity? How will you explain to her that you have lied to her all this time?*

Her voice, expressing pleasure over the gift, chased away the taunting sound of Thomas's voice. Once again Philip promised himself that he would tell her. Soon.

But not today.

CHAPTER 12

The church in West Easton was an ancient building. Construction had begun during Norman rule, but successive generations added decorations and made repairs in the style of their times. The most recent change had been made during the war. Then the exquisite stained-glass windows, which had adorned the building since the rule of King Henry V, were knocked out by Puritan sympathizers for being idolatrous. Now plain glass was fitted in the casements, but for many years the windows had been boarded up, mute testimony to freedom lost and idealism taken to extremes.

The interior of the church had also been altered. Raw scars, where Gothic carvings had been chipped away from the stone, bore mute testimony to the destructive forces unleashed by fanaticism and war. The beautiful wooden pulpit, set high above the congregation, had been torn down and replaced with a less ostentatious podium. It was there that the Reverend Randolph Graystone, Vicar of West Easton, stood on Sunday morning after the service was over and addressed his parishioners.

"I have asked you all to linger a few minutes today in order—" There was a commotion at the back of the church. The vicar peered down the long, dim aisle toward the door, trying to make out what was going on. The members of the congregation turned in their seats, craning their necks. A low whisper, almost a growl of anger, erupted as a half-a-dozen armed men marched into the building.

"Yes, do come in. Everyone is welcome," the vicar said, making the best of something that was happening with or without his approval.

At the head of the troops was Lieutenant Weston. He swaggered down the aisle, the sword at his side slapping ominously against his leg as he walked. One hand rested on the hilt and his eyes flitted from face-to-face, looking for something—or someone.

The vicar did not move from his austere pulpit. He placed his hands on the encircling balustrade and watched calmly as the lieutenant strutted toward him. When Weston halted at the altar rail the vicar said placidly, "I fear that your timing is unfortunate, sir, as you have completely missed our morning service."

"My men and I are not here to worship," Weston said curtly.

"I see." The vicar bowed his head innocently. "Then you are here to offer your help in rebuilding the smith's forge and barn. How very kind of you."

The church was suddenly so quiet it seemed as if the whole congregation had paused to draw breath. The lieutenant's gaze bored into the Reverend Graystone's mild eyes. "Is that what this assembly is about?"

"This gathering is a service to worship God," the vicar reprimanded gently. "The people of West Easton have stayed behind to do His work and help succor one of His own who has been beset by misfortune. What else would it be?"

Weston deliberately turned his back on the vicar. His eyes slowly scanned the congregation before he spoke. "Information has been laid that this is a meeting to plot rebellion against the Lord Protector!"

Lord Strathern jumped to his feet. "Really, sir, you are absurd!"

Eyes narrowed, Weston retorted, "Am I? I think not."

Strathern's comment and the lieutenant's brusque reply broke the spell that held the congregation silent. Angry voices protested the intrusion and the insulting tone of the military man. Heads nodded and men got red in the face.

Weston listened to all of this with an expression of annoyance on his face. He allowed the protests to continue for a few minutes; then he pulled his sword from its scabbard and raised it high. Evidently this was a sign to his men, who had been standing at the rear of the church. They moved into position along the aisle, their swords drawn and raised.

"For shame!" the vicar bellowed, mild no more. "That weapons should be drawn in God's house! Tell your soldiers to sheath their swords, Lieutenant. Then leave this building. You are not welcome here in the guise of violent men."

"I will go when I am satisfied that nothing improper is being done." The lieutenant did sheath his own sword, however, before he sauntered back down the aisle to the pew that housed the Leighton family. He looked at each person there, from the stiff and haughty Edward, still standing defiantly, to Abigail who sat straight and firm beside him. Slowly, in a deliberate attempt to intimidate, Weston's gaze scanned Alysa with the dangerous thoroughness of a masculine predator. Alysa's eyes sparkled with anger and she met his gaze boldly, her head high. The lieutenant began to redden and looked over at Prudence, repeating his silent harassment. Less composed than her sister, his gaze made Prudence look away, fear lurking in the depths of her eyes.

A nasty smile of satisfaction curled Weston's lips, until he happened to catch the hard promise of retribution in the expression on Lord Strathern's face. Weston's hand tightened on the sword hilt and a muscle jumped in his cheek as his eyes dueled with Strathern's, trying to force the older man's gaze down. But it was Lieutenant Weston whose gaze faltered. He turned away with an angry flounce.

"I have information that this church is being used for more than religious services. I intend to stay until I have found proof of that."

"Of course it is, Lieutenant," the vicar said patiently. "As I told you, the people of West Easton are staying behind today to discuss what is to be done about the tragic loss suffered by

Master Wishingham, our village smith."

Barnabus surged to his feet. "And right kind it is of all of you. My good wife and I cannot imagine how to thank you for your thoughtfulness."

The vicar beamed and nodded in the direction of the smith. "Now then, Lieutenant, may we get on with our meeting? Although it is Sunday and our day of rest, I know these good people cannot linger overlong and we have much to discuss before we are finished."

The lieutenant sneered. "Go ahead, get on with your meeting. But my men and I will not leave. If this is simply a ruse to try to confuse us, it will not work! But do go ahead and try."

"Most kind," the Reverend Mr. Graystone said, inclining his head. "Very well, you all know why we are here. A week last Saturday Master Wishingham's forge and barn burned down. Apart from the hardship this will cause the town, now that we no longer have a proper smithy, I believe it is our Christian duty to try to set to right what some evil man has done. We will rebuild. If we work as a team I know we will be able to quickly reconstruct the buildings. Now, who is willing to help?"

There was a sudden outpouring of voices and one after another the men stood up and promised to do their part.

The vicar beamed. "Wonderful! Now, who is to do what?"

More voices were raised in promise. The result was general confusion.

"Dear me." The vicar appeared to be quite perturbed. "I think we need a committee. Lord Strathern, will you volunteer to head a planning committee?"

Strathern, who had seated himself once the meeting began, stood and bowed. "Certainly." He glanced around the church, then pointed to several men as he said their names. All agreed to help. "Now then," Strathern continued, "it seems to me that we need to discuss what is to be done. Should we simply recreate the buildings as they were, or would Master Wishingham like to see some improvements?"

"Well," the smith said, stroking his chin thoughtfully, "the forge could be enlarged a trifle, if that is not too difficult. The old foundations escaped the fire and I assumed that I would simply rebuild atop them, but I admit that more space would be a treat."

"Why Master Blake, the stonemason, is amongst our number today," the Reverend Mr. Graystone said, sounding as pleased as a child with a new toy. "Why don't we ask him what he thinks?"

The stonemason was a ponderous man with a slow, thoughtful way of speaking. He rose to his feet with a heavy grace, then considered his reply a time before beginning. "From what I remember of the construction of the forge, the foundations could be lengthened a few feet without difficulty. But is that how you'd like the building enlarged, Barnabus? Would it not be better for you to widen it as well?"

Wishingham allowed as how that would be nice.

Blake, the stonemason, nodded. "Aye, I thought as much. Now that might be a more difficult task." He looked down at his large hands. "Problem is, I'm not that familiar with wood construction. Now, if you was to consider rebuilding the forge in stone—" His voice warmed to his topic and his sentences picked up speed, his tongue tripping over itself as he spoke. "A forge should be constructed of stone, I think, what with the fire burning all the time and the sparks that are thrown with the working of the metal. Seems to me that a fire there was inevitable. I vote we rebuild the smith's forge in stone. What does everyone else say?"

"I'm for it!" Wishingham announced, not surprisingly.

Peter Graham, a prosperous merchant who owned the town gristmill and sawmill, protested. "An excellent suggestion, Master Blake. But where do you expect to find the materials for such an enterprise? Stone is expensive, unlike wood. Since there are no quarries in this area it must be cut and hauled from miles away."

"Your timber must be felled, cut and aged," someone said.

Graham nodded. "Aye, it must, but I promise to donate a portion of the materials. Would a quarryman not of this area be willing to do the same?"

And so it went on for the next hour, suggestions made, rebutted, agreed with. Everyone had an opinion and none was shy about speaking up. Men like Lord Strathern, who were in on the real reason for the meeting, could almost forget that they were not here to discuss the smith's sad loss, but to consider the possibility of a restoration of the monarchy.

The hour lengthened into the next and still the good people of West Easton found reasons to continue the debate about how to rebuild the smith's lost forge. When it should be done was argued over, as was who should direct the construction. Eventually the discussion came round to what refreshments should be provided when the work actually commenced.

It was during the exhaustive discussion on what each lady would consent to bring on the days chosen for the rebuilding that Lieutenant Weston lost patience. "You people are impossible!" he announced, his face flushed.

The vicar looked at him innocently. "Why, my dear man, whatever do you mean?"

"You argue about the merest trifles! What does it matter if two women bake the same kind of biscuits? Food is food!"

"I can see you are a man of limited taste," said Mistress Thompson, who happened to be the sister-in-law of the smith's wife's cousin. She was also the individual who had protested that they could not allow each and every woman to bring whatever foodstuffs she chose, or there would not be a healthy balance for the men laboring to rebuild the forge. She drew herself to her full height, a mere five foot two of imposing feminine outrage. "You clearly do not have an understanding of what is needed to keep men working willingly and well. And you call yourself an officer! You should be ashamed of yourself! Soldiers, like any other men, will work harder and go greater distances if they have a belly full of good, nutritious food. You claim to be a leader of men, yet you don't know this! I say again, shame!"

"Now see here—" the lieutenant began belligerently.

Philip broke in, before Weston could finish. "Lieutenant,

the lady is entitled to her opinion, as are all the good people here. There is no wrongdoing occurring, only a desire to help one of our own. Why don't you take your men and leave? There is no need for you to remain." He looked at Mistress Thompson and smiled slightly. "Indeed, I think we may be on this topic for quite some time."

Weston chewed his lip indecisively. Mistress Thompson sniffed triumphantly and continued her pronouncements as if Weston did not exist. Abruptly, the lieutenant motioned for his weary men to lower their swords and leave the church. Without so much as a word of apology, he followed them from the building.

After the troops were gone there was a long silence in the church. One member of the congregation tiptoed to the rear and peered stealthily out the door. He returned a few moments later to report, "They're gone. The lieutenant mounted his men up, every last one of them, and rode off."

There was a collective sigh of relief; then Lord Strathern said, "Good. With your indulgence, Vicar, I propose we get on with the real business of this meeting so that we can conclude it as quickly as possible."

Nodding, the vicar relinquished his place to Strathern.

"Very well. You were all told the purpose of this meeting when you entered the church this morning, so I will waste no further time with long introductions. You all know my son," Lord Strathern indicated Thomas, who was sitting beside Barnabus Wishingham and his wife. "He is here on behalf of the king, to discover if now is a suitable time for His Majesty to attempt a return to England. What say you on this subject?"

"Now is not the time," a voice said. "You've all seen what just happened. We've been harried by those troops since young Leighton arrived in England. How much worse would it be if the king were to land? The Protector is still too strong. We could not win."

"Few are loyal to the Protector anymore!" Cedric Ingram shouted. "I say the king returns! His supporters will flock to his standard the moment he lands on English soil."

"A fine sentiment," the smith said warmly. "And a month ago I would have agreed wholeheartedly with it, but today—" He shook his head. "We've become used to living under the harsh rules that govern our land now. It takes something out of the ordinary to show us just how hard those rules can be. The Lord Protector will not give up his power easily. As loyal as a man might be to the king, he must still look to protecting his own. The late wars taught us that. I say that the king should remain in Europe. Now is not yet the time for him to return."

"One might expect such sentiments from a man of Wishingham's sort," Cedric jeered. "What say the gentler members of the congregation?"

Philip had been debating whether or not to speak. He was torn between his duty and what he perceived was right. The sight of the troops marching up the aisle of the church with swords drawn had shaken him more than he could ever have expected. He was a military man. He had seen atrocities committed and he had watched men die, but he had never been involved in vandalizing a church. Nor had he willingly bullied frightened civilians the way Weston had. When the lieutenant had stared so insultingly at Alysa, Philip had felt the full effect of the impotent fury of the vanquished and all he wanted to do was plant his fist in Weston's smirking face, not once, but a dozen times.

He was certain that the dragoons had been sent to the church because the local spy had informed Osborne that the people of West Easton would be lingering after the morning service in order to discuss the possibility of a Stuart restoration. That narrowed the likelihood of who the spy was considerably, and confirmed what Philip already suspected. But Osborne and his spy had been outwitted once more by the resourceful people of West Easton and the meeting was now taking place. Thomas Leighton, dressed in a worn jerkin and looking nothing like a courtier or the son of one of the local gentry, would hear the opinions of the people of West Easton and be on his way, back to the Low Countries with his hard-won information.

What news would he take back to the Black Boy? The saber-rattling promise that England would rise for her Stuart king? Or a more moderate suggestion that war ought to wait?

Philip did not think that the king could win against the military machine Oliver Cromwell had built to police his country. It still functioned too efficiently, despite the erosions that had been made since Richard Cromwell had taken power. However, an attempted rebellion might be enough to show how brittle the new Lord Protector's hold on power was.

But war had a way of binding men of disparate beliefs together. A rebellion might aid the Protectorate, rather than harming it, and yet another defeat could dishearten the Royalists disastrously. Today, the victim of a cruel policy of repression, Philip realized that he did not want to see the Royalist opposition destroyed forever. "I say Master Wishingham is right. Now is not the time to test the new Lord Protector's strength. It is too close to his accession. The troops are still loyal to the memory of Oliver Cromwell. Give them time to know their new master and the king's return might be easier than you could ever expect."

"You've been out of the country for years, Hampton. What makes you such an expert?" Cedric Ingram demanded, obviously annoyed.

"His brother is an officer in the Lord Protector's cavalry," Lord Strathern remarked mildly. "I think Sir Philip comments are well-taken. Somewhere in our midst is a traitor who has laid information with the Protectorate on more than one occasion. That is bad enough. Even worse is the government's response to that information. It has been quick and thorough and potentially brutal. All that to capture an agent of the king. How much more thorough would they be if it were King Charles himself who was about to set foot in England? No, I too agree that now is not the time. The king must wait a while longer before he attempts to regain his crown."

There was a general muttering that signified agreement. Thomas Leighton stood up. "I want to thank you all for your wise words today," he paused and grinned, "and for the excellent ruse you used on the lieutenant. When he learns that he looked the man he was seeking straight in the eye and never knew he had his quarry within his grasp, he will be furious! Thanks to you, good people, I shall be long gone!"

His sally was greeted with laughter. Thomas bowed and the congregation began to disperse, smiles still on many faces. Philip idly watched Thomas move amongst the crowd, bowing to the gentlemen, clapping the shoulders of those who had helped him, kissing the hands of the ladies.

With luck, Thomas would be gone from here before Osborne knew that he was leaving. Then there would be no reason for Osborne to remain in West Easton. However, with the local Royalist organization intact, it would be in his interest to leave his pair of agents in place to watch over what was happening. That way there would be no need for him to dispose of the local spy and Philip would not be forced to defy him. Philip could remain at Ainslie and get on with his life.

Thomas reached his sister, Alysa, and said something that made her smile in a sad way as he bent down to kiss her cheek.

It looked like a farewell. Philip hoped it was. He did not want Thomas Leighton exposing his identity before he was ready. Alysa Leighton had become the center of his plans for the future. He wasn't sure what he would do if he thought he might lose her.

He hoped he would never have to find out.

The afternoon was much advanced when Philip rode over to Strathern Hall to visit Alysa. When he was announced, the family had just finished eating dinner and were relaxing in the small, shabby parlor as was their custom.

As Philip bowed over her hand, Abigail said mildly, "How pleasant of you to come by, Sir Philip."

Lord Strathern's eyes twinkled as he noted the fine blue silk doublet Philip was wearing. It was a richer garment than the sober brown one he had worn at the church earlier. "I will hazard a guess that you have come to see Alysa, Sir Philip. Am I right?"

Philip had the grace to color. "I am always happy to talk to you, Lord Strathern. In fact, I did want to tell you how pleased I was at the way the meeting was handled today. I was delighted to see Weston thoroughly mislead."

"It is not often that I feel such satisfaction in fooling my fellow man," Strathern mused, "but I do not think there were any in West Easton who were not glad to see the lieutenant completely trounced."

An impatient expression on her face, Prudence nudged Alysa with her elbow. She said fervently, "I was more than happy when the odious lieutenant was forced to leave with his tail between his legs. Did you not feel the same way, Alysa?"

Alysa had been blushing and staring shyly down at her hands, which she clutched together in her lap, from the moment of Philip's arrival. Prudence's unsubtle nudge and her deliberate attempt to bring Alysa into the conversation made Alysa smile and look up at their guest. The expression in her eyes was warm with affection. "Indeed I did. I thought too, Sir Philip, that your remarks in the real meeting were most sensible. I am glad that you were able to be there."

"As to that, I merely spoke my mind," Philip said. He smiled at Alysa and in that moment there only seemed to be the two of them in the room.

Lord Strathern laughed. "Go on, you two. Go out into the ornamental garden and catch the last of the light on this fine day. Tomorrow it may rain."

Alysa shot her father a teasing look as she stood. "You must talk to Master Bailey and find out for certain, Papa."

"There is time enough for that tomorrow, child. Now, go and enjoy yourselves with my blessing."

Alysa cast her father a surprised, but delighted glance. For him to give them permission to be alone together, then to add that the excursion had his blessing, meant that he was open to receiving an offer from Philip for her hand. Trembling slightly, for this was an important step, Alysa allowed Philip to take her arm and guide her from the room.

When they were alone, she found herself feeling shy again, but she hid the emotion beneath the need to give him directions on how to get to the formal garden, which graced the west side of the house.

Once there, it seemed a good idea to open conversation with comments about the garden itself. "When we came to live at Strathern this garden was so overgrown that it gave the property a melancholy air. My stepmama took it upon herself to restore the beds to their former beauty. It has taken several years, but now the garden is a showpiece." Alysa looked up at Philip, a trifle defiantly. "As the rest of the estate soon will be. We Leightons do not easily give in to misfortune."

Philip smiled down at her, the light in his eyes teasing. "A fine recommendation for a lady wife, don't you think, Mistress Alysa?"

She blushed and hastily looked away. Then she laughed. "If the man looking for a wife was a typical Royalist lord who had lost most of his estate to the rapaciousness of the Commonwealth, I think it would be a fine trait to have. If the man were more settled," she cocked her head mischievously as they walked along a gravel pathway, "why, then I think it might make the wife a rifle hard to handle."

"Spirit in a wife adds spice to a marriage," Philip murmured.

The heady excitement that presages a personal success buoyed up Alysa. "Marriage is a serious business, sir. Have you not been told that?"

Philip stopped and drew Alysa to a halt beside him. The late-afternoon sunlight made the blue satin of his doublet gleam and deepened the rich burgundy of Alysa's velvet gown. "Oh, yes, I have been advised of that old homily. I do not believe it though. Not when the two people involved in the match care deeply for each other." His eyes burned into Alysa, telling her without words that what he felt for her was a love as strong and deep as an emotion could be. She swayed toward him, irresistibly drawn by all she knew of him.

He caught her shoulders and drew her snug against him, molding his body to hers and catching her lips in a kiss that confirmed all that Alysa had read in his passionate gaze. Their lips clung together, tasting, savoring, fulfilling, until it seemed that the only response to the fire they had started would be to quench it here in the newly restored formal garden.

The repercussions of such an impetuous deed would be horrendous, however, and although they were both far gone in passion, enough sanity remained for them to end the kiss before all was lost.

"Perhaps your father was wrong to allow us to come out to the garden alone," Philip groaned as he dragged his lips from hers. "You intoxicate me, my lovely lady. When I am with you I want nothing more than to take you in my arms and make you mine."

Still cuddled against him, Alysa promised softly, "I would give myself to you freely, Philip. It is against all I have been taught is right and proper, but when I am with you I forget what I should do and obey my instincts."

"Come," Philip reluctantly drew her away from his body, then tucked her arm through his. "Let us walk and talk of less incendiary things, as your father no doubt expected we would do when he allowed us to come out here alone."

Still full of the heady pleasure, Alysa tossed her head and laughed. "What a wonderful day today has been! It began with our thorough defeat of the odious Roundheads and ended with—" she squeezed his arm "—well, with the opportunity to walk in the sunshine with a handsome, charming man who delights me."

A shudder went through Philip as he forced himself not to respond as he wished to Alysa's saucy comment. Instead, he addressed the first part of her remark. "Lieutenant Weston was indeed mislead, but I pray you, Alysa, don't imagine that he is completely vanquished. The Roundheads know that there is an active Royalist movement here in West Easton and they will not patiently allow you to plot rebellion without repercussion."

Nothing could penetrate the bubble of pleasure that surrounded Alysa at that moment. "Pooh! We have trounced them once; we will do so again." She smiled coaxingly up into Philip's grave features. "But we are worrying over nothing, Philip. The consensus today was that rebellion would not be in the king's best interests and that is what my brother will tell the Sealed Knot and the king, so it is unlikely that the government will have any reason to interfere with us once Thomas is away. Come, sir, do not look so gloomy. I know that England is not as it was when you left it, but it is still a fair land and a better place to live than anywhere on the Continent."

At that, Philip did smile. "Yes, you are right, lovely Alysa. And I am glad to be living at Ainslie." He drew her to a stop and reached out to gently stroke her hair. "Had I not returned to Ainslie I would never have met you and I do not think I could bear that."

Alysa's breath caught. His words flowed like honey, sweet and silken, while his eyes once again burned with promise. She swayed toward him and he grasped her waist.

"You are so tiny, my hands can span your width," he marveled. "Yet you are strong enough to control a powerful horse. Fragile and resilient in one. You fascinate me, Alysa Leighton. Come to me."

Willingly Alysa lifted her hands to his shoulders and eased her body against his. The passion that had been cut short earlier blazed forth again, hotter than before. He dipped his head and Alysa tilted her chin up so that their lips met and clung. As their tongues touched and mated, desire bathed her in its golden spell. Her fingers tightened on his shoulders, for her knees were swiftly losing strength. She was dependent on him to keep her safe, but her heart knew that he would. Above all, she trusted him to do what was right for both of them. And if that went beyond the bounds of convention, Alysa didn't care. She was so lost in the magnificent feelings his touch aroused that she did not hear the crunch of boots on gravel. Nor did Philip at first, but as the footsteps came closer he wrenched himself away from her.

"Damn!" She looked up at him through dazed, hurt eyes. "Listen, Alysa. Someone is coming. Put your arm through mine and walk with me. Do you understand?"

She obediently did as she was told, but she shook her head.

Philip sighed, touched her cheek fleetingly and whispered, "For myself, I do not care if we are seen in each other's arms, for I am not ashamed of what I feel for you, lovely Alysa. But I would not for the world have you subjected to the unpleasantness that would occur if we were caught in an embrace. So walk with me now and pretend that we have been chatting as carelessly as old friends who have not seen each other in years."

His explanation revived Alysa and she was able to laugh softly. "The feelings that fly between us cannot be masked by light conversation, dear sir, but I will try. Who is it who is following us? Do you know?"

Philip shook his head. "Your father, perhaps, or a servant."

He was wrong. It was Cedric Ingram whose boots crunched loudly on the gravel path. Though he was dressed with his usual sumptuous glory, in Alysa's eyes his gaudy green doublet and breeches with golden ribbon loops and rosettes could not hold a candle to the elegant blue doublet and black breeches that Philip was wearing.

As he drew near, Cedric glowered at the picture Alysa and Philip made, standing close together and intimate in a way only a man and woman with an understanding could be. His expression darkened further as he neared and when he spoke his voice was shrill with agitation. "I was told you were out here, Mistress Alysa. I could not believe my ears when Strathern informed me he had permitted you to walk alone with Sir Philip. Come, I will take you back to the house." He held out his arm, expectation writ large on his face.

Alysa didn't move. She shot Philip a mischievous look, but when she turned to Cedric her expression was grave. "Sir Philip and I were having a pleasant conversation, Master Ingram. You are welcome to join us, but we are not yet ready to return to the house."

Ingram's eyes narrowed ominously. "Mistress, we have an

understanding. You are duty bound to obey me."

Alysa swallowed. She did not want to have a bitter falling out with Cedric Ingram, but she could not allow him to go on believing that he merely had to ask for her hand for it to be bestowed upon him. "I am not, Master Ingram. Though you have assumed these many months that we would one day be betrothed, no promises have ever been made, by my father or by me."

She lifted her head proudly, tilting her chin with an oddly vulnerable defiance. "My father gave his permission for Sir Philip to walk in the garden with me and I am not ready to return as yet."

"And when she does return to the house I will take her," Philip added. His voice was a low, dangerous growl that Cedric could not help but understand.

He colored furiously. "I cannot believe that I am hearing this! That you would prefer this stranger to me is unimaginable. Why, he could be the spy who has been plaguing us, yet you take him into your confidence with the blind trust of a child!"

"And why not?" Alysa demanded, furious. "Sir Philip cannot be the spy, Cedric, because he was not privy to all of the information that was given to the Roundheads. Moreover, he has told me of himself and I believe him. Yes, I do trust him and I will thank you to keep your vile comments to yourself!"

"Alysa," Philip said very gently. "I thank you, dear lady, for your passionate defense of me, but I would much prefer to deal with Master Ingram myself." His cold eyes bored into Cedric's. "I believe we have a score to settle, Ingram. Let us discharge it tomorrow at dawn."

A light flickered in Cedric's eyes, then was quickly hidden. "Preposterous! You expect me to duel with you over a woman who has the bad taste to prefer you? I think not! I will leave you both here to bill and coo like disgusting peasants. I intend to have a few sharp words with Lord Strathern before I take my leave of Strathern Hall."

Philip watched him leave, his expression hard. "So be it,

Cedric Ingram. We will settle our score another day, you can be sure of that."

Alysa looked up at him, her face grave. "I'm sorry that you were subjected to that unpleasantness, Philip, but I am glad that it is done. I did not want to marry Master Ingram, but I could never bring myself to say so aloud. I feel much better now that it is over."

Philip gently touched her cheek. "Beware of him, Alysa. He did not take your rejection of him easily."

She wrinkled her nose distastefully. "No, he didn't, did he? But what can he do beyond complain to my father?"

"I don't know," Philip said slowly. "But I would put nothing past the man. Nothing at all."

CHAPTER 13

"Thomas leaves in three days." Lord Strathern looked into the dismayed blue eyes of his daughter and sighed. He knew that Alysa had hoped that there would be time for a proper visit with her brother while he was in England, for they had been close since childhood. During Thomas's exile in Europe she had missed him terribly. "Thomas wants to see you before he goes. He will be at the cottage of John Gardner early tomorrow morning. I promised him you would be there."

"I will, Papa," Alysa said fervently, but there was a dark, worried expression in her fine blue eyes. "Papa, is it safe for me to visit Thomas? Since he returned we have discovered that we can no longer trust the people of West Easton. It is a difficult lesson to learn."

Lord Strathern shook his head somberly. "Only one man is guilty of betraying us, Alysa. We cannot condemn all the people of this area because one is a traitor."

"But who is it, Papa?"

"There were very few people who knew that we would be holding our meeting after the church services last Sunday. One of those men betrayed us. I believe I know which one it was, but I will not act until I am sure. Nor will I whisper a name in case I am wrong."

Affectionate pride made Alysa smile for the first time during the conversation. Honorable and just, Lord Strathern would not condemn a man without proper evidence to prove his guilt. "But is Thomas safe, Papa? I don't want to visit him if it puts him in any more danger!"

"Thomas has been taking extra precautions, Alysa, since we realized that the traitor is a person I have long trusted. No one knows where Thomas is, except me, and he moves about frequently, in random patterns. After you meet him tomorrow he will leave Gardner's cottage for another safe haven. Trust me, Alysa. Thomas is as dear to me as he is to you. I would not jeopardize him."

"And the traitor?"

Lord Strathern's voice hardened dangerously. "When Thomas is gone and I am certain, I will act."

Deep in her father's eyes Alysa could see feelings of betrayal and sadness, as well as a ruthless resolution. Unnerved, she dropped her gaze. "Tell Thomas that I will be glad to see him. I too would like to say a proper good-bye."

The next morning dawned wet and gray, excellent weather to keep men abed and to discourage watching eyes. At her father's suggestion, Alysa had donned a heavy black cloak with a roomy hood, which served two purposes. The thick woollen cloth kept the rain from soaking her, but it also served to disguise her familiar blue riding habit and glossy blond hair, for both were well known in the area.

Lord Strathern had dressed with similar circumspection in a dark brown suit covered by a long enveloping cloak that was an uninteresting mud-brown color. His hat was an old one with the feather gone and brim frayed about the edges. Even the horses were unremarkable animals that would not be out of place in any man's stables, a far cry from the highly bred animals Alysa and her father usually rode.

Although it would not be possible to fool anyone who looked closely at the two shabby riders out in the early morning, from a distance a casual observer would not guess that the pair were Lord Strathern and his daughter. The precautions proved unnecessary when there were no chance meetings on the way to the cottage, but the need to present an unremarkable appearance did not end with their arrival there.

Together Alysa and her father entered the small, well-kept cottage. Inside were Thomas and John Gardner, while the rest of the Gardner family waited in the shed behind the house, at Thomas's request. Lord Strathern greeted his son with a gruff good morning and an affectionate clap on the shoulder, but then he deliberately left the cottage with John Gardner. They walked to the shed, Gardner talking earnestly and pointing from time to time, as if he had a complaint about something. From a distance it appeared that he was conversing in an animated way with a friend, nothing more. Alysa and her brother were left alone in the house.

Thomas was oddly reserved as he gave Alysa a quick kiss on the cheek. "I'm glad you came."

The tension in her brother made Alysa draw back and observe him uneasily. He was wearing a jump, a loose jacket favored by the lower orders, made of a coarse fabric over leggings of an equally rough cloth. The tunic hung to mid-thigh and was belted at the waist with a leather thong. Alysa thought that even though he was dressed as one of the common folk, with his long, curling hair tied by a string at his nape, Thomas looked what he was, a well-bred aristocrat. There was an aura of reckless authority about him that could not be denied.

"I wish you did not have to go back," she said at last.

A small smile cracked the grim lines on his face. "I too, little sister. I too. But I made my choice long ago and I do not regret it. I will go back to the Continent this time, but the next—next time I return to England it will be behind my sovereign lord!"

"How can you be so sure, Thomas?"

He strode restlessly across the small room, which was the cottage's living room, dining room and kitchen combined. A small casement window looked out over a tiny flower garden, where daffodils made a bright splash of color in the gray morning. Thomas stared through the opening, his eyes a little misty. "England is changing, Alysa. Ferment is beginning to grow amongst all levels of society. The new Lord Protector is not the man his father was and he will not be able to control the changes that will inevitably come.

People are not yet ready to rise up against Richard Cromwell, but soon they will be." There was a smile on his lips and in his eyes when he turned away from the comfortingly English scene out the window. "And when they do, the king will be ready!"

Caught up in his enthusiasm, Alysa clapped her hands together. "Oh I hope so, Thomas! I truly do."

"In the meantime—" Uncharacteristically, Thomas hesitated. "Alysa, Papa tells me that you are, well, that you would encourage the courtship of Philip Hampton."

The phrasing sounded ominous. Alysa stiffened. "I do not find him unattractive, if that is what you mean, Thomas."

"Take care, Alysa. He is not what he seems."

The words hovered in the air, deadly, vicious words that cut with the ruthlessness of a rapier. Alysa's eyes widened with horror and she drew in her breath with a sharp, hissing sound. "Then he *is* the Roundhead brother!"

Thomas nodded.

"Thomas, why is it you who are telling me this, not Papa?"

"Because Papa does not know—yet. I am going to tell him today, before he leaves here."

Alysa opened her mouth to say something, then shut it again firmly as she considered her brother's motives. "Then you are certain that Philip is not the Royalist brother."

"I met Anthony Hampton many times before he died. Exile was not kind to him. He was bitter about his misfortunes and drank heavily. He resented too that his brother had chosen the parliamentary side. I think it was the estrangement that hurt him the most, for when he was in his cups, he would talk about Philip in a most affectionate way. Indeed, I came to feel I almost knew the man, even though I had never met him." At the stricken look in Alysa's eyes, Thomas concluded gently, "I can assure you, Alysa, the man living at Ainslie Manor is Anthony Hampton's younger brother, Philip Richard Hampton."

The answer was essentially what Alysa expected. She nodded slowly, her eyes fixed on her brother's face. "You must have known that Philip was not what he claimed as soon as Papa mentioned him. Yet you did not tell Papa this. Surely he deserves to know who the spy in our midst is?"

Thomas sighed heavily. "Hampton is not the spy."

Alysa shuddered. "Thank God! When he first arrived, I was suspicious of him, but as I got to know him better—Oh, I don't know! I began to think that he could not be a spy. He is too straightforward, too honest to indulge in that kind of subterfuge!" She took her brother's hands and said urgently, "Thomas, who *is* the traitor?"

He drew a deep breath. "Alysa, if you knew you might inadvertently alert the fellow to the fact that we had guessed his secret. He has no scruples and there is no telling what he will do. For your own good I cannot tell you who it is."

She allowed his hands to drop. With a little sigh she said, "Papa would not tell me either." Tilting her head, she looked up at her brother. "Very well, if Sir Philip is not the spy, why are you warning me against him?"

"Because he is a Roundhead," Thomas said gently. "He is our sworn enemy. And one day, when it is time for the king to return, he will be forced to choose. Could you live with yourself if your husband was an officer in the Roundhead army while your brother and father fought for the king?"

Alysa paled. "A pox on this endless war!" She covered her eyes with her hands. "Oh, Thomas! When will it be over? Must it continue throughout our lives?"

"The war will end when our sovereign lord is safely on his rightful throne once more." Gently, he pried her hands away from her face. "Alysa, look at me. Hampton is just one man. Turn your eyes elsewhere. You are beautiful. You will have no trouble finding a husband among our kind."

"Too late," Alysa said softly, gazing up into her brother's concerned features. Tears shimmered in her lovely blue eyes. "It is too late, Thomas, for I have been foolish enough to give my heart to Sir Philip Hampton." Her lower lip trembled. "Oh, what am I going to do?"

"I don't know," Thomas said somberly.

With a woebegone smile, Alysa removed her hands from

his. The bright future she had envisioned only yesterday now loomed impossibly dark as decisions she didn't want to make hovered over her. Thomas was right. If she married Philip Hampton she might one day find herself on opposing sides with the rest of her family. But if she loved him would that matter? Should it matter?

Above all, Alysa was a realist. She had no doubt that, if Philip were to choose the Roundhead cause over the Royalist one, it would put unendurable strains on their marriage. Perhaps Thomas was right—it would be better to cut her ties to Philip now, before they became so strong that the breaking of them would destroy her.

There was one good side to what she had learned today. At last she could be sure that her instincts were right. Philip Hampton was not the traitor who had betrayed her brother. But if he was not, who was? For the moment the question was of no matter. Thomas would soon be gone and after that her father could deal with the spy in West Easton.

"Thomas, take care," she said softly.

"You too," he replied. He bent to kiss her cheek and Alysa hugged him.

"We will miss you." She wiped a tear from her eye. "Safe journey."

He nodded, then strode from the building. Outside she could hear him talking to their father, then the sound of a horse's hoofbeats as he rode away.

A few minutes later Lord Strathern entered the cottage. "He told you about Hampton?"

"Yes, Papa."

"Alysa, I do not think you should encourage the man any further."

She lifted her head proudly, her eyes flashing. "I am loyal to the king, Papa, and I will not consort with a rebel. Sir Philip will no longer be welcome at Strathern Hall on my account."

A small smile formed on Strathern's lips, but his eyes were sad. "Good."

The approval should have made Alysa feel better, but it did not. Her mouth drooped despondently.

"Come, let us go so that these good people will no longer be in danger from our presence," Lord Strathern said briskly.

Alysa nodded. She had no desire to remain any longer.

"Alysa, Sir Philip is waiting for you downstairs. Aren't you coming down?"

Alysa lifted her brush and calmly pulled it through her long silken tresses. She was dressed in an informal gown of aquamarine silk that was bound at the waist by a darker sash. The garment was meant to be worn only in the intimacy of the family setting, for there was no boning in the bodice and the flowing skirt was not opened to show a petticoat. "No."

Prudence stared at her aghast. "But why not?"

"I have a headache." Alysa stared at her reflection in the glass and was amazed that her inner turmoil was not apparent on her face.

Prudence cocked her head in a puzzled way. "You don't look terribly unwell. Are you sure you don't want to come down, Alysa?"

"Quite certain." She turned to smile at her sister. It was a rather woebegone attempt. "Mama knows how I feel and will explain to Sir Philip."

Prudence sat down on the edge of the daybed set in front of the fireplace. The skirt of her primrose gown fanned out about her in a pool of bright, cheerful color. She frowned. "Alysa, is there something occurring that I don't know about?"

Sighing, Alysa put down the brush then moved to sit beside her sister. Taking Prudence's hands she said gently, "All kinds of things. Even I don't know the half of what is going on."

A glum expression settled on Prudence's features. "Does this mean that you will accept Cedric Ingram's courtship after all?"

Alysa laughed. There were times when Prudence

expressed herself with the straightforward self-interest of a child. "No, Prue, I will not. I told Cedric the other day that I was not bound to him in any way and he became quite perturbed. I do not think he will ask me to marry him now, and even if he did I would refuse him."

Prudence's eyes lit up, but she still appeared puzzled. "I do not understand, but if you are happy with that arrangement, then I shall continue my study of him. But what of Sir Philip?"

Alysa had to turn her face away, to hide the shimmer of tears in her eyes. "I have decided that Sir Philip is not a gentleman I wish to encourage. I will not accept his calls anymore."

"But why? What have you learned of him?"

"Nothing and everything." Alysa was hanging on to her self-control by a mere thread. Much more of Prudence's probing and she would start to shriek. "Prudence, please go. I really do have a headache and I would like to be alone."

With a shrug Prudence complied. Alysa watched her, relieved and dismayed at the same time. Now she could be alone with her thoughts, even though the thoughts were ones she didn't want to have.

It had only been a day ago that Thomas had told her the truth about Philip Hampton, but it seemed like many long, miserable weeks. Her waking hours were spent asking herself what she should do. She brooded over her options, considering which would be best for her family, the people of West Easton and the Royalist cause. She even wondered which would hurt Philip the least. But she never asked which was best for her, for she knew that the only alternative that would keep her from hurt and make her happy would be to spend her life with Philip Hampton and that was no longer possible.

She could cut him off immediately and absolutely, but if she refused to speak to him again, he was bound to find a way to ask why she had changed so in the space of a few days. She did not believe that he would accept a soft answer meant to deflect him from the truth and she feared that with her emotions so close to the surface he would easily realize that her love for him was, to her shame, not diminished at all. Breaking with him was an act of honor, nothing more.

Moreover, there was an additional problem that went beyond Alysa's personal reaction. Philip's courtship of her had become well-known in the neighborhood. A sudden cessation of it would lead to questions and, ultimately, to Philip's true identity. People might also brand him the spy in their ranks. Alysa was loath to subject him to the kind of hostility those assumptions would create.

In the dark reaches of her mind and in the willful comfort of her dreams, Alysa sought refuge from bleak reality by imagining what could happen if she continued to allow Sir Philip to court her.

She had no doubt that what Thomas had told her was true. Philip Hampton was the Roundhead brother. However, she found it difficult to believe that he was still deeply committed to the Protectorate and its causes. Many men had turned their coats throughout the war and after. It was possible that Philip's loyalty to the Lord Protector could be undermined by a clever and determined Royalist wife. When the time came for the king to return she would not expect Philip to fight on the Royalist side. All she would ask was that he remain neutral. It was a tactic that had been successfully used by many of the great Royalist lords to keep what estates remained to them after the execution of the first King Charles.

The difficulty was whether or not Philip could be persuaded to do that.

Alysa didn't think he could, and that was why allowing him to continue his courtship was nothing more than a wish and a dream.

Still, she could not bring herself to make the final break with him. So, she hid in her room and begged her stepmother to extend her excuses. Perhaps tomorrow she would feel stronger. Then she could send word that his attentions were no longer wanted, or she would confront him with his subterfuge.

Tomorrow.

Alysa put her head in her hands and wept.

The Reverend Randolph Graystone, the Vicar of West Easton, was a spare man with a high forehead and deep-set brown eyes that were always compassionate. Well, thought Alysa as she accepted a glass of sweet wine from his wife, almost always. At this moment, as they discussed the invasion of his church the previous Sunday, his eyes were quite ruthlessly cold.

"The man who notified the Protectorate troops that a meeting of Royalist sympathizers was to take place after the service is obviously without scruples," the Reverend Mr. Graystone was saying in outraged tones.

"Obviously," his wife repeated soothingly, offering him a slice of apple cake.

The vicar took it and began to munch. "Excellent, my dear, as always," he said around the crumbs, before continuing his tirade. "To have given away his neighbors and friends in that underhanded manner is despicable."

"Entirely without shame," his wife echoed cheerfully. She offered the cake plate to their guests—Alysa, Prudence and Abigail, Mistress Wishingham and Mistress Thompson. The purpose of the meeting was ostensibly to arrange victuals for the raising of the forge and barn, which was to go ahead as outlined during the false planning session.

"Whoever he was, he certainly did as much good as he did bad by calling in the soldiers. After all, we would not have organized the raising of Master Wishingham's barn so effectively had we not been forced to have a town meeting about it last Sunday," Abigail remarked peaceably. "This really is an excellent apple cake, Mistress Graystone."

"The result may have been good works," the vicar said forcefully, "but the intention remains wicked."

"Granted," said Mistress Wishingham. "But Lady Strathern is right, my husband and I are in Sir Philip's debt, in a way."

"Sir Philip?" Alysa repeated sharply. "Are you suggesting

that Sir Philip Hampton was the one who reported on us?"

"Who else could it be?" Mistress Thompson said reasonably. "You can't believe that it was one of us!"

"It could easily be anyone in the vicinity," Alysa retorted, spots of red flaring in her cheeks at the knowing looks of the ladies.

"I think that Alysa has allowed her emotions to run away with her good sense," Mistress Wishingham whispered in a conspiratorial undertone to Abigail.

Sparks flashed in Alysa's eyes and Prudence hastily jumped in before she could speak. "Mistress Thompson, why do you believe the spy is Sir Philip, beyond the fact that he has only recently come to live at Ainslie Manor?"

"His brother is a Roundhead," the lady said simply.

Abigail shot a quick look at Alysa, then said reasonably, "Many families were torn asunder by conflicting beliefs during the war. What makes you think that Sir Philip, who spent years in exile, would betray other Royalists to the Protectorate?"

"Most likely that was the price he had to pay in order to be allowed to succeed to his property," Mistress Wishingham said tartly. "Ainslie is a rich estate. Any man would sell his soul to get it."

"Sir Philip wouldn't," Alysa said furiously, rising. It didn't matter that Philip had betrayed her trust. Or that he was a Roundhead. He was not the spy and she could not bear to stand by and hear him maligned in this way. "Excuse me, Mama. I cannot stay any longer. Mistress Graystone, I will be pleased to help wherever my services are needed. Good day to you and to the Reverend Mr. Graystone." She left the room, her steps sharp and hurried.

Outside the vicarage, she stopped to take a breath of fresh air. The conversation made her realize that she could not simply cut Philip cold without explanation. She would have to confront him and explain why their relationship must not continue any further. Then they could meet as friends and avoid the tittle-tattle that would surely occur if she were to refuse to speak to him.

She went round the side of the house to the paddock at the back, where her horse was tied. There she was joined by Prudence, whose expression was that of a truant who had just escaped and was free at last.

"Mama said I should join you, so that you would not be riding home alone. I thought that was an excellent idea. I was falling asleep in there." Her eyes sparkled as a servant tossed her up into the saddle and an irrepressible grin curled her lips. "I think Mama felt I should leave because all of the old tabbies had begun to speculate on your relationship with Sir Philip. It isn't the kind of conversation she likes me to hear."

Alysa had to laugh, even though she was feeling rather low now that the righteous anger had left her. "There is no relationship. I hope Mama convinces them of that."

Prudence shot her a disbelieving look just before she kicked her horse into motion. "Come on. We have the whole afternoon free to do whatever we want. Let's not waste it here worrying about gossiping old hens." Without waiting for Alysa, she trotted her horse out of the yard. Alysa shook her head, but there was a smile in her eyes as she followed her sister at a more decorous pace.

She was about to round the side of the building when she heard Prudence call eagerly, "Master Ingram, how good to see you this afternoon." Alysa emerged onto the street to see Prudence staring crestfallen at the retreating back of Cedric Ingram. He hadn't bothered to respond to her greeting, let alone stop to chat.

"In truth, there are times when that man has the most appalling manners." Alysa stared at Ingram's scarlet-clad back bobbing up and down in a regular motion as his horse trotted down West Easton's main street. At this moment she could happily have strangled him for his rudeness to her sister.

"Alysa," Prudence said slowly. "I'm going after him."

Alysa stared at her, aghast. "Prudence, why?"

Prudence's eyes were sparkling with curiosity and determination. "Alysa, he was so deep in thought, he didn't even see me. You know how I have been trying to discover what is dear to his heart so that I can prove to him how much I care. Nothing I have found out so far seems to be of importance. But today—why today he was so serious I think he may just be on his way to whatever or wherever it is that is important to him." She urged her horse forward. "I must go, surely you can see that."

Alysa had to kick her mount into a trot to keep up with Prudence. "Sister, I don't think this is wise."

Prudence shrugged and shot her a look that said wisdom was not on her mind at the moment.

Alysa tried again. "What if he is on his way to a place where a woman cannot follow?"

"Do you mean a cockfight or a bullbaiting or some entertainment of that sort? At least then I will know where he has gone! Alysa, I cannot allow this opportunity to slip past me!"

"Then I shall come along."

"No!" Prudence slowed her horse to a walk. Ingram's form was still visible in the distance, bobbing along at a steady trot. "Alysa, if for any reason he stops and sees me, I will be able to talk to him. But if you are there he will have eyes only for you and he will ignore me. I might lose my chance to show him just how much I care for him."

Alysa felt gloomier than she had when she emerged from the vicarage, for she believed that nothing Prudence could do would arouse Cedric Ingram's interest in her. She knew Prudence would never accept this fact, however. Troubled, she gazed at Ingram's insignificant figure ahead of them. Surely he would not go far. "Very well. Follow the man, but take care, Prudence! A lady alone is fair game. Do not track Master Ingram if he goes too far from town."

"I won't," Prudence promised, smiling fiercely at Alysa.

"I have some shopping to do. Meet me back here in an hour." Alysa made the words an order, hoping her sister would obey.

"I will, if an hour is enough," Prudence said irrepressibly, digging her heels into her horse's side. She looked over her shoulder, her eyes sparkling, as she cantered away. "Wish me luck, Alysa!"

Alysa watched her go with some foreboding.

When Prudence did not return in an hour she wasn't sure what to do. Her shopping had been taken care of and she had no more reason to remain in the village. Reluctantly, she returned home to Strathern Hall.

CHAPTER 14

As Cedric drew farther and farther away from the village, Prudence began to wonder if she had been a bit precipitous in her decision to follow him. At the same time, her curiosity was running rampant. Was Alysa right? Was Cedric going to a clandestine activity such as a cockfight?

For some reason, the idea of a cockfight being staged in broad daylight seemed unrealistic to Prudence, and since she couldn't think of any other nefarious event for Cedric to be attending, she continued to follow along behind him at a discrete distance.

When the village was behind him Cedric slowed his horse to a leisurely walk, then, to Prudence's surprise, plunged into the dense undergrowth that bordered the road. Prudence dug her heels into the flanks of her mount, to hurry the beast to the spot where Cedric had disappeared. She had been traveling far enough behind so that Cedric wouldn't particularly notice her, unless he happened to deliberately turn in his saddle, but the distance between them now seemed to yawn wider and she was afraid of losing him completely. As she neared the spot where he had entered the trees, she realized that the road forked and that Cedric had turned into a narrow path that led deeper into the thick forest. Undeterred by the atmosphere of peril, Prudence followed the man of her heart into the woods.

Tall trees bordered the path and their branches, high

overhead, reduced the daylight to dusk dimness. Thick bushes fringed the rutted roadway and in places the branches were scarred with marks of fresh cutting, while withered fronds lay on the ground, further evidence that the road had recently been widened. None of the twists and turns of this little-used route had been straightened out, however, and there were several times when Prudence thought she had lost Cedric. She kept her spirits up by telling herself that there was nowhere for him to have turned off.

Then she came upon the inn.

The place was old and decrepit. Built in ages past and added on to by successive generations, it was an establishment that had fallen upon hard times since the Civil War had shattered the fabric of English society. Prudence only vaguely knew of its existence, for it had a reputation as a place where men came to do things that a lady, especially a young lady, shouldn't know about.

Pausing in the shelter of the trees to figure out what she should do next, Prudence told herself that she was mistaken. Cedric Ingram hadn't come to this dismal place. Somehow she had lost him in the woods. He had gone on to another destination, while she continued blithely along without realizing that she had missed him. Then she noticed that the handsome bay stallion he had been riding was standing in the courtyard of the inn, being held by an ostler, as if Cedric had thrust the reins into the man's hands as he strode impatiently into the building.

The dismay that filled Prudence as she identified the horse rapidly turned to panic as she saw a man in the bloody-red coat of one of Cromwell's Ironsides saunter from one of the outbuildings. His pace picked up as he noticed the ostler and changed direction so that they would meet.

Cedric was in danger! Prudence almost galloped her horse into the courtyard in order to create a diversion and warn him that he should depart immediately, before the redcoats found him there. Before she had moved, however, the crisis was over. The soldier said something to the servant, making him laugh; then the two settled into the comfortable lounging positions of people indulging in a good gossip. Evidently, the trooper was known to the ostler and well liked.

Dazedly Prudence watched the scene as she tried to figure out what she should do. Her beloved Cedric was inside the inn, doing who knew what, while outside was one of the dragoons who were terrorizing the area. Although Cedric had done nothing wrong, Prudence remembered another time when he had been out riding and had been accosted by the troopers. That day it had taken him over an hour to talk his way out of danger. Today it might take him as long. Or even worse, he might not be able to convince them that he was not someone who should be arrested.

There was no doubt in Prudence's mind that Cedric was in danger. He was a confirmed Royalist, one of the very people the dragoons had been harassing ever since they had arrived in the area. Should he be caught in a compromising situation he would be vulnerable to whatever pressures they chose to bring to bear on him. The very idea of Cedric Ingram being hurt by the military made Prudence shudder, but she reassured herself that there was only one soldier at the inn and Cedric would not be overpowered by just one man.

That romantic supposition was blasted to pieces by the arrival of another trooper, who spoke to the first one and jerked his thumb in the direction of the inn, as if giving an order. The first man nodded and strode off, leaving the ostler to tend to Cedric's horse. The second soldier watched the servant blandly. Clearly he had no intention of indulging in a quiet chat with an underling.

Prudence gnawed at her lower lip. The presence of two dragoons made her wonder if there were more in the area or at the inn. Whatever he was doing, Cedric must be warned of the danger he was in. But how?

The most sensible thing for Prudence to do would be to retreat down the little path and ride as quickly as possible for Strathern Hall, where she knew she could get help. But that would take an hour or more, and by the time she returned the soldiers could have kidnapped Cedric and taken him anywhere. Clearly it was up to her to rescue him.

Prudence had absolutely no idea how she should go about freeing Cedric, but she had the strength of first love on her side and the brave boldness of the Leighton family to draw upon. Slowly, carefully, so as not to alert the occupants of the inn's yard, she dismounted. Leading her horse deeper into the trees, she tied it securely. She didn't want the animal to wander into the stable area looking for a mouthful of hay and the company of other horses while she was in the middle of her rescue.

She scurried from the trees to the inn as silently as possible. Having safely crossed the open area without being seen, she pressed up against the side of the building, her body shaking and her heart pounding. Drawing a deep, deliberate breath, she paused to decide what she would do next.

She had no idea where in the building Cedric might be. If he was in one of the rooms on the ground floor she would be able to find him and warn him. She refused to believe that he was upstairs, in one of the bedrooms. She could not accept that the man she had fallen so desperately in love with would waste his time with one of the trollops who frequented this place. Stealthy, she began to creep along the perimeter of the structure, hugging the wooden wall as she tried to keep herself as inconspicuous as possible.

The first window she came upon looked into a large and surprisingly clean kitchen. Several servants and a somewhat better-dressed woman, standing with arms akimbo, were in the room. The woman shouted an order, making the harried servants jump into action. Prudence guessed that this must be the innkeeper's wife. A comment about too much meat in the stew drifted out into the fresh morning air, confirming the assumption.

Prudence was about to smile when the woman made a remark that froze her where she stood. "The whole lot will be back in an hour and we're only half done here! Get a move on, or we'll have twenty-five grumpy men complaining about the lack of food."

Prudence's knees buckled and she sank to the ground, her heart beating rapidly. If she interpreted the woman's words correctly, the whole troop of dragoons were staying at this inn. Moreover, they could return at any time. That meant Cedric was in even deeper peril than she had first imagined. The knowledge spurred her into action once again.

Prudence crawled on her hands and knees, so that she would not be seen passing the window by those inside. She bit off an unladylike curse as a sharp stone dug into her knee and at the same time tore her gown. She gritted her teeth and fortified herself with fantasies of Cedric thanking her extravagantly for saving him from the cruel Protectorate soldiers.

On the other side of the window she straightened again. This time she hurried to the next window without the careful stealth she had initially used. Peeking inside she saw an empty room. Impatiently, she scurried to the window beyond. This one opened onto what appeared to be the private apartment of the innkeeper and his wife, for it was a combination bedroom and sitting room that was none too tidy. Like the previous room it too was empty.

Prudence was beginning to get a little desperate. Heedless of the danger of being seen, she ran to the fourth window. This looked in on a room that apparently was an office, for a crude but sizable desk had been set up so that the person working at it faced the doorway to the room, with the window casting a generous light over his shoulder. Opposite the desk was a chair that was equally old and just as roughly constructed.

In this whitewashed room were two men. As Prudence peeked cautiously in the window, her heart began to beat quickly with excitement.

She did not recognize the man sitting with his back to the window, but on the other side of the desk, lolling indulgently in the high-backed chair, was Cedric Ingram. For a second, Prudence assumed that Cedric had been captured and was now being interrogated. Then his voice drifted out to her, the tone contemptuous.

His words shattered the dreams she had harbored for months. "Your men are fools, Osborne! As soon as they left, the subject of rebuilding the smith's forge was abandoned."

Dismayed, Prudence slid down to a crouch as she shook

her head helplessly. She did not want to hear what Cedric was saying.

"Lieutenant Weston could not have known that," a different voice, evidently the man called Osborne, said mildly.

Cedric was not to be put off. "I told you that Thomas Leighton would be there that day, and he was. Leighton could still have been taken into custody whether the discussion at the church was about rebuilding the forge or welcoming the Black Boy back to England. Thomas Leighton is an enemy of the state. Weston didn't need a reason to arrest him!"

"The lieutenant had to know which of the men there was Leighton. How was he to identify him when Leighton wasn't sitting in his family's pew and he was disguised as well?"

"'Od's blood! What did Weston expect? That Leighton would stand up and say, 'How do you do? I'm Thomas Leighton and who might you be?' Don't be absurd, Osborne."

Prudence felt slightly sick. Cedric Ingram was the spy who was selling the secret of her brother's movements to the government. How could this be? Cedric was the man she had decided she would marry. Cedric had been a friend of her father's for years.

As unpalatable as the knowledge was, Prudence was a Leighton and she knew her duty. She must return to Strathern to tell her father all she had discovered. He would want to know who the spy plaguing them was.

In her anxiety to be away she jumped to her feet, forgetting to pay attention to the heavy skirts of her riding habit. She stumbled as the tailing hem tangled between her feet, and in her efforts to right herself, she briefly wavered before the open window.

Osborne's voice said nervously, "What was that? I thought I heard something."

Then Cedric yelled damningly, "There! A woman running for the trees. Quickly!"

Osborne's voice merged with Cedric's as they both shouted, "Guards!"

At that point a chaos of movement broke out as Cedric and Osborne fought to push the casement window completely open and climb out. A half-dozen soldiers appeared around the side of the building, some mounted, some on foot. A horse whinnied as its rider kicked it hard and from within the trees came an answering neigh from Prudence's horse.

Her heart pounding as she raced for safety, Prudence watched with dismay as a soldier rode for the trees and emerged with her mount. Now, even if she reached the woods, she would never be able to get back to Strathern Hall quickly. However, she might just be able to lose her pursuers in the dense underbrush. She doubled her speed, panting with the exertion.

She had almost reached the edge of the forest when she felt a hand grasp her upper arm. Desperately, she tried to shrug off the restraint, but inexorably her captor dragged her to a stop. Turning, she looked up into the cold gray eyes of Cedric Ingram. "Od's blood!" he gasped as the man called Osborne came up beside him. "'Tis Prudence Leighton."

In a frenzy to escape, Prudence fought to free herself from his hold. But Cedric was too strong for her. Moreover, he now had the assistance of Osborne and several troopers. Soon Prudence was subdued, but not cowed.

She glared at Cedric, her eyes snapping with outrage. "Now what do you intend to do, Master Ingram? Betray me as you have my brother?"

Cedric's head snapped back as if he had been slapped. "You know?"

"How could you?" she flared. "You claimed to be our friend! You were courting Alysa!"

Cedric sneered, "I still am." His features hardened into the frightening mask of a fanatic. "And I will marry her."

"Not when she learns how you have betrayed our family, Cedric Ingram! She will have no more to do with you than any other person of quality in this area will."

Cedric's eyes glittered with cold brutality. "She will learn nothing until it is too late."

It was at that moment that Prudence began to feel real fear.

CHAPTER 15

Prudence was missed by Abigail that afternoon when Alysa and she met in the family salon to enjoy a few minutes of quiet talk and a cup of herbal tea. "I haven't seen Prudence since I returned from the vicarage. Do you know where she is, Alysa?"

Alysa jumped nervously. Prudence had been in her thoughts ever since she had watched her sister ride gaily after Cedric Ingram's retreating form, but she had not been sure what she should do. On the one hand, she had promised that she would not tell their parents what Prudence was up to, should she be missed for any reason. On the other hand, Alysa couldn't shake the fear that Prudence had gotten herself into trouble. If such was the case, the sooner Alysa told her parents, the sooner Prudence could be rescued.

"Perhaps. That is…. Yes." Relief fought with guilt in Alysa. Relief that the story could finally be told. Guilt at betraying a confidence. Relief that someone else could decide what should be done. Guilt that she had withheld information from her stepmother.

Abigail's expression was mildly amused. "Well, which is it? Yes or no?"

Alysa knitted her fingers together in her lap and wished desperately that Prudence would sail through the door to the room at that very instant. When she did not, an answer became inevitable. "It's not really so bad, you know. What she's doing, I mean."

The amusement fled from Abigail's features. Imperceptibly she straightened. "Prudence is up to something she thinks I should not know about."

It was a statement of fact, not a question. Alysa took it as such as she nodded agreement.

"What has she done, Alysa?" Abigail's voice was stern.

Alysa knew that tone of old. Through the years Alysa had been the daughter who did the daring, dangerous things and gotten herself into trouble. Abigail had responded with a firm hand, gentling Alysa into a lady, rather than breaking her spirit. Thus, Alysa knew that when Abigail demanded an answer she expected it to be honest and truthful. Alysa could not lie to her now.

Her expression pleading for understanding, Alysa said, "Prudence has been following Cedric Ingram and today—"

"Following Master Ingram? Whatever for?" Abigail interrupted incredulously.

Alysa leaned forward earnestly. "To get to know him, Mama. She believes that if she discovers his interests she will be better able to talk to him, and so to gain his regard."

"Good heavens, wherever did the child acquire such an idea?"

"From you, Mama. You have always told us that gentlemen like to talk about themselves and that we should always ask them questions on the subjects dearest their hearts."

"Dear Lord," Abigail said weakly, "I didn't mean her to take my advice quite so literally."

"No." There wasn't much that Alysa could say at that moment, even though she sympathized with her stepmother.

Abigail shook her head. Her expression was bleak, but she spoke with her usual brisk authority. "Very well, Prudence decided she must learn all she could of Cedric Ingram by following him about. What happened today?"

"He passed by when we came out of the vicarage.

Prudence told me she was going to follow him and perhaps speak to him. She rode off after him. He was just beyond the village when I last saw him. Prudence was some distance behind him."

"She had not reached him? They were not conversing?"

Alysa shook her head.

Abigail nodded decisively and reached for the bell to summon a servant. "We must notify your father and then we will go over to Ingram Abbey. If Cedric Ingram did speak to Prudence he may know her current whereabouts."

When Lord Strathern was apprised of the situation his expression darkened angrily. "She rode after Cedric Ingram, you say, Alysa?"

Alysa nodded apprehensively. Her father's expression was forbidding enough to make the stoutest heart quail and Alysa was already so consumed by guilt that she began to fear that Prudence was in real danger.

"We will have to speak to Ingram, but I do not have much hope of learning anything positive from him."

Lord Strathern's voice was grim. Alysa hastened to reassure him. "Papa, I am sure Master Ingram must have seen her and even talked to her. Prudence was so determined to find out his secrets that I doubt she was willing to remain in the shadows."

The grimness deepened on Strathern's face. "Cedric Ingram is unlikely to give us the help we need, but we must begin by talking to him."

An hour later, when the Leighton family was seated in a recently redecorated parlor in Ingram Abbey, Cedric Ingram was ruefully dismayed and very apologetic. He had not seen Prudence that day at all.

"I cannot think where she might have gone," he said earnestly to Lord Strathern. "When I left the village, I returned to my lands and stopped by one of my tenant's cottages. The poor fellow broke his leg two weeks ago and I have been checking up on him regularly to be sure his family is not wanting. After that, I rode back to the abbey. I did not see Mistress Prudence at all."

Something in what he said struck Alysa as being false, but at that moment she could not identify it. She frowned and Cedric immediately hastened to reassure her.

"I promise you, Mistress Alysa, if I knew where your sister was I would be delighted to tell you. Indeed, I wish I did know so that I could chase the concern from your lovely blue eyes and see it replaced with pleasure."

After their last meeting, when she had told Cedric that she would never marry him, the flowery promise sat ill with Alysa. As she considered how to respond, she forgot the question that had been puzzling her. "You are very kind sir, but when I last saw Prudence she was determined to speak to you. I cannot understand why she would have allowed herself to be diverted from her project."

"Perhaps her horse threw a shoe. Or perhaps she saw a friend and decided a quiet gossip would be much more entertaining than chasing me. I cannot think why she would be so intent on speaking to me in any case."

Alysa looked uncomfortably at Abigail. If it was true that Cedric Ingram had not spoken to Prudence that day, she did not think it fair to her sister to give away the secret of her infatuation.

Abigail interpreted Alysa's dismayed glance and quickly improvised an answer. "We had been at a meeting at the vicarage, discussing what was to be done to arrange for the rebuilding of Master Wishingham's forge. She must have thought you would wish to be involved in the preparations and rode after you to mention it to you."

Cedric seemed to accept this. "Of course. Mistress Prudence is such a compassionate young lady I should have expected something of the sort from her."

Again Alysa felt his remark grate against her sensibilities. Something was definitely not right here. Cedric Ingram had never before expressed such a positive attitude toward Prudence. Most of the time he seemed unaware that she existed, and when she forced her presence upon him, he acted as if she were an annoying insect to be swatted away.

Lord Strathern was looking grimmer by the minute. He put

his hands on his knees in a gesture of frustration and stared at Cedric with hard eyes. "My daughter is missing and the last time she was seen she was following you, Ingram. I cannot take this information lightly."

Cedric bristled. "What are you saying, Strathern? Are you implying that I had something to do with Mistress Prudence's disappearance?"

Strathern's expression didn't change. "Did you?"

Cedric jumped up from his chair in a fine display of cavalier temperament. "I cannot believe that you would say such a thing to me!"

"Is it true?" Strathern growled.

"I must ask you to leave this house at once!" Cedric pointed dramatically to the door. "When your daughter returns home with a dirty riding habit after taking a tumble from her horse, or chagrined because she stopped to gossip with some other female and forgot the time, I shall expect an apology, Strathern!"

Lord Strathern stood, indicating to his family that they should do the same. "I will be happy to apologize, Ingram, if Prudence has, as you say, already returned home. Otherwise...." He let the words hang in the air for several long seconds. "I look after my own, Ingram. Remember that."

Outside the abbey they paused on the steps as the carriage was brought round, along with Lord Strathern's horse.

"What are we going to do, Papa?" Alysa asked anxiously. Responsibility for this whole mess weighed heavily on her. If she had refused to allow Prudence to chase after Cedric Ingram, her sister would be home safe now. Moreover, the rift between her father and Ingram would never have occurred had she not denied Cedric's right to court her and then let this latest problem arise. Until now the two men had worked so closely together it seemed impossible that they should be enemies.

"You and Abigail will return to Strathern Hall in case Prudence does return. I am going to go to the village to see if I can learn anything further."

There was a bleak look on Strathern's face that said much more than the words he was speaking. He didn't think Prudence would return home on her own, anymore than he would find out her whereabouts by asking about the town. But something had to be done. A start had to be made somewhere.

Abigail nodded acquiescence as the carriage arrived. After seeing the ladies into the vehicle, Lord Strathern mounted up and rode off. Abigail and Alysa watched him go with troubled eyes. As the carriage gained momentum, Alysa said diffidently, "Mama, would you mind if I did as Papa is doing? Go to speak to certain people, that is?"

"If it helps find Prudence, do whatever you like," Abigail said, her voice shaking.

Alysa nodded. She knew what she must do.

Philip had no idea of the events that were rocking the Leighton family. He had spent the day with one of his tenants, helping to repair a barn with a badly leaking roof. He knew that his uncle would never have stooped to such manual labor, or his father for that matter, but times had changed. Ainslie and the people who farmed it were his responsibility now and he would deal with problems as he saw fit. His years in the army had taught him that the lower orders respected an officer who was tough, brutal and distant, but they gave their hearts and loyalty to one who demanded much, but gave more. He planned to manage Ainslie and his tenants in just that manner.

Now he was comfortably ensconced in front of the fire, casually dressed in black breeches and a fine lawn shirt, browsing though a book from his uncle's extensive library. He remembered his father saying that Richard Hampton had been obsessed with books. The collection that Philip had inherited seemed to bear that comment out.

He was a bit surprised when Ashton, his butler, opened the door to announce that Mistress Alysa Leighton had called, but he was even more surprised when the lady did not wait to be properly announced by Ashton, but stalked in even as he spoke her name. She was dressed in the dark blue riding habit that suited her so well and the strands of her hair that had escaped from beneath her broad-brimmed hat told him that she had ridden to Ainslie at an indecorously swift pace. The loose, tousled hair clustered around her face in a wild, wanton way that bewitched Philip. Slowly he closed the book in his hands.

Deliberately, he kept his eyes hooded, his features expressionless. "Do sit down, Mistress Leighton."

Alysa shook her head. There was a peculiar expression on her face, as if seeing him had freshened an old wound. When she spoke, her tone was sharp with desperation. "No, thank you. Philip, I need answers. Now."

Something in her eyes and voice warned him that all was not as he would wish it to be. He raised one eyebrow inquiringly and kept his tone light. "What makes you think I have the answers you seek?"

Her lovely mouth tightened into an angry line. "Because you do. Philip, I know who you are!"

A muscle flickered in his cheek, but that was the only evidence that her remark had hit home. "Indeed. And who am I, pray tell?"

"The Roundhead brother." She said the words flatly, watching him with a kind of despairing hope.

Philip sucked in his breath, but he did not deny the accusation. There was no point. Alysa had not asked a question; she had made a statement. "How did you find out?"

"My brother told me."

Philip nodded, for the information fit. He wondered who else Thomas Leighton had told. "Is that why you refused to see me the other day?"

She shuddered, but she kept her head high and met his gaze squarely. "I could not decide what to do. My heart told me it did not matter which side you followed during the war, but my head said that I must not consort with a rebel."

"Your head and other members of your family," Philip said roughly.

"It is true that my father and stepmother know who you are, but—"

"And the amorous Cedric Ingram?"

Alysa was surprised by that, but he saw her eyes kindle as she responded to the inadvertent jealousy he had allowed to creep into his voice. "Heavens, no! At least, I don't think so. Thomas told me and later Papa, but he said nothing about discussing you with Master Ingram and I am sure Papa has not done so."

Philip drew a deep breath. "Why are you here?"

"Because…I need your help."

A bitter irony twisted his mouth. "The help of a Roundhead?"

"I think," Alysa said softly, "that a Roundhead is the only one who can solve this puzzle." Her eyes pleaded with him, begging him not to reject her out of hand. Philip was not immune.

He dropped the book on a table beside his chair. "Why? What has happened?"

Alysa put her hand on his arm. The touch of her skin burned through the thin lawn of his shirt. He could feel her desperation in the clutch of her fingers and knew that she was frightened and vulnerable.

She said in a shaky voice, "Prudence has disappeared and it is all my fault!"

Responding to her despair, he caught her hands in his and squeezed them reassuringly. "Hold a moment. What do you mean, Prudence has disappeared?"

"Exactly that! She went riding off after Cedric Ingram this morning and has not returned. Nor has Cedric seen or spoken to her. Philip," she said anxiously, "With soldiers in the area I am so afraid! What if a group of them found Prudence alone and unprotected and fell upon her? She could be lying somewhere unbearably hurt or even…even dead!" Her hands trembled in his. "You know these people. You are a man of the Protectorate. You can find out if any of them have seen Prudence or…." Tears started in her eyes and she couldn't go on.

Philip gently pressed her into the chair, then crouched down beside her. "At one time I would have boasted to you that your sister would never be molested by Protectorate troops, but an army is only as good as the officers who lead it and I must admit that discipline in this troop is very lax. I promised Lieutenant Weston that he would have me to deal with should he allow his men to harm any of the people of this area and so he shall. But first we must discover if Prudence has been harmed, or if she has been captured."

Alysa rubbed at her damp eyes and sniffed. In the past Philip had observed Royalist ladies shedding copious tears while they judiciously batted long, wet eyelashes at the man they had decided to twist into doing their wishes. More than once he had been the recipient of behaviour of that sort and he had been immune to the woman's wiles, but Alysa's defiant yet very vulnerable sniff overwhelmed him with a sudden protective urge. Smiling with a whimsical tenderness, Philip handed her a handkerchief, and when she returned his smile with one of her own, his heart leapt.

"Who would have captured Prudence? And why?" she asked, kneading the fine linen handkerchief into a knotted ball.

Drawing a deep breath, Philip made a decision. Once he had given his loyalties freely to Oliver Cromwell, but the Lord Protector was dead and the nation was fragmenting under the rough care of men like Sir Edgar Osborne. Loyalty, he knew, was a precious commodity that had to be earned. It was time for him to place his where it belonged— with the lady he loved and her family.

"Alysa, I am not what you think. It is true I am the Roundhead brother, but I was not allowed to inherit Ainslie freely. I was sent here to spy on the people of West Easton, on your family particularly."

There was no surprise in Alysa's eyes. Philip could not even read disappointment there.

"At first I did wonder," she said, "but I could not believe that you would do the underhanded tricks that the spy in our midst has done." She watched him steadily. "As I have come to know you, I realized that you are a man of honor, whatever your political beliefs. You would not betray those you called friends."

Philip's expression was serious, despairing. "I thank you for your faith in me, Alysa, but—"

"Did you notify the authorities of the day and time of my brother's arrival?"

"No."

"Did you set fire to the smith's forge and barn?"

A small smile cracked Philip's set features. "No."

"Did you suggest that the troops should intrude on our Sunday worship in the hope of capturing my brother?"

The smile hardened and died. "No."

"Then you are not guilty of the crimes that have been committed against my family and the people of West Easton." She stretched out her hand, reaching for him. "Philip, forget why you came to Ainslie. Remember only that you are innocent of the crimes that have plagued this area. Help me now to find my sister."

"Alysa, I may not have done those things, but I am a spy. I report to a man called Osborne who is staying at an old inn some distance from the village. This is also where the troops are stationed. The last time I saw Osborne, he admitted to me that he was receiving information from someone else, a man who has lived in this area for a long time and who is trusted by the Royalists." He hesitated, unsure how she would react when he told her who he believed the spy really was. "I think that man is Cedric Ingram."

Alysa gasped and sat bolt upright. "Cedric Ingram! But that cannot be! Why, we have known him for years. His family is connected to the most ardent Royalist families in the realm! His position is beyond censure."

"Exactly. But remember, he is not the owner of Ingram Abbey, he only manages it for his brother, the Earl of Easton, who is in exile. Should Charles Stuart be reinstated to his throne, the earl would return and Cedric would lose his power, his position and his income. All are persuasive reasons to pretend to support a cause, while at the same time to work against its success." Philip watched while Alysa considered that. When her eyes clouded he knew that he had made his point.

"Then, if Master Ingram is the spy, he could well have been lying to us when we spoke to him this afternoon," she said slowly, thinking things through.

Philip stood. "He undoubtedly was."

Alysa stared ahead of her, her eyes focused inward as she remembered the conversation at Ingram Abbey. "There were several things he said that struck me as odd at the time. I did wonder, but—" She shrugged and looked at Philip, her expression baffled. "He is my father's friend! How could he consider putting Prudence in danger?"

Philip's mouth twisted. "He is a desperate man, grabbing whatever opportunity arises. Think, Alysa! If the Lord Protector continues in power Ingram has proved that he is worthy of reward. If the king regains his throne, Ingram will claim he has been loyal through the hardest of years. His statement would have the backing of your father and, through him, members of the Sealed Knot. Cedric would become a man of influence in the new government. Either way he wins."

Alysa's eyes began to sparkle with outrage. She stood up and started to pace impatiently. "What you are suggesting is abominable! Philip, we must thwart him as well as find Prudence." She stopped, all business now. "Have you any suggestions?"

The abrupt change from a frightened, vulnerable woman to a decisive Amazon was so typical of his Alysa that Philip almost laughed. Instead he tamed the inappropriate pleasure surging through him and concentrated on the problem at hand. "If Ingram captured Prudence he would not be such a fool as to keep her at his house. He would hide her elsewhere. Osborne would also be involved. Even if Prudence didn't know of his existence, he would consider her to be an first-rate tool for bargaining."

"What do you mean?" She stood tensely, her hands balled into fists at her sides. As Philip strode over to her, she watched him with an alarmed frown in her blue eyes.

He sought to soften the words he had to say by cupping her cheek in his palm. "Your sister would be an excellent hostage to exchange for your brother, Alysa."

Her eyes widened in dismay. "Is that what this is all about? Was Prudence captured so that she could be exchanged for my brother? Did Cedric plan all of this when the soldiers were once again foiled at the church?"

Philip thought about that as he gazed deeply into her lovely eyes. Her suggestion had merit, but from what he had learned, Prudence's disappearance seemed to be an act of impulse. "I don't think so. I would guess that Prudence had the misfortune to see Ingram in a compromising position. Once that happened he had to keep her from returning to her family and disclosing what she had seen. Now that she is in their hands, however, she has provided them with an unexpected but excellent counter for your brother."

"What can we do?" Alysa asked, gazing hopefully up into his eyes.

Philip answered with more assurance than he felt. "Find Prudence before any damage is done."

"How?"

She trusted him. Without a shadow of a doubt, Philip read her faith in her eyes. Suddenly anything seemed possible. "We'll start by visiting the inn where Osborne is staying. It is possible that Prudence is being kept there under guard. If she is, it will be no great matter to rescue her."

"And if she is not?"

"Then we must look for her elsewhere." Philip ran his thumb down Alysa's cheek. "Fear not, my lady. Your sister will come to no harm. Nor will your brother."

Alysa caught his hand in hers and turned it over. Softly she kissed his palm. "Thank you, Philip. I knew I could rely on you."

He let his hand rest in hers for what seemed an eternity. From that moment he was committed heart, loyalty and honor to Alysa Leighton.

CHAPTER 16

Darkness was falling as the aged coach that had served old Richard Hampton for most of the days of his life drew up in front of the decrepit inn. Testily, Philip jumped down from the vehicle without waiting for his coachman to come to his assistance. He was dressed in one of his new suits—a short, skimpy doublet of blue silk and black breeches adorned with bunches of blue ribbon loops and rosettes at the knees. Over his shoulders was draped a silk cloak in a blue that matched the doublet and on his head was his wide-brimmed felt hat with the rakish feather.

With his long, curling black hair, he looked very much the aristocratic Cavalier gentleman, and as he spoke to the driver, he assumed the curt, arrogant tone that had given many Royalists a bad name in the past. "Once again your faulty sense of direction has placed my lady and me in an awkward position. You are just fortunate that you were able to find a place for us to stay the night." He sent a brooding look at the old building. "If there is a room to be had. Help my lady from the carriage while I talk to the proprietor of this establishment." He stomped off without waiting for a reply.

The coachman, who had been fully briefed on his part in the action, climbed down from his place on the box, muttering darkly. He was still scowling as he lowered the stairs and helped Alysa down.

On her lovely features was the haughty expression of a gentlewoman pushed to the end of her endurance and she too spoke sharply to the servant. "Pray assume a more pleasing mien, coachman. As my husband said, it is your poor judgment that brought us to this pass." She sniffed and cast a scornful glance around the courtyard. An ostler dressed in a grubby tunic was headed toward them. Deliberately, she raised her voice so the man could not help but hear. "Had you not insisted that you knew a quicker way, we would not have become separated from the coach bearing our trunks and servants. Now we shall have to endure a night in this…this place without the comforts of our own sheets and fresh clothes. I hold you responsible!"

With that she swept away, her full, silken skirts rustling an imposing accompaniment to her feigned annoyance. She was robed much more elegantly than she had been when she rode frantically over to Ainslie Manor, for she had returned to Strathern long enough to change and leave a note for her father explaining the desperate plan she and Philip had embarked upon. Behind her the coachman announced to the ostler that he was a good parliamentary man and shouldn't have to put up with these high and mighty Cavaliers. The ostler nodded agreeably and started to unhitch the horses.

Inside, Philip had taken a quick look around to assure himself that neither Osborne, Cedric Ingram, nor the lieutenant were in the taproom before he shouted lustily for the landlord and demanded accommodations.

The innkeeper was a skinny, harried looking man who was not used to having so much company all at one time. He gaped at Philip and repeated blankly, "A room? A private parlor? For the night?"

Philip raised his eyebrows haughtily. "That is correct, innkeeper. For my wife and me. Do you or do you not have rooms to rent?"

"Aye, we have rooms," the man said hurriedly. "I mean we do rent rooms. But, at this time…you see, we have a troop of cavalry staying here and, well, I hate to say it, but there are no rooms left."

Philip narrowed his eyes. "Do you mean that you would turn me away so that a *soldier* could have a soft bed in a warm room for the night? You would make my lady and me sleep in our carriage in your courtyard so a *soldier* could stay in his warm bed? What kind of nonsense is this?" Philip's voice rose as he spoke and with each increasing note the landlord cringed a little more.

"Your point is well taken, sir," he said hastily, hoping to stem Philip's rising tide of anger. "Perhaps if you returned to West Easton—"

"West Easton? What is that? That tiny village we passed through a few miles back?"

"Aye, sir, it is—"

"Absurd! There is no inn there."

Philip was quite correct; there was no inn in West Easton. The innkeeper rushed in, his tongue tripping over itself as he tried to explain. "No indeed, sir, there is not. But—"

"But what then?"

"Well, sir, there are several fine houses in the area, owned by most respectable people. I am sure any one of those families would be happy to help a traveler in trouble."

"You expect me to go to the home of a stranger, knock on his door and ask for sanctuary for the night?" Philip repeated, aghast.

Put that way the innkeeper could only agree that his suggestion sounded farfetched.

Alysa, who had entered in the middle of this dialogue, pulled off her gloves in a weary way and said in a bored tone, "Simply tell one of the soldiers that he must vacate his room for the night." She looked around the little inn's hallway disdainfully. "I suppose it is too much to hope that it will be possible to arrange for a private parlor as well."

The innkeeper's mouth gaped open.

"Yes, I can see that it would be." She flicked her gloves in Philip's direction. "I shall leave you to make the arrangements, my dear. I shall be in the common room soothing my parched throat." She drifted off, a vision in magenta and white.

Philip stared with amusement at the innkeeper, whose expression said that he had been totally overwhelmed by Alysa's autocratic charm.

"Which soldier should I evict?" the man asked dazedly.

Philip raised his brows again, but the amusement remained in his eyes. "The one with the most comfortable room, innkeeper. Would you expect my wife to accept anything less?"

"That would be Lieutenant Weston," the innkeeper said, musing aloud.

Much as Philip liked the idea of the lieutenant spending a night sleeping in the stables, he did not want the man asking questions and demanding answers, so he pretended to be shocked. "Not an officer! 'Od's blood, even in these times the man might well be a gentleman. Evict one of the rank and file."

The innkeeper looked relieved and said that he would do it immediately. Philip nodded and strolled into the taproom at a leisurely pace.

There he found Alysa seated in one corner, sipping gingerly from a tankard. The loud voices and raucous laughter that had echoed from the room before Alysa entered it were hushed now as the uniformed soldiers seated at several tables silently stared at her, some surreptitiously, some openly. Philip glared at each and every one of them, as furious at this ogling of his lady as any true husband would be. The men responded to his hard, challenging glances by lowering their eyes or turning their faces away. Only one or two continued to look on for a short time after he had silently challenged them. Then even those bold souls quailed under the hot blast of fury that shot from his dark eyes.

"This is ale," Alysa said in a loud, querulous voice as he sat down at the table. "They were able to serve me nothing better. They do not even stock a decent wine here!" She fiddled irritably with the tankard. "Did you make the arrangements for a room?"

He nodded, afraid to say anything lest the laughter in his

voice be audible to their eagerly listening audience.

Alysa's lips tightened, in temper apparently. "Good." She pushed the tankard aside with a disdainful flick of her fingers. "I shall go up immediately. Pray order me a plate of supper and, my dear, do try to wheedle a decent beverage out of the barkeep here. I fear the man is a trifle hard of understanding. Perhaps conversation with another man would help convince him that I *do not* thrive on such coarse beverages as beer or ale!"

Philip lounged in his chair as he watched her sweep from the room; then he lazily called one of the servants to the table and ordered the best meal and bottle of wine the inn was capable of producing to be delivered to their bedchamber. That task done, he returned to his indolent contemplation of the taproom while he consumed his own tankard of ale.

The plan was for Alysa to search the upper floor for Prudence while most of the residents of the inn were out or down in the taproom enjoying a glass of beer or their dinners. Philip would wait in the public room to keep the occupants there from returning to their chambers.

Once she had checked the second floor, Alysa would return to the taproom, announce that the bedchamber they had been given was simply not suitable and insist that they continue on their travels or do as the landlord suggested and return to West Easton to throw themselves on the mercy of the owners of one of the great houses there.

The plan would have worked, except for the inopportune arrival of Cedric Ingram. Philip heard him in the hallway loudly demanding to know if Osborne was in the building. The innkeeper's frightened voice squeaked that Sir Edgar was in his room, but he was not expecting…. Then the sound of footsteps told Philip that Ingram had headed upstairs. Philip downed his ale and rose to his feet, trying not to seem hurried, but desperately afraid that Ingram would run into Alysa in the upstairs hallway. At best this would ruin her reputation. At worst Ingram would have another hostage to exchange for Thomas Leighton.

At the top of the stairs Philip didn't know whether to be relieved or worried when he found the silent hallway empty. He paused, wondering which of the rooms hid Alysa. He was about to go down the passage, trying doors and damning the consequences if he barged in on Osborne and Ingram, when a door at the far end opened a crack and Alysa's blond head peaked out. She saw him and motioned for him to come to her. Philip strode down the hall, relieved beyond measure that she was safe.

"What happened?" she hissed as she closed the door behind him.

"Ingram arrived demanding to see Osborne," Philip said grimly. "The innkeeper sent him upstairs directly."

"He almost caught me." Alysa sighed. "Now what do we do?"

"Stay put for the moment," Philip said after considering their options. "We cannot very well leave until Ingram does."

Alysa looked around the small, spartan room. "No, I suppose not. Very well, let us eat the dinner the landlord will be sending up and see what happens afterward."

There was silence for a space after that. By the standards of Ainslie Manor and Strathern Hall, the room was quite tiny. Of necessity, the furnishings were simple. A wide, plainly made bed was pushed against one wall, with a narrow chest at its foot. A straight-backed chair had been placed by the fireplace, but there was little distance between it and the bed. Alysa had sunk down onto the chair, leaving Philip the option of sitting on the bed or standing.

He eyed the surprisingly clean spread covering the white sheets dubiously, thinking of all the implications of a man and a woman in a small room dominated by a double bed and decided that standing would raise the fewest expectations in his own mind. He wondered if Alysa's thoughts were as outrageous as his and glanced her way.

She was staring into the fireplace, biting her bottom lip. Philip decided she hadn't considered the big bed and all it implied and thought he should be relieved. Insensibly, he was piqued. Perhaps she didn't share the fierce attraction that had drawn him to her against all his beliefs and good sense.

Under the intense scrutiny of his eyes Alysa shivered. The tension in the room tightened. Slowly, almost reluctantly, she lifted her gaze from the safety of the leaping flames and turned her eyes toward Philip. Triumph filled him, for in her eyes he saw a need that could be quenched by him alone. Desire filled the room, warm and enticing.

"Alysa," he said, taking a step toward her.

Her lips parted, but she never made her reply, for there was a knock on the door.

Philip stiffened. Soundlessly he moved to the door easing his sword in its scabbard as he went. Alysa sat immobile, hardly daring to breath. The change, from the heat of passion to the promise of danger, was almost too sudden for her to take in. So she waited silently while Philip eased the door open a crack.

The hesitant voice of the innkeeper made them both wilt with relief. "I brought the food you requested, sir," he said, coming into the room as Philip opened the door wider.

Alysa noticed that Philip was careful to keep away from the opening so that a casual glance would not reveal who was inside.

The innkeeper put the tray onto the chest and looked around the room rather dolefully. "Is there anything else you'd be wanting, sir?"

"No," Philip said. "That will be all for the evening."

The man nodded and began to back out of the room. "Very good, sir. There's a bell by the bed if you change your mind. Good night."

"Good night." Philip closed the door behind him with a snap. He looked at Alysa. "Shall we dine, madam? Such as it is?"

Alysa laughed. "It seems we do not have much choice, sir."

They made no effort to rush the meal, even though the food was not the best. As they ate they talked, not of

Prudence, who had not been in any of the rooms Alysa had checked, but of themselves—their beliefs, their hopes, what they wished for England in the future. In this way they passed a pleasant hour while outside the evening darkened into night.

At last, when the bottle of poor claret had been finished off and the last of the stew and coarse bread had been consumed, Philip said reluctantly, "I'll check the taproom and see if Ingram or Osborne is there. If not, I'll seek out my coachman and pretend to berate him about his poor directional skills. At the same time I'll see if Ingram's horse is still in the stables."

Alysa nodded, but as she watched him head out the door, she said softly, "Be careful, Philip." She wasn't sure whether he heard her or not.

An agony of waiting later, he returned, his expression grim. "Both Ingram and Osborne are in the taproom and look to be making a night of it. We will not be able to leave as we had planned."

Looking at the practical side, Alysa said, "With them both downstairs we will at least be able to check the rest of the inn. Let's do that now, Philip, while we know they are otherwise involved."

Philip nodded. If they found Prudence they would then have to create a new plan of escape. If they did not—well, they would work out that problem as it became necessary.

It was a simple matter to finish checking the rooms on the second floor. None housed Prudence, nor was there evidence that she had ever been held here. Except in Osborne's bedchamber. There, on the floor by the bed, Alysa found a ribbon that she swore belonged to Prudence. Her mind instantly wondered why the hair ribbon would be here, in this particular spot, and her concern for her sister's well-being intensified. But there could be no doubt that Prudence was not in any of the guest rooms of the inn.

By the end of the search, Alysa was desperate. Back in their chamber, she whispered, "Philip, she was here! Where could they have taken her?"

"I don't know," he replied grimly. He was beginning to wonder if Prudence was even alive, but he could not say such a thing to Alysa. She was already frightened enough.

Suddenly, her eyes brightened. "Philip, we haven't checked the other rooms downstairs—the kitchens and the innkeeper's private chambers. Perhaps she is there!"

Philip was loath to extinguish the hope in her eyes, so he said cautiously, "It is possible, but I cannot think of a way to search the back rooms of the inn without arousing suspicion."

"I can!" Laughter sparkled in Alysa's eyes. "I shall go down the back stairs looking for the innkeeper's wife. When I find her I shall plead a headache and demand a tisane of some sort to cure it. With any luck, the poor woman will not be where I first look for her, so I will be able to poke around at my leisure."

"That will still not get us a look into the cellars," Philip pointed out. He added reasonably, "And that is the most likely place for them to hide Prudence, if the landlord is involved in her abduction."

"That is where you come in." Alysa laughed and came to stand beside him. Her vivid blue eyes gazed up into his dark ones, mesmerizing him. Lightly she touched his shoulder. "After I have returned with my tisane, you must go down to the kitchen and demand a decent bottle of brandy from the landlord. Tell him in your most obnoxious manner that you want to see his cellars. I am sure that, if you press hard enough, he will show them to you."

"And if he refuses we can be pretty certain that Prudence is being held down there." Philip looked approvingly at Alysa. Her mouth was only inches from his and the words of praise he'd intended to say were lost as instinct overcame good intentions and he bent to kiss her.

His mouth touched hers, tentatively at first, then more firmly when she didn't pull away. Alysa made a soft sound of pleasure and her eyes drifted shut even as her trembling lips opened under his, allowing him to deepen the kiss. Philip slipped his hands around her waist, gently drawing her against him, letting her feel the proof of his desire.

Feelings Alysa had only experienced with Philip began to intensify as their tongues met and mated in a slow dance as ancient as time. She was beyond thought, beyond fear, for she had long since surrendered herself to Philip's keeping. His kiss was making her body clamor for something more, even as it filled her with a tremendous lethargy. She melted against him, wanting the kiss to never end.

Shakily, Philip pulled away. For a moment he rested his forehead against hers. "We had best find out what we can and make a plan to escape—tonight."

Blushing, Alysa agreed in a whisper. She looked up at him. "Philip?"

He put his finger over her lips. "No, Alysa. Not here. Not like this. I had thought, when this was all over, to speak to your father, but until then—" He drew a deep breath. "Go, and be careful."

Alysa slipped down the back stairs and was able to check the pantry and the kitchens, before she found the innkeeper's wife in her private room. Alysa's quick search told her that Prudence was not there, for these were active, busy places used constantly by servants. She got her tea and crept back up the stairs. It was up to Philip now.

He waited a long, difficult half hour before he tromped down the back stairs on his own quest. He found the landlord easily enough and was able to convince the man to show him the cellars without relying too much on the high-handed theatrics expected of a Cavalier gentleman. The cellars were much as Philip expected them to be—dark, dank and full of articles of all shapes and sizes. The candle the landlord carried made frightening shadows on the walls, distorting the shapes of the goods stored in the oppressive dungeon. Many areas were left in gloom, but Philip doubted that Prudence was being held down there. There was no sound of movement, no muffled or muted cries from someone desperate to escape. There was only silence, broken by the innkeeper's harried description of his meager horde of wine and the clump of their boots on the earthen floor. The poor man did not even protest when Philip grabbed the candle away from him on the pretense of getting a better look at the bottles of wine.

No, Prudence was not in the inn. At least not now.

Then where was she?

Philip couldn't answer that. He still believed that Ingram would not be foolish enough to try to hide her on his own grounds. Nor would Sir Edgar Osborne be willing to stash her away in a place where he had no control of such a prize.

After scorning the innkeeper's selection of wine, Philip angrily stomped up the narrow stairs, then left the inn through the back door, saying that he was going to check to be sure his coachman had seen to the horses properly. A short conference with his servant told him that Prudence was not being held in the stables or outbuildings. Hope began to die in Philip. Where could she be?

He returned to the inn through the main entrance so that he could check the public room before going upstairs. He noted grimly that Ingram and Osborne were still there. Cursing softly, he crept back up the stairs to the little room at the end of the hallway.

"She is not here," he reported baldly. The door was closed behind him and he and Alysa were alone in the room once more. Already tiny, it now felt claustrophobic since the kiss.

Alysa turned away. "What can we do?"

Unbearably touched by her dismay, Philip came up behind her. He took her shoulders in his hands and rubbed them comfortingly. "There is nothing we can do, sweet Alysa. Not tonight. Since Ingram and Osborne are still in the taproom, we cannot escape without danger of being caught ourselves. Although I am of no interest to either man, I fear for your safety should Osborne set eyes on you. With both you and Prudence in his clutches he is sure to have Thomas handed over to him. We must stay here tonight and hope that tomorrow we can leave as any normal traveler would."

She turned in his arms. "But—"

He silenced her protest with a kiss. He knew he was not giving her any chance, that he was not acting the gentleman, but he could not help himself. Her scent was heady in his nostrils, her body warm against his. If she pushed him away, he would not force her, but....

She did not push him away. Instead her hands crept up his body to his shoulders, while her mouth opened and her tongue twined with his.

He heard a low groan from someone and was surprised that it was he who had made it. Alysa clung to him, her fingers digging into his shoulders. At last he eased the pressure of the kiss.

"What did you mean," she asked breathlessly, "when you said you planned to speak to my father?"

Philip touched her lips with his tongue. "I intended to ask him for your hand in marriage."

"Were you going to ask me? Or was my father's consent enough?" She caressed his chin with tiny, featherlight kisses.

Philip laughed. "Would you have said no?"

Yearning was in Alysa's eyes as she looked up into his. She knew what her father's answer would be to a marriage between Sir Philip Hampton and his daughter. It would not be the same answer that Alysa's heart would give. "I would have cried out yes in the loudest voice imaginable. Philip, I am yours. Tonight. Whenever you want me. Take me into the bed we have both been trying to ignore and make me yours. Please."

"Are you sure, my love?" His eyes searched her face, seeking the reason for the desperation he read there.

She smiled. "Yes. I am sure. Tonight, Philip Hampton, in the eyes of those around us we are man and wife." She laughed softly. "And your wife has the reputation of being a demanding shrew, so tonight you must obey, or I shall make your evening so despicably awful—" She squealed as he lifted her off her feet to carry her over to the bed.

There he paused once again, a smile in his dark eyes. "If you are sure."

"I am. Oh, Philip, I am!"

He laid her on the bed, then knelt down beside her. The

bodice of her magenta gown was cut low. A diaphanous scarf modestly covered her throat and was tucked into the neckline above her breasts. Philip plucked it out, then slowly pulled it away.

Alysa shivered voluptuously, then smiled as his lips caressed the flesh he had just exposed. His thick hair brushed her skin as he kissed her. Tenderly, Alysa stroked it back. Philip looked up, a question in his eyes. "You tease me unmercifully, sir," she said huskily.

"This is only the beginning, sweet Alysa." His hand traced the edge of the cloth, from her shoulder all the way down to the place where her breasts rose enticingly from the fabric.

Alysa raised herself on her elbow. "Unlace my bodice, sir, for I cannot do it myself." She bit her lip, wondering if she was being overly bold.

His hands fumbled with the laces that bound the bodice closed and as he worked she reached up to caress his cheek. Philip groaned and worked faster.

At last the laces were undone. Philip slipped the boned garment from her body, then made short work of unfastening her skirt. Alysa rose up to her knees and pushed the bulky material over her hips so that she was dressed only in a loose shift made of a finely woven linen that was so soft and light it was virtually diaphanous. Philip's eyes narrowed; then he drew her against him and kissed her hard. Alysa responded fiercely, hungry for more.

After a moment, Philip pulled away, but only to disrobe himself.

Alysa kicked off the heavy folds of her skirt and watched him with unabashed interest. She wanted Philip and wanted him badly, but the sight of him shedding his clothes with indecent haste created its own kind of pleasure.

When the last of his garments were gone, he smiled at her intense expression. "Do I pass muster, my lady?"

Alysa was more awed by his muscular frame than she had expected. She said on a shaky breath, "Philip, I had no idea! Am I as pleasing to you as you are to me?"

"Oh, yes," he said, coming down beside her on the bed.

She shivered with fear and excitement. His mouth closed over hers, steadying her, filling her with the promise of gentleness and passion to come. His hands strayed over her body, stroking, caressing, easing the shift from her skin.

She hardly knew when that last barrier between them disappeared. She was more than ready for whatever was to come. She trusted Philip and was prepared to give herself to him freely. Her body ached for him, and murmuring softly, she urged him closer.

When he moved atop her, instinct told her that this was what she wanted. She opened her legs to cradle him securely against her and with a little groan he lowered himself upon her.

His entry was a shock that broke through the heady mists of pleasure that held her in thrall, but she trusted him not to hurt her and he did not. He eased himself deeper inside, gently but insistently, until she was full and he was anchored deep. Then he paused, a thumb teasing her hardened nipple, his mouth dropping nibbling kisses at the edge of her lips. "You are mine now, Alysa Leighton. Say it."

"I was yours before, Philip. Yesterday, today and tomorrow." Her body needed to move. She stirred against him and he gasped.

"Yes," he groaned. "Alysa, you are enough to drive a man wild."

Her neck arched and her body twisted, obeying instincts as old as time. She felt as if she was climbing a great peak, slowly, tortuously, each moment an ecstasy of its own, but with the promise of something more still to come. It was that unknown thing that kept eluding her, making her writhe beneath her lover.

She knew what she was seeking when Philip moved within her. A gasp escaped her lips, followed by a little cry of pleasure. As if this was a sign he'd been waiting for, he crushed her mouth beneath his and moved more forcefully inside her.

Pleasurable sensations ripped through Alysa as she surrendered herself to his direction. Together they reached the top of the peak and slowly they slipped gently down the other side.

They lay quietly afterward, neither speaking. Philip stroked Alysa's skin in an absentminded way that she found both endearing and soothing. Gradually, she slipped into sleep.

Awake, Philip knew that he should not have done as he had. Alysa had been a virgin when he'd taken her, as he'd assumed she would be. A young lady of her class and breeding would be expected to be pure when she went to her legitimate husband's bed and Alysa was not one to use illusion to cover truth.

So, knowing that, why had he deliberately taken her tonight?

Because he loved her. Because she was his. Because she would be ruined in the eyes of the world after spending the night alone with him whether something had happened between them or not.

When he had conceived this idea of bringing her to the inn to search for her sister he had not stopped to think what might happen if they were unable to leave as intended. He should have. He had planned enough actions to know that the unexpected was far more likely to occur than whatever had been anticipated.

Yet when the unexpected had happened, he'd taken advantage of it, as any good commander would. After tonight Alysa would be his. Always.

He had read the doubt in her eyes when he had spoken of asking her father for her hand and he'd guessed that Lord Strathern would probably have refused his suit.

Not anymore. As little as her father might like it, Alysa had given herself to Philip. Now they must marry.

It was up to Philip to make certain that when they did Alysa would not be separated from her family as a result of her impetuous actions. He drew her against him so that she was settled more comfortably in the crook of his arm.

There was one way to do that. He could find Prudence Leighton and ensure that Thomas Leighton was safely away about his business for the king.

Philip smiled to himself. A momentous task. One he found he was looking forward to.

He bent and kissed Alysa's lips again. They fluttered beneath his. Satisfied, he deepened the caress at the same time as he began to tease her breast. She stirred, exciting his manhood.

Opening her eyes, she said sleepily, "Philip?"

"Tonight is ours, love," he said huskily. "Let's not waste it."

Alysa looked at him searchingly for a moment; then she laughed softly. Her answer was to slide her arm around his neck and touch his mouth with the tip of her tongue.

The promise of passion to come made Philip groan and draw her close. "My lady," he said, "I am yours."

Alysa sighed with pleasure. "And I am yours. Forever."

CHAPTER 17

Alysa woke to find herself pressed tightly against the length of Philip's long, hard body. She felt wonderful, in a lazy, exhausted sort of way, and she was content to remain snuggled against him while she contemplated the events of the previous day.

When she had gone to Philip, she had not intended to give herself to him, either emotionally or physically, yet she had done both. She had ridden to Ainslie Manor angry and frightened over Prudence's disappearance and certain that Philip knew where Prudence was, or could at least guess her whereabouts. She had not expected that her anger would have as much substance as a puff of smoke in a strong breeze or that she would find herself defending Philip against his criticism of his own actions. Sometime during the last weeks, trust, as well as love, for Philip had crept into her heart, so that when he had suggested that they go to the inn to search for Prudence, she had agreed without so much as a mild objection. Philip would find Prudence. She knew it in her mind, in her soul.

She still believed it now, even though Prudence had not been at the inn and she had just given herself to a man who was not her husband. No matter what his political background, Philip had promised her that he would not let Prudence come to any harm in the political games that were being played in West Easton. Alysa snuggled closer, listening to the steady beat of his heart and inhaling the heady scent of his body. What Philip promised, Philip would make good on. She had his word and that was enough.

A lock of his hair tickled her nose and she burrowed deeper, trying to escape the thick, dark strands. His hair was tousled, as she was sure hers was, and she almost giggled at the thought of how very different they must look right now, compared to their elegant appearance when they arrived at the inn.

Returning to Strathern Hall to change from her riding habit into one of her more fashionable gowns had been a gamble. Alysa had been certain that her stepmother would demand to know what she was doing and where she was going. Instead, Abigail had asked distractedly if Alysa had had any word of Prudence, then ignored her after she had said she had not. Thereafter, escaping from Strathern Hall without either of her parents realizing she was gone had been ridiculously easy. Abigail had hardly noticed her change of clothes and Lord Strathern had come in, announced he had no news, then promptly departed again to return to the search. When Alysa slipped out to meet Philip a short distance from the house, no one had noticed. The family and staff at Strathern Hall were too distracted by Prudence's disappearance and Abigail's distress.

Alysa had expected to return shortly after nightfall. Though she didn't think anyone would worry about her, she had been left a note with her maid, to be given to her parents should they inquire about her whereabouts. The note was damning, for she had been truthful when she composed it, and now, as she lay beside her lover, she could only assume that her father would have read her missive and become furious at her. However, at least he wouldn't be despairing over the loss of both of his daughters.

Alysa gently probed her emotional reaction to the fact that her parents were by now most likely aware of where and with whom she had spent the night. Foremost, she felt relief. Relief that she could now freely admit her love for Philip Hampton and her desire to be married to him. Relief that she need no longer oppose that love with the ideals and beliefs she had held for so long.

Side by side with relief was a gentle melancholy that her love had to be exposed in this sordid way. She knew that her family would do its utmost to keep the news of her indiscretion from spreading, but inevitably it would, which meant that she and Philip would now be expected to wed. As there was nothing more she wanted to do than to marry Philip, this was not the cause of her sadness. Rather, she felt sorry for those who would happily gossip or smile behind their hands, for they would not understand the wonderful feelings that she and Philip had for each other.

Alysa sighed and caressed Philip's shoulder with a feather-light kiss. She was a practical woman who was not going to waste time moaning over what could not be helped. If it took an indiscretion for her to be together with Philip, so be it. She would happily endure the consequences now so that she could enjoy the rest of her life with the man she had fallen so deeply in love with.

None of this had any bearing on finding Prudence. Alysa felt a little guilty that she had spent a night in heaven, while her sister had undoubtedly spent one in hell. She hoped that, wherever Prudence was being kept, she was being treated generously, but with Cedric Ingram involved, Alysa was doubtful.

Under the gentle caress of her lips, Philip stirred. Alysa felt her body respond to his movement and to the prospect of his hungry gaze upon her. Slowly he opened his eyes and at the sight of her he smiled.

"I was afraid that last night was but a dream," he said in a husky voice that sent little ripples of pleasure up and down her spine. "I hesitated to open my eyes in case I found myself in my own bed at Ainslie Manor, alone. Then I felt your softness move against my rough skin and I knew I had not imagined our night together."

Alysa touched his lips lightly with her own. "No dream, dear heart, unless I am dreaming the same dreams you are."

Philip deepened the kiss. "Perhaps you are. Perhaps we are

lost in the sweetness of our own imaginations. I have wanted you for so long, I can hardly believe you are mine."

Alysa gasped and rubbed her hand along his side. "This is real, Philip, believe it. This bed is real, this room is real, the feel of your body against mine is real." She paused, then added softly, "My need for you is real."

He looked at her, a tender, satisfied smile in his eyes. Slowly he lowered his head to catch one of her nipples between his lips and gently suck. Alysa arched against him, her body responding to the promise of passion to come. He growled deep in his throat and gently nibbled the tender flesh. Alysa cried out in surprise, but the sensations were an exquisite pleasure. Philip ran his palm down her taut belly to the heartland of her desire and Alysa melted against him, her body already damp with promise.

His mouth left her nipple and Alysa relaxed a trifle, only to tense again as his fingers toyed with the sensitive bud his teeth had aroused. "Tell me you want me," he demanded huskily.

She laughed. "Philip, I want you. Right now I can think of nothing else but my desire to be joined with you. Oh, yes, I want you!"

Her hand stole down his torso to his engorged manhood. She touched him a little shyly. He had shown her what pleased him last night, but a man's body was still new territory for Alysa. So was pleasuring it. Still, she thought it only fair that she try to give back some of the wonderful sensations he was giving to her.

Philip groaned and took her mouth in a rough kiss that gave no quarter. If Alysa had not already been deep in the throes of her own passion, she might have frozen at the roughness of the embrace, but its hardness only deepened her need to be joined with Philip. Her legs slid open while her fingers tangled in his long hair, keeping his mouth on hers even as he entered her in one ruthless thrust.

As he slid deep within her, Alysa felt herself soar. Her mind cried out with pleasure, even as her body fought and twined with his until they both reached that far place where heaven seemed very real. There they were one and the same, no longer fighting to reach their separate goals, but united in their success.

Philip was panting as he pulled himself off of her. "I didn't mean to be so rough, Alysa. Forgive me."

She nuzzled his neck with lazy enjoyment. "You gave me pleasure the way I needed it. Your touch made me wild for you, dearest heart. There is nothing to forgive."

"Alysa," he groaned, "you are a very special lady. Have I told you yet how very much I love you?"

She laughed softly. "You have now, in words. Last night your body told me in a thousand silent ways. Just as I hope mine told you. I could never have given myself to you so freely, if I had not already loved you, Philip."

He sighed and stroked her cheek. "It will not be easy when we return."

"I know." She smiled, a mischievous look at odds with the gravity of the situation. "I left a note. My father will be seeking your head if he has had time to read it."

"I would gladly face him to settle your future between us, but at the moment I think Prudence's fate is more pressing. Forgive me, Alysa, but I must put off asking for your hand until I have discovered what I can from Osborne. When Prudence is safe I will speak to your father."

"Do whatever you think is best, dearest heart." Alysa's gaze was steady. She refused to accept the common assumption that, having had her body prior to marriage, the man would then scorn the woman. Alysa trusted Philip and knew that he would ensure that all worked out as it should.

He pulled her tightly against him. "Sweet Alysa," he said on a sigh. "You are far too good for me."

Alysa only smiled.

Philip arranged to meet Osborne on the little rise on Ainslie property later that afternoon. Knowing that time was of the essence, he had simply sent one of his servants to the inn with a note and had him wait for a reply. With the time confirmed, Philip was able to secret Alysa at the meeting place well ahead of Osborne's arrival, yet allow the man to appear to reach the site first.

"So," Philip said as he dismounted from his mettlesome black stallion. "You got the jump on me this time."

Osborne's expression was smug. "You must be getting soft, Hampton. Usually it is I who seek the meetings and you who arrive first. What is it that is so important that you must needs send a message to me at the inn?"

Philip's bland expression hid a flood tide of relief. He had been worried that someone might have mentioned to Osborne that he had been at the inn, but he was certain that the man would have alluded to it somehow if he had been aware that Philip had been there with a woman.

His ignorance gave Philip a hard-won sense of advantage. Now was the time to drive hard into his enemy's weak spot. "You seem to be a trifle nervous, Osborne. Have matters begun to slip from your control?" He tied his horse to a tree and casually patted its smooth black neck. He was at pains to appear as if this meeting was of little more concern to him than any other.

Osborne snorted. "Though Thomas Leighton has eluded me so far, I am not without resources. I've a troop of horse to subdue this neighborhood if I must, but I do not think I will be obliged to use them. I have other methods of capturing my quarry."

Philip finished rubbing his horse's neck and turned. "Such as Prudence Leighton."

Interest flickered in Osborne's eyes. "Yes, indeed, but how did you know?" He waved a dismissive hand. "No, let me guess. Strathern must be distraught at his youngest daughter's disappearance. Did he come to you for help? How vastly amusing."

There was no humor in his eyes, or in Philip's, however. "When I agreed to aid you in monitoring the activities of Royalist sympathizers in this area, I did not agree to become involved in the kidnapping of a gentlewoman. Return Prudence Leighton to her family, Osborne. She has no part in this deceit."

"Unfortunately she knows more than she should," Sir Edgar retorted dryly. "Besides, I must use whatever bait is to hand to entice my man into captivity. If it means subjecting a woman to a few days of discomfort—" He shrugged, his meaning perfectly clear.

This was much as Philip had expected. Though he had hoped for an easy victory, he was prepared for a long, hard campaign. His purpose at this meeting was to undermine Osborne's confidence, so he countered with a small shake of his head and a steady, thoughtful reply. "Lord Strathern will not betray his cause by trading his son for his daughter."

Osborne shrugged again, still certain. "Thomas Leighton could feel differently. He might be willing to surrender himself if he believed his sister was in danger."

Philip snorted. "The sister he hardly knows? Prudence was but a child when he went away to war and after that into exile. He is tied more strongly to the Black Boy than he is to his sister."

Doubt appeared on Osborne's face, but it was only momentary. "Idealists like Leighton tend to be a soft lot. Mistress Prudence might not be as close to him as the lady Alysa is, but she is a woman and in danger. Thomas Leighton cannot fail to respond to that."

As Osborne mentioned Alysa's name, a shiver ran down Philip's spine. He suppressed his fear ruthlessly, for he did not want Osborne to attach any more importance to Alysa than necessary. Instead, he acknowledged the truth of Osborne's observation with a nod, then added, "If he hears of it."

"What do you mean?"

It was Philip's turn to shrug casually. "Thomas Leighton is well away from Strathern Hall and has no contact with his family. Unless someone notifies him that his sister is in danger, he will not know. Lord Strathern is not likely to do that, so…."

The doubt in Osborne's eyes turned to dismay. "A pox on the man!" he muttered. "I hadn't thought of that."

"I take it your spy doesn't know Leighton's current whereabouts."

Osborne grimaced. "If he did I wouldn't need to dangle Prudence Leighton as bait."

"It seems," Philip said softly, "that your turncoat is not quite as useful as he first appeared to be."

Osborne grunted with some degree of disgust. "I've no use for men of his sort. None of these self-serving Royalists can be depended on in a pinch."

Philip acknowledged that with a sardonic smile. He allowed himself a moment to wonder if Cedric Ingram was as cold-blooded in his attitude toward Sir Edgar Osborne as Osborne was toward him, and decided he probably was. The two men deserved each other. Once Philip had Prudence Leighton safely out of their clutches he would sever his relationship with Osborne. The knowledge was a relief.

Now though, he had to concentrate on extricating Prudence, preferably without danger to her. "There is a way of getting a message to Thomas Leighton."

Osborne cocked an eyebrow. "Through you?"

Philip nodded.

A calculating look appeared on Osborne's face. "I suppose you were able to romance the details of his whereabouts from Alysa Leighton."

Anger flared in Philip, but he quickly suppressed the emotion. The situation called for cold, hard reason, not hot-tempered passion. If Sir Edgar Osborne wanted to believe that Alysa could be swayed into betraying her brother by a few honeyed words, so be it. "Lord Strathern and his daughter have always been close. He tells her more than most fathers tell their female off-spring."

Osborne nodded, then said briskly, "Very good. Tell me where Leighton is and I will arrest him. When I have him, I will release the girl."

Philip put up a hand and laughed. "Slowly now, Sir Edgar. I said I could get a message to Leighton. I did not say I knew where he had gone to ground."

Osborne cursed. "State what you mean in the future! All right, if that is what it takes, send a message to Leighton.

Tell him to come to the inn and surrender himself. The girl will be sent to her family afterward."

Shaking his head, Philip said scornfully, "Have some sense, Osborne! Thomas Leighton is a courtier-in-exile, not an innocent from the country! He will no more trust your word than you would trust his. He will demand to know that his sister is truly safe before he surrenders himself." Philip paused to allow that to sink in, then pushed his advantage. "Give Prudence Leighton to me. I can assure her brother that she is safe and where she is. If he wants to check on her whereabouts he will find I speak the truth. Then he will be free to surrender himself with good conscience."

Osborne almost accepted Philip's reasoning, but at the last moment he shook his head. "Can't be done. The Leighton girl is presently under the control of my local spy. He would never agree to hand her over to you."

Philip guessed that Cedric Ingram was intent on keeping his identity as a turncoat secret. If he believed that only Prudence and Osborne were aware of it, Prudence's life was forfeit. The time had come for Philip to reveal that he too knew the name of Osborne's other agent. He said in a hard voice, "Ingram need not worry. I have no intention of using Prudence Leighton for anything but the cause we both believe in. Why should he keep her?"

Osborne's eyes widened in surprise, then narrowed ominously. "How did you find out my turncoat's name?"

Philip's mouth twisted contemptuously. "Through reasoning. I worked out who was heavily involved in the Royalist movement, whose background wasn't as pure as it was supposed to be and who was not where he claimed to be at certain times. The person who fit all the categories was Ingram."

"You are brighter than I thought," Osborne replied with a thin smile. "And perhaps more dangerous. Ingram will keep Prudence Leighton until we have her brother fast. I have no control over that."

"Then tell me where he is holding her. Surely you know that much."

"I do, but I am not certain I want the girl in your hands any more than I want her in Ingram's."

Philip set his jaw over an annoyed remark and shrugged instead. "Very well. Capturing Thomas Leighton will not be quite so simple then."

"How so?"

"He will want proof that his sister is safe. What will be needed is an exchange in the open. Would you agree to that?"

After thinking about the suggestion for a moment, Osborne nodded. "I will ensure that Prudence Leighton arrives at the meeting place. You will guarantee that Thomas Leighton will be there?"

"Yes."

"Very well. Where shall this meeting take place?"

Philip had worked out the site ahead of time, just in case he wasn't able to convince Osborne that Prudence should be given into his care. "There is a place called the Fenwick Cliffs. It is an open area, but the ground drops off abruptly one side, while trees cover the other. You can see for miles in all directions, which makes it a good place for what we are planning. I will bring Thomas Leighton there tomorrow at midmorning. Agreed?"

"Agreed." A smile lit up Osborne's face as he reached for his horse. "I shall be glad to be gone from this area and back to London. The comforts of that inn are few and I have come to enjoy the privileges my rank has given me."

Philip didn't reply. He watched with hard eyes while Osborne mounted, then rode away. When he was sure the Londoner was beyond the sound of his voice he said very cautiously, "Alysa?"

She emerged from a thicket deep within the trees. Philip grinned. There were leaves on her riding habit and her hair had been mussed by the touch of the branches. Though her expression was somber, she looked adorable to him.

"Did you hear?"

"Most of it," she said, brushing bits of twigs from the

velvet skirt of her riding habit. She looked up, her eyes searching his face. "Prudence is in very grave danger, isn't she?"

He nodded. "Ingram will not let her live."

She shivered. "Philip, why did you tell Osborne—who is an odious little man, by the way—that you knew that Cedric Ingram was the turncoat?"

He caught her shoulders and rubbed them lightly. "So that Osborne would not go along with Ingram if he demanded Prudence be killed to ensure her silence. Dear lady, above all, Sir Edgar Osborne is a realist. He has no interest in Cedric Ingram beyond his usefulness as an agent. If he finds that Ingram is no longer able to serve him, he will cast him away without compunction. But if he thought Ingram would remain useful after all of this is over, he would not hesitate to allow the most heinous crime to be committed."

She looked up into Philip's eyes, her own miserable. "Do you think he will be able to persuade Cedric that Prudence should be exchanged?"

"Yes. He will bring Prudence to the meeting place." Philip hid the grim remainder of his thought from Alysa. Osborne might bring Prudence to the meeting place, but he would make no guarantees that she would be allowed to leave safely. To ensure that happened was up to Philip.

A tear trickled down Alysa's cheek. "What a wretched choice! To sacrifice a brother or a sister! How can I do it?"

Philip gently stroked away the moisture. "You will sacrifice neither. If this follows as I plan, Prudence will return to Strathern Hall, Thomas will successfully escape and Ingram will be rewarded for his betrayals as he should be."

Alysa smiled through her tears, her eyes trusting. "Can it be?"

"With a little luck and a lot of planning, yes, I believe it can."

She snuggled against him. "Now all I have to do is convince Papa to talk to you."

Philip smiled over her head. "Was he very angry?"

Alysa sighed. "He will be once he has time to consider

what my absence really means. He is beside himself with worry over Prudence and was simply glad to know I had returned home safely. I did not realize that the note I left was more than a little ambiguous, you see. I said you and I were going into the lion's den to find the spy and make him tell us where Prudence was. Papa sat up all night worrying about my safety, not my honor, I'm afraid."

Philip's hands stroked down her back in a comforting way. "So that is why you were able to slip away to meet me this afternoon?"

She looked up at him and smiled. "I would not have allowed anything to stop me, Philip, for I promised I would come. However, neither Papa nor Mama forbade me to see you, although I am afraid my stepmama guessed that we had become lovers. She said that I looked too happy. Papa, fortunately, wasn't about when she spoke to me, but I am sure she will tell him soon. I do not know what he will do then."

Another detail to be sorted out. Philip didn't want to think about what he would say to Lord Strathern, not with Alysa warm in his arms and the woods silent around them. Planning could keep until later. For now he pushed the future out of his mind and thought only of the present.

He tilted her chin up for a kiss, giving her plenty of time to move away if she did not want to accept the embrace. Instead her lips parted and she moistened them enticingly with the tip of her tongue. He drew a deep, sizzling breath. "Alysa!"

She raised her hands to his head and urged him closer. Their mouths met and soon the only sounds to break the quiet of the woodlands were those of two people in love.

CHAPTER 18

Philip's plan to save Prudence Leighton had all the precision of a military engagement. After choosing the field, he walked over it, hunting for its weak points and its strengths. Then, having assessed the terrain, he analyzed the people involved to decide how they would act and react. Finally, he created a plan, then tested it for flexibility. If the unexpected happened, how well would his design hold up? Did it have the capacity to bend or would it break, and thus lead to Thomas Leighton's capture?

When he was satisfied that his overall strategy would be successful, he set about organizing his forces. His first recruit was Lord Strathern.

By the time Philip saw him, Strathern was nearly frantic with worry over Prudence and to a lesser degree over Alysa. He was in no mood to listen patiently to a man he knew was in league with his enemies, not to mention the fact that the same man had taken his eldest daughter into danger and ruined her reputation at the same time.

As Lord Strathern's participation in the exchange was crucial, Philip let him vent his anger and frustration. When the man had pretty much run down, Philip said flatly, "Lord Strathern, my knowledge of Osborne and his activities is our greatest strength, not a weakness. It is a motto of every military man that to know the enemy is to defeat the enemy. Sir Edgar Osborne does not care about Prudence; he is just using her to get what he really wants—your son, Thomas. If he thinks Thomas will give himself up freely, he will gladly hand Prudence back to us. If he believes Thomas will prove elusive, he will keep Prudence as long as is necessary for him to make the arrest he seeks. That is why it is important for Thomas to *seem* to be giving himself up."

Strathern eyed Philip warily. "I understand what you are suggesting, Hampton, but this exchange is all in Osborne's favor. He will be there with his troop of dragoons—"

"We agreed that the exchange would be done quietly, with only the principals there," Philip interjected quickly.

Strathern brushed this off with a flick of his wrist. "Osborne is a traitorous Roundhead. He will not honor his word. Mark me, the dragoons will be there."

Philip was inclined to agree on that point, so he didn't dispute Lord Strathern's pronouncement. Instead, he said evenly, "Osborne might have his troops, but we will have the element of surprise."

"Will we?"

"Yes!" Anger flickered in Philip and filled his voice. "Listen to me, Strathern! I know Osborne. Moreover, I know his sort. He's a minor functionary in the Lord Protector's court who has been given a task that he can only do if people act as they are supposed to. He's never learned that success is the result of careful planning and hard work. He won't go to the Fenwick Cliffs and walk the ground, looking for defensive positions and escape routes, as I did. Oh, he may go to the cliffs so he knows where they are, but he won't put in the extra effort that a good commander needs to make his strategy work."

Strathern frowned at Philip from under his brows. "What exactly are you saying, Hampton?"

"At the Fenwick Cliffs there is a grove of trees to the east. The ground does not fall off as abruptly there. Do you know the place I mean?"

Strathern nodded.

Philip continued in a flat, even tone. "Very well. When I walked amongst the trees I discovered a path that led down from the high land to the flats below. It is a steep path, little more than an animal track, but a man could scramble down it without too much difficulty, as I did. If a horse were waiting for him at the bottom he could gallop the short distance to Fenwick Cove and meet a boat there that could take him far away from West Easton."

"Your idea might well be possible," Lord Strathern said slowly after a moment, "but I see some flaws."

"Such as?"

"If Thomas could scramble down the hillside, then anyone pursuing him could do the same."

Philip smiled and nodded. "A good point, but as long as Thomas reaches the bottom first he will be safe, for there would only be one horse waiting there. If he was followed down the hill, his pursuers would be left standing in the dust of his passing."

Strathern nodded thoughtfully. "A well-reasoned argument. I find it difficult to believe, though, that Osborne will allow Thomas to get close enough to the trees for him to reach the path."

"Once again Osborne's weaknesses will serve us well. Thomas and I will get to the cliffs first, so that we will already be in place when Osborne arrives. Because he has no sense of the importance of positioning, he will not object to where Thomas is waiting. The trick is to have Thomas nearing the woods when he and Prudence pass each other. If he is relatively close to them, he need only kick his horse into a gallop and he will reach the cover of the trees before anyone has decided what to do. Osborne, as I said, does not react well to the unexpected."

"What about Prudence?"

"The moment Thomas gallops for the trees, I will ride to Prudence's side and protect her."

"Then she will go from Osborne's hands into yours."

There was a contemptuous note to Lord Strathern's voice. Unspoken were the words *and she will be in just as grave danger then as she is now.*

Philip's voice hardened at the intended insult. "On the contrary, Strathern. Your daughter will go from the hands of Cedric Ingram into mine. I would feel far more comfortable about Prudence's safety if she were being held by Osborne. He, at least, has nothing to hide and no reason to harm her. Ingram, on the other hand, still believes his perfidy to be unknown. He is capable of anything to keep his position here intact."

At the mention of Ingram's name, the frown on Lord Strathern's face hardened into a grim mask. "What do you want me to do?"

"Contact Thomas and have him meet me at Fenwick Cliffs tomorrow at ten in the forenoon. I have asked Osborne to be there an hour later, so Thomas and I will be able to walk the ground together as we discuss the plan. Osborne will be late—he always is—so he will suspect nothing if he finds us at the meeting place ahead of him."

Lord Strathern said slowly, "How do I know that you will not have the dragoons waiting for Thomas?"

"You must trust me," Philip said softly.

"Why should I?"

Philip drew a deep breath and answered honestly. "I wish to marry your daughter."

"And if I told you that would never happen?"

"I love Alysa. If I allow Thomas to be captured or harm to befall Prudence, I would hurt Alysa. I cannot do that."

Strathern eyed Philip from under his brows. "Is that your only reason for turning your coat?"

Philip flushed. He was not used to hearing himself referred to in that derogatory way. "Lord Strathern, I am offering you my help. Will you take it?"

Slowly, Strathern nodded. "I will, but only because I must."

Philip nodded. He hadn't expected that Lord Strathern would be easy to convince, or that he would look happily on the union of his eldest daughter and a Roundhead officer. Persuading him that he should bless the marriage of Alysa and Philip Hampton was a battle that Philip knew he must put aside until a later date. For the present, he had achieved his goal. Strathern would do his part in arranging the meeting at the Fenwick Cliffs.

It was all he could ask. For now.

Thomas arrived at the hour Philip had specified and Philip pointed out the entryway to the path, the direction in which Osborne would be coming and the point where Thomas should wait so that when the exchange took place he would be heading toward the trees as he rode to Osborne.

Though Thomas was suitably attentive, Philip noticed something disconcerting lurking deep within his eyes. He thought the expression might be amusement, but he dismissed the idea. How could a man in danger of losing his freedom and worried about a sister who was being held captive be amused? It didn't make sense.

A little before the appointed meeting time, Philip and Thomas remounted their horses, so that it appeared as if they had just arrived. Philip was careful to position himself away from Thomas so Osborne would not become suspicious. He wanted Osborne to believe that Thomas Leighton was alone, friendless, and therefore vulnerable. That would keep Osborne's guard down and make Thomas's escape all the easier.

Osborne arrived late, as Philip had predicted, but he did not honor the terms of the agreement he had made with Philip. With him he brought Prudence Leighton, but she was riding in the middle of the troop of dragoons, led by a very smug-looking Lieutenant Weston. Philip noted that, although she was very pale, she was riding with her head high and her back straight, good indications that she had been frightened by her incarceration, but she had not been molested by her captors. Philip allowed himself to relax a little. Even with the troops here he still believed he and Thomas could carry off his plan. Their timing must be perfect and luck must be with them, but it was still possible.

The troop halted a quarter of a mile away. Philip and

Osborne each rode forward to discuss the terms and agreements.

Philip didn't bother with a polite greeting. Instead, he jerked his head in a peremptory way toward the dragoons. "What is the meaning of this? We agreed that this meeting was to be between the four of us—there was no mention of your soldiers being involved."

Osborne smirked, apparently well pleased that he had outthought Philip. "I brought the troops as a simple precaution, Hampton. I did not want Thomas Leighton deciding that his horse could outrun mine once his sister was safely in your hands."

"Then the exchange will not be impeded by the soldiers?"

Osborne nodded his head. "Lieutenant Weston has orders to stay in his position unless something unforeseen occurs."

"You trust Weston?" Philip retorted incredulously.

"He will do as I order. Now then, shall we get on with it?" He gestured toward Thomas, who was sitting his horse stiffly, his back to the cliffs, his eyes narrowed as he watched the two men talk. "I see you were able to persuade young Leighton to give himself up."

Philip glanced over his shoulder and shrugged. "Family ties have a way of making a man do what might not be in his best interests."

"My good fortune, Leighton's bad," Osborne said cynically. "Very well, let's get this exchange over and done with, shall we? I'd rather not linger here any longer than I must."

Philip nodded. "Leighton is ready to do it now."

Osborne raised his hand in a prearranged signal, and Prudence was allowed to begin her ride toward her brother's position. At the same time, Philip looked back at Thomas and nodded. Thomas glanced at Osborne, his look full of loathing; then he concentrated on riding toward his sister while keeping his horse at a slow walk.

Tension mounted as Prudence and Thomas moved closer and closer to the middle ground where they would pass each other. That was a crucial point, for after it Prudence would be increasingly safe and Thomas would simply have to choose his moment to make his escape.

When Prudence and Thomas were within a few yards of meeting, the hush was broken by the sound of galloping hooves. Prudence stopped, unsure what to do. Thomas also stopped, for he would not go on while she was not moving. They stayed that way, frozen, as the swiftly moving horse and rider gradually became larger until it was possible to discern who was interrupting the exchange. It was Alysa.

The thin line of dragoons held their position as she galloped headlong toward them, but they looked uneasily at their officer, waiting for instructions. In his turn, Lieutenant Weston glanced at Osborne, clearly as disconcerted by this change in plans as his men. Osborne made a slight motion with his hand and magically the line of troops parted to allow Alysa through.

She reached Prudence and pulled her mount to a snorting stop. "Thank God, you are safe!" she cried, leaning over to embrace her sister.

"What the devil are you playing at, Hampton?" Osborne snarled, shooting Philip a furious look.

For his part, Philip had no idea what was going on. Alysa had been included in the details of the plot, but because she too would be a valuable bargaining tool, she had been told by her father that she should remain at Strathern Hall. And she had agreed, seeing the sense of his words. Yet she was here. Why?

Alysa gave Prudence a final hug, but she continued to talk in an animated way, to reassure her sister, Philip guessed. Then he noticed Prudence glance surreptitiously at Thomas, then at the forest. Philip almost groaned. Apparently Alysa had decided that Prudence needed to know the details of the plan in order to carry out her part and so had decided to risk everything to speak privately with her sister.

Afraid that Osborne's thoughts would mirror his own, Philip did his best to distract him. He turned to the Londoner, his mouth set in a grim line. "I did not expect to see Mistress Alysa here today, though I know how close she is to her sister. I must assume that she was desperate with worry and felt she had to come."

Osborne's eyes narrowed as he looked at Alysa and Prudence, still talking excitedly. He shook his head. "These Cavalier women are as undisciplined as their men. The lady needs a strong hand to beat her impetuosity out of her." He snorted, then laughed in a rather evil way. "And the man who plans to wed her will do a good job of that, I wager."

"Are you speaking of Cedric Ingram?" Philip asked coldly.

Osborne nodded. "Aye. He's hot for the wench. That's one of the reasons he didn't want to give up Prudence Leighton. He was afraid that he would lose his chance to secure the sister."

"Surely he doesn't expect that Lord Strathern will allow him to marry Alysa now?"

Osborne laughed. "Lord Strathern's fortunes are about to take a serious blow, my dear Hampton. His son, the traitor, is soon to be captured, then executed. Strathern himself will be accused and condemned for insurrection. After the estate has been sequestered, the daughters will be glad to take whatever marriages are offered."

Philip didn't comment. He kept his eyes on Alysa and Prudence, warily watching for any movement that might put them, especially Alysa, in danger.

Prudence began to cry as she and Alysa separated. She said something as she gestured at Thomas, who shrugged and looked uncomfortable. Clearly she was distraught that her freedom meant his capture. Alysa patted her on the shoulder, but Prudence was not about to be comforted. Thomas looked at Osborne and Philip, frowning. Evidently he did not expect Alysa to get Prudence moving any time soon.

Osborne swore.

"Careful," Philip drawled tauntingly. "You wouldn't want word to get back to the Lord Protector that you use that kind of language."

Osborne laughed. "When old Ironsides was alive, I'd have made sure I didn't curse aloud. His son—" He shrugged, allowing the implication to make itself. Richard Cromwell was not the man his father had been. Even those intent on keeping him on his false throne knew that. "Come on," Osborne shouted. "I want this farce over with. Mistress Leighton, move your horse now!"

Prudence bit her lip. She glanced over her shoulder at the soldiers. They had closed up ranks again, creating an effective barrier between the Leightons and freedom. The riders sat immobile, but their horses were clearly uneasy, playing with their bits, tossing their heads or stamping their feet. All were good indications that the riders, too, were far from calm. Prudence said something to Alysa, who also looked at the soldiers.

Osborne's impatience turned to grim annoyance. He lifted his hand and with a flick of his wrist Philip's carefully laid plan dissolved.

The troop of soldiers jerked into the action they craved. Fanning out and moving inexorably forward, they advanced toward the Leighton position at a steady, controlled walk.

Philip turned angrily to Osborne. "What is the meaning of this?"

Osborne shrugged. "Obviously, these Royalists plan to break our agreement. I'm just ensuring that I do not lose Thomas to his scheming sisters."

"Signal your men to stop," Philip said angrily. "Allow me to talk some sense into the ladies."

Osborne looked amused. "I doubt that is possible, but all right, you can try."

Although his plan had been seriously compromised, Philip was not unhappy with this latest development, for it would allow him to be close to Alysa and Prudence and thus able to protect them when Thomas bolted for the woods. He was just about to put his heels to his mount when another rider, galloping recklessly, appeared in the distance. Once again everything stopped.

This time the rider was Cedric Ingram. He was flushed and his eyes stared wildly. "Stop them!" he shouted as he approached. "Don't let them get away."

Osborne sighed. "This was supposed to have been so very simple. What happened?"

The urge to ride into the fray was almost more than Philip could bear, but he forced himself to remain calm. With Cedric Ingram once again involved, quick wits could be more important than brute strength.

Ingram was panting as he reached Osborne and Philip. "None of the Leighton family is at Strathern Hall. None! I sense a betrayal! Arrest Thomas Leighton now. And the ladies too."

"An excellent idea," Osborne drawled. He lifted his hand to make one of his dangerous, silent signals.

Philip, desperate to distract him, said bitterly, "You are obsessed with treachery, Ingram. You have been so deeply involved in betraying your friends that you see it in the actions of everyone else."

Cedric brushed off his remarks with the ease that one brushes off a pesky fly. "Where else would the whole Leighton family be, but here, trying to ensure that their beloved Thomas gets away scot-free? Sir Edgar, I beg of you, listen to me! A plot is afoot to keep Thomas Leighton from being taken. You must act, now!"

"You really are a turncoat," Philip said contemptuously. "Do you think the gold Osborne gives you will be enough to pay for the loss of your home and the respect of those around you?"

Cedric looked at Philip amazed; then he laughed. "Money is not the issue. Power is. Osborne has offered me a position at the Lord Protector's court. I shall be a man of importance, as I deserve to be."

Philip laughed without amusement. "I wish you joy of your new post, Ingram, but I doubt the power you attain will be quite as heady as you expect."

Cedric frowned. "You sound as if you know of what you speak."

Osborne laughed. Unlike Philip, he was amused by the conversation. "He does. He was once offered a position at the Protector's court, which was a good deal more respectable than yours will be." When Cedric frowned and looked about to question that remark, Osborne added, "Enough! I want Thomas Leighton under guard immediately!" He signaled to Weston, who ordered the dragoons into a trot.

At that moment, Thomas Leighton looked back at Philip. A silent communication passed between them. He nodded and put his heels to his horse, urging it into a gallop. Philip did the same. While Thomas bolted for the trees, Philip headed for the vulnerable Alysa and Prudence.

For a moment there was chaos. Weston wasn't sure how to react to this unexpected twist and his men milled about behind him, anxious to be in action, but unable to act until the command was given. Osborne and Cedric Ingram shouted and fought with their nervous, prancing horses, issuing orders that only confused the lieutenant further.

Alysa saw Philip heading toward them and urged Prudence to ride to meet him. They were almost together when he heard Ingram scream, "The woods! He is heading for the woods. There is a path there! He can escape!"

Philip spared a desperate glance over his shoulder. Thomas was closing on the trees, but a half a dozen of the troopers were now thundering behind him. All that was needed was for one man to bring Thomas down before he reached the path, and escape route or not, he would lose his freedom.

Philip's job, though, was to ensure that Prudence and Alysa were safe. Most of the soldiers were intent on capturing the ladies, for it was obvious to all that Thomas would surrender if he thought that his sisters were in danger.

As Philip neared, he shouted to Alysa, "Stay by me. I'm going to ride through the troopers and head back to Strathern Hall."

"What about Thomas?"

"Thomas must look to himself," Philip said grimly.

"But—"

"There is no time for argument, Alysa! You must do as I say now, or all is lost!"

Slowly, she nodded. Thomas had reached the trees with the troopers hot on his heels. Alysa turned her horse to ride for home, still unsure whether or not her brother was safe.

"Stay behind me," Philip said grimly. He eased his sword in its scabbard. His plan was to fight his way past the troopers, for he had cut a path through the enemy's line and ridden to safety on a number of occasions. The drawback now would be Alysa and Prudence, unused as they were to the violence and bloodshed of combat. "When we are through, ride as fast as you can for Strathern. Once inside the house, your servants can protect you."

"Philip—" Alsya said in a shaky voice.

"Please! I will not be far behind you."

The time it had taken for Philip to convince Alysa to follow him was enough to allow Osborne, closely followed by Cedric Ingram, to reach them.

"The devil you say, Hampton! I'm not about to allow the ladies to escape while Thomas Leighton is still at large."

His sword raised, Philip turned to confront this fresh danger. "Your men will have Leighton secure in a few minutes. Path or no, your soldiers are close enough behind him to capture him, even if he does reach the woods. Let the ladies go."

Behind him, Alysa and Prudence shifted closer, knowing that he was their only protection.

A nasty glint appeared in Cedric Ingram's eyes. "Don't listen to him, Sir Edgar! The path he speaks of is a footpath! Leighton can leave his horse, climb down to the bottom of the cliffs and disappear into the countryside before your men can do anything about it!"

"A footpath!" Osborne half turned in his saddle to shout a warning to his men, but Philip stopped him with the point of his sword.

"The ladies return to Strathern Hall, Osborne. Without hindrance."

"The devil you say!" Osborne drew his own sword.

For a moment the two men, allies once, enemies now,

stared at each other. Then Philip nodded. "So be it."

Their swords clashed, steel meeting steel in an angry clangor. From the first it was clear that Philip would be the victor. He was the one trained in hand-to-hand combat on the back of a horse, not Osborne, who had been a member of Parliament during the war and more recently a courtier and a man of influence. Moreover, Philip was riding his spirited black horse, trained in the arts of war. The stallion responded to hidden signals Philip gave to position it more effectively and the clash of swords did not make it nervous, as it clearly did Osborne's mount.

Philip did not want to waste time in pointless dueling with Sir Edgar Osborne, so when Osborne's horse shied, Philip took the opportunity offered. He gave the leg and hand commands that caused his horse to rear up on its hind legs and lash out at Osborne's frightened mount. In that moment Philip raised his sword and with a sweeping movement brought it down hard on Osborne's blade.

Osborne's horse shied and bucked at the same time as Philip struck. The sword fell from Osborne's hand as easily as if it had just turned into a hot iron poker.

Osborne swore as he steadied his horse. "Stupid beast!" He laughed through his annoyance. "A fine move, Sir Philip, and worthy of the warrior you are, but I fear honorable battle does not always lead to victory. In defeating me, you have lost your prize."

One quick look told Philip the rest of the story. While he had fought Osborne, Cedric Ingram had grabbed Alysa from the back of her horse. She was struggling desperately, flailing at him with her riding whip, but she could not break his hold.

A silent command, which was an almost invisible combination of the rider's hands and knees, made Philip's stallion rise on its hind legs, then whirl in an elegant leap that brought it directly in line with Cedric Ingram. When the stallion's hooves once again touched the ground it was galloping toward the enemy.

Prudence screamed a warning, and Alysa began to punch

Ingram's chest and kick at his legs with her feet. Though she was impeded by her heavy riding dress, her wild flailing was enough to unsettle Ingram's horse. Like Osborne's, it spooked, bucking and shying. Within seconds both Cedric and Alysa had tumbled onto the ground.

There Alysa was able to roll to her feet first and she ran, not caring which direction she was going as long as it was away from Cedric Ingram.

Hoofbeats sounded beside her. She looked up to find Philip reaching for her and a smile as bright as sunshine broke over her face. Without hesitation, she grabbed his outstretched arm and let him swing her up onto his mount. Shuddering, she wrapped her arms around his waist and buried her face in his strong chest. She was safe now that she was with Philip.

Across the open ground, Thomas slowed his horse to a trot and vanished into the shaded grove. The dragoons were not a length behind him as he disappeared. Philip feared that he would not be able to get deep enough into the gloom to successfully escape.

But as Thomas entered the trees there was another flurry of motion. Two dozen or more of the townsfolk of West Easton stepped from the shadows carrying pikes, swords, some muskets and a variety of other weapons. They stood silently, their expressions grimly determined as they faced the soldiers.

Their leader was Lord Strathern. He stepped forward. Shouting, so that his voice could be heard by all, he said, "Sir Edgar Osborne! Kidnapping is a reprehensible act and unacceptable to civilized men, no matter what their political beliefs. Thus, no one who has been victimized by this crime is required to deal honestly with those who have perpetrated it. My son will soon be gone from England. Allow my daughters to freely return to their home."

It was doubtful whether Lord Strathern and his motley band of adherents would be any match for the disciplined men of the New Model Army, but the mere fact that they stood defiantly before the soldiers was enough to give Osborne pause.

"This is treason," he shouted back, remounting his horse and brandishing the sword he had just retrieved from the ground.

"No, sir, it is not!" Strathern retorted, unimpressed. "I am merely exercising the right of every Englishman to protect the honor of his family. Call off your men."

Osborne looked from Strathern to Philip, who protectively cuddled Alysa against him, and to Prudence who had guided her horse very close to Philip's. Between them and Strathern Hall were perhaps a half a dozen of the dragoons, but Philip still held his sword raised and the expression on his face said that he would gladly fight his way through to keep his lady out of Osborne's hands.

In that instant, Sir Edgar Osborne knew that he was beaten. It was merely icing on the cake that the sound of hoofbeats drew him to the edge of the cliff to watch Thomas Leighton, mounted on one of his father's fast horses, gallop toward the little cove beyond. Osborne could see a boat waiting there for him. Clearly, Thomas Leighton would be bound for the Continent before too much longer, for there was no way that he could be caught now.

Grimly, Osborne turned away from the scene. "Very well. The ladies return to Strathern Hall, unharmed." He glared at Philip. "You, sir, will regret this act of betrayal!"

"I regret having ever agreed to aid you in your scheme," Philip said evenly. "I shall never regret thwarting it." He saluted Lord Strathern. "Pray allow me to escort your daughters home, sir."

"I think not," Strathern said coldly. "I would prefer to know that my daughters are safe in the hands of an honorable gentleman."

Philip stiffened. Alysa exclaimed, "Papa!"

"Hush, girl, and do as I say. You and Prudence will ride home with me."

She looked up into Philip's eyes. "He is just being cautious, dear heart. It doesn't mean—"

"Do as your father says," Philip replied, gently lowering her to the ground. "He and I will have much to discuss later."

"I love you," Alysa whispered, her eyes searching Philip's.

He smiled, but didn't reply. His expression was hooded as he watched her mount up behind her sister and ride past the troopers to the protection of Lord Strathern and the sturdy yeomen of West Easton.

Behind Philip, Osborne laughed. He glanced over his shoulder at the gloating face of the Roundhead.

"A turncoat can never win, Hampton. Look at this fool, Ingram. I bought him with the promise of power and position, a promise I had no intention of keeping. It appears that you sold out for a promise that was just as insubstantial."

Philip didn't reply. He turned his horse's head and rode away, without looking back.

CHAPTER 19

The four occupants of the shabby drawing room were very still. Lord Strathern stood by the fireplace, his expression remarkably difficult to interpret as he read the missive that had been smuggled in from the Continent. Alysa, her sister and her stepmother watched him in strained silence, waiting. It seemed to Alysa that she had been waiting ever since Thomas had sailed from Fenwick Cove two weeks before. Two very long weeks.

Strathern smiled as he crumpled the sheet of paper and threw it into the fireplace. The news was good. Alysa heaved a silent sigh of relief.

"Thomas has successfully reached Amsterdam. He reported his findings to the king. As these are much the same as the arguments that the gentlemen of the Sealed Knot have been making, His Majesty is now better able to assess the promises spouted by hotheads who claim that a rebellion now would inevitably succeed." Strathern's cheerful expression faded as he looked at his two daughters. "So, I will be able to tell my associates in the Sealed Knot that a true and considered report was given to the king. Thus I can say that Thomas's time was productively spent while he was here. I wish I could say the same for both of you."

Alysa bit her lip and looked guilty. Prudence lifted her chin defiantly. "Papa—"

Strathern held up his hand. "No more protests, Prudence.

Today we must decide what to do about your future. 'Tis not an auspicious prospect, I fear."

"How could you be so silly as to follow Cedric Ingram?" Abigail said wretchedly. Because Edward had felt it necessary to invoke the aide of his tenants and neighbors to rescue her, everyone in the vicinity knew that Prudence had been kidnapped by Cedric Ingram and why he had been able to lure her into his clutches. She was an object of pity to all and a severe embarrassment to her mother.

Prudence hung her head. "I thought it was a way of learning about him. I was simply doing as you suggested, Mama!"

"Don't mock your mother that way!" Strathern snapped. His temper was very close to the surface, for he had been sorely tried by his daughters these past weeks. Moreover, he didn't like being placed in the position he was now in. The decisions that would be made today would last for the lifetimes of his daughters. Those were decisions that should not be made lightly, or because current circumstances made them inevitable. Yet that was what he was being forced to do. He wasn't happy with the situation.

"No, Papa," Prudence replied meekly. "I'm sorry, Mama."

Abigail's bout of self-indulgence was characteristically brief. Her voice resumed its usual brisk tone and her expression became gently concerned. "I accept that you wished to make Master Ingram notice you, my dear. What your father and I need to know is how you feel about him now."

Prudence diligently pleated the smooth peach cloth of her petticoat. "When I heard him talking to that odious Roundhead, I was repulsed, but later—" Her fingers closed into a fist, crushing the bright fabric. "He hid me in an abandoned cottage on his lands and he came to visit me there. I was desperately lonely and bored and frightened and I think he sensed that. He would pause to talk to me when he brought me my meals. During those hours, he told me quite a lot about himself. I came to I believe that he was not the black villain I had first thought him to be. In fact, his motives were much misunderstood." She drew, a shaky breath. For the first time she seemed to notice her clenched fist and the crushed material. Slowly she relaxed her hand, then smoothed the crumpled peach cloth.

Abigail sighed. "Prudence, you disappeared for three days. Your reputation is undoubtedly ruined."

Prudence looked deliberately at her mother. "If Master Ingram would have me, I would wish to be married to him."

"You cannot!" Alysa burst out. "Cedric Ingram kidnapped you so that our brother would be captured!"

Prudence turned lost eyes to her. "I know that, but I love him still. He fascinates me as no other man ever has."

Strathern snorted. "He fascinates you because he is— was—the most influential unmarried man in the region. Should another such come this way, you would find him as exciting as Cedric Ingram!"

"I do not think so, Papa."

Prudence's rebuttal was said with such quiet dignity that afterward there was an uncomfortable silence in the room. Prudence blushed, for the silence was the silence of pity, not respect.

Abigail cleared her throat. "We will say nothing more on this topic for the moment. There still remains the question of Alysa's conduct with Sir Philip Hampton."

It was Alysa's turn to blush. "I did not stay out all night with Sir Philip on purpose, Mama. You must understand that we were trapped! There was nothing—"

Abigail held up her hand. Her expression was stern now. Prudence's transgression could not be mended. Alysa's could. "There was everything you could have done! You *could* have refused to participate in Sir Philip's mad scheme in the first place! You *could* have left the inn through a back door!"

"We were afraid of being caught by Osborne's men!" Alysa retorted, defending herself on the one charge that could be defended. "Philip was certain that Osborne was holding Prudence. It would have been madness to allow him to have a second hostage for Thomas! Moreover, if we had been caught, Osborne would have learned that Philip was no longer his ally. I do not know what would have happened to Prudence then."

"I would have been fine," Prudence interjected. "Cedric would not have harmed me."

Abigail ignored Prudence's interruption and concentrated on Alysa's crimes. "I will not be placated, Alysa. The whole sordid incident could have been avoided if you had not gone to the inn. Now your reputation is in shreds and I despair of ever finding a husband for you."

Alysa set her jaw. "You need not worry about that, Mama. Philip will marry me."

"He hasn't asked for your hand yet," Lord Strathern growled.

Two weeks had passed since the exchange at the Fenwick Cliffs. Two weeks in which there had been no communication between Strathern Hall and Ainslie Manor. The last Alysa had seen of Philip Hampton was his back, as he rode away at her father's command.

Alysa looked at her father through clear eyes. "He will, Papa. I know he will."

"I am not certain that I wish my daughter to be allied to a Roundhead," Strathern said bleakly. "We are Royalists, Alysa. We have been true to our sovereign lord through the worst of times. How can you betray him now?"

"In marrying Philip I would not be betraying the king, or my own beliefs." A subtle triumph gleamed in Alysa's eyes. "I would be gaining a convert for the king's cause!"

Abigail's expression softened, but when she spoke it was with her usual brisk manner. "I do not think it is wise to generalize on men's behavior, Alysa, but I cannot see you delude yourself unnecessarily. If a man has his way with a woman before marriage he loses respect for the lady in question. Furthermore, he no longer needs to endow his hand on her in marriage."

"Philip is not like that!" Alysa said fiercely, although butterflies were busily at work in her stomach. Over the past fortnight she had told herself too many times that Philip loved her and would marry her. She had reassured herself that although her reputation might be in shreds, her future was not in doubt. Each day it had become harder to believe and her protestations sounded weak even to her own ears.

Once again Abigail's expression softened. This time she said quite gently, "My dear, I can see that your heart is involved and I am truly sorry. This is a hard lesson for you to learn. Lessons such as these are difficult, all the more so when one wants to believe passionately that they are not true."

"Mama, Papa, I beg of you, do not give up on Sir Philip so easily! He will ask for my hand in marriage. I know he will! He has promised me!"

Abigail shot a look at Lord Strathern, who turned away. Alysa felt her heart give a sudden, painful lurch. What if they were right? What if Philip didn't love her and wasn't about to marry her?

Then she reminded herself of his words of love that night at the inn, of the way he had risked his life and his future for her at the Fenwick Cliffs, and she wondered how she could ever have doubted him. Her head went up proudly and her eyes were defiant.

Abigail said gently, "As hard as this is for you, Alysa, we must plan what to do in the event that he does not ask you to marry him. First there is the matter of a child—"

"A child!"

Abigail nodded, brisk once more. "There is always that possibility. If you are with child we will send you to live with my aunt in Yorkshire. She will take care of you and her house is sufficiently remote that your condition will not be remarked upon. The baby can be given to a local family to raise."

Alysa's eyes kindled. "There will be no need of that, Mama. If I am with child, Philip will marry me."

"He will not be given the opportunity." Strathern's voice was heavy, but firm. "The man must ask for you of his own free will. I will have no hand in a forced marriage."

"Papa! I would rather have him because he must marry me, than not have him at all!"

"You do not know what you are speaking of, Alysa," her father said gruffly. "A lifetime tied to a man who does not want you is an eternity of regret."

Alysa leapt to her feet. "Better than an eternity spent pining for the man you love and cannot have!"

"Sir Philip Hampton." The butler's deep voice cut into Alysa's passionate outburst and silenced her. It also silenced everyone else in the room. For a moment all were still. The only movement was the servant standing aside to allow Philip to enter the room.

At the sight of him, Alysa's face lit up. She turned to her father, her eyes sparkling with triumph, and not a little relief. "You see?"

Strathern looked at her from beneath his brows, then went forward to greet their guest. "Good day to you, Sir Philip."

Philip bowed. He was dressed in a plain, well-made doublet of dark blue cloth and his black breeches lacked the froth of ribbon loops that would adorn a Royalist's clothes. "And to you, Lord Strathern. May I have a moment of your time, privately?"

Strathern nodded. Prudence slid past the two gentlemen, glad to be released from a further, more uncomfortable interview. Abigail followed her. As she passed Philip, she shot him a curious look, but she merely nodded politely and wished him good day.

Reluctantly, Alysa also prepared to leave, but her father stopped her. "I believe you are the reason Sir Philip has come today. Please stay with us, daughter."

Alysa nodded and smiled into Philip's eyes. He took her hand and kissed it with an elegant flourish. "Indeed, my lord, you are quite correct. I have come to ask for Mistress Alysa's hand in marriage."

Strathern made an indecipherable sound in his throat as he watched his daughter and Philip Hampton together. There could be no doubt that Alysa was deeply in love with Sir Philip, and although Lord Strathern believed Philip Hampton to be a just and honest man, he could not forget that the younger man had fought for Parliament during the war and had given his loyalty to Oliver Cromwell. It was difficult for Lord Strathern to accept that his daughter would choose a Roundhead as her lifemate, but the evidence was there before his eyes.

Now what he had to do was make sure that the man she had chosen would treat her properly, at this moment and throughout their time together. "I trust, sir, that you are prepared to set aside a part of your estate for my daughter's use as her marriage portion?"

Philip looked surprised; then his eyes narrowed. With amusement, Alysa thought. She said hastily, "Papa, should I be a party to this? I mean, after all—"

"It is always wise for a woman to know her rights," Strathern said tranquilly. "Please sit down, Sir Philip, and you, Alysa. I do believe this will be a lengthy discussion."

Numbly, Alysa sat. Philip was careful to choose a place away from her and opposite Lord Strathern, so that he could look his future father-in-law in the eye while they negotiated.

The bargaining lasted an hour. During that time the amount of Alysa's dowry, her widow's portion, funds to be settled directly on her children, and other financial matters were hammered out by the two men. Alysa listened, a little dazed at the details, but well aware that her father was acting in her best interests. Moreover, Philip was as generous with the amounts he bestowed upon her as his estate would allow, indicating that his feelings toward her could not be anything but warm.

At the end of the financial discussion Lord Strathern nodded approval before saying, "There remains one matter to be settled."

Philip stiffened. "If you are referring to the night Alysa and I spent at the inn—"

Strathern's eyebrows rose. "In truth, I was not. Although that is an incident in which I feel your judgment, sir, was seriously impaired."

"If Alysa and I had tried to leave the inn she would have been in as much jeopardy as Prudence was." Philip's eyes flashed as he made the statement, but his tone was even. "I did not take her there with the express intention of harming her in any way."

"Had I believed you did, Sir Philip, I would not allow you to marry my daughter, for any reason."

Somewhat mollified, Philip nodded. "The only other topic that might hinder my suit, then, is my affiliation with the Lord Protector."

"You are quite correct, sir." Strathern's expression was grave. "I fear your actions the other day will not endear you to the authorities in London."

Philip's lips twisted wryly. "You are quite correct, Lord Strathern. Osborne returned to London and did his best to blacken my name. However, I have friends whose influence outweigh his, especially since he was not able to fulfill his mission. Officially, my refusal to participate in a kidnapping and ransom have been lauded as evidence of my high moral fiber. As I have made it known that I do not plan to return to the army, but will live quietly at Ainslie, no one is inclined to punish me. You need have no fear that bestowing Alysa's hand in mine will place her in any danger."

Strathern shot him a hard look from under his brows. "That is satisfactory for the present, but what happens when the king returns?" At Philip's surprised expression he added softly, "He will return, sir, and we both know it. The Commonwealth is dying of its own weight. Either a new republic of fanatics will be formed or we will return to the old ways, but with a new, young king to lead us. Which would you prefer?"

Philip did not take his eyes off Lord Strathern. He said slowly, "You place me in a difficult position. If I tell you that I would gladly espouse young Charles as our king, would you believe me?"

"Yes," Strathern said simply, "if you gave me your word of honor that that was your true belief."

"You have my word that it is," Philip said steadily. "I

joined the parliamentary army full of idealistic fervor to fight a monarch who had lost touch with the needs of the common people of England and the rights of all her citizens. Then the war ended and our new government became, over time, as arbitrary as the old. I owed much to the Lord Protector Cromwell. I gave him my loyalty long ago and I kept my oath to him until he died. But my true allegiance is to England. Richard Cromwell is not the man his father was and he is proving daily that he is not able to govern this nation. If we must have an hereditary ruler, then it should be one born of the rightly anointed line."

Fixing Philip with a stare that sought to see into his soul, Lord Strathern said, "Well spoken, Hampton. I am satisfied that you will make a suitable husband for my daughter." He smiled, almost mischievously, as he stood. "Now all you have to do is persuade Alysa to accept your proposal. I shall leave you alone together to discuss the question."

As the door closed quietly behind him, Alysa looked over at Philip and smiled tremulously. "Papa told me earlier that a marriage made because the partners felt duty bound to agree to it was one of eternal regret. I must ask you now, Philip, if you have asked for my hand because you feel you must, or because you wish to be betrothed to me? I pray you, answer me as honestly as you answered my father about your political beliefs."

Philip came to sit close beside her. He took her hands and held them in his, his thumbs rubbing the soft skin on the backs. "When I was young I told myself I would never marry a Royalist woman. I had seen them at court, so smooth and sweet on the surface, but full of venom and fury on the inside. Their very polish made them too conniving for any man to believe in. I thought a straightforward, trustworthy woman of the Puritan persuasion would be much more to my taste. A lady who was serious and thoughtful and would never make me wonder whom she was with or what she was planning."

He smiled ruefully. "In time, I discovered that a Puritan woman could be as deceitful as a Royalist one. And so I learned that I must look at the individual and see what she was made of before I judged her. When I came here I was not looking for an emotional entanglement. But I found one and I do not regret it. You are a woman of spirit, intelligence, guile and charm, Alysa Leighton. You are the perfect woman for me, the woman I love. I would not change you and I cannot live without you."

Alysa smiled and moved closer to him. "Philip, I am a Royalist. I always will be. What happens if the Protectorate continues and you wish to return to the Lord Protector's court?"

"I have made my decision, sweet lady. I am finished with the Protectorate. I will not return to London, except to visit now and again." He smiled tenderly. "Besides, this is not about politics, but about us. I love you, Alysa. Do you love me?"

A smile trembled on her lips and her eyes filled with tears of emotion. "Oh, yes. I love you with all of my heart, Philip."

"Then you will marry me."

He made it a statement, but Alysa answered as if it were a question. "Yes. Oh, yes."

CHAPTER 20

May, 1660

All over London church bells tolled joyously. The city was festive with new hope for the future, for the king was returning. The long years of the Commonwealth were over.

Thousands of people came in from the country to join in the celebrations, to greet returning family members or to remind the newly returned monarch of their loyalty through the extended period of adversity. King Charles had been heard to remark wryly that if the Stuarts had had as many friends in England as was claimed, his father would never have lost his throne and he would not have spent ten years in exile. Despite this cynicism, Charles was gracious to all those who came before him. Compromise was the rule of the day for king and subject alike.

Lord Strathern and his family journeyed to London, more to see Thomas than to join in the festivities. The purpose of their visit was certainly not to petition the monarch for a return of the lands lost as a result of the war. To Strathern's mind, the family had much to be thankful for. Thomas was safely home once again and Alysa was truly happy in her marriage. His only worry was Prudence, who continued to be infatuated with Cedric Ingram, even though he was being shunned by the people of West Easton.

The rooms they had rented were on the first floor of a

timber frame house that jutted out over the street at a crazy
angle. Beneath their windows they could hear the constant
noise of traffic and the loud, often drunken voices of
revelers. As annoying as these outside sounds were,
Strathern was glad to get the rooms, which consisted of three
bedchambers and a private parlor, an almost unheard-of
luxury in the capital during these festive times. Thus it was
that Lord Strathern was able to invite his son to a private
dinner several days after the family had first gotten together
at a public ordinary.

During that first meeting there had been some constraint
between Thomas and Philip, but Thomas was rapidly
learning the art of compromise and Philip had long ago been
taught the skill. Once Thomas saw that his sister was happy
in her marriage, he was willing to accept Philip as part of the
family. Now, with the restraint between his son and son-in-
law mended, Strathern was able to preside at a table where
his whole family sat in harmony. It was as much a cause for
rejoicing as the return of the king. Perhaps more so.

Conversation flowed freely as the various courses were
brought and enjoyed. A dish of pigeons was followed by a
plate of carp and a boiled capon. The main dish was a joint
of beef, roasted upon the spit. Several bottles of fine claret
enhanced the meal, and by the time a sweet fruit tart was
brought, any last constraint that might have lingered between
Roundhead and Royalist was long gone.

Lord Strathern had ordered a well-aged brandy to end the
special meal, and as he poured the glasses, Thomas slid a
speculative glance at him. "Papa, were charges ever laid
against you for your defiance of Sir Edgar Osborne?"

"I am told that Osborne attempted to charge me with
treason," Strathern said somberly. "I have no other indication
of it, for Sir Edgar was unable to make the accusation stick.
It seems that his inability to complete his mission put him at
some disadvantage. His word was not enough to convince
his masters that my actions were those of a traitor and not a
man justly outraged at a crime against him." He looked over
at Philip. "I must thank Philip for using his influence to

ensure that few accepted Osborne's version of events."

Thomas said with some relief, "Then I have no need to speak to the king on your behalf."

A small, rather tender smile touched Strathern's mouth and was gone. "None, though I thank you for the offer. I am delighted His Majesty has returned, but I am a free man, I do not want a place at court and I do not expect to have my lands returned to me. My family is together again. That is all I care about."

Thomas toyed with the food on his plate, then said cautiously, "There is one other matter I believe we must discuss before we finish with that time."

"What could that be?" Alysa asked curiously.

"Cedric Ingram," her brother said flatly. "The king received a petition from him today."

"From Ingram? What for?" Strathern demanded sharply.

"He claimed to be a loyal Royalist whose fortunes have been adversely affected by the years of Roundhead rule."

"Is he demanding compensation?"

Thomas nodded, smiling at the indignation on his father's face. "Of a sort. He wants a place at court."

There was a shocked silence; then Prudence asked slowly, "Will he get it?"

"Probably. Ingram's brother, the Earl of Easton, went into exile with the king and the family is tied by blood to some of the most powerful magnates in the country. His Majesty knows what Cedric did, but he does not want to antagonize the old nobility so early in his reign. He will find a place for Cedric where he can do no damage."

"There is no such thing at court," Philip said softly.

Suddenly, Thomas looked tired. "Perhaps not, but what is His Majesty to do? If he turns Cedric Ingram away without a soft word the fellow will be sure to make mischief. At least King Charles and his supporters will be able to keep an eye on him if he is at court."

Prudence was frowning. Though he remained at Ingram Abbey, she had not seen Cedric since the kidnapping and the ill-conceived passion she had developed for him continued unabated. "Thomas, are you sure you are correct in this matter? I cannot understand why Master Ingram would want to claim he was a true Royalist. Why, in words and actions he admitted he preferred the Protectorate!"

"But the Lord Protector has tumbled from power and Cedric must discover a new way to find advancement," Alysa said gently. She added a bit more tartly, "He appears to have found it."

"But—" Prudence bit off whatever she was going to say. "His actions are not very honorable, are they?"

"No, my dear, they are not." There was a gleam of speculative hope in Abigail's eyes, for perhaps Prudence could be cured of her besottedness for Cedric Ingram after all. "Thomas, is it possible that Prudence might spend some time at court? I believe the experience would be of great value to her."

"I shall ask," Thomas said, looking a little surprised.

Philip, who had immediately caught on to Abigail's idea, enlightened him, although in a rather oblique way, so as not to make Prudence obdurate. "As I am sure you already well know, Leighton, court life has a way of bringing out elements of a person's character that one does not expect to find. Your sister would do well to learn what happens in the greater world. Perhaps she might even decide that West Easton is a better place to be."

Which meant that if Prudence could see Cedric Ingram in the broader scenario of court life she might well realize just what sort of man he was. Or she could very well attract a suitor more acceptable to her family.

Thomas looked thoughtful. "Indeed, I shall ask. Would you like to go to court, Prue?"

A determined gleam leapt into Prudence's eyes. "Above all things, Thomas!" She clapped her hands together with delight. "Just imagine! I will be able to see the king every day. Me! Oh, I am so thrilled!"

Thomas laughed. "Don't get too excited. I haven't found a place for you yet."

Prudence laughed gaily. "But you will, Thomas. I know you will." She turned to her sister. "Are you not jealous, Alysa? If you had not married Philip, it might have been you who was going to court."

There was a brief moment of constraint, until Alysa looked at Philip. The smile on her face was serene and contented as well as beautiful to behold. "I would have forfeited more than I gained, if that was so," she said softly. "Philip is the most precious thing in my life and I would be lost if we were not together."

"Is that why you rushed the marriage?" Prudence asked irreverently.

"We did not rush anything!" Alysa retorted. "We waited three months. Three *long* months." She shot a teasing look at Philip. "And I am not sure my husband would have been willing to put off our vows any longer than we did."

"At least the neighborhood cannot say that you were with child and forced to marry Philip," Abigail said practically. "By waiting the three months you made it clear that the wedding was no hasty union to bless an early child."

Alysa sighed. "I know a child conceived too soon in our marriage would have set tongues wagging, but I do wish I could have one now." She glanced at Philip, love brimming in her eyes. "Philip's child would make my life complete."

Prudence made a face. "Well, I would prefer to be at court, myself."

Alysa smiled. "Maybe that is how you feel right now, but when you find a man you can love, as I love Philip, you will think differently."

Later that evening, after they had all retired to their beds, Philip said to Alysa, "So you want to have my baby, do you?"

As he nibbled the corner of her mouth, Alysa sighed voluptuously. "More than anything else in the world."

His hand drifted down her side in a slow, sensuous caress. "Let's think about making that baby tonight."

She turned toward him. "I'd like that."

Their lips touched in a sweet embrace that soon heated into passion. As their bodies met in tender communion, the thought was in both of their minds that this joining would create the new life they so desired. Later they lay quietly, their bodies still touching and their hearts still twined together.

"Philip," Alysa said quietly.

His eyes were shut and there was a tiny smile of satisfaction on his lips. "Hmmmm?"

"If Thomas was able to get you a place, would you want to return to court?"

His eyes snapped open and he looked at her sharply. "Would you like to go to court? If so, Alysa—"

She hushed him with a finger over his lips. "I meant what I said, Philip. I am happy at Ainslie. But I have never known anything else, while you have. Your father was a powerful man at the late king's court and you were brought up there. Sometimes I wonder if you pine for the life."

"Never," he said, drawing her to him again. "What I want, Alysa, is you. Your love, your happiness, your desires. If you wish, we will go to court, but not on my account."

"Then we will not." She curled against him. "Hold me, Philip, and tell me you love me."

"With all my heart, Alysa. I bless the day Edgar Osborne suggested I should go down to the estate I had inherited so I could keep an eye on the Royalists there. As nefarious as his scheme was, it brought me into your life. You are my other half and I could not exist without you."

She reached up to touch his face. "Nor I you. I love you, Philip, my Roundhead husband. Once I would have scorned the idea that I would wed one whom I considered to be the enemy. But you taught me that honor and trust and faith know no boundaries. You are all I want in a husband and as the years pass our love can only grow." Her eyes grew misty. "Together we will help to create an England where people of all persuasions can live together freely and in peace."

"Together," he echoed, drawing her close. "Always together."

Turn the page for an

excerpt from

DANGEROUS
DESIRES

The Hearts of Rebellion Series
Book Three

Louise Clark

She lifted her chin, tilting her head in an oddly vulnerable little movement. She could not gauge the effect her gesture had on the Earl, as he, too, had his defenses well in hand. They stared at each other across the dimly lit room, each measuring the other's resolve as the candlelight flickered eerily.

Stephanie made the first move. "I think, milord, that I should bid you good night and retire. I am wet and tomorrow—"

"By tomorrow you will have had the time to create a neat little explanation for your unorthodox behavior. Oh, no, I think not, Mademoiselle."

Amusement colored his deep voice. Stephanie stiffened angrily. "I protest, Monsieur! It may amuse you to malign my character, but I am far too fatigued to be in the mood for jesting. Tomorrow I will be happy to discuss the evening with you. But for now I will retire." She turned toward the door, intending to sweep out in a grand, imperious exit.

Instead, forgetting that she was not wearing a fine gown, she stumbled over her own booted feet and the clinging folds of the heavy cloak. Stifling an unlady-like curse, she twisted, trying to save herself from falling.

As her shadowy form swayed, then pitched forward, Nicholas moved quickly, familiar with the layout of the room and sure of his path even in the gloom.

Stephanie felt his hands catch her waist, stopping her fall. The momentum pressed her body against his hard chest and his hands slid round her waist to wrap her securely in his strong arms. Her heart thundered—because of the narrowness of her escape, she assured herself, patently ignoring the sensations that his long, lean body was arousing in her.

"My, my. Mademoiselle, I had no idea you knew such colorful language." His words were light and mocking, but there was a telltale unsteadiness in his voice. Evidently the Earl was as much affected as Stephanie knew herself to be.

The house was very still: silent evidence that they were truly alone. Stephanie knew that there was danger, not because Lord Wroxton would do anything to hurt her, but because he roused feelings in her that she was hard put to control. The absence of others freed her from constraints that would normally have kept her safe. "Please, milord," she whispered.

She put her hands on his chest to push him away, but as her palms touched him, they seemed to take on a will of their own. Slowly, she smoothed the fine fabric of his shirt with her fingers, savoring the warmth of his skin beneath. His heart pounded, beating as erratically as her own.

"Mademoiselle." Nicholas caught her roaming hands. His voice was ragged, and he cleared his throat before speaking again. "Mademoiselle, I am now sure of what I only surmised before."

She looked up quickly. "*Q'est-ce que c'est?*" Instantly, she realized that she had made a mistake. Her mouth was inches from his and the temptation to rise up on her toes to eliminate the intervening distance was almost irresistible. Their eyes locked and she thought he was moving toward her. But then he drew back, deliberately breaking the spell between them.

Shakily she said, "*Pardon*, milord. I forget my English at times. What was it you were asking?"

Before responding, he prudently stepped back. Still holding her hands, he paused at arms' length to examine her. Even in the gloom, Stephanie was able to watch the passion that had darkened his eyes being damped down, until it was nothing more than a pale smoldering gleam in the blue of his eyes. That he had himself well under control was confirmed when he spoke in a cool, amused voice. "Apart from the dampness of your outer garment, which you have transferred to my own apparel, I cannot help but be aware that you are not clothed, er, shall we say respectably?"

Stephanie offered no resistance as he gently guided her toward the fire and the incriminating light. Bravely, she turned to face him and boldly she met his challenge with one of her own. "I am dressed for riding, Monsieur. What of it?"

DANGEROUS DESIRES

available in print and ebook

THE
HEARTS OF REBELLION
SERIES

Pretender's Game
Lover's Knot
Dangerous Desires

Louise Clark is the author of both contemporary and historical romance novels. These two genres are combined in Fighting Fate, a time travel story set in contemporary Boston with an 18th century time traveler who comes forward into his future, and Ridgeway, a

historical time travel that takes place in post-Civil War North America. Ridgeway is available as part of the seven book time travel boxed set, Swept Through Time. In 2014 she was a quarter finalist in the Amazon Breakthrough Novel Award contest.

In addition to working on new material, she is also republishing her out-of-print titles—Dangerous Desires, Lover's Knot and Pretender's Games—in e and print format. Louise holds a BA in History from Queen's University and a Master of Publishing degree from Simon Fraser University. Her books have been published in fifteen countries worldwide.

For more information please visit her at
    www.louiseclarkauthor.com
    www.facebook.com/LouiseClarkAuthor.